Orenda Rising

Volume One of
"A Prospect for Orenda"

R. D. Taylor

To Janet Slone Taylor,

The light of my life.

Author's Note:

ORENDA RISING opens a three-volume alternate history fiction that tells the 300 year story of a different and more positive indigenous-settler relationship in North America.

I hope many readers will read the exciting story that follows, before reading this note. Those who want to position themselves about my fiction before even reading it, will likely read it first. So be it.

I can understand Indigenous wariness and concern that two recent fictions under the name of one of their great spirits, Orenda, have recently been written by white guys, even though the non-Indigenous writers concerned strongly identify with the cause of Indigenous restoration in North America.

A Prospect for Orenda has its title because its story gathers the genius of that spirit of one side of its combined people to energize both their sides. That helps drive the prospect of their combined progress in the world. The story evolves naturally from and necessarily draws from the strengths of both sides of the O'dan people. Otherwise, there would be no story. The fact they draw their very name from Orenda is not only because their leading founder was a Longhouse Chief. It is meant in veneration and respect of that spirit's side of the O'dan.

However, I must pause, as may some Indigenous readers, at any notion that there should be "a prospect" for Orenda, as the series title suggests. Orenda, on the Indigenous side, is what Orenda is and always has been. I too, and the characters in my novels, reject the idea that Orenda must be lost when Orenda too, faces progressive change. Indeed, there is a scene among main characters in the middle novel, PAX ORENDA that actually addresses this very concern.

Let me too, explicitly declare that I am non-indigenous and that mine is a non-indigenous voice.

While I strongly believe in indigenous rights restoration, my life experience, underlying views and the imagined story do not speak as an indigenous North American and I cannot even guess how the trilogy will be received or made any use of in the Indigenous communities. Since the novels rework the terrible actual historic relationship, including renaming rivers and places as they might have been once named, and I do not write about one side, I can, like anyone on either side of that relationship, write about it.

I have already been asked: might such a project of alternative history detract from current efforts to ensure the awful actual history of this relationship is better understood and acted on?

My firm answer is no, alternative history as a genre will not be a distraction in this case. One thing that can still block progress is a sense that the history of the relationship was inevitable, that nothing could have been different in the confrontation of two such different civilizations, the one all but overwhelming the other. I think there exists a good deal of such fatalism. I think it can limit the open mind and vision now needed on both sides of the current relationship to build a more equal future together.

My intent is to return the reader to earlier times that held people in situations who faced active history-making moral choices in those times, too – choices that could have produced a different outcome. This sense of the past as a path of possibilities and not the only possible path, can help empower us to think and act boldly together now as we seek to remake the Indigenous-Settler relationship in the present. I believe that will need to be a very open-ended process, with less sense than anyone would like, about what the future will bring, only serious efforts as we go to make our relationship together a better one.

I also alert the reader that the alternate characters, situations and events and the scenes among actual historical persons in this novel are, however plausible, my own invention. The distinction between actual and the alternate history of the novel should be, in my view, apparent to any high school educated reader.

To help those concerned about which is which, I include a table of the trilogy's essential historical points of departure from actual history, in my Afterword on the writing of the Prospect novels in the second novel, PAX ORENDA.

R.D. Taylor
Richmond Hill, Ontario

"Beware if the light skinned race comes wearing the face of death. You must be careful because the face of brotherhood and the face of death look very much alike. If they come carrying a weapon ... beware. If they come in suffering ... they could fool you..."

"In the time of the Fifth Fire there will come a time of great struggle that will grip the lives of all native people. At the waning of this Fire there will come among the people, one who holds a promise of great joy and salvation. If the people accept this promise of a new way and abandon the old teachings, then the struggle of the Fifth Fire will be with the people for many generations. The promise that comes will prove to be a false promise. All those who accept this promise will cause the near destruction of the people."

From the Anishinaabe Prophesy of the Seven Fires

"White people nearly always write sentimentally about the Indian. . . But the Indian is not in line with us. . . A man cannot belong to both ways."

D. H. Lawrence

"Much later in life I learned the middle was the place to be, I can walk both ways."

Patricia Wonture, Awahande

Part One:

Trouble in the West

The Forest is still

In the starving winter camp
Death's fingers fondle through the damp
Finding all but an old one left to brood
Her dreams her staying food.

She dreams of a way too late to tell
Of southern cities and their kings
Of long forgotten things
And with her last knell
Things that will be lost
To the northern hunter spell.

.

Chapter 1

I am Water Bear.

I am about to dream.

I know that, because I have prepared myself to dream. For me, it means being alone with no food for a few days. It's been five days this time, out here in the Bay of the Huron.

I know it will be a fearsome dream. I know that, because I feed my dreams with my own story. The last year of my story is a potent mix indeed. It will be good food for a powerful dream.

As a child, my story began when I earned my strange name running to get my father to free a bear trapped in the slippery rocks far out in the bay. The lucky bear escaped back to the forest. Some crows watched the whole thing and chased the bear further into the forest.

The naming shaman truly foretold what all that meant. Crow knew Bear had foolishly made himself vulnerable to me, a mere boy, having to save him. Henceforth, I would take on some of Bear's magic powers, but with the cunning of Crow.

The shaman was right. From a boy, I dream with Bear's extra powers and with Crow's extra cunning.

I should admit: I come by my dreaming from a dreaming people. We are guided by the vision of past dreams. Our guiding vision is the Prophesy of the Seven Fires. The Prophesy sprang from an ancient dream. It instructed my ancestor people to move westward from the coast of the great ocean. From the ancient time, the Anishinaabe had come west by different routes, some curling back on themselves, gradually surrounding the other inland native peoples.

According to the Prophesy, we are now at the time of the Fifth Fire. It warned that a new people would come behind a false mask. As it foretold, the palefaces, the hairy ones, have come.

I am in another way like my Odawa people. I am a trader. Now, in a year said to be 1681 by the palefaces, I am widely traveled in my woodland world. My own Odawa people now live with their close Anishinaabe cousins, the Ojibwa and the Chippewa, along the rapids between the Upper Lakes which everyone called "water pitching over the rocks." The French ones called such a rapids a "Sault" and the Jesuit explorer Marquette named it after Mary the Mother of Christ. Hence the French now call it Sault Ste. Marie. To my people of that Sault, it remains the place of the leaping waters.

The big dream coming to me all started when I left my village near the Sault late last summer. I should have known then that I had left too late. I sure came back too late.

But do not let the dreamer tell the story. Let the story teller tell it. That way, it will be passed on. In a good telling, the story teller is not the only one the spirits will smile down upon: they love the listeners. Some of you could be the next story tellers.

* * *

Water Bear remembered the exact moment when the story began for his coming dream. He was sloshing through the woodland at the hardest time – the breaking of winter into spring. During the late winter of 1681 he had travelled further west than any of the trading Odawa had done before. His feet had travelled by the end of winter beyond all the stories of his own people. He was now only a few leagues east of the Michissippi, the Father of Waters.

On that first thaw day, the sounds of the melt were everywhere. The forest dripped and gurgled as the melt water rushed down the slopes, into the surging rivers and swollen lakes, towards the great father river and onward to the great southern gulf and southern sea.

All the people told in their origin stories of the great solar fire in the sky giving energy to the woodland realm. The sun was from where their great spirits around and near the big lakes came: Gitchy Manitou, so named by the Ojibwa and other Anishinaabe; Wakunda, so named by the Eastern and Northern Sioux; Orenda, the spirit giving the people energy, so named by the Iroquoians.

Just after the sun reached its highest point, the sounds of Water Bear's party moving through the forest could be heard. The crunch and squelch of the wooden racquets they wore on the now sodden snow. The snapping of twigs and branches in bare spots. Heavy breathing. Occasionally, the sound of human speech itself, but only its meanest expression: mutterings; sharp oaths; sudden shouts of warning, as brush beneath the snow gets tangled with the racquets, or one of the men sinks into unseen water or another encounters a treacherous crevice still covered in the snow.

There were six men in the party. The two leading and the last three in the party were men of Siouan tribes, becoming known as the Iowa. Water Bear was in the middle of the party. He was the tallest, a feature of his distant eastern Odawa nation.

The Iowa were returning to their own western countries from a winter near the great Lake to the east, spent disagreeably, but to a purpose, among their haughty kindred, the Winnebago. It was a foolish trip through the soggy woods.

Only one reason caused them to continue their trip at such a hazardous time. It was something new and astonishing they were carrying through the woods. They were eager for the renown it would bring them among their own peoples.

In truth, it was not the Iowa members of this party who were the bearers of the wondrous new thing at this moment. It was being borne by Water Bear.

He was not only the tallest of the men, he wore dramatic clothing, most prominently, now loosely thrown over his shoulder, a black bear skin and a formidable bear claw necklace. His chest was tattooed and his face on the left cheek was dramatically painted with a jagged black slash he wore as a mark of his dreaming gift. And, literally above all, there arose a profuse fountain-shaped coiffe of greased black hair. Any of these features would have made his appearance more formidable than his modestly attired, unpainted squat companions. This not being a war party, they cared little for their appearance.

Water Bear knew the feelings among the others, that they tolerated his youthful vanity only because of trade. Only a few, even of his trading nation traveled the far western countries at this time with the knowledge of many languages and how the trade is entered for the astonishing goods of the paleface ones.

Thoughts about his special mix of Bear and Crow had always given Water Bear energy and strength beyond others, as they had done on this trip, further west than he had ever been before. Despite his youthful vanities, his fellow travelers knew that he was strong medicine.

But Water Bear presently laboured with less dignity than he would have liked. Because the toboggans were no longer efficient for the purpose, for a time it had been his turn to carry upon his own shoulders the item which, more than any other trade goods the party carried, was the reason for this forced journey through the woods.

He was carrying a large blackened copper kettle.

The going became even more difficult as the men entered a deep ravine. After a time, one of the Iowa ahead of Water Bear became so entangled in roots that he lost balance completely and pitched headlong down the steep slope. Then, Water Bear could not keep hold of the kettle, and it too was pitched down the slope, making an audible 'Clunk" as it hit a rock near the unfortunate Ioway, now in a heap at the bottom.

The others watched these mishaps at first with alarm, and then with growing amusement. Their fortunately unhurt companion managed to disentangle himself and began to struggle toward the kettle through the still deep snow at the bottom of the slope. When he reached it, he awaited the others, who were now plunging down the slope toward him. With more curses, he prepared for the derisive comments that would be his inevitable due for having so disgraced himself.

As the others reached the ravine bottom, Four Horns, the leading Ioway, began the barrage of sarcasm.

"The kettle spirit made only one oath at having fallen thus, but Stone Shoulder carries on with many," he shouted. "Perhaps Stone Shoulder would have us carry him upon our backs as we do the kettle," another of the Ioway said mockingly.

Stone Shoulder glowered as the others whooped with laughter. It was the first laughter in weeks of humourless travel together.

In retaliation, Stone Shoulder put the kettle aside and made several large snow balls which he hurled at the group, taking special aim at Water Bear's still kempt coiffe of hair. The rest threw off their packs and soon they were all caught up in the hilarious frenzy of a snow fight. They gave in freely to this long overdue eruption of play, the more so knowing the end of their long journey was close at hand.

Yet the diversion could not last long. They had not eaten for two days and felt lucky to be as near to the Michissippi as they were. Now they were still some leagues east of their original destination. The journey was quickly resumed.

By mid-afternoon, the party had passed through the roughest of this wrinkled country of steep ravines. The light in the woods brightened and the undergrowth began to thin. They were now able to move more quickly, and for some time had been beckoned by the sound of distant drumming.

Soon, they emerged at the edge of the forest. They stood upon the high ground of a northwest-facing ridge.

Water Bear marvelled at the scene before him.

In the foreground was the broad valley of the Michissippi. It was Water Bear's first view of the river, known by all peoples as the Father of Waters. The great river was enlarged at this point, into a lake over five leagues in length, with several islands at the northern end where it narrowed. Beyond, on the far shore, the cane breaks, marshes and wet meadows ran to a line of treed bluffs. An opening in the forest along the ridge gave a glimpse of the grasslands to the plains stretching to the western horizon.

The others waited as Water Bear took in the wondrous view.

After a time he said, "the setting sun has a vast country in which to rest the night through."

Four Horns knew the impact of first seeing this view. He had been with the Frenchman Nicolet's party when that trader first espied the vast western prairie.

"My cousin and some of the Turtle band went into that country. They traveled for two moons and found no end to it."

"It is there that our people will settle after the season of storms, unless there are problems at the Spring Council," added Stone Shoulder.

He was about to say more, but Four Horns gave him a sharp glance. Four Horns looked over at the Odawa. He seemed relieved that Water Bear was still distracted by the view and had not seemed to hear these careless remarks by Stone Shoulder.

Along the near shore, a small settlement could be seen. It was to this that Four Horns now pointed, hoping to further cover over Stone Shoulder's remark.

"The cabins of Burnt Foot are there. His drums tell of the breaking of the ice on the inland rivers. We are well pleased to see on the other side of the river the smoke from cooking fires. Unless someone got there before him, those smoke columns tell us that my father and the main body of our people have arrived. It was agreed we would stay there until the time to depart to the Spring Council up river."

Indeed, trade at the Spring Council hosted in the territory of the Lakota had been their original plan. At a time of peace along the upper Michissippi and with much recent tribal movement into the area resulting from disturbances to the east, it was increasingly necessary to negotiate hunting grounds at the beginning of each season. Conflict among tribes who were not traditional enemies could thereby be avoided.

What was different this season, and a cause of concern, was that some bands of the Iowa were proposing to cross the Michissippi for the first time, with the intent to settle permanently. Four Horns had kept the knowledge of this dangerous issue from Water Bear. It was the prospect of this historically peaceful trade meeting of large numbers of different native peoples still little aware of the paleface or his goods that had drawn Water Bear so far west in this uncertain journey at the end of winter.

There would, Water Bear had imagined, be no better time to whet the appetite of these western peoples for trade with the new pale-faced ones. For his part, Four Horns had been sent east to the Green Bay by the elders of his tribe to find out more about trade with the pale-faced spirits. Already, a few paleface adventurers had been through their area but direct contact this far west was still sporadic. At the Green Bay he had met Water Bear who seemed quite willing to accompany them back west with the sample of the trade goods Water Bear had brought to the Bay, including the great kettle, but insisted on attending the Spring Council of which he had learned.

Four Horns had agreed to this, although it had not been his instructions to bring anyone else to the Spring Council, partly because of the potential disagreements and dangers there, and partly because the elders of his tribe had considered the prospect of gaining the paleface trade for themselves.

Four Horns knew that few outside his own river band could make progress up the Michissippi at the time of its strong spring currents, and had thought Water Bear would be deterred from trying once he saw the strong currents. But he had come to realize the strength and capabilities of Water Bear. He now recognized Water Bear's determination to reach the Spring Council despite thirty leagues of rough travelling to get to it, on and off the water.

Being the first visitors from the east after the season of cold, Four Horns and his party were warmly welcomed by Burnt Foot.

He was a squat old man, and gimp-legged, but full of humour. He was known, along the great river as a spreader of news of all nations and teller of stories, which included many variations on how he gained his gimpy leg.

For the six travelers, it was an agreeable end to their long weeks of hardship. They rested and smoked Burnt Foot's fine calumets which came, he assured them, from the famous Pipestone quarry in the far west. They also took the revitalizing pleasures of his excellent sweat lodge.

At the sumptuous evening meal, Water Bear ate heavily of the freshest river fish. The meal was more tasty even than the whitefish of his own country because of their preparation with salt and hot peppers from the south.

At the meal, Four Horns prompted Burnt Foot to tell his story, thinking Water Bear would be a good listener.

"My grandfather started this settlement and my father and I have kept to it. He came here with three rejected Illini women who would have been short-lived in their villages because of their strong spirit. Yet somehow he delighted in them, and now I take such complaining women from the Illini as did my father, because they delight me too with their mischievous thoughts, so reviled by the Illini men, who still wish their women to be quiet. I give back to the Illini most of my sons. The youngest here stays with me. He has the knack for sorting out real information from false – he shall carry on this village after I go to the spirits."

"What is it then you do here, that gives you such independence?" asked Water Bear.

"Oh, we take and give information on all the waters, up and down this great river to its furthest extents, and the inland rivers beyond each of its shores to the rising sun and the setting sun: the tales of the peoples, the news of the forming and breaking of ice and the movement of game and the buffalo herds, and especially, the movement of peoples. We see and hear it all. We weigh it all. I and my women are smart talkers. Then we know what talk is the best value and tell that truth to all those who seek news of things they need to know every season. In exchange, they leave us what we need to live a good life. And we are given back a rich lazy life"

They all laughed.

"But do not listen to any of his brave stories about his name and how he withstood pain in that foot." It was the oldest woman, Pecking Bird, still at the fire who now spoke. "He never tells you all of it. Long before, he had lost the sense in that foot, because of a childhood accident. When, shortly after that he had burnt his foot in a fire and showed no pain, he was given the name Burnt Foot. His ability to withstand pain in the foot made him famous and, the best thing for him was he got his name changed from Cooing Pigeon."

The women laughed merrily.

"I was never called Cooing Pigeon. You make my first name sillier each time you tell that story," Burnt Foot said, while chuckling himself.

Water Bear loved the story. He spoke through Four Horns, "So, there is more to you than you say, Burnt Foot. Does your stomach too, burn, but not have sense, like your foot? You burn mine with these hot peppers from the south that I cannot even eat, and yet you show it not." All around the fire laughed again.

When the laughter was over, Water Bear again spoke. "I welcome your stories Burnt Foot, for in them is the wisdom from a life long-lived. My wisdom is not yet of that kind. I am learning much here. But, when my naming vision came, in that dream too there was fire in the forests. It chased Bear in front of it, to the water, where he waited for me in a terrible death throw. He too had a burnt foot from the forest fire that drove him to the far shallow place in the bay, to drive his foot too deeply under a sharp rock. So, I know my way to your fire is a true one."

Burnt Foot nodded and the rest around the fire were silent for a time. Even Stone Shoulder, who resented this Odawa's frequent interpretation of other stories to his own story, thus making it seem to assume some greater importance, gave Water Bear the respect he was due.

When the others had gone from the fire, Water Bear was left alone, deep in thought about what he had learned from Burnt Foot and the strong-talking women. He thought of his world as great nations living beside each other – yet here was not a nation: Burnt Foot's place was less than a village and yet he and his son and the women lived well here and meant much to the nations here and afar. When he finally began falling into a welcoming sleep, he could not wait until he would awake, to seek more of the stories of the peoples hereabouts.

Chapter 2

The following morning, the season had changed and the first spell of mild weather was upon them. As the day dawned it brought the first clear sky in more than a moon. Here and there in the brightening sky, lines of geese and other migrating birds could be seen riding northward on a strengthening southwest wind.

Even before the cooking fires were lit at Burnt Foot's cabins, a small flotilla of large canoes and dugouts was crossing the great river. Four Horns was pleased to see his father in the lead boat. The boats, their company all a-song, approached the shore at Burnt Foot's cabins and when they saw Four Horns waiting on the shore, the shouts back and forth were so clamorous that the great rafts of geese and ducks that had settled along the river the previous night began to take wing.

Seeing this and with only the briefest of introductions to Four Horns' father, Sun Behind the Cloud, and his party arriving at the river's edge, Water Bear chose the moment to produce the great black kettle. Water Bear set it aside while he produced his other European goods. At each small metal knife, axe or utensil, or trinket of glass, the wonderment grew. After a time, Water Bear produced two small looking glasses. Only after the excitement and delight from seeing these mirrored spirits reflecting their own image had begun to quiet down, did he finally move to the large copper kettle. This he now raised above his head and hurled upon a nearby rock. The resounding clunk which issued forth caused fright among the Iowa and scared some even back to their boats.

Four Horns had to speak quickly to lessen the alarm among his people.

"You see, Father, a kettle of this spirit will not break. And it never leaks. How many times in travel have our pots broken if they were made of clay or leaked if they were made of bark so as not to break? This kettle does neither!"

These being a people in the last generations most often on the move, understood the truth of this and the practical advantages of such a kettle. After a few moments reflection, Sun Behind the Cloud took up the kettle from where it lay, and, with a loud and courage-giving "Eieee," hurled it likewise upon the rock. He did so twice more. All were delighted to see that after the third loud clunk it remained unbroken.

"We have never seen this, though if it be some part copper we know of such a thing worked by peoples to the north and west. Surely the spirits will only make one black one for this man of magic,' concluded Sun Behind the Cloud.

Four Horns carefully explained to his father that many more such kettles and other wondrous things besides could be obtained in trade with the pale-faced ones who came from beyond the morning sun, in exchange only for beaver skins.

Several of the more enterprising warriors began to go to their dugouts for their winter robes so that they could at once obtain what most pleased them among Water Bear's trade goods. Only the strongest interventions from Four Horns and then from his Father, quick to grasp the matter, could prevent this premature trade for all of Water Bear's goods, since it was these goods that Four Horns hoped would clinch the deals for beaver furs his people wanted to work at the spring parley with the Lakota, thirty leagues further north up the great river.

As the party settled in at Burnt Foot's early morning fires before setting out on their arduous journey north, Sun Behind the Cloud, on Burnt Foot's bidding and despite Four Horn's misgivings spoke of the challenging circumstances that they would face at the traditional spring gathering.

"We learned that a great chief of the Lakota died in the winter season and that there was much trouble among their villages as a result. For a time it was in doubt there would be a Spring Council this year although there had always been one at the great bluff where a river to the far west meets this Michissippi. But we have just learned that that the Council will be held, though earlier than usual, to help them make peace among themselves, by having to show a good face to others. Those peoples may not be in a mood to parley with us, but they have said we are once again among those they welcome to the Council, as we Ioway have for the past six seasons. We shall be leaving at the half moon."

For the rest of the day, Water Bear crossed and re-crossed the Michissippi, spending time both at the Iowa encampment on the west side and at Burnt Foot's cabins on the east side. He learned much at the fires on both sides of the river.

He listened closely to the long story of the Iowa. Over unimaginable distances they had for a time reached as far west as the red stone pipe quarry far to the west of the Michissippi and even presided over that hallowed neutral ground for a generation still within telling. Then they had been expelled by other Siouan nations back so far east that they had again dwelled on the eastern side of the Michissippi in a place well south of their older generations. Sun Behind the Cloud summarized that as a "path for our people east to west, and then west to east as winding as the great river is north to south."

In the evening Burnt Foot said, "Sun Behind the Cloud is here on my side of the river. He wants us to trade stories. Will you trade a story?"

Water Bear eagerly agreed.

Sun Behind the Cloud said, "Can you tell us why those far away Iroquois force so many other nations further west to the father river?

"Maybe I can tell of that. What story would Burnt Foot give in exchange?"

Burnt Foot said, "If you tell us about your east to west things, I will tell you about south to north things."

There was a large gathering at the evening fire.

Water Bear wanted to tell the best east to west story he could. There was none better within the current memory of the old ones than the Iroquois expansion into Huronia, the country on the great bay of the middle lake of their own cousins the Wendat. It well summed up the issues other nations faced. Water Bear told the story of the last year of the Huron in when they were driven away from their gentle country of rolling ridges, marshes and planted fields.

"It forced all those villages to empty and their people were forced further west, just as has happened below the lakes. Those lower Iroquois did it to take over the paleface fur trade. But they did it with guns supplied them by the palefaces calling themselves English and because of the impact on the Huron of those other palefaces calling themselves French and their martyred black robe priests, which had weakened the spirit of the Wendat villages. My uncle told me the Wendat were foolish to weaken themselves by accepting those priests into their country. He said to me if they can weaken one of our nations, they can weaken all the rest of us. He warned me that this is the time of the Fifth Fire, by our ancient prophesies. It tells us of a time of strangers coming with true and false promises. I will never forget that."

Even Burnt Foot, the great river's garrulous source of news, was silent at this.

Water Bear concluded, "We all desire and want to trade for the paleface goods, but it seems hard to do that and not face their disruption of the balance in our own ways and among our nations. They sometimes make us take things in trade we do not need, like their fire water. It is my desire to trade their goods beyond the divisions they cause in ourselves. Yet your stories of their wandering traders and their two-sided influence shows they have already begun to reach even this far west."

Burnt Foot said, "That is a good story. It tells of how the palefaces can disrupt our own peoples. It should be well told and remembered here. You have earned my story in exchange."

"One day in the time just after I settled here a long ago now, I saw three canoes approaching from down river. They took a long time to get to my spot and when they got to my new landing, I found out why. The middle canoe, loaded with all their belongings, was taking in water and needed repair. Not only that, while the sole man in the middle canoe handled it well even while bailing, the six people in the other canoes were three women, one very old, and three children. What a sad lot they turned out to be. They stayed with us for a time, while I helped them repair two of their canoes and gave them some of our stored food to maybe get them to their destination: cousins of theirs, they said, among the Santee Sioux, who were at least a moon to the north."

"They told me their story and I tell it now. They were the last of a family who lived on the edges of the country of the Cahokia. Those people live near the great Mound, where they say their ancestors are all buried, a half-moon down the river beyond the Illini. But this family, which once numbered in the hundreds, was not of the Cahokia, whom they in turn claimed were not the true people of the country in the ancient time. Their family claimed they alone carried the true memory of the big settlement there and that had many places in it built from stone and was ruled by chiefs who were the same as the sky spirits who wanted a way in one place that would not move and made all obey them in a way no nation knows today. They told the story that the whole ancient way and the spirit chiefs ruling it, disappeared."

"Their family, they said, were the last of its people, far after it went back to the forests and its people abandoned the place that never moved. Most of them long since had moved northwards and are called the Santee, though some moved further west to the Great Plains. They claimed the people now calling themselves Cahokia came to settle that country much later and that they are not the true descendants of the ancient people."

"They went on to tell me of the enmity this caused between their diminished family and the present Cahokia. Most of their remaining family had recently died or been killed off by those new Cahokia. They – those seven –

they said were all that had remained of that ancient town there, and now they too now sought the northern countries."

"I'll tell you one thing – my early thoughts to move here and there from time to time along the river never came back to me after I said goodbye to that family. I've stayed in place ever since, as a way of holding their story and honouring those ancient times. You're the first I've dared tell the story to. No-one else would care."

Water Bear was well pleased with this south to north story of long ago. He marvelled at the scope of the human movements that coursed up and down as well as across the great river, matching its own deep energies. The last ripple of a kind of left-over energy from that ancient time along the river had been experienced by Burnt Foot in his own lifetime.

Water Bear could only conclude that it must have been some large ancient event, which shattered and scattered the fixed in place people at Cahokia, who had lived in a heavy way on the land, like the palefaces. It was more than anyone now could understand, except that no current nation could be a perfected thing under the spirits and that all was still astir along the Michissippi as it was in the east.

It made Water Bear wonder: was the more freely wandering way of the woodlands only something temporary, something in between, something that could not survive the will of the fixed in place peoples from which even his own western cousins may have come?

Water Bear slept a restless night with these thoughts, and whether and how he might dare share them.

In the morning, the half-moon was visible in the sky and the Ioway party made its departure northward, bidding fond farewells to Burnt Foot. Water Bear was pleased when Burnt Foot hugged him tightly and said to Four Horns and his father, "Let me hear by the end of the season that you and this Water Bear have fared well at the spring parley." Then he said in his hand signs

and a broken Ojibwa, "Be careful of those questions of yours, tall fellow –
some may be troubled by the one who asks such questions!"

As he was taking that in, Pecking Bird approached him and asked for
Four Horns to translate. She said, "We think you have gifts. For the people.
You will travel far. Give those gifts back to the people. We are waiting for
those gifts."

* * *

The following days were spent in an arduous journey fifty leagues up
the great river toward the spring council with the Lakota.

Water Bear came to appreciate the skills and knowledge of these
peoples who knew the great river. He learned much from the river man who
lead the party and his friend Four Horns' own knowledge of the river,
especially "further to the south, where its spirit is darkest." Water Bear kept a
keen eye on the scenes along the river. So frequently did he ask questions that
the Iowa grew weary of his trader's curiosity, so much the greater than their
own.

As a trader, Water Bear sought in his persistent questioning not only
the information it gave, but also the practice it gave him with their language.
He began to speak with the Iowa in their own tongue. Some were clearly eager
to hear more about the palefaces especially in their own language. Others were
little moved to learn more. Many seemed still barely to perceive the possibility
of a new people so strange. But most appreciated someone who listened
intently to them and appreciated their own ways and skills.

On the sixth day they approached their destination. Just ahead, the
Michissippi took a sharp turn, in the midst of which it received the sluggish
waters of a western tributary, before resuming its northerly course. At the
confluence of the rivers, a high bluff on the north-western shore overlooked the
surrounding bottomlands through which the larger river made its way around a
line of gently treed islands. Cliffs rose above the bottomlands to the south and
west.

And, as if these views were not enough to delight the eye, another wonder was situated just to the north of the high ridge they approached that divided the greater from the lesser river. Here extending straight across the Michissippi was a line of water, broken dramatically in the middle by a sandstone outcrop, falling to a frothy base.

As the dugouts drew nearer the shore below the high ground atop the bluff, Water Bear could see up that there was already an encampment.

"That is the place of the spring council," explained Four Horns, pointing in the direction of the great bluff. "You see there the first of the Lakota. It looks to me as only an advance party. We are in good time after all."

Indeed, a large area had already been prepared with piles of tree boughs and numerous stands of bare poles to receive the skins, which the main parties would bring. The party of Sun Behind the Cloud that now arrived prepared their own adjacent camp.

Apart from a brief meeting of the leaders of the two groups, there was little contact between nations on the first day. The rest of the day was spent making camp, all anticipating the grander events when the main parties of Lakota and western Siouan peoples would arrive from the north and west.

The next day, a bright sun was overhead when the main parties arrived. Leading the party were several of the principal chiefs. They moved slowly toward the single host Lakota chief awaiting them at the place already carefully prepared for the main council fires.

Each chief wore colourful robes, some made of buffalo hides, a few of bear and wolf skins. Water Bear watched in the background with the other Iowa, behind the leading members of the Illini and other tribes from east of the Michissippi. Each of the Siouan chiefs carried a long smoking pipe, most from the red stone quarry, superior to any pipe Water Bear had seen before. Most also wore handsomely wrought copper and shell work jewelry. The Lakota and Sioux chiefs wore impressive feathered head dress, the feathers arranged fully around the heads of the leading chiefs. Water Bear noticed many wore the quill work leggings worn by some of the chiefs. He knew that his own Ojibwa peoples were the source of most of the porcupine quills used by many nations.

The manner of the chiefs was grave. Unlike some of the younger warriors accompanying them, and the women and children who followed bearing the main loads of the great party, the chiefs seemed either uninterested in the presence of the tall Odawa at the camp or were better able to resist a look in his direction, as they preferred to have all eyes focused on themselves. Only one chief, Water Bear thought, seemed to indicate the slightest sense of someone unexpected being present and glanced briefly toward him.

"It is a Santee war chief who has noticed you," said Four Horns, responding to the unspoken question in Water Bear's glance at him. "Better he notices you, than the medicine man who dances in circles around the leading chieftains. He will ask the Illini about you."

Chapter 3

Though new groups arrived all the time, by the end of the afternoon the main party was settled. The first of the smoking ceremonies began with the Illini and other chiefs of nations east of the Michissippi. The spring council was a peaceful meeting among even sometimes warring nations.

The Iowa party was not invited until late the following day. It was known that the Iowa had difficult matters to put before the parlay. Only after that, Water Bear was introduced at some of the meetings, though he was not invited to smoke among the chiefs.

By the third day, as large a throng of peoples had assembled above the bluff as Water Bear had ever seen before. As he looked out across the spring meeting ground, he was delighted to see hundreds of teepees, wigwams and other temporary dwellings of various forms on the now crowded table land. Though there were several nations around the Great Lakes, his trading had previously moved between only one nation at a time. The even more frequent state of war in the east now prevented such a gathering of nations. He wondered how long the hosting of a peaceful spring meeting could last among these western peoples.

With an accepted peace among these peoples, at least for the duration of the spring council, trade and information involving the strange new pale-faced people should have caused quite a stir. Yet, Water Bear was not pleased with his initial efforts to interest the Santee and other Sioux in matters of trade. What contact he attempted, without the mediation of someone trusted among them as Four Horns was with his people, seemed each time to arouse suspicion, annoyance and even fear. The Lakota, though they had seen paleface trade goods before, refused even to look upon the large black kettle, fearing an evil spirit within it, as had the Iowa first feared.

By the eve of the main parley, Water Bear had followed Four Horns' advice and concealed the kettle from view. He had no wish to arouse the medicine men against him. He would have to await a better opportunity to take up matters of trade with these chiefs and their people, who seemed preoccupied with other things. In the meantime he witnessed the main events.

On the fourth day, all the chiefs assembled for the most important matters to be considered at the spring council. For a long time there was silence as the pipes were shared and passed around. Until well into the afternoon there had only been a few vague speeches by minor chiefs.

Four Horns had foreseen correctly that the main speeches and any unsettling harangues would not begin until later in the afternoon, when the matters being raised by the visit from the Ioway would be considered. He and Water Bear now slipped into the group of other Iowa behind his father.

This serious talk was finally begun by Black Arrow, who had been chosen by the Lakota to speak to Sun Behind the Cloud.

"I, Black Arrow, chief of our outward face, speak now for all the villages and clans of the Santee whose country is the land of many waters above this place. This has been our country and that of our ancestors from the time all was stone and no man lived beneath Father Sun."

He pointed to the northern and western areas of the encampment that arced about the bluff's edge, and listed the divisions of the northern Sioux.

"I speak too for our cousins who dwell in the west and who have come here in larger numbers than ever before." He listed these kindred Siouan peoples and his outstretched hand slowly signified the southwest portion of the large encampment where their tepees stood.

"The spirits have blessed my people, as others know, with the harvest of the wild rice. This we share with our cousins and other peaceful nations when they are in want or when they would give to us in trade what we seek from them." Here he looked in the direction of the Illini and Iowa.

"We Siouan peoples have come to this place above the two rivers here from the time of the oldest ancestors to remind ourselves and all neighbouring peoples of the rules by which we hunt the buffalo. But the buffalo herds belong to all nations and to no single nation - nations at peace or nations at war." He listed the names of many more nations further to the west who shared the buffalo herds.

"The buffalo wonders free, up and down the great country beyond the Father of Waters. So it is for the nations of this place. So it will be for any nation who would move within us from the wars in the east." He said this last with much emphasis.

He now looked at Sun Behind the Cloud.

"When you Iowa come to say you must again cross the great river, we can listen to your talk. But when you ask us, what are the boundaries in the country of the buffalo, we think you must mean something which is true for some things that are in only one place, but not true of the buffalo herd. It was not true of the pipestone quarry to where you once wandered. Any nation that talks of making a boundary for that which has no boundary, must also be speaking soon of war to all of us who live on this side of the river."

As Black Arrow reached this loud climax, there were "Ho, Ho" sounds of approval among the Lakota and other Siouan elders.

After a time, Sun Behind the Cloud rose.

"You speak well, Black Arrow of the Santee."

He turned toward the two most senior Santee chiefs, Stone River and Gathers Rice, as he continued.

"It will always be known to us Iowa who once lived as part of you, that we are but one part of you. We know that you in the north of this favoured country are the greater part. It is as you say, we who come to you in these matters upon which my people's fate depends: it is your wisdom we seek and your protection we ask for, now that we must move our villages again across the Father river."

To these agreeable words there were more "Ho Ho's" and Sun Behind the Cloud continued.

"Hear this, then, our northern cousins. We Iowa seek not to put boundaries in the buffalo lands where none should be. We hear you well on this matter. Nor do we wish to change boundaries of other people where they dwell and where they should be. But we are of necessity a people who must move, as the red star moves among its cousins in the night sky, but does not change their position. This is because there are now too many of the Illini and others pushing at us from the east because of wars with the Longhouse league."

He looked around at each of the Santee chiefs. He saw that they were listening.

"We are not like our haughty cousins, the Winnebago, the Ho Chunk, who as you know, in their big village choose sometimes and sometimes not to war, but argue with numerous cousins as if they were enemies all about them. We are different. We have come to need only lord buffalo around us, as he is around you."

Many of the chiefs nodded at this.

"Already the main village of our people awaits where the Ohio meets the Michissippi to again cross the great Father River and travel up the muddy river west to where the winter sun lies on the ground at the end of the day and the buffalo sniff the winds. We think we are bid by the morning star to make our final crossing of the river this season and make our villages on the other side, not just for the season of the hunt, for which we have parleyed in the past."

There were many nods showing this was an understanding shared around the western nations.

"And, so it is that we have come north to smoke with you at the spring parley. For, it is told that there is still a country of no villages, below that of your western cousins and up the river of slow water that we see before us now."

Sun Behind the Cloud pointed down the wandering river splitting into the Michissippi in the bottomland below the bluff.

"Even now, those of my people left behind down the Michissippi await a message to head again into the western country, knowing that I am here speaking with you, for it is reached from our winter villages by the big muddy river to the south as well. In this, we mean only the greatest respect. It is so that we do not again encroach upon the boundaries of your own country, that we now seek to know what those boundaries are."

With this said, to emphasize the peaceful intent, Sun Behind the Cloud placed a shell-work collar before the Santee and Sioux chiefs. But, all of this was met with a stony silence. At this point, the Illini main chief rose to speak.

Sinissippi, the senior chief of the Illini, rose. "I speak for our confederation. It is to us first the Iowa should have come. We are the senior power on the east side of the river. We have the first right to cross the river to settle should we so desire. We have crossed before and a few of our settlements are on that side of the river. But for now, we accept the nations that are there now and would not disturb them with new movements to settle. We say, deny the Iowa a crossing until we Illini have decided."

The Santee chiefs understood and seemed to approve this.

Another stony silence was broken by the words of the greatest Lakota chief, Dust in the Sun.

"Anyway, if there is such a land of no villages, it must be in the country of the pipestone quarry your nation briefly occupied many seasons back. Many nations prefer it remain unoccupied and available to all nations. That way, with only a few there at any one time, only to take the pipestone. In that direction, there are also other gathering places like this one. Those empty countries keep our own countries known and apart except for the councils when nations must meet together. When nations crowd together, as they do east of the Michissippi that means war. Your Winnebago cousins and many others are too often at war with the Illini for that reason. Their chiefs here separately tell me they may soon again not to be able to avoid war."

He paused for effect. The Illini chiefs nodded their agreement.

Sun Behind the Cloud pleaded, "But we are your cousins and known to you. Would you not vouch for us settling somewhere there in those usually empty lands, now that we have no choice but to move?"

Dust in the Sun looked upon the ground. "It was the distant past when your villages were swept away from the pipestone and back down the great river. It is a story told now by none of our elders. It has little meaning to us. It is only your presence here now that tells us of this."

Sun Behind the Cloud held up his arms in appeal. There was no response. All looked at Dust in the Sun, who shook his head slowly.

"For now, we cannot take up the request you have made. We must think longer on the matter. You may do as you wish this season, but we do not give you any guarantee. If you make your villages up that river to the pipestone, you will know soon enough whether it is our will that you live there. Other nations may make their wishes known to you as well. If they do, it is no business of ours. They too will wonder about this talk of more boundaries in the land of Lord Buffalo. If there is to be an answer from us more definite, you will know within this moon. But, if there cannot be an answer, you move at your own risk. See that we are not offended. We cannot say more. There is a troubling spirit here."

He looked in Water Bear's direction. "I cannot say we will smoke together tomorrow."

With little thus gained from the parley and with a second breakdown in negotiations with the Lakota the following day, the mood around the Ioway camp fires was a gloomy one.

In the mid-afternoon, Sinissippi, the Illini chief, led a group of Sioux chiefs to the Iowa teepees. The Sioux were led by their most feared shaman, Red Hand, so named for a large birthmark running down from his wrist. He was a wizened old man, but still moved swiftly. He called for Sun Behind the Cloud and said,

"Bring forth that black pot - it is time we confront its spirit."

Water Bear brought it out from his teepee and dropped it unceremoniously in front of Red Hand, as if to say he would let the pot take care of itself.

Red Hand was holding a large round stone. He brought it full force against the pot and jumped back at the clunk it made. He then pounded the kettle in several places. After that, he stood back, and shook some amulets he wore.

"This pot has too strong a spirit for a pot. It is the bad spirit released in this camp. The daughter of our greatest chief lies sick after she stole a look at it the other day. This pot must go from here, with that Odawa man, He would leave it here in trade only to give us more sickness."

Red Hand shook his amulets toward Water Bear, turned and strode away with his entourage.

That evening, Four Horns had spoken to his father before he again spoke to Water Bear.

"There seems little chance of repairing the day. The Illini oppose us and the Lakota choose to misconstrue our talk. They say we wish to put boundaries on the common buffalo herd not just the pipestone quarry, as if the buffalo herd were in one place and harvested there like the wild rice. It is a reason they have invented. My father says that they have been too much disturbed by their own recent troubles and have not given our proposal to move our villages back toward the pipestone quarry any serious consideration, though we told them at the last spring council that we would come to the council this year to talk of these things."

Water Bear was not surprised.

"Ho. It is perhaps for the same reason they refuse to consider my offer to trade. From what I hear from Stone Shoulder, jealousies among them weaken their ability to decide. He heard one among them say they could not even organize the buffalo hunt this season, because of divisions in the western villages. The buffalo will outrun them this season. It is lucky for the Santee that the wild rice does not move on four legs."

Four Horns did not smile. He looked seriously at Water Bear and said,

"You know my father has a liking for you, and my people were well pleased with you, Water Bear. But we cannot deny any longer that your presence here has been a bad influence. Nor can you yourself deny that as long as the Lakota believe that the black kettle is a bad spirit, at least as brought here by your hand, and they will not be trading with you."

Water Bear began to protest that he had been making progress among some of the Santee, but Four Horns waved this aside, and continued determinedly,

"You do not know the untrue things that have been said about you. Spread to them, I am sorry to relate by the Illini chiefs, goaded on by our own Stone Shoulder, who is part Illini, even as he spreads worse rumours about the other nations to my father. He and the Illini disrupt all sides."

"Hah! He too and the Illini wish to take the trade from the east himself," Water Bear interjected. "But they know nothing of how it is done."

"That may be true. But, my father now fears a plot against you as a symbol of Iowa bad mischief, if you remain here any longer."

Water Bear shrugged.

"Listen well. I must go back down the Michissippi to lead the main part of our people across the Michissippi and up the biggest river into the western countries to some new place of settlement for us. That is what we have been trying to negotiate here. I will be leaving here tomorrow for our southern village. It is a half-moon down the Michissippi."

"So?"

"My father wonders if you would travel with me. You will have our protection and will see more of the great river, as you have said it is your wish to do. This, only on condition my father sets, that our people shall have a preference in the trade for the goods of the pale-faced ones when you bring them to the western countries. How would you answer this, Water Bear?"

Water Bear did not answer for a time. He had concluded earlier that it was not just his presence which had upset the Iowa plan of settlement in the northwest. He thought Four Horns was making too much of this. He could not help the feeling that he was being made the excuse for the Iowa failures at the spring council.

Yet, his own Odawa people were as proud as any and Water Bear could understand the Ioway not wanting to admit that the real reason for their inability to secure an agreement with the Sioux was that their northern cousins no longer cared for their cousins to the south, living among the Illini for whom the northern tribes were often at ear and had little respect except meeting them sometimes in the spring. And, there could be other reasons. This was only one undercurrent in the speeches that Water Bear had listened carefully to.

Finally, Water Bear looked over at the Lakota encampment and said,

"I know and care little about any plots and threats against me. A simple look at their shaman protects me. They know I am a man of dreams, and that my dreams are strong medicine, beyond those of a crazy man. It will take them more time to move against me. This is not their own land, and they know they cannot be so powerful in this mixed place of meetings among many peoples, as they can be in their own villages."

He looked over the vast encampment and then back at Four Horns.

"Yet, I must remember that I have very few goods for trade itself on this trip and that it was the interest in trade that I sought here. I have learned where it is that the beaver is best traded and some tell me in secret that they would trade it and other furs for my goods in another season."

Four Horns smiled at this show of good sense.

Water Bear continued, "As I would contact as many nations as possible before returning to my own lands above the lakes, I will accept this offer to travel with you to the south and the condition upon which it is made. I can know little of the prospect to the south, but that I would be in the company of a brother whom I have come to love well and to trust as few others."

"Good!" exclaimed Four Horns, obviously pleased and relieved at Water Bear's decision. "We will leave tomorrow. "

Later, Water Bear, lying outside the teepees in the warm spring night, fell into a fitful sleep. He was unused to the inactivity of the past few days and frustrated with his largely failed trading effort.

Once, he came awake and saw a piercing star flash across the southern sky. This was an uncertain omen for him and it unsettled him the more.

When he fell back asleep he dreamed of a circle of wolves, yapping incessantly at each other. When they began to tear at each other's flesh, he once more came awake.

This time, Water Bear heard something new in the night.

It was the sound of movement just beyond the nearest teepee.

He tensed. Although there was no sound for a while, he slowly drew his knife under the blanket while he continued to feign sleep.

Then there was movement again. He could now make out a single figure approaching him, also with knife in hand, slowly at first but then making a final rush toward him.

The attacker was almost upon him before Water Bear countered the attack with a suddenness and finality that he could not avoid, if others were not to be disturbed.

Only after the dead man was lying on the ground with the moon shining full upon his face did Water Bear realize that he had just been forced to kill an Illini youth.

He quickly placed the lad face down upon his own sleeping boughs and headed noiselessly to the tepee of Four Horns to alert him to what had happened. He managed to gently shake Four Horns awake without causing alarm among the others.

When he explained what had happened, and described the youth he had despatched, Four Horns whispered in reply,

"That is indeed the oldest son of Sinissippi whom you describe. He is the hottest head among the Illini and has been condemned even by his own father for his treachery. We must leave here immediately. If he is on your boughs leave him there with his knife. But gash yourself with it and leave a trail of your own blood as if you too were wounded."

Four Horns thought some more.

"I will tell my father. He must try to smooth things over with at least the Lakota chiefs and can say that he has banished you for this untimely death at their hosted camp, though already wounded, you simply defended yourself to prevent a mortal wound at the hand of whoever attacked you as you slept. He can say that I was sent to assure that you leave this country. Those Lakota chiefs may accept the explanation. But the Illini never will. They have a relentless will. They will send a war party after us as far down the Michissippi, likely well beyond their own lands. Go to our biggest craft below the bluff. It will take us fastest down the river, which still surges. Can you carry the bad spirit?"

"Yes, I will bring the kettle – with the blankets covering it, it holds all my remaining trade goods."

A short while later, Four Horns had said good bye to his father and joined Water Bear below the bluff.

They took the heaviest of the Ioway dugouts and were soon headed swiftly southward, borne by the great river's strong spring currents into the dark before the dawn.

Chapter 4

For the next week, the two men paddled the swift river currents a hundred leagues down the Michissippi. Early on, they had ditched one of the dug-outs, and now travelled together with the black kettle and Water Bear's remaining trade goods all wrapped in a woolen blanket inside the kettle.

They had sped past Burnt Foot's settlement in the dark of night and then passed the last of the Illini villages further south with growing confidence they had outdistanced any Illini pursuers.

"The anger of the Illini will be focussed on you and it will not spend itself. Those in their own country do not know of you yet. But, we must go further down the river to escape them."

The next afternoon Four Horns headed their craft to a small island and they went ashore into its meager woods to make spears to catch fish. He turned to Water Bear after they started a cooking fire.

"We are just above the inlet on the far side where the River of the Illini joins the big river. If we part here, you could return almost directly north back to your country of the big lakes. It is a half-moon on the waters, but you lack a proper canoe and there is no birch bark until you get nearer the lakes. It is longer taking the trails and they would take you through possibly hostile villages."

Water Bear pondered the situation as he ate the last of the fish.

"I say this: From what you say about the uncertainties with the Illini, I may prefer another route home. What option is left?"

Four Horns said, "If we still face those Illini who would chase us down the Michissippi, the best option for you to return home is the river of the Ohio where the rest of the Iowa await me. It flows into the Michissippi from almost as far east as the Longhouse Confederacy. We will reach its mouth in the next day. Before it empties into the Michissippi, another big river the Illini people call the Wapaashi - maybe to your ear, Wabash, or White River because it flows over white stone in some parts, comes to it from the north. That river you can take to one of the lower big lakes and back to your country. It goes mainly through the country of the Shawnee, though those people now move and swirl about their lands as do the twisting winds, caught as they are between the Iroquois on one side and the Illini on the other.

Water Bear tried to take in this complicated geographic information. "I have heard of those Shawnee."

"The Shawnee are very strong, but they take less to slights than the haughty Illini. They speak a language similar to you Odawa and are related to the western Lenape people and the Miami, who live further up the Wabash on their own big river. All I think meet your Prophesy of coming from once living along the big eastern ocean. Many Wendat also came to the area after the Iroquois destruction of their home country of which you have told me. The Shawnee think of those Wendat as their "uncles." All those nations are a new mix from an old mix, I think. They might help you make a lighter craft for the northern rivers, when you get up to the country of birches. I hear they have good land trails there too. But you never know where an Illini war party may be – they can be like the Iroquois when it comes to ranging beyond their own lands during the season of war."

Water bear said, "I can run along a trail if I have to, but not like some of my brothers who can run all day on a trail, sometimes longer and faster than a canoe. You have helped me decide: I choose to take that Ohio River and then the Wabash, north."

The following day, they passed along a big winding bend in the great river with high white bluffs forming the east bank of the river. Four Horns pointed to the high rock cliff looming above them.

There, to Water Bear's astonishment, were two painted monsters. He saw in the monsters something of every creature that could scare or threaten a man: fearsome red eyes, the beard of a big cat with horns, claws, scales, enormous slashing tails twice the size of the bodies, and yet the faces seemed almost human. The colour combination, which had blotches of green, as well as the black of the outlines and the burning red eyes: astonished Water Bear.

As Water Bear gazed at these giants, Four Horns said, "We do not look on them very long. We think they should not be there. They are surely meant to be very bad medicine."

Unable to avert his gaze, Water Bear heard Four Horns' low chant as he made a tobacco sacrifice into the water.

Water Bear said, "We have pictures on rocks in some parts of my country, but they just seem to show things we see – a deer, a wolf, a big bird. But, this is different. You say they are "meant" to be what they are. Is that a warning of some kind? It is surely a story on the cliffs that is meant to give wisdom to all the people who see them, maybe a story not just to be feared alone?"

"You can say those things, Water Bear, but no-one else has. We Iowa just wish those monsters weren't there."

Later, while Water Bear was still asking him about the cliff paintings, Four Horns steered them onto an eastern coil from the main river where they camped. "If someone still chases us, they will not see us here."

"Do you think anyone would still be coming after us this far?" said Water Bear.

"Not really - we are well beyond the Illini country, now."

The next morning, they passed another wide river entering the Michissippi from the west

"That river flows from far distant countries. It brings a lot of mud into the big river here."

Water Bear already could see the brown water from that river swirling into the Michissippi waters.

"That is the river called the Missouri I will travel west with the rest of my people who await me at the Ohio." Water Bear saw the mud stain from the Missouri surging into the Michissippi from the western shores.

But before we approach that, we will see another marvel where the great river meanders until it turns back to its main course. I will take us up a side stream to see it."

Along the stream Four Horns pointed to a high mound that rose in an unnatural way, with almost straight walls, above the surrounding ground.

Four Horns explained, "The villages of the Cahokia are down the big river a half day from here. They claim this is the burial mound of their ancestors. Burnt Foot told you of this. As he said, he was told this mound was built by some ancient ancestors buried there. There are other mounds all along the Michissippi but there are few as big as this. It is a mystery. The Illini say that it is just a hill like any other. They seem to fear any other way of thinking of it."

Back in its main channel, later in the day the swift river currents took them to a place of narrows where a great limestone rock formed an island in the middle of the river. As they shot through this narrow portion of the river they fought cross-currents in the waters as treacherous as the rock-strewn white waters in the rivers of Water Bear's own land.

"From here to the southern sea, the flood plain of the big river gains widens and is in some seasons raging with floods. The river winds about these flat countries like a snake." Even as he said this, Water Bear's paddle hit a large water snake coiling through the waters. He raised his paddle to shake off the snake, but it struck at him, before slithering off.

Four Horns laughed at this.

"Do you know, I've never before seen that happen? Think not of it. I have heard that they are not poisonous. That little bite will heel."

Though bothered by the snake incident, Water Bear's strongest impression of the great river in the past two days, as it received the waters of other large tributary rivers, was that it had formed its own powerful and brooding spirit.

This sense of the river's growing powers made him restless.

"Those large trees touch the river with their bending arms," said Water Bear, pointing to the cottonwoods, now numerous along both banks of the river. "I hope they give a better spirit to the river than I have sensed of late."

"But, it is said they are the reason for the river's coils. When they fall along the banks, and on the islands, they change the flow of the river. This makes the whirlpools that I told you about."

Water Bear appreciated this kind of truth about things causing other things – it sounded like the palefaces' talk he had heard at times.

"But, I would not say they give the river a better spirit."

Even as Four Horns said this, they headed into a strong eddy that was forming before them. It was the first of several they could see ahead.

Water Bear now faced a palpable reason for his growing fear of the great river's powers

He began to feel the inner pull of the swirling water, a force so strong that the first and second of the strange pools could only be resisted by the strongest paddling.

They seemed to be finally free of these and were headed closer to shore, when a third much larger whirling pool loomed before them. He had never before felt so helpless.

Water Bear saw it as huge coiling snakes, his only fear. He cried out in terror. He could not hear Four Horns' shouted instructions. Panic overcame him, and he made a mighty leap out of their craft, grabbing at an overhanging branch, ignoring Four Horns' fate.

Luckily, the dugout's forward reaction to Water Bear's violent motion had powered it beyond the strongest central force of the pool. The monstrous coil of water now moved slowly up river and away from their craft, only the occasional splashing of waves on its receding edge making apparent its powerful forces.

Four Horns managed to return to where Water Bear still clung in terror to the overhanging branch. It took a clever talk for Four Horns to persuade Water Bear back into the dugout. "I understand your fright, not knowing that bad spirit that has taken even many a seasoned river man."

Exhausted from their experience they camped early. They spoke little. Four Horns knew that Water Bear had to come to terms with his fear of the river and his failure in courage. After a time, he thought a few words would help.

"Today, you faced the worst of the river. Even I needed your help to overcome its power. It was the force of your kick away from the boat that pushed me out of the worst of the pool's coils, or I would have been taken by it. Yet, look. It washed a bunch of fish into the dugout, for us to dine well on tonight!"

Water Bear looked at him, but felt little consoled.

"I have not known such fear before. I was not a brave, there. I was shown a mere child, when I foolishly thought I was even more than a mere man. I shamed myself before my overlooking spirits. I hope they do not turn on me."

Four Horns shrugged. "You are a man only if you have known real fear, Water Bear. You are a man who now learns more about his limits. And yet, I still see before me no mere man! You are a man who draws the spirits to your story."

Water Bear nodded slowly. He started to think that this might still be true.

Four Horns continued, "Anyway, you do not lose a feather. Those pools have taken good river men who know them best, and all are like small children when they first experience those treacherous spirits. That was one of the worst I have seen."

"Yes, they are like that twisting wind the other day, but coming up from below. The fifth and sixth directions, from above and below, are well sensed in this open country."

"Tomorrow will improve your spirit," reassured Four Horns. "We should enter the Ohio and arrive at my people's village just up that river. Come, let us smoke a pipe, Water Bear," he said, and opened the last of his tobacco.

At first light the next day, Water Bear awoke refreshed as Four Horns said he would. His irrational fears were gone.

The morning brought them to a point opposite the mouth of the Ohio. By the time it converged with the Michissippi the so-called "beautiful river" was larger than the mighty father river itself. Four Horns had already told Water Bear it flowed all the way from the land of the Longhouse carrying the waters of many other rivers. It took the rest of day to fully enter the Ohio and they made camp for the night.

Four Horns talked at the night fire of his southern self.

"When my father's ancestors explored the Michissippi to find a new settlement, a huge flood took them far south. It is thus that I am the son of a Quapaw Mother. Quapaw is a pretty place, just enough away from the river's big floods. Our feasts are famous. We use the local persimmon fruit in many different ways. Down river to the great gulf, there are many nations. On the eastern side, the Choctaw and the Chickasaw until there are many smaller nations near its shores. On the western side the Quapaw have many surrounding nations: the Otoe, the Kansa, the Osage and the Caddo."

"Those Caddo brought us stories of the Spanish settlers to the southwest and even below the Gulf. Once, when I was down in the southeastern forests near one of the big inland rivers running to the Gulf our party was disturbed one night by a big and dangerous wild cat known as the jaguar. We had to kill it. The jaguar is rare there – far from its normal grounds in the Spanish dominions where it remains a great spirit of the native peoples. We brought its skin to Quapaw. When some Caddo saw it they were very impressed – the Spanish had traded them just such a skin from many moons to the south west.

That night, Water Bear dreamed that he and Four Horns had set a camp on a trail far to the south crossing a big river. He was talking, but Four Horns cut into his words.

"Do not move, Water Bear. Listen. There is a spirit moving this night."

Even as Four Horns said this, Water Bear could feel the presence of something different. His ear began to separate the remaining sounds carrying through the sultry evening air. The little white dog traveling with them since they had passed through a village had been restless even before their meal. But Water Bear had not heard its low growling for a time and it had now disappeared. A roost had been attracting half a sky full of birds into the woods behind them, but that sound, intensified by the heavy air, had also quieted sometime during their meal.

Distant thunder rumbled in the west. A procession of clouds leading the storm, their deep red undersides seeming to Water Bear to be dripping with blood, now nearly covered the fading sunset. The only sound remaining was a background hum of the masses of insects anticipating the storm. That sound, too, seemed less than it had been a few moments before.

"There is something new out there. It is now too silent," Water Bear whispered to Four Horns.

He reached for his knife and bow, and began to get up.

Four Horns knew his thoughts at doing so. "It is not the threat of other men, Water Bear. I have felt its presence once before on this trail, on a hot night like this one."

Water Bear now moved twenty paces to the edge of the firelight and set on his haunches to listen. He thought he could hear something, down a slope behind their encampment, along a stream bank, which was now dimly lit by an early evening full moon not yet concealed by the approaching storm clouds.

But he heard nothing more. After a time on his haunches, he arose to return to the embering fire.

He had taken a few steps, when two sounds rent the night – the yowl of a terrified little dog, and the terrifying roar of a much bigger animal.

In his dream, Water Bear ran to the edge of the slope. In the moonlight, he could make out the shape and the black and orange blotched coloration of a large wild cat standing on the other side of the stream. It was even bigger than the cougars he sometimes saw in his own lands. Beneath the big cat, he saw the torn motionless form of their sometime companion, the white dog.

The cat now entered the water and looked menacingly at Water Bear, who was about to run. But then, a little up the river a large black bear emerged from the woods. Both Water Bear and the big cat were astonished. The big cat growled. The bear rose on its haunches, but did not advance on the cat. It just staring at the cat, making no noise. Water Bear watched in fascination as the cat slowly turned around and receded into the forest.

Water Bear was shaken awake by Four Horns.

"You catch a late sleep. But we must leave."

Later as they paddled up the Ohio toward the river of the Shawnee, Water Bear told Four Horns of his jaguar dream.

"You do have vivid dreams. What meaning do you give it?"

"This dream matters much to me. Often the meaning of my dreams gets frozen in the cold of my own country. But this dream gives readily of its meaning. It must mean that the strongest spirits of different countries respect each other, no matter how different. So too, must the people of different countries. That is not a lesson much appreciated. But it will now become part of my own story I think."

"You have gained the right to tell of such things. You have travelled more countries than any other, now, even in your dreams."

"This jaguar dream tells me that if the spirit of the South can mix with the Northern Spirit, so too can the East with the West. As the smoke from our pipes rises, the white with the black, the dying red sky comes from the middle of the day blue; all of those spirits can be mixed. Even the smallest thing, with the greatest thing. Do you see?

"Our nations already try to mix these things. What are you talking about?

"I think it is an even grander truth we must understand. That is what that magically mixed black kettle brought us from the east and from those new people there. A great people must become a mix of all things, not just one or two of anything. The powerful jaguar spirit and bear spirit came in my dream to tell of that."

"Sometimes, Water Bear, I think when you talk like this you have been dreaming too hard. For most of us, dreams are a tricky way to find out things."

"The Trickster wants to tell us things in a way we will remember.

"You are a strange one, Water Bear, to see such things."

"Let it be, for now. Increasingly though, I see the truth of these things even when I am not dreaming.

"You may be lucky, Water Bear, if these dreams do not interest the spirits, Water Bear. They would come and take you I think. So, let us resume our journey with no more such talk.

By the end of that day the Iowa camp at the confluence of the Michissippi and the Ohio was within view along a break in the towering elm woods along the river.

Four Horns pointed to a long line of dugouts pulled up on the shore saying, "You are in luck. Two of the dugouts there are Shawnee. They must be here on a peaceful mission and they could take you up the Wabash.

When they landed and introductions made, the Shawnee agreed to take Water with them up the Wabash. They would be leaving at daybreak the next day. This left Water Bear and Four Horns little time for good byes.

As they sat at the night fire, Water Bear said, "You know, we have travelled like brothers for four moons and I have never asked you about your own strange name."

"Well, I once headed off two large buffalo toward the rest of the hunting party. It was an unusual feat for a youth. That night, the hunting chief presented me with the four horns to take back to my family's lodge. He called for a naming ceremony and my family did not disagree that henceforth I would be known as Four Horns."

Water Bear was impressed. "You earned your strange name as well and strangely as I earned mine. No wonder we travel well together. Let us rise then and embrace. Let us hope we meet again before the spirits. You have taken good care of me in the west."

"Yes. We are now like brothers. There are tears in my eyes as I bid you a happy retrun to your own land."

Water Bear also wept in the parting. He did so again at sun-up as the Shawnee dugouts pulled away from the shore and began to make their distance from Four Horns standing and slowly waving there. With that, Water Bear began his long journey north back to his homeland.

The Shawnee decided despite his protests that the Ojibwa would travel as their passenger along the Ohio itself, which required expert knowledge with their heavy craft.

As Water Bear sat the dugout, a hot sun burned away the morning mists. The waters began to glisten as he stared into them. He lapsed into a reverie of what he had experienced in the months along the Michissippi. The mix and movement of peoples and spirits was astonishing. Their behaviour and that of the father river was mysterious. Both ranged from smooth acceptance of his presence to a raw rejection. Everywhere there was a talk not heard – his own questions much of the time, that of those seeking peace and those fearing war and even trade, and the painted monsters speaking silently to and ignored by all nations.

Water Bear fell into a trance, until an explosion of flushed ducks loomed out of the shimmering waters. For a moment they seemed as the painted monsters, as if some giant new unsettling spirit was going to follow Water Bear north.

Part Two:

The Dream of Water

Bear

Chapter 5

The next spring, Water Bear was paddling up the eastern side of the Bay of the Huron. He had deliberately sought a water dream. To bring on the dream, he had not eaten for five days.

He had paddled along the shore of the Bay south-east from his Odawa settlement at the leaping waters, taking a route through the emptied countries of the Wendat. It reminded him of their destruction thirty years before and the destruction of the black robes and their fort among the Huron. He paddled through a weedy pass into it. It was now a ruin.   The silence was broken only by a few cawing crows that had followed him in, as if to tell him nothing more was left here.

He thought the French priests' mission had been a foolish and doomed quest without more defenses against the Iroquois. He and most of the nations around the Lakes held the black robes mostly to blame. At least in their new spirit forts around the upper lakes they and their sometimes native allies were less vulnerable to Iroquois attacks. Huronia remained the most vivid symbol of the divisions within and between his world and the palefaces. Now being reminded of it in the very place it occurred would add power to his dream.

As the Prophesy foretold, they were at the time of the new people coming behind a false mask. He himself both marveled at and dreaded the powers of the hairy ones and their beguiling talk. Most in his native world wanted the paleface goods. Yet, the paleface powers were so different from the powers of his people. He had seen what their fire sticks could do; he had seen how heavily they settled the land. How some of them would cheerfully die for their Christ out of some kind of love, not as his peoples in unending mourning wars against their merely human enemies. He had already dreamed that they would make his people dance as sparks on their fingers, and then would drown them in their holy water. He feared any new dream of his peoples would be about an epic struggle. A struggle already happening that was bringing the indigenous people against themselves even more than against the palefaces.

Some shamans said Water Bear's dreams were too strong and that the evil spirits of the trade goods had entered Water Bear himself. Some said he now was possessed with the two-edged magic of the paleface's mirrors, blankets and kettles. Some said he would deny the Prophesy and would threaten the tradition.

And, when he had returned home, his home village and his family was gone. He told the shaman it was because they doubted him, but he could not forgive himself. He had not had a good dream since.

Finally, now he sensed the coming dream would be a visionary dream. But, the spirits would not give back to him any easy vision. They would give him a new challenge, full of uncertain things.

Water Bear stopped trying to paddle. He felt the pains from hunger. The strange weather had for most of the day brought mists swooping and lifting from the bay as if the spirits were dancing upon its waters. In the early evening the sky was full of uncertainty: clouds scudding in opposing directions, only occasionally revealing the rising full moon.

By nightfall he was slipping into and out of delirium. He clutched his bearskin, waiting for the dream Spirits to come. As his canoe drifted, lightening winds moved his canoe in different directions, until a dying puff of west wind pointed his canoe toward yet another small island.

The moon reappeared from behind the clouds.

The island was rocky. In the middle of it, Water Bear could make out a small woods. The branches of its wind-blasted trees formed jagged shapes in the changing moonlight. Water Bear could sense the spirits were there. He shifted his position and bid the spirits to carry him swiftly and without more mischief to the land of dreams.

Even as he did so, the spirits manifested themselves.

The now brilliant light of the moon seemed to focus on the near edge of the island's central woods. There, a white rabbit had emerged and sat motionless.

Water Bear gazed upon it. At least this timorous being was not a threatening spirit.

For a time, the rabbit seemed to become an even more brilliant white. As new clouds crossed and blackened the moon, the rabbit drew to itself all of the previous moonlight until it alone shone upon the shore. All about was a deep blackness. But then, the white light began to pour forth from the rabbit and flowed along the shore to a rocky point a short distance away.

Water Bear was seized with fear at the spectre he now beheld, illuminated by the light from the rabbit. Upon the rocky point there loomed a monster bear, standing at full menacing height, yet making no sound.

All remained silent. Water Bear no longer felt fear. The Spirits were speaking to him.

The bear went down on all fours and the light ebbed from the huge form, flowing back along the shore once again to the rabbit. The small creature looked again timorously about, even as it seemed to control the flow of light.

Then, the light flowed away from the rabbit, down to the water's edge. Water Bear groaned and was seized with a new fear, as the white light began to undulate and took the form of glittering white snakes, slithering into the water and coming rapidly toward Water Bear's canoe.

Water Bear clutched at his throat but could not move otherwise. Within moments this most evil Snake spirit, his own Bear clan's worst enemy, suddenly appeared over the side of the canoe.

The first snake, and then many others slithered into the canoe. They coiled, in a ball, at first seeming to consume each other. They turned from white to black. Then one, and then others plunged at him. He could not stop his mouth opening in horror. He would have preferred they had bitten him to the next moment, for he could not stop them from entering him by the mouth, engorging into his throat, until he swallowed them and awaited the terrors within.

But, in that instant, the whole lake around him began to shine in a blinding white light, which then resolved itself into thousands of brilliant glints as the friendly Fish spirits converged on Water Bear's canoe, bringing now with them the wondrous light from the moon Rabbit.

First the canoe, and then he himself took on the brilliant light. He felt a great surge of energy. He coughed up the snakes and grabbed and threw them from his mouth.

That moment brought him awake, pulling at his face.

Water bear was now assaulted by his own confused thoughts. The shadows across the moon had started the dream – he knew they were the black robes. What had been a flow of white moonlight flowed to and through the animal spirits – to Rabbit and only then to Bear. That was a reversal of their normal role in the world. Somehow, the snakes brought something dreaded that had to be done – he gagged again at the thought he had swallowed them and regurgitated them in the dream.

What strange mix of different spirited things could this be? The Bear spirit was from his own country, Rabbit was in many. The Fish spirits were in all countries. They told him his dream must be shared with all people and it would somehow be widely accepted. But, what did the reversal of Rabbit and Bear and the terrible actions of the Snake and his own spirit really mean?

His mind was clear on only one thing: he knew that he had been touched by the Spirits for some great purpose.

The clouds disappeared and the moon was brilliant in the night sky. By the time it set, Water Bear had slipped again into unconsciousness. Responding only to the winds and currents, his canoe drifted away from the island into the darkness toward the eastern shore of the Bay of the Huron.

Water Bear was awakened the following morning by the sunlight and the sound of weeds brushing against the side of his canoe. He was surprised - it seemed that he was alive and not on the way to the Spirits.

The previous night's dream had been a monstrous vision. But, far from leaving him even weaker and near death, he felt somehow refreshed. His fever had gone, and although he had long since run out of food, some of his strength had returned to him. In fact, he marvelled at how well he felt despite the hunger. He drank deeply of the cool water surrounding him.

He could recall every detail of the dream. Yet, he could not understand its meaning. Why had it been driven by Rabbit, one of the weakest forest spirits, and not the monster Bear? Why had it made him swallow the snakes? Though the snake was sometimes a "serpent of good luck" in some Anishinaabe nations, Snake was the spirit Water Bear himself most dreaded.

One thing seemed clear: the fact that he had awakened somehow restored surely attested to something the Spirits had in mind for him.

He strongly felt this most powerful dream was not just a personal dream. He sensed that this dream was intended to be shared among the people. He vowed that by the time he saw his own people again he would know the meaning and could share its great purpose with them.

Water Bear decided he had to head for shore where he could find food and make a medicine lodge and take the necessary measures to regain his health and interpret his dream.

In the distance, he could see the outlet of one of the rivers coming from the country of the Nipissings. He headed toward shore well north of the outlet to avoid any Iroquois war party which might be lurking at the outlet.

He came between two islands. Emerging from the channel between them he headed toward the mainland shore. Too late he saw the smoke of campfires along the shore. He would suffer the consequences of his unwariness. Two Iroquois war canoes were converging fast on his canoe.

With his normal strength and lighter craft Water Bear might have had a chance to escape. But, he did not have his normal strength.

The two Iroquois war canoes were now quickly cutting him off. Water Bear had to make a rapid decision. Instead of trying to escape, he turned his canoe and paddled directly toward the nearer of the two canoes approaching him. It held Onondaga warriors. Water Bear could not make out whether any of these was a war captain. But they were more given to reasonable talk than the Mohawk he could see in the other canoe, who saved their reasonable talk only for the palefaces.

Chapter 6

Many Axes, an Onondaga, shifted his squat but kept staring at the fire. He was a big heavy man. His hair was a single dangling tuft, to which were affixed two feathers. At twenty seven years old, by his feats already as an Onondaga sub-chief, he could have worn many among the Iroquois nations. He usually chose two crow feathers – he said they represented his only two truly important achievements, "being born" and "staying born." For him, the life of a man meant many new births before death. "Without that, the stones are alive, too, if that's the way you want to be," he said.

His hair tuft dramatically set off the axe scar on the left side of his neck running onto his shoulder. Ten seasons before, the war club of an Erie brave had gone deep. It took all his older brother's strength to staunch the bleeding. Many Axes had been near death for days. The women elders of Onondaga said his coming out of death long after even the medicine men had given up on him was a spirit-given thing. Many Axes had then and since been a favourite of the women elders.

But the axe mark was not the reason for his name. When even younger, he had thrown axes that split distant wooden targets four times in a row, the third throwing with his left hand, the last, with the longest successful axe throw witnesses had ever seen. He had learned how to throw an axe with the help of his younger brother – a scrawny sickly kid whom Many Axes fiercely defended and who in return would sit with crossed legs for a whole day watching Many Axes throw axes. He would gauge the distance, speed and angle of the thrown axes so Many Axes could become increasingly proficient. And then, at his little brother's suggestion, he learned to throw with either hand.

After these feats with the axe, the youth Many Axes was given his new name. Now his prowess with the axe was widely known, well beyond the

Iroquois. He laughed each time he embarked on a war party. He would throw several axes, some now made from the palefaces' iron, into his canoe and wore one at each side. "You never know which arm I might lose," he would say.

Because of his menacing presence, the great peace chiefs of the Mohawk started bringing him along to their palavers with the Dutchers and the New Yorkers. There, Water Bear learned the arts of persuasive diplomacy. Now the women loved him more – he was both a war chief and a peace chief.

But he was not loved by everyone. Many Axes looked across the fire. Loud Dog was there, sharing a meal with two of his Mohawk warriors. He was a lean man, his face marred with several scars from warfare. He was older than Many Axes and accordingly outranked him in the war party. They were in fact rivals in seeking the favour and agreement of the leader of the war party, Dancing Pipes, one of the occasional women war captains among the Iroquois. She had from childhood insisted on playing a fluted pipe when joining the dances at the Mohawk and Onondaga fires. She was a rarity in that and in her skills at Iroquois leading war parties, especially when they were a mix of the five nations of the Longhouse people, which they did now this far north.

Many Axes was on the water-facing side of the fire. He was one of the first to see far out emerging from some islands a canoe paddled by a single high hair Odawa. The canoe was close enough to the Iroquois war camp for the Odawa to see it and warn others of his nations further north that there was an Iroquois war party approaching the French fur-trade river.

But, if this man was who Many Axes thought he might be, he had to move quickly to head off his sure death at hands of his Mohawk companions. Even as the Mohawk shouts from the shore summoning Loud Dog rang out, Many Axes waved for two paddlers from his own fire.

Choosing not to flee, Water Bear instead had closed on the leading Onondaga canoe and had a moment to speak to the leading man he had met once before the second Mohawk canoe reached them. As he came within talking distance, Water Bear raised his hand in a sign of peace and said in his best Iroquoian,

"Ho. Many Axes. I see the Great Tree of Peace spreads even wider. We Odawa have wondered whether it will soon grow even to the upper lakes." He slowly waved his hand in the direction of Huronia, and then to the northwest. Many Axes saw that this man was indeed Water Bear, the visionary Odawa trader whom he had agreeably met once before.

As the three canoes converged, one of the young Onondaga warriors laughed at Water Bear's opening words and raised his war club, about to strike him down. But Many Axes made a quick move to prevent him from doing so.

"Hold! Do not be so quick with this man. That necklace that he wears makes him Bear Clan, as are many of our Longhouse brothers. Look at his hair. He is an Odawa. He has wide knowledge. He is a worthy enemy."

Many Axes made a secret sign of friendship to Water Bear, but spoke out loud to him as if he did not know of him,

"Tell us, man of the Bear, what would make you worthy of the stake that we should hold off our present blows?"

"I speak not to insults. I am Water Bear. I pass and trade among all peoples, speaking their languages, yours more than once. You are not a full Chief. I would see your captain first, but do as you will."

"So! And I am Many Axes. I have heard of you. You are the latest in your family of Ojibwa, dreamers more than traders I would say, though whom among you people would have a dream worthy to tell to us Longhouse? Do you have a dream for us? Hah!"

The others shared his harsh laughter.

Many Axes and Water Bear had met two seasons before, when Water Bear could not make a trade with some Seneca, unless approved by Many Axes, already much respected among his brothers though he was only an Onondaga sub-chief. They had said he was a favourite of all the mothers because he saw wisdom on all sides on many matters that fired young Iroquois braves only in one direction or another. Many Axes had briefly appeared and being on the war path against northern nations kindred to Water Bear he approved an unusual trade for some needed guns with Water Bear and spared his life.

As he eyed the Mohawk canoe, Water Bear similarly realized he could not speak to Many Axes as he might have, if they had been alone.

"I may have had such a dream, but as I said to you: I speak not to insults."

Loud Dog, now within earshot, was uncaring of this talk and gave Water Bear a mighty blow with his war club, knocking the Odawa senseless into the bow of his canoe.

"We will let this man dream some more. But let us hear no more of his talk, Many Axes. You give him spirit by not throwing him immediately to the fish."

Many Axes looked warily at the tall warrior. Many Axes spoke carefully to him.

"You will see, Loud Dog. Our war captain Dancing Pipes knows of this man. He trades widely, but he is a powerful vision seeker. He has been of value to more than one of our war parties in the Western countries with useful goods and information. If the Seneca were with us now, you would be told these things. "

"Too many things already distract this year's war party," the scarred man replied in disgust. But, Many Axes, though younger, was a favourite of Dancing Pipes. His wishes in this matter could not be ignored.

Loud Dog turned away and waved to one of his men to board Water Bear's canoe. He gave a sign, and the man began to paddle the senseless Water Bear toward shore.

"Your cowardly blow will not gain you a feather, Loud Dog."

"I gave only a glancing blow - he will be awake again well before tonight's fires."

The three canoes headed for shore without further talk among the men.

Later in the day, Many Axes saw that Water Bear had gradually regained consciousness and was looking up at the branches forming the lean-to over him. Dancing Pipes had deputized Many Axes to find out more from Water Bear, especially if, as he had hinted, he had a vision of interest to the Iroquois.

Many Axes brought corn sagamite in a wooden dish and water in a second bowl. Though Water Bear had a splitting pain from the blows he had received earlier, he managed to take the food and water. By nightfall, Many Axes sensed that Water Bear was feeling a little better.

"Tell me exactly your thoughts, Water Bear. They may help in this situation."

Water Bear looked up, first warily and then, sensing the beguiling Many Axes' genuine expression of sympathy, and wondering if he was being approached to trade a dream for his life, he dismissed his concerns about his chances among the Iroquois war party and thought quickly about how he would tell his story.

He knew that his dream was of much greater importance than any he had before. But, he would not speak of such a dream without a sign, and even if such a sign came, he could not yet understand an uninterpreted dream, so there was nothing to tell of the dream's meaning, only its literal content. That it was a dream of black and white powers, Water Bear swallowing and spitting up snakes or that somehow the Rabbit spirit, not Bear was central to it, would hardly satisfy the Iroquois war party. He must stall for time.

But Many Axes, sensing these thoughts of his captive, gave him no chance to stall for time.

"Speak now, Water Bear. Tell it all. "

Water Bear could not resist Many Axes' order.

"Just last night, I was given a dream – a vision of the future for our world, yours and mine."

Many Axes listened to the literal dream.

He marveled at the strangeness and power of the dream, but equally asked, "So Water Bear, what is the interpretation of such a dream? "

"As yet, I know not, so it can only be told as I dreamed it, not its meaning. I have nothing yet to satisfy what will be demanded at your fires. I need the time to interpret it."

Many Axes left Water Bear. He headed for Dancing Pipes, sitting at a fire across the camp from both the Mohawk and Onondaga areas. He saw that she was alone and that Loud Dog was nowhere to be seen.

He took the chance to offer her an idea. She asked a few questions and then agreed with it. They parted, just as Loud Dog re-entered the camp from a morning sortie to meet their scouts along the main river of the Nipissing. He could tell by Loud Dog's scowl that there was no news yet of any approaching fur congees from the west.

At the end of the morning, Water Bear was roughly taken from the lean-to and tightly tied to a stake close to their smouldering central fire.

Many Axes approached the tethered Water Bear nonchalantly. Loud Dog had again disappeared, but there were a few Mohawk at the fires. He carelessly dropped a wooden bowl beside the Odawa, spilling out some of its fish soup, and spoke quietly.

"Take what is left. You need it. And listen to me carefully. Say nothing. The others in the camp must have no idea of our talk. I will make loud threats and show you my contempt. React as if I were making you squirm with vile thoughts of your coming torture. As you do, I will give you my decision with Dancing Pipes. You are my captive, though she is the war captain. You are lucky you can speak our language a bit."

"I am a trader."

"I said say nothing!" He now yelled at Water Bear and kicked him. The kick was vicious but it mostly hit the ground. Water Bear recoiled and went into a fetal position. He made a low cry that those watching would not mistake for anything the sound of pain and fear.

"Good. Keep that up. Now I can begin my talk. We know you have powerful dreams – you are like all the Ojibwa. They have the best dreams we think. I am interested in dreams. So is Dancing Pipes. She is Mohawk. Those at the Eastern Door of the Longhouse Confederacy have learned to distrust everything, even powerful dreams. She alone seeks them."

He kicked at Water Bear again, and shouted terrible oaths at him. But he then quietly continued.

"She pleases the grandmothers: she not only talks well to the Dutchers, she is also the best eastern war captain, because she understands those tribes and only wins. She not only keeps the peace across our federation, she beguiles us with the old dreams in the depths of winter. Best of all, she values me highly: I am Onondaga and my grandmothers love me. I could sit all the time and do nothing and still be sought out for the final wisdom on things when the older brothers of the Mohawk and Seneca and the younger brothers of the Oneida and Cayuga come to the central fire with their decisions. But I am also, at thirty seasons, the best war captain for the Seneca who hold the Western Door and I speak the best talk with our western foes, as you were once told. After you waited for me two seasons ago to approve that trade, my brothers told me of your interesting dreams. Even hearing it second hand, I thought they were powerful. It made me think: what is the black and white? Why does Bear seem the weakest power in your dream, not Rabbit and why are you forced to swallow the snakes? And then I thought, when it comes to our nations and the palefaces, why are not the Bear of one Nation not the best cousins of the Bear in any other? We divide ourselves, it seems. I will return to you later, with a plan."

Seeing Loud Dog emerge from his lean-to, Many Axes kicked Water Bear again, dragged him back to his lean-to and laughed harshly, before striding away, still laughing mockingly and saying to the Mohawk,

"Leave that Odawa out of sight – until he gives us his dream he disgraces our fire."

That night just after dark, Dancing Pipes slipped into Water Bear's lean-to.

He was not surprised that she would visit him, not Many Axes, given the tensions between Many Axes and Loud Dog, and that she was doing so in stealth. What he witnessed of her was widely known: by her tongue and manner, she made even her fiercest warriors listen to and obey her.

He had watched her during the day. He knew the Iroquois tribes appointed women as war captains, sometimes for their own merit, more often because of conflicts among the men who might have been selected. In this case, it was probable that merit had been the reason.

She was shorter than most of the men around her, but perhaps a little broader and stronger looking than most women. She was painted as the others, but wore no particular war clothes. Her main feature was her way of looking directly at whom she was talking, more directly than any Iroquois he had known, even the young Many Axes, who had looked at him once or twice in the eye. She now looked directly at him. He could just make out her face in the falling darkness.

"Ho, Water Bear. You are Bear Clan, as are some of us. It is two seasons since I once saw you at the Seneca fires. Despite the enmity of our peoples, you gave freely of your dreams and their wisdom at that fire. I have not set eyes upon you since. But, from that one time I know your dreams have value. I later made its lesson work against hot heads in my midst"

Water Bear looked up at her, drinking in her sympathy as healing medicine, as she continued.

"Many Axes says he thinks you had an important dream just before you were taken out there in the bay. He told me its details, and I shared that with Loud Dog. It is now hotly disputed between Many Axes and Loud Dog, my top warriors. The one blames the other for trying to knock you senseless and making you uncooperative; the other says you are worth nothing."

Water Bear remained silent.

"Some would have you put to the stake and be done with. I will not permit that, though it is a bad business to keep a camp for so long as we have and have yet a new thing unresolved between key warriors."

Water Bear kept his silence. Dancing Pipes shifted her position and began to show impatience. She continued to look at him directly.

"The scouts reported today to Loud Dog that the Nipissing villages along their river are abandoned with no pelts. Our main objective to intercept a Frenchmen's trading party has so far been frustrated and it is getting late in the season. None approaches."

"Now we linger here. This seeming indecision is not my usual way. Most in my war party are beginning to share Loud Dog's displeasure. All this grows into doubts and opposition on other matters. Only Many Axes, blessed with unusual patience for a leading young warrior, and his few braves here remain fully accepting of my leadership. I was close to deciding to return to our own country when you were captured. This brought the current disagreement, and is seen as fouling and delaying us more. They would have their way with you at the torture stake and be gone."

Water Bear looked up searchingly at her. "You tell me that it is hard to lead. But, continue, I think you have more for me to hear."

"I do. Let me then tell you why I do not permit the fate for you that is so eagerly sought by the majority of my war party. Only now do I see some meaning may emerge from this diversion north and that you and your latest dream must be it. If there are no furs to be had, I do not see meaning in one more enemy's death. And, I have warned that yours is not a spirit to release at our stake. You Ojibwa peoples can hurt us. Some of our own medicine people could also find this a bad mistake. But, you say you cannot give us the interpretation of this dream. I cannot hold the others much longer if you continue to refuse to give us all the dream's meaning. What say you to this?"

Water Bear had been increasingly troubled at what Dancing Pipes said to him. His expression darkened as he finally spoke to her.

"I seek not your protection if it cannot be given. But you have spoken the truth and so must I. The dream of which I foolishly hinted when first captured was indeed a dream of great importance. But, it is not mine to relate as yet, even if my life may depend on it."

He now looked pleadingly at her.

"As I told Many Axes, I do not know its meaning! Though it was a dream more vivid than any I have ever had, the Spirits deny me the meaning. I cannot know why, but only that some further sign must come and some time must pass before I know the dream's meaning or can speak of it."

Here he raised face to her again, in anguish.

Dancing Pipes was thinking quickly about this.

"But is this not the first sign? Your first chance to relate it is to a war party of an enemy nation? I sense from that it must surely be an important dream, perhaps then for all our nations. And, if it will take a little time, by this sign, Many Axes and I agree: the interpreted dream must be told first to an Iroquois fire!"

She spoke these last words very strongly.

Water Bear remained silent for a time. Then, he turned to her and said,

"Ho. The sign seems clear enough and I accept what you say. I cannot say it makes my northern spirit happy to accept such a thing. But if there is not yet a meaning to relate on which all can agree, then the dream cannot now be told at your fire, or at any fire. It anguishes me that I do not grasp its meaning. I can only relate it as I dreamed it."

"Yes, just as Many Axes related it to me. I too am mystified.

"I know only that it speaks of a mighty contest between subtle spirits, perhaps neither the black nor the white wholly good or evil – perhaps somehow we must learn to pick out what we need from each. There is no meaning yet for your fire."

She said, "I am afraid that dream is so strange that my warriors would laugh at it, except Many Axes."

He sank back. "You can see. The spirits have cursed me with this confusing black and white dream. Just as they have cursed is nations with the white people and the black robes. I can only say that there is in the dream some power that turns black to white and then white to black and the terrible snakes and only after that, the friendly fish."

His face was wet with tears as he spoke these words.

Dancing Pipes was moved.

"Perhaps its meaning will come to you soon. Of the black robes, we urge you to think nothing. We think they are too clever for their own good and they cannot persuade most of us to take their Jesus seriously. Even the other palefaces warn us about them. Their God works more mischief than even the spirits of your Wendigos. We think all those people really understand is war. Let the Iroquois carry that war."

Water Bear gave her no response, and rolled to his other arm, looking up at her for some answer.

"I will give you another day. If you have not called for me by midday tomorrow, something else will have to resolve the matter. We must break camp before the new moon." Dancing Pipes walked away from the lean to.

Water Bear spent another feverish night. By mid-morning Many Axes again came to him. He could see that nothing had changed with Water Bear concerning the dream – he would not be telling it without its meaning before the present fire.

He concluded the meeting this time quickly and with a surprising direction.

"Here is a war band from Dancing Pipes' wrist, Water Bear. Although she wears it only into battle, it is beautifully made of shells and the porcupine quills gathered from your own people. It is a prize of her family. It is decided that you are to be put to death tomorrow. I gained you another day. Dancing Pipes and I would rather it be arranged for you to escape with your uninterpreted dream tonight."

Water Bear was not fully relieved. He had been preparing for his fate at the torture stake.

Many Axes continued "Dancing Pipes has agreed with me that we have seen that you must interpret the dream in your own way and in your own time. You must only give me a promise that none other must hear the interpreted dream before you have related it to an Onondaga fire at which Dancing Pipes or I attend. This is why I give you her wrist band. It will give you passage into my country through the Western Door. Take care not to enter through the Eastern Door. I think the Mohawk will continue to reject you. Do you accept my proposal?"

Water Bear looked at the red and black wristband. It reminded him of the strange patterns that the Iroquois worked so well from shells in their wampum belts. At this moment, Water Bear was more of a mind to accept an honourable death at the Iroquois torture stake than go along with this ignominious escape offered by Dancing Pipes. But, he realized that the dream now seemed to mean as much to this Onondaga war chief as it did to him.

He murmured his agreement to the plan.

"Good. When I return for you this night, be ready to follow me as fast as you can. When the time is right, she will tell our elders that you are sworn to bring the interpreted dream to our fires before any other as soon as you can. Nothing will be revealed of your arranged escape, save it must have been arranged by the Spirits and that it must be to give you the time needed to interpret such an important dream meant first for the people of the Longhouse. You seem well enough recovered. Find a fast trail, Water Bear of the Odawa. Loud Dog may decide to chase you."

Water Bear watched Many Axes as he went quickly away. He had not imagined such an outcome. But he trusted her and Many Axes to do as she promised. He would try his best in the future to meet the condition.

By the middle of the night the soup he had been given through the day finally began to improve his spirits and increase his energy. He eagerly awaited Many Axes. It was a long wait. The moon had long risen at a low angle and passed from the sky and a drum had begun at fires on the far side of the camp when Many Axes appeared, gave him some cornmeal and told him a paddle had been placed in the canoe which awaited him where it had been left where the river of the Nipissing entered the Great Bay.

With an appreciative glance at Many Axes, Water Bear slipped out of the Iroquois camp.

He moved as quickly as he could through the forest before the day dawned. As the morning sky first brightened, he was able to locate the canoe. He stood a moment, watching some deer drinking at this place. He knew that he had little time to decide his course, since his escape would soon be known and some of the Mohawk might even had decided to come after him. Then he launched his canoe into the Bay and was able to find a steady stroke northward.

He thought of his own people at the leaping river from the Upper Lake. They would likely know about the Iroquois northern war parties this season. If he headed west, back to his own peoples, there would be some black robes at the fort there. He wondered if that was a vain hope. Then he wondered at how they had lasted as long as they had in the time of Huronia.

He thought maybe a better choice was to go around the Iroquois camp to the north and rejoin the river of the Nipissing and make his way to the great ancestor river of the Odawa traders. There he could seek out the leading black robes in their own place with the other Frenchmen at the end of that river to find out and whether to accept or reject their role in his dream. He need to replenish his trading goods. Perhaps, if necessary, he could pretend he wanted to become one of the "praying Indians" there.

If he went east, he would have to avoid the Iroquois scouts. And he might even find fur caches, in secret places he knew along the main trading routes, if the Nipissing had indeed fled west to escape the advancing Iroquois. If he met up with spring trading party headed down from the northwest, so much the better. The French traders knew him, as did his own people who did the trade and the other trading nations.

His decision made to go east, he turned his canoe again northward to the nearest outlet of the river of the Nipissing. It would take him back to his own father river, the river of the Odawa and down to the paleface settlements.

Chapter 7

Water Bear had spent a season in Quebec. His quest for a sympathetic Jesuit to help interpret his dream's black content led him to a priest much experienced among the native peoples and now retired in the Jesuit College at Quebec. At first the priest had seemed quite interested, but, in the end, he told Water Bear it would be best to forget it. The priest thought that maybe all it foretold was he would father a mixed blood child, or if it had larger implications surely it meant his people should embrace the faith in Jesus and more civilized ways and exclusive trade with the French at their chain of forts. Water Bear was disappointed that these weak one-sided interpretations had replaced the priest's initial enthusiasm in talking about the dream. He thought the priest must have shared the dream with other priests, perhaps in confession, and had been told to close his mind.

Not seeing any further promise in New France, Water Bear journeyed back to his Odawa people living along the chutes from the Upper Lake. He had begun to have doubts about the dream until it occurred to him the black robes never had doubts about theirs. He had all along thought of their Christ story as a kind of vision. It was a dream he now doubted, not so much because of its strange ideas of a God, but because it was the God of someone else, not that of his own people. They said they had had that vision for more than 1600 years. But the creation stories of many woodland nations and the Prophesies of his Anishinaabe people had also been told from an ancient time. Maybe they had come to the ancestors as more than just personal dreams, just as he had believed from that first morning after his own most important dream that it was meant for all the people.

The problem was his own dream seemed to point to something combining both spirits. Perhaps he was foolish to have thought any vision in a dream of his own would suggest some shared fate of his own peoples with the ways of these new people. It now seemed absurd to him. Maybe it was only within his own world his dream would be interpreted. The palefaces had their own dream to contend with. It still badly conflicted them too. So said the Dutchers and New Yorkers.

Water Bear felt disgust at himself for having spent so long a period in Quebec and disgust at the Iroquois for alliances that had destroyed the balance of peoples around the Lakes and thus were forcing the Huron and the Odawa and so many other tribes of the Anishinaabe to flee in all directions from their native countries.

As he got nearer his home country he began to feel pure again.

On the last night of his journey, he stood a long time on a ridge, watching the sun set. He came to a peace with himself about living with an un-interpreted dream. He would be its guardian: he would simply tell it as he had dreamt it, at all the fires. Let others help him bear the burden of its interpretation.

It seemed a gentle country, the land of low treed hills that lies between the Upper Lake and the Lake of the Huron. Yet the great volume of water carried by the river flowing from the upper lake to the lower ones, and the narrowness of the rushing river's many channels, make its waters leap wildly about the ancient rocks which it has scoured since the time of the Ice.

In the spring sun, the rocks and leaping waters glisten. It was the season when the whitefish run. They leap with the waters in such quantity as to make this a strategic place in the Great Lakes world. Who sets the seines across the surging river at the right time and place, feeds not only his own people but the many neighbouring peoples in all directions who trade for the fish that are caught and dried here.

On one such spring day in 1680, two men watched from a nearby hill as their younger cousins worked the nets across the river for the second time in the day. The two men had been making a peace with each other.

One was Water Bear. He spoke carefully to his companion about the meanings of the ancient spring fishing rite they witnessed before them.

"This is not really a hunt with a hunting spirit. It is a more studied thing, and a thing always in one place. And, like the wandering buffalo herds I have seen massed beyond count in the western countries, the fish run feeds all the peoples. All around need fish more each year. The ways of the hunt yield less and constant war destroys the ways of the hunt as it destroys our best hunters. The rabbit dream speaks of powers I thought were those of the pale face ones that are not like the hunting spirit. Yet, is not our own method of fishing, with the man-made nets out there, one such thing? Do you hear any meaning in my talk, Whitefish? "

The man to whom Water Bear addressed these words was the only man outside his own immediate band of loyal followers to whom he would speak of such things searching for meaning beyond the un-interpreted content of his dream.

Whitefish was even taller than Water Bear, gaunt and with a more angular countenance and redness to his skin. He wore the extra feathers of an Ojibwa chief and was strikingly tattooed all over his body, more so than even Water Bear.

The man did not avert his gaze from the scene on the river, when he replied to Water Bear.

"You observe things I do not know. When you had that dream, I think a net descended upon you, just as those settle in front of us now. Even if it was a net that the fish spirits carried, it turns inside out and opposes things we know."

He looked directly at Water Bear.

"The black of the dream that must be the black robe, as you first said, seems to twist our peoples' fate. Yet, are not the French and their traders among us our fast friends? They would not take our lands, only some of its bounty for good trade of their things in return and a few forts far and wide to protect that trade. They are not like those pale faces from New York obeying another far king, who would take our land for their own settlements. You yourself have told us those English are told by their God that they must have our land, because they think we make too little use of it. The French do not tell us that."

"Yet, my dream seems to tell of something we must do to control all of that pale face power – even perhaps the subtler invasion of the French upon us, though I cannot say that for sure."

"Well, unless you are clearer on the meaning of your dream, especially in the respect I just told you, it is dangerous for you. Our shaman, Leaping River hurts you, as do the other medicine men who would dream as you, but expect others to seek their help in interpreting their dreams, and who think dreams are only matters between each man and the Spirits, through a medicine man's intercession and not for all to know."

Water Bear showed a flash of anger at the mention of his most dangerous rival.

"Ho, those medicine men would trap that power of dreams as if it were not for all, just as the pale face would trap the land as if it were not for all."

Whitefish murmured an acknowledgment of this insight.

"The dream gave me more power to see these things than I ever had before, though I still do not understand all the things of which it speaks. They do not seem directly ours. But, this is a thing all councils must consider: why does the paleface master these powerful things that are both about and yet seem not about what their spirits say to them? As we want their things more, they give us their things and we lose our own spirit. Can we not somehow put the spirit of the hunt into their things and thereby take back new spirit for ourselves?"

This was answered with a grunt of disgust. "I cannot think what you mean," Whitefish said dismissively this time. "But as I have said to you, I sense it may be important to our people, so you have my protection Water

Bear. Whatever protection that can be against the evil spirits that Leaping River would summon against you."

"Your protection is of great value, my cousin. It keeps Leaping River from gaining the support of too many others, though I fear him not myself."

Whitefish departed down the hill. Water Bear was pleased that he had for the first time in several attempts won the full support of his powerful cousin.

As he walked the two leagues back to his own small settlement, he knew that he had an additional reason to make the trip between his own lodges and the settlement of Whitefish's people, nearer the black robe mission at the place of the rapids.

On each of these occasions, as Water Bear reached the low rise which offered a pleasing overlook of these settlements along the river between the Upper Lakes, he had seen a young woman in a field planted with corn, beans and squash at the eastern edge of Whitefish's main village. Her dark hair was striking, and more to one side than the way worn by women of the nations around the middle Great Lakes. She was sometimes alone tending the fields and sometimes with others.

She was near enough to return his smile. But each time, she quickly averted her eyes from him, discouraging him from approaching, though he wished more each time that he could get close to her and maybe be able to speak to her.

He knew he was drawn to her and wanted to know her. But until he did, he also wondered whether having to pass her by silently so many times had itself increased his attraction to her.

She was older than the other girls who sometimes tended the field with her, possibly as old as Water Bear himself, but she still moved with a child's quickness among the rows of crops. He had passed her a few times, before he realized that she moved with a slight limp. By several more passes he thought of it as an intriguing limp, a kind of slight hop to correct a slight imbalance from any previous two seemingly normal steps she made.

When she had turned away from him for a sixth time, Water Bear made enquiries at the village. Few seemed to want to speak of the girl. Then, after a day or so of such inquiries, he spoke to an old woman named Blue Duck whom Water Bear had told him fed the gossip of the villages.

"So!" Blue Duck said excitedly. "You speak of that pretty Lakota girl, passed to this country from the country of the Western Cree. She was brought here as a child, the only survivor of one of the frequent raids into the land of the Santee Sioux by Cree war parties. At some point during her captivity she had been hurt in a fall down a stony slope and even now has a slight strange limp from that time. Though she is not much impeded, the Cree band she was traveling with left her at the trading fires as spoilt goods. Thus our village, the last to leave that year, picked up a useful interpreter of western tongues."

"There seems to be some shadow about her."

"I am afraid that in her case the usual adoption into another nation never went well. She was not fully accepted in our villages. Some think possibly, it is the work of Leaping River or others of our suspicious Ojibwa shaman. It was said that the Cree refused to keep her. Nor could they simply do away with her, because she was herself the daughter of a famous medicine man among the Sioux – one of the few medicine men among those people whose terrible influence the Cree and Ojibwa genuinely feared."

"Among her birth people, she was from the small Snake clan, and that undesirable fact about her was always passed on as she was passed on from tribe to tribe. Here she lives as the adopted child of Pounding Thunder. From a girl she tended the fields with the children, as her other special task, besides interpreting. She keeps to herself."

Water Bear studied the gnarled Blue Duck as she made to leave him. He wanted to learn more.

"What languages does she speak?"

The old woman turned again to him.

"Well, she speaks all the languages hereabouts and as I said some from the west. It is her other special gift. When she speaks, that is. She says little and is rarely spoken to, because people still think her strange."

"What is her name?"

"When she came to us as a girl, the village women all laughed when we heard Pounding Thunder joked he would call her Runs and Walks, after her peculiar gate,. But that name stuck, until one day she had saved a young child from a dangerous snake by moving very agilely despite of her limp and the child she saved said she did a magic walk. That little girl's family persuaded Pounding Thunder to give her 'Magic Walk' as a grown-up name. The naming was accepted, though the girl herself, sometimes still is not accepted, because she is the one to interpret the "never good news", in Pounding Thunder's words, from visiting western traders coming for the spring fish. But, anyway we had a good enough naming feast that day."

Water Bear shook his head in wonder at how a lonely girl from another tribe far away growing up became a valued but still estranged member of her adopted village.

"But, because she speaks so many languages, and walks as fast and long as anyone, though a little strangely, she travels with Ojibwa trading parties. Even a war party against her own Santee two seasons ago. But the best thing for us is that she speaks all the news of western nations when they need to come here for the whitefish and that makes the Ojibwa here stronger."

This surprising new knowledge made Water Bear all the more interested in the girl.

When a half moon later he passed where the girl was once more working the field, he saw she was alone and decided he must approach her. He was not put off his purpose by her refusal once again to notice him. Even as he came close to her and addressed her, she continued her hoeing.

"Magic Walk, I have seen you in this field many times this summer when I come to these villages. I have wished to speak to you. I am Water Bear, the Giver of dreams. He used the new name given to him by his followers.

She still did not acknowledge him.

"I am told, Magic Walk, you are a true daughter of the Sioux, brought here by the Cree as a child, twice removed from the country of your people. I know that country from my travels as a trader. It is a pretty country.

"Those people are now my enemies," she said, but did not look up and continued to hoe around the bean plants.

"There are too many enemies in our countries. I will stay at my village tonight and would welcome you at my fire."

As she continued to hoe in silence, his patience was finally rewarded by a shrug.

"I speak the language of the Odawa and all the Ojibwa. Yet I am from the enemy. As you say, many think the pale faces are the enemy. I have heard you speak the language. You can teach me to speak as well."

She spoke all of this in already well inflected French, or at least in the French spoken in the woods by the voyageurs out of Quebec and Montreal.

He marvelled at her ability. It reminded him of the prowess in other languages of the Jesuits who were excellent at the native languages.

"You speak many languages. I think you might have been better named 'Magic Ear.'"

Even as he said this, she had just pulled an ear of corn to test its nearness to harvesting. She turned it over in her hand and looked up at him, this time with a warmer smile.

"There are ears and there are ears, eh?"

She said the latter to him in English. Recognizing that, he was even more astonished.

"How do you know the language of those people?"

"Oh I learned it the same way I learned French: as the interpreter in trade journeys. Once we went around the bottom of the Lakes through the Iroquois country in a time of peace and some of those English were there."

So maybe that is her interest in me, he thought.

"Well, now that I know this, I will ask for you to accompany me in my trade journeys."

She looked at him with added interest.

"Do you also speak the Hollanders' language?"

"Yes. Even that, though I do not like them. Tell me, do you tell your dream at all the fires?"

"Yes. It is still not interpreted. You could help me do that. Something foretold in the dream will happen soon I think."

It pleased him that she wanted to talk about this.

"I think though that some would not trust such a one as Water Bear sharing his dream. The shaman says dreams should be kept to oneself, especially strange ones that are not interpreted. Why do you tell it when you do not know its meaning?"

"If you can ask that, I think you too share the dream. I understand most of it by now, but I fear a bad interpretation or more than one interpretation."

"I have heard you tell it now many times. Even I have ideas about what it means." She shrugged and turned back to her hoeing.

"Perhaps I will see you at your fire tonight?"

She resumed hoeing in silence.

He departed without looking back, but he sensed she was secretly eying him.

That night, when Water Bear made his place at the fire of Magic Walk's adopted father, Pounding Thunder, she came and sat near him. He could only think she had made a decision about him: the attraction he had had from the beginning was now a shared one. When the others had gone, she moved closer to him and said with a smile, "So, brave man of the dream, we are alone."

"Maybe we should become one, never more to be parted?" he smiled down at her,

She smiled warmly in return. Since childhood she had never really smiled, except at the children. Now she felt something that transformed her always guarded and troubled state to one openly giving and receiving love. She took his hand and held it very firmly. He knew he did not need to ask if she would return with him to his own camp.

Chapter 8

Within the moon, Water Bear was happy to have finally found himself a good wife and Magic Walk believed she had been unexpectedly blessed with a good husband. Together they strengthened their resolve to help find the full meaning of the dream. He began taking her on his trading journeys. Sometimes he would let her tell the dream at distant trading camps.

One night they were at a western trading camp. It was in the country of the POdawatomi, but it was at the western edge of Seneca territory and other nations were represented there to parley about the next fur-trading season.

Many Axes had arrived with a Seneca trading party earlier in the day. He was now watching Water Bear and Magic Walk at their fire. He made a decision and walked over to them.

"So, again this season we have not seen Water Bear at our fires in Onondague. I hear two things - the dream is not yet interpreted, and worse, it is opposed by your shaman. I begin to think Dancing Pipes and I should have squeezed it out of you in that northern camp."

Water Bear refused to react to this jibing talk.

Magic Walk who now spoke a passable Iroquoian rose and stood behind Water Bear.

"The promise to bring the interpreted dream to your fires first is his commitment. Nothing has changed to break his honour. The talk of Leaping River, our medicine man is true. He has followers too, who oppose the dream. That it is against our Prophesy, that it is against our tradition. They know our every move. We cannot yet stop his malicious influence. They will surely strike soon, but it is a battle my husband is prepared for. We shall prevail over that shaman."

Water Bear added,

"It is an uneasy balance of strength between us. I know it cannot last much longer. My own powers have so far been greater than his..." He cut of his words.

Many Axes gave his final comment. "You had better use them or I will soon turn our own medicine men upon the dream." He strode away.

Magic Walk was concerned about a new weaker tone in Water Bear's voice.

"You must speak the truth to me, husband. What is it?

"My powers..."

"What, husband?"

".My powers are weakened because I now spend time with you. That has diverted me from the great struggle I have with that shaman."

Water Bear now shifted uneasily and then arose to stir the fire. The sparks exploded by his action seemed to set his mind. He looked again at Magic Walk.

"Our few followers cannot last much longer with Leaping River as their enemy. Young Copper Star and his family are strong and brave, but the Spirits can move around them if bid by Leaping River. It is no problem when White Fish is there. He has long understood the importance of the dream and that it must be properly interpreted. It is the strongest medicine and meant to make a change in our way, though it will take an unknown time to do so. But Whitefish must leave soon on a voyage to the upper lake."

They sat in silence for a time.

Water Bear spoke again.

"I will tell you one thing, Magic Walk, dream or not, I have seen the energy of the people weaken since my youth when I once was told by an Illini chief that it may be the spent energy of an older time that burst in all directions from a too intensely lived place at great ancient cities along the Michissippi. What energy is left in our way from the ancient time drains off even more to this new way, which our people wrongly seem to feel threaten our tradition and yet they seem to want at the same time."

"And, your dream may answer that?" Both silently wondered if it would.

As he lay later with Magic Walk, Water Bear spoke more of his frustration, and growing anger with not just Leaping River, but with the tradition he accepted as his own.

She said to him, "You are in a weak position still. You must wait. Give me your trapped energies on this; enter me, and forget all else." He entered her and forgot all else for an ecstatic moment.

A week later when they arrived back at their village by the Rapids, everyone was unsettled. Followers and enemies of Water Bear alike feared the great struggle between Leaping River and Water Bear must soon reach some terrible climax. It was being foretold by other medicine men.

Water Bear was trading at the black robes' mission at the Point of the Pines, when Copper Star came in a rush with dreaded news.

The young brave said, "Come quick. I think it is bad. Leaping River has become crazed with a vision that he must kill you to destroy the dream. He is looking for you. He has a musket."

Water Bear and Copper Star hurried back to their cabins east of the fort.

Pounding Thunder was standing there. The chief had become more interested in Water Bear and his dream since his adopted daughter had become the dreamer's wife.

"There was nothing we could do to stop Leaping River. He went into his Shaking Man and was given bad new thoughts against you. Anything is possible." he said.

"Where is he?" cried Water Bear.

"He awaits you at your dreaming cliff. He has a musket."

Water Bear hurried there. He knew this would be a final confrontation with Leaping River. He slowed to avoid indicating his presence as he neared the high promontory that was his spirit cliff. The last red of the evening was bleeding into the western horizon. He saw the figure of Leaping River on an outcropping half way up the cliff. Even as he saw him, a musket shot shattered the evening stillness.

Water Bear felt a burn in his shoulder and was thrown to the ground. Copper Star had come to the edge of the forest and took in the scene, bounded up the slope, only just in time to prevent Leaping River from reloading for a second shot.

Copper Star grabbed the weapon from Leaping River and lifted him off the ground.

"You come to this place only for your own death hateful shaman."

Leaping River spit foul oaths at him and screamed hideously, trying to summon the young man's fear of a shaman. But, Copper Star's iron grasp was as strong as his purpose. He moved rapidly with his still screaming burden, on the path upward to the edge of the high rocky overlook, where he intended to hurl the screaming shaman over the edge to his death, when Water Bear's cry stopped him.

"Copper Star listen to me. Bring Leaping River to me – he is bested!"

Copper Star stopped his upward progress. He did not release his terrible lock on Leaping River, but he set him down.

He then walked back down to Water Bear, pushing Leaping River ahead of him.

Copper Star looked miserably at Water Bear, seeing that there was blood on the front of Water Bear's shirt.

"What can you mean, Water Bear, that this foul man is bested when he has nearly slain you?"

"It is a grazing wound. He has failed in that. I will recover. But he has failed more than that, for the wound was made not by his powers. He abandoned his own powers and came at me with the pale face's power."

Leaping River stared at Water Bear for a moment and then made an agonizing groan as he came to the same realization.

"He knows that. He falls to the ground. He moans at his own failure. Unless I restore it, his power is wounded far more grievously than my shoulder."

Water Bear looked sympathetically at the Shaman who now sat back on his arms had begun to shudder in self-loathing.

"I was the greater fool to challenge you, Leaping River. I see now, it is only together that we may unlock the secrets of the dream."

The Shaman had quieted. He finally looked appreciatively at Water Bear. They waited for him to dare to speak. He slowly said,

"What evil spirit possessed me to use the fire-stick? It is as if those paleface devils made this happen. It fouls our tradition. I have been the greater fool."

He tried to clear his throat so as to speak up more clearly, as if the sudden truth had remorsefully dawned on him. "I should have seen the dream as new strength and not an old prophesized weakness. That story was in my medicine bundle all along. I kept myself blinded from it by the stronger evil spirit within me. I drove away any other thing seeking my attention. Now you have driven away that evil spirit. I saw Water Bear worse than the Wendigo and by any means his spirit must fall soon onto the path to the Spirits. The musket was at hand. I..."

Leaping River could not go on and wept.

Water Bear said, "Leaping River, though we have been in great conflict, can we make a pact that you and I will travel together, along the rivers of the long channel to the east? Each of our spirit powers must struggle on to find the dream's true interpretation. We will gather a new medicine bundle to help interpret the dream and that will ensure healing through the dream - both of us should together seek truth of the dream. Each of us will know if the full truth of the dream is revealed to our people."

Water Bear said, "Copper Star, let us retell the dream, now that we have a good ear from Leaping River."

Copper Star related the literal dream story.

Water Bear said, "Though I felt both the black and white and the strong and weak powers strongly I know not what they are, though they passed through all things. How can Rabbit control those powers? Rabbit, not Bear is the key to the dream, and then the snakes and then the fish, but I still know not what all this could mean."

Water Bear winced from the pain in his shoulder. Leaping River said, "Here Copper Star, give him this root for the wound."

After a moment, Water Bear said, "Yes that is soothing. "Anyway, those snakes coiled and seemed to devour each other, and then, then, my greatest horror: some escaped their own consuming coils and sprang at me. I had to swallow them. Yet spit them out before I awoke, feeling better, almost joyous. Can meaning be found in so terribly strange a dream?"

Water Bear clutched his wounded shoulder.

"But, this is not the worst thing. The truth of the dream, when I know it, must be told first at the Onondaga fires of the Iroquois, south of the Lakes, to Many Axes and Dancing Pipes there."

Leaping River recoiled at this. But his new respect for Water Bear made him speak softly about this awful truth.

"Those promises were forced on you, Water Bear. They are our enemy still."

Water Bear quickly replied, "No. No. I cannot avoid the commitment I made to those Iroquois, who freed me to try to find the meaning of the dream to help all our nations on that one condition."

Leaping River gazed up at the spirit cliff for a time. He saw two eagles circling and then landing in a tree. It was an omen.

He looked again at Water Bear. "I see your dream as a living thing, needing a medicine bundle to give it the balance necessary for continued life, for it to thrive, for it to be interpreted and live among our people."

Water Bear and Leaping River agreed to find the medicine bundle for the dream. With a good medicine bundle, both men could begin to explain the dream to their respective networks, Water Bear far and wide at the trading fires, Leaping River to all the shaman of neighbouring tribes.

They were accompanied on their medicine quest by Magic Walk, who insisted that she would make their trek as comfortable in the eastern direction of meager food as possible, and who thought, without telling them, that she might have as wide a knowledge as they to decide the ingredients for the new medicine bundle.

It was at the last moon of the change to fall colours when the medicine party turned back. The men were feeling dejected about their quest. Nothing seemed to address the dream's puzzle, though they had collected a few plants they thought would somehow help. A yellow flower, with browning leaves, they knew as corn mud which grew widely and cured madness, and a special tiny star shaped lichen from the great rocks they passed. But these did not give them meanings for the dream.

At this moment of despair, Magic Walk had cooked a rabbit and served it with a potent soup from the ferns she had collected. Then she spoke to them strongly.

"You men have missed what I have seen. It gives the dream to you. There are things you have seen everywhere, but not seen. The blue berries grow all around the Great Lakes. The dream must have its meaning everywhere in our countries. There is a part that goes to each individual of us, to cure many things, but only as each person is made up, so that the public dream becomes a private dream. I see that can only be wild garlic, with a tea that is made partly of the balsam fir whose berries are here. Those must be in this bundle, for they work differently for every person, not a sermon from a French priest which must be the same for everyone. This bundle means the spirit of the dream will be in each person."

The men thought on this.

"The reversing part of the dream is so easy to see that you have missed it: the very tea of the Ojibwa. It is, as Leaping River knows and as you do my husband, Water Bear, made of several magic ingredients, but its starting point is also a root found in all our countries, the Burdock root. Is it not true, Leaping River, that it sometimes reverses the worst sicknesses? Perhaps the sickness we have been given by the pale face?"

"And there..." She pointed to a pleasing flower of white ears surrounding a yellow centre. "What of Yarrow, found everywhere as well? When the Sioux war parties went against the Cree, they carried that flower with them, just as they had learned the Cree staunched their wounds from it. I was told to bring it to where too many warriors lay wounded. Even the Cree and the Iroquois know it can stop the bleeding wound. Is that not the bleeding wound what we all will suffer, like Water Bear, if we continue to war amongst ourselves on behalf of the pale faced ones?"

Leaping River thought for a time. Before, he would have taken this as yet another challenge to his power? But now, he had learned to welcome others to strengthen his power.

He looked more carefully at her than before.

"You are more magic than your walk, for you tell us what we should have known all along on this journey. What you give us is the reversing root. And a flower all around that stops the bleeding. They too must be in our bundle, with the other plants we have gathered that make each one of us, some differently, or some the same way, whole from sickness. They give much more to the bundle than those we have chosen."

Water Bear embraced his wife.

"I am proud of you, Magic Walk. You help make us what the Spirits want of us."

But two weeks later, back at the chutes on the day of the first snow, Water Bear was very troubled.

Magic Walk sensed this strongly and approached him at their fire one night.

What is it, my husband? I think you want to tell me something, but cannot yet. What is it?"

He drew her to him and said, "I fear that the dream is still too strange for me to interpret and that our people will never grasp it, even if I do. The other side in their colonies and beyond the great water, is very strong and is also very strange – not like the fur traders among them we have easily made friends with. Like our peoples, the French and the other palefaces are more than one thing - they are many more things than we know or understand; even many opposed things that they themselves don't understand about each other. How can we take them into us or make them part of us?"

She hugged him more closely.

"Surely there are some common things about paleface ways that could meet the requirements of the dream. Perhaps one dream and its medicine bundle does not hold all the herbs and remedies in the forest."

"The Paleface's medicine bundle is his writings and his books. They make him remember and keep fighting over every story in them– every herb in their forest - all of the time, not just the main drift of things in their world as we remember the stories in ours. The great powers they have learned to use are much misused by only a very few over the many. Very few are at peace in their world, even the powerful. The fur traders here feel a freedom they do not have. Their chiefs fear that and try to control their traders. So our side must hold much truth."

Magic Walk spoke to him "I am mixed people. Many of us are mixed people. Then in some way, why not all of us? We must try to interpret that from the dream, do you not think, husband?"

"Yes. Of course, Magic Walk, we must try," he replied. "But what the dream seems to call for will be a strange mix."

He looked up at the brilliantly starlit night sky.

"Even if we can, it will be hard to know what to take from the palefaces that we can ourselves control."

"Well, I have taken you, good husband, so influenced by those palefaces in your dream and it seems little strange to me that I easily control you." She kissed him. "You must at least tell me all of you know of those Europeans."

"I will do that, but they are far more than I know alone. As I said, good wife, they are very strange."

Part Three:

To the New World

The Music is Resolved

The vaulted stone heights
Gather the stringed sound
Heavenward
Taking it into
God's infinite surround

Point begetting counterpoint
Pleasing atonal epiphanies
Theme begetting variations
To multi-textured harmonies.

All so pleasing to Heaven
And to the cultured ear
That the noblemen weep
And noblewomen seek
The answer to their prayers
That such sonorous beauty
Call back the helmeted horde
Their sons, well ordered to begin
Hell-bent to cacophonous war
God driven, vassal to lord.

All falling faithfully into
The unimagined dissonant
Chaos of distant battlefields
Where, in a day
Even the still hooting near-dead
Are soon, well dead
Mingled with the mud, stones and hay

So triumphantly there
Is all of horrible, clanging Hell involved

Though the music is resolved.

Chapter 9

You might think that I, Jean Paul Laliber de St Triste, could write a good story about the New World. My Jesuit predecessors in New France sent many "Relations" back to France and Rome for much of this 17th century.

But, here, I make only a first few comments about my part in a much larger story. The rest I cannot write as myself. I can only give it to the story teller. Each page is so shaming to me. For each page of the story I must pray that Christ will forgive my sinful willfulness in this world. I could not bear to write it first person, though it tells of a signal achievement before God's eyes.

My course here in the North of the Americas was set beyond my four traditional Jesuit vows by a fifth vow to His Holiness himself and then, beyond that to a sixth vow to my own anguished soul. I vowed to find the truth of the good spirit in native peoples that challenges and at least matches whatever superiority we Europeans think we have. I was left with no option – my own undeniable will made it clear that I had to escape, even as their leading warrior for Christ, the clutches of a purblind church here among the native heathen.

By their own visionary dreamer, Water Bear, I know, as God's witness, that the native vision of themselves can bring them and us again independently to Christ by a strange new mix of our own and their own visionary inclinations.

So, let my story be told under God.

* * *

It was a damp evening in March, 1683. Ghost shapes loomed in the mists along the roadstead at La Rochelle, France.

A dark human shape pushed away his supporting companion and stumbled onto one of the ships' gangplanks. He slumped at the posted sign bearing the ship's name: the Saint Bartholomew.

Two ship's crewmen came to his sunken body, pulled him up by his black robe and took him aboard and below ships where they lay him on a plank bed. His companion, pleading with the crewmen to be careful, followed and sat on the second bed in the cabin.

"This priest is already a holy ghost before he dies," said one crewman, as they left the cabin.

The priest stirred, rolled to one side, and vomited.

He fell into fitful sleep.

He dreamed of his past.

He lived again the three years he had been in the Reductions of Paraguay. He once more hated himself for having summoned the soldiers there to take the one man among those worthy savage people who had had an inspiring dream for them. The dream had seemed to some of the Jesuits to speak against the colonists and the Christian mission among them. Yet, it was a mission that was proving well enough to his own eye, if not to the others. They were converting to Christ, with their own added beliefs. The souls were being won; in their own settlement, in their own way, away from the Spanish colonists. They who would rather have enslaved the natives and destroyed their ways.

But, then he had been stricken with a fever, and in that fever, he had doubted himself and could not overcome the other clergy in their rejection of the native dream.

He was there the hot dusty day the dreamer was executed in Buenos Aires. He watched the execution from the edge of a square fronting the first towered church in the town. He was there with two young donnes, who now as eagerly supported him physically as they did spiritually, though he was even younger than they. The dreamer, a spindly native called Ingunio by the Spanish who sounded out his native name thus, seemed a pathetic figure as he was led to a crude gallows that had been set up. A crow had landed on the top of the gallows just before the makeshift floor fell. Ingunio dropped, neck broken and had twisted violently and then in smaller jerks full minutes before he was finally horribly dead. The priest had vomited all over his acolytes. The Reductions experiment was never the same after. Its real promise was all gone now.

The priest turned over in his bunk and vomited anew.

He had been brought back to Rome and was called a hero by his Jesuit brothers. The Jesuit Superieur himself introducing him to His Holiness, who took a liking to him, and made him a diplomat. And somehow he found that skill and made it work to avoid several scandals in Rome, Paris and even London.

And then what? Being called before His Holiness. Why? Because of another savage dream in another part of the new world.

The priest struggled to turn over again to his other side. He vomited once more, all over himself. He finally fell into deep undreaming sleep.

An hour later, a six-horse caleche noisily arrived at the St. Bartholomew's birth along the roadstead and disgorged two gentlemen who were lead up the gang-plank and then disappeared into the ship.

The two gentlemen arrived below deck and entered the priest's cabin.

They looked alarmingly at the priest, as his companion bent over to take his pulse He pulled a handkerchief and wiped the priest's feverish brow.

The three men knew and nodded to one another.

The priest's bending companion was Isaac Kastler. He was an average looking man in every sense except for his large eyeglasses, from which if one looked closely, peered out a blue eye and a brown eye. In fact he was a well-known Paris physician, whose patients included the two men beside him and, when he was sometimes called on referral, ministered to the Sun King himself. He was now more famous as one of the King's travelling botanists having been once to and now returning a second time to the new world for exotic new specimens for the King's botanical gardens and green-houses.

Of the two gentlemen standing, the taller was Roche de Verdelieres. He was a dilettantish courtesan known for his biting tongue. Because of that, he was famous in Paris for avoiding the direct presence of Louis XIVth. That was because he occupied one of the King's properties in Paris which could be seized from him at any moment should he be the cause of regal displeasure, which all agreed in the King's presence he would be with his acerbic wit.

The second man, Henri du Moulin was a shorter solid man with a massive forehead beneath his thinning hair. He had been at sea, commanding the King's ships for almost twenty years, and then returned to the status of a minor land-holding noble. He had joined the King's administration under Colbert in which he had steadily risen and become much valued by that great bureaucrat, just now on his death bed, as being not only shrewd but especially knowledgeable about France's empire abroad.

Du Moulin said, "Can you reassure us, Kastler that our dear Father Paul is not as he appears to be, on his death bed? We know you have tended him before, as you do others in our circle."

"Father Laliber has a returning fever from the tropics. It comes and goes, often violently. As do the scourges of his restless soul. He always seems to survive it."

Du Moulin shook his head in wonder. "Well, I am glad we have placed him in your care on the sea crossing."

"He is actually sleeping well at this point. I will occupy this cabin with him. Let us return above decks where we can have a last drink together at the tavern opposite."

They emerged on the main deck and headed to a tavern across the roadstead.

"Ah yes," said de Verdieleres, "the venerable Black Cormorant.'"

Looking along the roadstead, his companion, Pierre du Moulin, said, "What were once half a dozen masts at this place has become a forest."

La Rochelle was indeed a crowded port in 1683. Its line of ships and buildings stretched far along the roadstead. The busy port had begun to rival even the Dutch ports as an entrepot and transfer point between the European seas and now the principal French port for embarking to the New World.

De Verdelieres said, "And what once were two taverns, is now a long line of forest weeds."

After they entered, stares from the tavern's rougher patrons followed the new entrants to their table. The tavern keeper tried his best to please the three men by immediately serving them a large pitcher of wine which de Verdelieres sniffed, tasted and declared "more or less palatable," and a sea food snack platter he tasted and declared "more or less delectable."

Du Moulin started the conversation. "Father Paul Laliber de St. Triste is well named, because there has never been a more perplexing creature under God's eye - a man who can take woe from the gayest thought and then change that woe into a joyous experience."

Kastler replied, "Or the other way around. I have known several men of his Order to insist upon contrary things. They teach natural science without any sense of it not being referred to by Christ nor that it is still doubted in the church."

De Verdelieres took up the story, "There is a most intriguing combination of freedom and sadness in the name, and in the man. Always bearing burdens of the soul no mere mortals could bear. But, we are close friends of this dear disconcerting priest. You will have to grapple with his indomitable will. The Pope himself has apparently bid him go and he is decided. And we who love him must simply accept that. Yet even when he is determined on something, he can be confoundingly unpredictable. It was no different when we were all students together at La Fleche."

Kastler knew of all the members of the la Fleche circle, but thought he should check. "Yours is a still-flourishing circle, is it not?"

Du Moulin said, "Yes we cooperate on some good works, including trying to keep Father Paul out of trouble. We were seven in that jolly group of students now twenty years back. We two, and Laliber, who was then only considering the priesthood, but relentlessly and openly so, in a way we all had to share. There was also Raymond Barseau, now rich beyond imagining as the bankers' banker in Paris and also rumoured to be the power behind Croix du Bois." He referred to a lay society furthering the interests of the French church throughout our empire.

De Verdelieres continued, "Not to speak of the noblest and most pious of us all, Francois Moreau, the Compte d'Amboise, then fifteenth and now second in line to the Dukedom of Tours. And two more, now married and in New France, Emil de Merlot, a senior official there and his wife Antoinette."

Du Moulin said, "Ah, to our school days. We debated such issues so intensely that Descartes himself would have been perplexed.

De Verdelieres recalled, "Antoinette had been part of the circle, not directly as a student at la Fleche, but because, as the daughter of one of the university's leading scholars, she had insisted upon inserting herself into its group of brightest students her own age. All the men had been in degrees in love with her – she was most vivacious. So unlike the man who finally won her – Emil was a dogged man, more so than even the infinitely calculating Barseau, and du Moulin here, yet she thought Emil the more desirable for that stupid kind of manliness. Wonders never cease. "

De Verdelieres looked about the smoky tavern.

"Ah, to our school days of rigorous philosophy," he swooned. In his smile was a trace of his own early scholarly enthusiasms and marked abilities in matters of extended abstract thought that had provided him an early rehearsal of his true gift - voluptuous verbiage.

"And, do you not recall that Paul was often merry company in those days!" said du Moulin.

De Verdelieres now fulsomely took up the cause.

"He was not destined to be near the Court as I – though God help me, not too near – nor part of grey officialdom as you are du Moulin – though the dear   recent diplomacy with, and then against, the Gallic tide makes one wonder. He was most certainly not intended to make money from money, as does Barseau hugely, nor bound to a life of aesthetic idleness as is d'Amboise our gentle near-Duke, only having in common a fate to share the new world with the de Merlots, now so rudely lodged in far off New France. Our Lord Laliber was made for the morally hazardous life of an atypical priesthood, which we all had long ago agreed, even before he, was to be his inescapable fate, did we not?"

De Verdelieres got through this flood of words to see that the other two had only just barely kept up with it.

"Oh dear, do I again lay my pretty bricks of speech too fast for the mortar of grammar to take hold? Anyway, as I say, his recent stay in Paris caused a stir."

"You did not say that," du Moulin said. De Verdelieres' non sequiturs bothered du Moulin. His career in the government demanded point by point discourse and no surprises.

"Well, I refer to the Gallican troubles. Rumour has it that there was in fact something Jesuit to the so-called Popish plot in England and that he had to feed the lies upon lies that covered it up."

"What lies?" said Kastler.

"It's a mystery – they must be good lies since no-one knows. Perhaps you can find that out, at sea? "

Du Moulin gave this little credibility. "Sounds like a rumour calculated to harm his reputation."

De Verdelieres shrugged. "Anyway, Kastler, I daresay Father Paul's biggest challenge at sea will be that humourless monsignor chosen as the new assistant to Laval, the Bishop of New France. Such a cleric will not be amused to have a Jesuit in ship's company, much less a very bold Jesuit, such as our dear Laliber."

Du Moulin agreed. "I would say that both he and the monsignor whom I once met are both hard men of the church, but in almost opposite ways."

"And with opposed earthly reference points – Paris and Rome," De Verdelieres added.

"Perhaps that accounts for each one's mission," Kastler said, hoping to gain as much information from the table talk as he could before leaving for the St. Bartholomew.

Thoughts on this were interrupted when the innkeeper spilled some wine on de Verdelieres and knocked the lit pipe from his mouth, scattering the ashes in sparks upon the floor.

"Brute! Can you not see whom you serve?"

Kastler tried to ignore the incident. He was beginning to realize the full burden placed upon him by the priest's circle of important friends and the importance of his potentially controversial mission to the new world.

He said, "Let us conclude. I should return to the priest. I can provide him what care is possible if, of course, he himself should so wish. His best hope is that the ship will not have taken on any spreading diseases from here and the sea air may in fact do him good and he will not die from sea sickness."

"If you do what you can, you have our gratitude. Here, take this little donation from our banker friend Barseau to assist your natural collections in that place."

The physician was astonished to see the amount that was placed on the table before him by du Moulin.

"I personally do not need funds. But, for my specific botanical mission, I would gladly accept a donation and add it to the King's own donation. I shall write to the King and mention this generous addition to his own.

"Oh no, no, no," De Verdelieres protested. "Please. You must never mention to the King my connection with this or with anything else."

"Well, of course, then. As you wish, I shall mention it to no one else. But, I shall see to it that you are kept informed of the fate of my charge."

"Make your addressee Moreau, the Count d'Amboise," said du Moulin. "He is far enough outside of Paris for his mail to avoid suspicion. Here is his address for such missives."

"I will do my best to keep the Count d'Amboise informed."

With that, the men took their leave of the tavern.

* * *

Two weeks later, a mid-Atlantic afternoon was almost cloudless. But, the captain of the St. Bartholomew, William Pinard, could feel the sea changing. He had been waiting for a strengthening of the swell. True enough, well before dark, scudding storm clouds had replaced that earlier blue sky. Everything not lashed down crashed about the decks of the hundred foot wooden vessel from New Rochelle.

Despite its latest sail design, by an Englishman named Chapman, the ship was being tossed relentlessly from one great wave to the next. Pinard braced himself on a rail of the mizzen deck. He smiled brokenly and spoke his usual thought on this voyage in a bad storm to the physician Kastler beside him who held onto a straining stay.

"What a tiny wooden spec we be, physician, between the endless sky above and the unknown watery depths beneath!"

"Well said, Master, with a flare of poesy – But can we survive this stormy sea?" Kastler shouted.

"Oh aye: much better riding out a near spar-breaker for one day than becalmed for three. Dead in the water means dead in the bunks, I say"

As he said this, a huge wall of water smashed against the ship, causing a stay to snap and several barrels to break loose and crash through the ships rails into the roiling seas.

Seeing Kastler holding a backstay, the captain warned, "You best hold on to something stronger if the stays are starting to go," the captain warned.

Kastler quickly moved to the iron binnacle holding the ship's new floating magnetic compass and grabbed the end of a rope tied around it.

With its latest mathematical adjustments to true north, the Captain had said, "the new instrument helps us zig and zag - do you know that nice new German and Dutch expression? Anyway, we French zig and zag a shorter more direct route to the river of Canada than do the Dutch and English."

In the next hour the fierce storm began to abate. But not before an old woman enveloped in black clothes came above deck to crow to Kastler,

"They are not good signs below decks for him you have a special care for. His right cheek burns. T'is a sign of death. His right nostril bleeds. T'is a sign of death. It is a terrible sign of death if a rat gnaws at a man's clothes. I saw these things. If a man as you stumbles coming out the door in the morning it is a bad sign. I saw these things."

Even as she said this, the suffering Laliber of whom she spoke came on deck and overheard the old crone.

"My dear, you are here to warn of these things – that is a good sign. But I am well enough and you have done your duty. Go again below, and rest."

She was astonished to see the priest up again, but seemed to take his comfort, and withdrew.

Kastler said, "Father you are too weak to be up and about in rough weather."

"I seek the fresh air..." was all he said as he sank back onto a rope truck and grasped a stay.

"You have an iron will, my Jesuit friend," said the captain.

The first mate appeared and reported, "Master: three more deaths below during the storm, but none caused alone by the storm. Damage is reparable. Things return to normal – the arguments everywhere that had been quieted by the storm, break out again."

Kastler mused to himself that the all too familiar human forces coursing among the under decks of the St Bartholomew could roil as unpredictably and as nastily as the stormy airs and seas the ship sailed through.

The ship was brought about again to head westerly, tight to the new wind. When order on the decks had been restored, the Captain loaded a pipe to smoke and said to Laliber,

"We are nearing the end of our crossing by my reckoning. Another few days and we'll see the Gulf of Canada that we seek. You may well survive the crossing, if you can move about now."

Laliber said, "Yet, until then the suffering aboard ship will continue."

"Believe me, there will be more gone to God on this trip. We are under-provisioned because we had to include in our company the new Governor of Quebec, Dennonville and the first of his new company of troops for the colony."

The physician nodded, "I am myself overly used and well beyond my resources."

The boson appeared.

"Sir, the monsignor approaches. He appears much vexed.

Captain Pinard inhaled the pipe smoke deeply. As a Huguenot "converted" back to Catholicism - a pretence unknown aboard ship and to its owners - he smiled ironically at the likely sour relationship between the haughty young Catholic monsignor and the doughty Jesuit priest. However Catholics fared and fought over truth, the stronger truth was that many of his own Protestant people were helping to make the Atlantic shores of the American New World a Protestant place.

Chapter 10

A commotion in the aft deck announced the appearance from his cabin of Monsignor Jean-Baptiste de la Croix de St Vallier, of Grenoble, newly appointed to assist and potentially succeed the ailing Bishop Laval in Quebec. Though still young, the man was already known for his severe manner. His long face already looked much strained. Brushing aside Kastler, he stood over and peered down at the now snoozing priest, jostling him.

Getting no response, he spoke callously, with no sign of sympathy,

"You are the Jesuit, Paul Laliber?"

The monsignor seemed irritated at having to raise his voice.

The priest's eyes opened. The monsignor was surprised by the strength yet left in their gaze, and the steadiness of the man's reply.

"And you are the new assistant to the Bishop? You have not sought me out during this voyage and I have not yet taken the liberty to present myself."

"If I take that to be a 'yes,' then I am given to understand that you summoned me earlier for last rites, being as you are, close to Jesus."

"I am always close to Jesus."

The monsignor narrowed his eyes in further irritation.

Laliber continued, "But indeed, I made no such request. Alas, I have made no sound at all this day until I gained the fresh air up here on deck. Some may have feared me near death, as perhaps I may be."

St. Vallier was perplexed for a moment.

"Well, let me tell you, Father Laliber, there is much work here on this ship for a priest. If you are not so near death as others think, then may I strongly urge that you rouse yourself to the pastoral duty that we clerics aboard, must all perform."

"Ah, but only in this way, with my deepest prayer and meditation, can I regain the strength I will need to complete this voyage to the New World and for the ordeals to come, Father…is that Father de Saint Valoir? "

"It is de Saint Vallier!' the monsignor sharply asserted.

Laliber continued,

"God has willed that I am on the mend and I shall be ready for my duty, as needed through the day."

"See that you are," said the monsignor sharply, no longer attempting to cover his annoyance with the man. "I do not expect again to have to enjoin you to do your duty."

The monsignor regained his full height and was about to head back to his cabin, when he stopped and turned to look back at the again motionless figure of the priest.

"There is one more thing. I have been informed that you were in the Reductions of Paraguay before your recent time in Rome and Paris."

"I was there." Laliber affirmed, without opening his eyes.

"Then have you the strength to explain to me your instructions for New France? As I understand it, you became, I believe the phrase was too "preoccupied" with indigenous community there and your return from Paraguay was greeted with great relief by all concerned. Let me warn you that I have been told your sole task in New France is one of instructing at the schools there and only in that way gaining souls to Christ."

"It is true that all were happy when I left Paraguay. Though the villages watched over by those of my Order are a brilliant Christian example, in the end it did not seem God's purpose that I myself should remain there. Others came to understand that."

"That is not the way I heard it and I must say I find myself not pleased with your wilfulness."

The priest shifted his position, so that he could look the monsignor directly in the eye.

"Well then, let it be. I regret you find my story offensive. As for my instruction for New France, yes, I am to instruct, at the Seminary in Quebec." He sensed the monsignor would not deign to press further.

Indeed, the monsignor concluded with more sharp words.

"See that you strictly adhere to that instruction to instruct, for I am sure his Grace the Bishop will not tolerate Jesuitical adventure. I shall so inform the Superior of your Order in Quebec. Good day."

As the monsignor turned to leave, he bumped up against the physician. After a cold stare at him but nothing said, the monsignor headed rapidly on his way.

Kastler said, "You have lied to the Bishop. I can see from here that you are far too weak to resume any duty priestly or otherwise this day or for some days to come."

The priest looked up to him.

"Actually, I feel a little better. I am given to severe ups and downs. It must have been that bad spirited young monsignor. That surely was what has raised me from my recent dolour."

Kastler looked down disapprovingly. "He is a testy one. Not one whom I think you should argue with."

"I did not argue, though he was most disagreeable. I have been near death before. I seem to come back to life."

The men were only now, after weeks at sea, beginning to speak easily with each other. They had become less formal with one another as they overcame the initial difficulty that both spoke a distinct French – the priest's a kind of Spanish French, Kastler's an Alsatian German French.

"This returning fever is a major reason I left the tropics, for it had weakened me in mind and spirit, as well as the body. I would have otherwise remained in Paraguay - God's work was being done there and many thousands of souls have been won in the past ten years, even as they make strides toward a more civilized way of life. Do you know of the Reductions, as they are called?"

As the priest spoke, the strength seemed again to return to him.

"They are small semi-independent settlements of native converts. I have heard tell of them."

"These were not so small; maybe several thousand lived in one of them and they were independent. Their leaders and we Jesuits were trusted to run them. For a brief moment, I thought it would work."

For a time the violent motions of the ship made any further talk difficult as they sought to support each other from being flung about the deck.

Kastler said, "There is so much sickness on this ship and I fear we will all carry it to our destination, only to spread it there. I fear it is our diseases, not our Christianity that spreads fastest among the savage folk."

Laliber shrugged.

"But, tell me, Father, when did you first develop this returning sickness? It seems it is given to Europeans in the Tropical regions. Can you remember the circumstances?"

"I see you seek a cause in this world. An important notion, as I sense you seem to conceive it as do some of my friends who think these days only in the terms of the natural sciences. The cause was surely God's will."

Another violent motion of the ship seemed to underline his point.

"Of course, if it is immediate circumstances you seek, I might hazard that a trip into the swamps somehow led to this pernicious affliction. One cannot escape such a trip without nature at its cruelest, not least the bites of the insects. I have noted over the years there that others came down with similar symptoms after such journeys. Yet, this could not be a sufficient condition, as I might put the logic, however necessary. Not all such hardy travelers as I were so afflicted."

"Just so!" Kastler was delighted at this talk. "I am excited that a priest so occupied with God's purposes would make such a natural observation.

These details of experience in other places can be invaluable to us scientists working out immediate causes. It is my own humble view that God does not wish us to ignore the immediate causes of things that He has created."

"There are two necessary ways of knowing God's world – that is a Cartesian premise."

"Did you see the ship's compass?" Kastler asked the priest.

"I looked it over and perceived it is a floating thing. Does it always point north?"

"With some adjustments to latitude, by magnetic lines of force, it tells how far or near to the pole or the equator of the Earth. But we know not how to use it or any other machine to calculate the longitude."

Laliber said, "I know of these ideas to place us on a chart. It is a worthy thing our scientists seek. I can teach some of that."

"Indeed. But we seek many more things."

"Such as?"

"How to do God's mathematics – it seems more and more to be the language of the immediate natural things around us."

Laliber shrugged. "I myself delight in teaching mathematics, including Galileo's physical laws of motion and principles of mechanics, but what could take it further?"

"More thinking, beyond Descartes, and even Pascal."

"But, we must also grasp St. Ignatius' truth."

"I recall that his words were 'Give me Thy love and Thy grace, for this is enough for me.'"

"Yes, exactly that," said Laliber enthusiastically, "That is what God wants back from us. Whatever few, tiny things we know otherwise than by faith alone, we must lovingly and graciously respect and accept God's higher purpose for creating and giving us his love. That faith alone is both necessary and sufficient for humanity, not the immediate causes. Our challenge is that His creation of this world includes so many more souls seemingly worthy of him, but who are somehow simply lacking the capacity of faith."

The priest said this as if he were making a sermon. But it lacked a complete inner conviction. He thought he should smile at Kastler. He did.

"Though God's love and grace was beginning to be felt among those simple people in Paraguay, it was through my actions that one among them who was disturbing the others with what my brother Jesuits took to be a Devilish dream that soldiers came and took the man away, later to die in a dank dungeon in Buenos Aires."

"But why, if you were intent on serving those people and serving God, would God be displeased with you?"

"I don't know." The priest gave Kastler an uncharacteristically helpless look.

"Perhaps I will have another chance with the savage dream rumoured to be surrounding New France. I am sure I will be faced with many tests there."

His first test came the next day as the ship's log recorded. There was seen an omen of such evil portent that nearly all aboard ship who saw it began shaking in fear, even the strongest of the sailors and soldiers.

The captain, finishing tucking in his shirt as he appeared on the quarter deck, was muttering to himself. He looked about at disarray even among his officers at the ship's wheel and immediately gave loud orders.

"Hold the course! What be this commotion?"

His second mate spoke to him with as much fear as the others showed,

"It is a black sail, sir. It bears directly toward us from the 'larboard quarter. No man has seen such a sail before. And, it comes from among those looming ice mountains. All are afraid and trembling, sir, lest it be the Devil himself, upon the waves."

"I see it," he said. "I need not a glass to see that it has veered and recedes from us, behind the iceberg, thus to avoid even crossing our path. Take heart! Whatever sail it be, it be the mischief of men to blacken a sail thus. I have not myself before seen such an omen. But, I am told in the Gulf seas there be more than one black sails these days, on the ships of one privateer or another. I cannot think it the Devil himself, except maybe a buccaneer, those ordinary human black sinners of the seas. Yet, upon my glass, it a strange sight indeed, against the white of those ice islands."

For a while, the ship's company watched as one until the frightening sail had receded and then vanished upon the horizon.

Laliber had come up onto the deck. His black robes whipped noisily in the winds and he seemed likely to be blown away, so thin was his body. But there was colour again in his face and enough new energy for him to hold his footing. The captain leaned to his ear explained the fears of many of the ship's crew and passengers.

"We just spied a black sail among those icebergs, though it has now gone. All but me mostly take it as a very bad omen that God deserts us. Perhaps you can set us at ease with some words and give us some reassurance, Father?"

"I understand. I will speak to those who wish to hear me," said Laliber.

It took only a short time to muster many of the ship's company to the main deck to hear what the priest would say.

Laliber looked over the expectant throng on the open decks facing him.

"All here have sighted a ship with black sail. Though your captain has said, it could be a pirate ship, why it would appear and then disappear seems most strange. But the captain has given you the key fact – it did not cross our path. I can but guess that, since it has disappeared, neither it, nor the evil omen we guess at, were intended to foretell evil in our future, much less that this black appearance against the white of the ice mount has some purpose to wound yet more, our already struggling spirits. I rather see that with God's will and God's good news, there occurs a brightening of our chances!"

There were murmurs of approval here and there about the now crowded deck.

"In fact, I think it a very good omen for us. For am not I, and are not many other men of God who spread the joyful news of Christ our Saviour, attired in the darkest black? And, are we not, on this ship among those glistening white ice islands that the black was easily balanced by the great masses of purest white? It is in such contrasts God gives our lives meaning. Take comfort in this. It is God's sign to us that our current suffering aboard this ship will soon enough give way to the reward of reaching our destination where we will see many more blacks and whites reminding us of God's great truths. Take heart and thank God for this most favourable portent."

He gave a blessing to all those assembled. But by now, though all had gained from his energy, his own energy was gone and Kastler had to help him back below decks.

The Captain smiled as they passed him. Though he himself did not much believe the words spoken by the priest, he could see that even the most cynical about religious belief among his crew, himself included, felt better about things. That was a blessing for sure in this dark voyage. He shared a word with Kastler as he passed, with the priest in hand,

"I say again this priest is different. He interprets God's purpose so that it stirs men to try to find some better understanding within them. It almost seems a Protestant position.

Laliber overheard this and stopped long enough to reply,

"My only purpose, Captain Pinard, is to save men's souls. That is blocked when men see only the Devil's business, as the Church keeps seeing with you Huguenots. If that is what it was, in reality or perception, it became my task to counter it, with the thoughts God cleverly gave to me."

How did he know I was Huguenot, Pinard wondered, as Laliber and Kastler disappeared below deck?

When Laliber was lying upon his bed and the physician was still fussing around him to make him as comfortable as possible in his again weakened state, there was the sound of men coming rapidly along the companionway. Within moments, the door flew open, and the monsignor peered in.

He spoke angrily.

"How dare you speak about God's purpose to all aboard this ship, without my permission as the senior cleric?"

The monsignor was as nearly red-faced in anger as his pale face could be.

"And you did this while I, the senior cleric, was praying in my cabin for God's mercy and deliverance from the self-same event, praying I may say with the Marquis de Denonville, the new military leader of our colony."

Shaking in his anger, he furiously pointed at the priest.

"Listen to me, Jesuit. I will be reporting to your Superior in Quebec what you have done this day, so freely as if you were Saint Peter himself, and advising him that he take steps immediately to have you returned to France. You have been given no gift from God, nor any mission to interpret His purpose beyond the correct instruction of the Church, or to be so familiar with these people about their fate, or to use such cheap and reckless metaphor as I was told, in referring to God's purpose in causing that event."

He was about to go on, but it was clear the priest to whom his venom was directed, had fallen asleep.

St Vallier rose in disgust.

"I warn you too, physician, Kastler. You also shall know consequences in Quebec if you continue to consort with this wrong Jesuit."

The monsignor whirled around and strode away, being careful to avoid bumping his head on the low door frame, but then bumping into it anyway.

Chapter 11

Some nights later, in a quieter sea, the priest heard his first confession

from the physician. It was a surprise to both of them. Kastler was no longer in the habit of such a thing. But he thought it would also be a good way of drawing out the priest.

The ploy had worked. The confession had been mutual and well before it was over, it led to the men opening one of Kastler's last bottles of brandy.

The priest seemed most understanding of Kastler's confession of weak faith.

"I fear it is a vocational hazard for you natural scientists in our midst. Ideas that persuade us to the immediate truth of things can block out ideas of God who is always there behind those directly sensed truths. If this science must be understood, I follow the precept of Canisius, that "only ideas can fight ideas." If a false view of science against God must be fought and indeed, a true view of science must be fought for, then the idea that nature is God-given, for us to study and make use of seems to me an obvious divine truth and therefore a powerful idea."

"That is an admirable position, Father. That God in nature can be known through natural philosophy, as well as directly through the spirit and religious knowledge. We can stand on much of the same ground together on that basis.'

"And how came you yourself, by these thoughts?"

"Though I followed my father in some ways, I did not in others. That I am a physician and naturalist is attributable to my father. My father, like some of the Pietists and many of his fellow Alsatians believed then in the unity of the church across all Protestant sects and even with the mother church itself. "

"A grand possibility," said Laliber.

"Yes. But when that ecumenism made no progress, he converted back to Catholicism at the time of my birth, and so I was baptized and raised a Catholic, though my older brothers in Mainz are Protestants. As I grew up, I came to see how my father was still poor in spirit, despite his many turnings of faith, I came to the conclusion that his search for a satisfying faith was too dependent upon this or that church faith, and since religion so divided men, I would settle for a more indirect path to God. It would be through the things and events I can see and know through thoughtful observation of his creation of and purposes in the natural world, based on a more immediate science upon which all can agree."

Laliber said, "And so, ever since, you have been a Cartesian! That position can be a deceptive dualism between God and Nature. It must be given most careful consideration, for it can be too easily contrary to a fulsome belief in God, as I learned during my days at La Fleche. I argued Cartesian dilemmas day and night with my friends there. What was, or was not a defensible Cartesian position fired us. And then, above all, there was Blaise Pascal: his seemingly indisputable mathematics we all struggled to grasp, thinking its indisputable purity was surely an essential part of God's kingdom."

Kastler asked, "Have you heard of Pascal's machine, the Pascalini machina? It is an invention as interesting as our ship's new compass."

"Yes, I have vaguely heard of it. My school teaching always included Pascal. It is very disciplining for the young mind to stress mathematics. Kastler continued, "Well, at one stage his father needed to calculate what taxes were owed, and that drove Pascal to invent a calculator, to keep track of tax accounts and add up what net sum was owed. "

"Yes, the Church could also use such a calculator."

"I have brought the machina Pascal sent my father with me on his voyage. It is, I think one of the cleverest information giving machines of our science to date."

Laliber stroked his beard.

"Some teaching Jesuits were told of it. But I heard that because of its great expense few could afford to use it, especially his last versions of it."

"True, indeed. Anyway, I had decided to send the machine we had and Pascal's last working notes on it to the Sorbonne. But when I knew I would be going to the new world again, I changed my mind, thinking since Pascal's work is now ignored in Europe it might be a gift to the new world in exchange for its rare botany."

"That is indeed a fine idea."

As they sipped their brandy, Kastler worked up the courage to inquire after the priest's own background. "Father, you have, may I say, a different way of speaking French or German. May I ask, having given you mine, what is your own family background?"

The priest was silent for a moment. But then he replied in greater detail than the doctor had expected.

"Let me begin where for me it began: I have always been cursed with a vivid imagination. When a boy of twelve, I had been learning the Song of Roland and I went once with my father to the furthest part of our lands where the armies of Christ had come through to conquer the Moor – an overlook where crows flew quite densely some years in their immemorial migrations back and forth across the Pyrenees. It was a time for the migration. I saw many that day. My father said the birds went some years in the autumn and brought back the spirits of the dead Crusaders in the spring. I asked my father why only some years. He shook that off as different weather from one year to the next. Then I asked if the crows carried the spirits of the black Moorish faith too. My father shushed me. But, I know it was at that moment when he decided I would be the priest in the family. He said to me, "Those crows are tricky and fiercely determined, just like a Jesuit. With a question such as you just asked me, you already think like a Jesuit. So you shall be. Until then, we will never return here. "

"I told him, 'But Father, I love this place. I would come here with you again and again.' My pleas were to no avail. My father died before I became a Jesuit and I never was to return there, though if I chose I would have command of the estate."

Kastler was much moved by this little story about the child Laliber at St Triste.

"Perhaps your father was wiser than you then realized – not to be diverted from the life of Jesuit."

"Yes, perhaps."

Laliber paused, before concluding, "It must be evident to someone well educated and experienced such as yourself, and who has met with some of my high born friends, that I am myself high born. In fact, I am descended of an ancient Mediterranean family which is also Spanish and Genovese, but also which joined an equally ancient French line over three centuries ago. Mine is the French family, though we are just barely French since our estate is closer to Spain than it is to Bordeaux, the business centre for the French side of the family. 'Laliber' is a short from for the original name, 'Laliberte', which latterly had too much dangerous meaning for the already powerful French side of the family."

"And the 'St. Triste'?"

"St. Triste is the name of our country estate far to the south-east of Bordeaux. It is indeed a place where pilgrims stopped, but usually because they had to turn back in tears when they heard of the early Christian defeats at the hands of the Moors who held all the countries to the south"

"The name - your name – does seem unusual though," probed Kastler.

"There is, of course, no saint named Saint Triste. But the name was allowed for the estate by Pope himself because of its prominence in the supply lines and solace for those on the early attacks on the Moorish capitals in Spain. It served my   purpose to give me a name of some distinction, though it was even more my mother's urgings, not his, until that special day of the migrating crows that headed me to the priesthood."

Kastler poured more brandy and encouraged Laliber to continue about his mission to New France.

"My own will is strongly to see once again the New World and the sweet souls of the savage that can be won there. Yet, it is a race with time: can those savage peoples discover civilized living and our Christian God at the same time, before our civilized living alone discovers and destroys them? Too many things that are not Godly in our European presence seem to prevent such a blessed concurrency of spiritual and earthly improvements for these peoples. I am most pleased that His Holiness agrees. I bear a Papal note to Laval. The monsignor will soon learn that he cannot be easily confine me to inside Quebec, though his Bishop must say nothing of the note itself."

Kastler felt that the priest had just confessed to him. Yet he continued.

"I have no desire to mix into the internal affairs of Quebec or in its fierce civil and even religious rivalries, but I know only too well however careful one is in a divided world, one gets taken by each side of such divisions to be a partisan of the other. Therefore, I hope to spend time away from Quebec in the native countries beyond. But, especially for the time I shall be confined there, I need others to tell me what they know of the true state of affairs in the whole colony and the fate of the surrounding savage nations. That is why I am pleased to be able to speak so directly to you. May I implore you to keep these things we have discussed to yourself, but beg also that you will keep me informed after your botanical missions as to that true state of affairs in your experience beyond Quebec itself?"

The physician held the priest's outstretched imprecating hands "I fervently agree to both of these things. I can only do what I myself am permitted, but I myself have sufficient Royal authority and plans to travel far and wide in and beyond the colony to gather botanical samples and other things of the nature of this New World."

Laliber now cautioned, "For a time, I think we should not be seen together in the colony. I will soon know whom else, if any, I can trust and then I will signal to you how we can meet without encountering the displeasure of those in power, including that preternaturally mordant young monsignor. You will have to send me things by message. If I do not immediately reply, it will not be because I am not reading your every word. "

The physician would have asked more questions, but he was worried that the brandy had made the priest speak more than he might otherwise have done and may be beginning to have ill effects.

Indeed, the priest said, "My head is beginning to ache. We can talk more another time."

The next, the sixty-fifth day at sea, dawned clear. Laliber was on deck and approached the captain with a hopeful expression.

"I am told we have entered the Gulf of the great river of Canada, Master. Can this be true? I see no land on any side?"

"Who told you this? I have not yet taken an exact reckoning." But, seeing the physician now so obviously disappointed, he had mercy on the man.

"My boson talks too much. Indeed, the cross currents tell any seasoned men of my crew that we have for some time been nearing the mouth of that great river, though it still be a sea empty to all horizons. This Gulf, do you know, is the size of all France itself! Its draining river from the interior penetrates into the new world for hundreds of leagues. Here, look at this map. It was copied from one made by the Portuguese fishers. Made by them from talk with the savages who once inhabited the coasts we shall soon begin to see. It is very old, but I have found it as good as any of the French and Dutch charts we have, for getting to the River of Canada."

The physician, whom the captain knew appreciated maps and charts, looked over the ancient map and whistled through his teeth.

"How could the savages produce such a map?

"It is a mystery to me. I was only told that one of the ancient peoples once dwelling along the coasts was asked to imagine the shape of the coast as if he were a bird flying over it and he pretty quickly made this map. Alas, those people are all gone. Some say they died from diseases - our diseases.

"My God, is it true - a whole people!"

They were interrupted by a cry from aloft.

"Land ho! To port!

The captain explained to the priest, "That is a mere sand island. We come about and must head north to the full Gulf. But sure enough, we have broached the edge of the Gulf leading us to the great River of Canada!

Chapter 12

By 1685, the settlement at Quebec, capital of New France, was an already imposing assemblage of civic and religious buildings on its heights, including the great Seminary instituted by its current first Bishop, Laval, and the religious complexes of the Jesuits and the Society of the Sulpicians. The latter owed their loyalties less directly to the Pope than to the Church in Rouen, whose Bishop had once unsuccessfully asserted Rouen's religious supremacy in New France, before Louis XIV and the Pope had agreed in favour of the Jesuit- trained Laval.

The great buildings were situated high atop the heights at the first accessible and still defensible point along the north shore of the River of Canada. Beyond the buildings of the promontory settlement, were cleared and cultivated fields on the slopes tilting away from it on all sides, themselves bordered and defined everywhere by the surrounding forests that stretched away beyond any reckoning points: a green sea as vast as the watery vastness of the great Atlantic itself.

For those arriving by ship, it was all the more pleasing a sight because its already densely built 'lower town' at shore level was set so cosily against the spreading settlement on its higher plain.

Kastler marvelled at the view of the lower and higher town in the fading red sun of a dusty late summer evening. He stood upon the deck of a small two-mast river shallop that had just left the southern shore and was headed directly toward the "lower town" landings of the settlement on the shore opposite. Equally pleasing him was the thought of how astonishing was the industry of the settlers who had within but a few generations made such a settlement in New France. This was also true along the south shore. He was returning from its linear ribbons of seignieurial farmlands running along and deeply back from the river after a two months summer visit to that area for both medical and botanical purposes.

What a pity, he thought, that since his own arrival in 1685, the main town had become even more racked with dissension and rival alliances, pitting the Governors group, the established clergy and various partisans of one or the other of the several companies contending for the fur monopolies and western forts inconsistently granted to the notables among the successive waves of newcomers to the colony. Even within these groups the tensions and disagreements were venomous.

The tensions were even greater within the clergy, since their disagreements had a more fundamental nature than the mere commercial interests of the lay population. And even within the different orders present, the tensions were now further divided by the strong and unsettling influence of Father Laliber, whose friendship Kastler had gained two years before aboard the St Bartholomew.

It was now well known that, the mysteriously independent Jesuit Laliber was especially contemptuous of the efforts and manner of the authorities of the colony to Christianize and otherwise deal with the surrounding savage nations.

Kastler's gaze caught the lights beginning to burn in the very church where Laliber was presently confronting the Jesuit Superieur in New France.

From the window of the Jesuit's chapel, Laliber had himself been watching the packet boat from the opposite shore approach the lower town below. He wondered if Kastler might be aboard, returning from his summer rounds along the south shore. He felt some relief - he had no other confidante in the colony, few indeed who were not now his enemies. It would be good to have the sympathetic ear of Kastler again. But, for now, he would have to contend alone with his Superieur.

The Superieur entered from a back door. He was startled to see Laliber before him.

"It is you! Why, I was told only the day before yesterday that you had gone to visit your friend, de Merlot, on the Island of Eyes. Most surely, I was told it was to help you find some peace with yourself. For what reason can you have returned so soon? And sought me out at this hour?"

"I have delayed that trip. I knew Henri and his wife well at La Fleche. I have not seen them since long before they arrived here. They have since finished a home on their fine seigniorial property on that Island. But, yours was a false supposition about my seeking peace there, Superior. For there can be no peace for me, least of all in greater solitude. The purpose of such a visit was only to seek a brief respite from the struggle here. Perhaps to hear the thoughts of those long-time friends on some of the matters that so greatly trouble us in New France."

He now looked searchingly at a dubious the Superior.

"Before that, I would ask that you take my confession."

"Well, yes. I know that we are all troubled. I know less of why you are so troubled, and I must admit a fear of what I do know. But as you are among the professed of this Order, please kneel with me here and I will take your confession."

"I seek you out because I now have little time for the normal relations of men and must have what blessing you can give in the time that remains."

"I cannot imagine of what you speak."

"Increasingly, Superior, I am unable to reconcile the role of us religious in our apostolic mission here as the army of the Christ and the universal church, directly avowed to his Holiness in Rome, with the state of the savage peoples hereabouts; in particular with that terrible nation with which we have so little success, and yet who so often harass our further entry to trade and win souls to the west."

"Well, if it is the Iroquois League of whom you speak, they also ply the unholy rum spirits they carry from the Dutch and English in New York to the surrounding tribes, but not the true Spirit whom we would carry to them."

"Yes. This past winter I have read letters from Father Lamberville in the Mohawk towns, telling of the evil influence of the English there. But I have come to agree with Lamberville, who has lived among the Mohawk longer than anyone of our brothers, that it is we religious who most of all may be blocking the spiritual progress of those nations whom we are avowed to convert."

"What a black thought you confess!"

"Alas, I confess only what I have read from Lamberville. We may well be the 'black' of his thoughts. You yourself have said on occasion that it is the ends of empire which spread from our efforts at conversion of souls, not the other way around.

The Superior found himself confessing to Laliber.

"I have thought that at times, the lesser cause has been furthered even as the greater cause has suffered – though I say that only as a coincidence of God's purpose here, which we cannot fathom."

"Whereas, Father Superior, I confess to you now that I do not believe God wishes us to make of Him an excuse in this matter. The problem is that we have not been allowed to do our true apostolic work. The facts of that are clear enough. Conversions among even the friendly tribes have declined. Too many of our bothers have been enlisted to spend more of their time in diplomacy for the Governor than they do in God's work. And the Bishop cares more about denying those people brandy and of the state of women's dress in the colony and the blasphemies of Moliere's plays than he does our holy mission."

The Superior was aghast.

"How can you hold such a view? Conversions among even the Mohawk are surely occurring plentiful enough, though perhaps less than desired at the Holy Sea. They have a Christian village here, on the far shore. If, among other Iroquois and other tribes that they are too slow, it is surely God's purpose that they be true. And we must not subscribe simply to our own earthly thoughts of such things. That is a false Protestant notion. We struggle against it everywhere back in Europe."

Laliber waited for more of the tirade.

"As for the work of our brothers, who can say they do not do what is earthly possible, especially among the Iroquois. If our brothers are able to serve the needs of ordering our borders, and are able to keep our own colony from being engulfed by vile heathen, so much the better I say. I can only agree with you that progress is much slower than we had hoped before our terrible martyrdoms in Huronia, now more than thirty years past."

Laliber was careful in his rejoinder.

"Father, there is little progress at all, that I can see. We delude ourselves. Those many nations who have become friends are lightly touched by any of our deeper truths – they seek only to trade with our traders, who enjoy an irresponsible freedom, while the main engagement between their peoples and we palefaces is south of the Lakes. Let me come to the main matter that is being missed here in Quebec – It is Lamberville's view: why is it that the vile barbarism of these peoples is matched by an equal virtue and simplicity of the spirit, that so many of them like our own martyrs, are martyred to the spirit they seek? Why is it that the hated Iroquois have learned how to speak in peace to the Dutchers and the English in New York, while we have not? Why is it, even more, our boldest and bravest Frenchmen seek out their strange kind of freedom – a kind of freedom we other French from Europe do not seem to know?"

"Oh, what you say must be false. They lack only the necessary steadfast purpose, to acquire on their own, all the methods of civilization and with that, a not too puritan Catholic spirit. To rely only on us French as do the trading peoples, without proper government as the Iroquois have among themselves, brings our wrong influence upon them, only to avoid God's modern world as long as they can. We Jesuits are an Order that must face reality, not hide from it. We are the advancing army of Jesus. Our Christian God expects us French to advance not just to hold our civilization."

The Superieur was reeling with this dismissal of everything he believed and had been instructed about as the French advantage in this new world – to offer an alternative to the English and their sense of divine purpose: to advance a farming and settlement frontier that would take away the lands extensively hunted and occupied by the native peoples in their own way, as if the native peoples were not "improving" the land as God intended.

"I find this all impossible to accept. Those English are seen as devils by our northern allies and so they are! The other nations put great value on our fur trade with them and allowing them to live in their countries as they always have. Of course, I have been told nothing since you arrived of special instruction to you from Rome."

Laliber looked sternly at the Superieur.

"As I once said to the monsignor, I have no need to invoke Rome in this. I have studied closely and tried to follow your instruction as best I can. But it is of little help in the cause of conversions hereabouts. And if our main business here is failing, how can I concentrate on my work at our seminary school, the school teaching that is all you allow me? You should hear the harangues of the Abenaki sachems in answer to the questions that I have asked for answers. I can but report to our Superieur in Rome: that, judging from their answers, our Lord's Name and the cause of winning their souls to Him seems less and less relevant as we try to speak it to them in a traditional way, as did the poor martyrs."

The Superior was stunned by this insubordination, but again recovered enough to reply "It is for Father Lamberville who labours among the Iroquois, to know any of the truth about them, not you hearing only stories at a distance. He counsels patience, patience, and more patience. We have several who have worked with the Abenaki and the trading nations, allowing them to live as they always have without loss of their lands. They will turn to the face of God in due course, from Christ's teachings. They must."

"What Lamberville and the others counsel is simply time passing. He has no strategic view. He has become too close to that one mission. Face the fact, Father: the English colonists vastly outnumber us! Theirs will be the future frontier with a disappearing Indian."

The Superior managed to look directly at the priest.

"Might is very often not right, Laliber. Anyway, you hardly know what you criticize - you have been here two short seasons. I now regret that I let you read the material in our Jesuit Relations. They are intended only for our Reverend Provincial in Paris and then, the best of them, from him to the Superior in Rome to share with His Holiness. Lamberville's own reports are often confused about the Iroquois."

"How can you be the judge of that – as you say, he is the one there. You are no Pijart or Rageneau who were well travelled among the native peoples. What do you know of those people, really?"

"Never mind. What I also regret is that I let you meet the Nipissing at their trading camp near Montreal or the Abenaki at their camp here across the river at the falls of the Chaudierre. I cannot imagine what you might have said as if Christ himself had said it. And the only French witnesses were those voyageur traders."

"I was with those people a brief time, and said nothing to them. But those couriers du bois told me the truth of things in their lives. Do you know that those French value their lives among those whom we call savages far more than they did their old lives in France, where they were caught in the many cruel bonds of our own ancient ways and not least the too often smothering effect of our Catholic Church? Do you not think the church must find a new way for those living in such a new kind of freedom?"

The Superior replied,

"Those ruffians are hardly the measure of our civilization. They are the criminal class sent here. Anyway, if you know so much, what would you do to break the haughty Iroquois south of us from their embrace of the English devil and who mock all our missions and who would break not only our favourable trade with the good Indians, but break their bones and spirits too?"

"None of you, even Lamberville seem to grasp the essence of the matter. It is not, what we would do to them, it is rather what those native people would do for themselves. I have told you of their strong sense of freedom."

Laliber tried to soften his tone.

"Those few of them I teach here along with our own French youth, mostly Mohawk as a matter of fact, have accepted Christ. They tell me they do so because Christ's message is not so much different from what they were told by their favourite medicine men and story tellers. It was the same in the Reductions of Paraguay. It is my belief as well that the wisest among them know full well we bring something more than our religious challenge to them with our permanent settlements here. In this, I subscribe to the views of our Superieur in Rome: too much contact with us "civilized" French here in our settlement but even at our increasing line of forts in the west has been unhealthy for the work of conversion thus far. It should be their forts out there, not ours. You cannot deny that the Abenaki, when baptised, regard themselves as French but do not change their adherence to their existing religious ways. When asked if they are Christian, they often know not the meaning of the question."

The Superieur knew that the straight truth in the reports back to Quebec from the Jesuits among the native peoples was a problem. He replied, his own tone now more earnestly seeking rapport with Laliber, as he sensed vulnerability.

"But I have been told by the monsignor you were brought back from the Reductions. There, they were not ready for any such talk. Why would this talk work any differently here? And how could our blessed Father in Rome support it or send you with any instruction in this regard? "

The Superieur again knew he was on tricky ground – the priest Laliber before him was not known for sure to be officially so instructed. Only that his work back in Rome had earned him the informal ear of the Pope.

"So, who has written something to you about this? Have you written letters, yourself?"

The Superior shrugged. "Others seem to know about what I hear only as rumours. Am I the only one in Quebec not to know? Do you have such special instructions, Father Laliber?"

Laliber shook his head, angrily.

"Well, at least you have asked me directly. Therefore, I think it is indeed time for me to tell you of its nature. You can judge my words against anything the monsignor has told you or that you receive in answer to your letters."

Trying to respect that he was in a confessional moment with Garnier, at his own request, however ironical, Laliber looked seriously at his Superieur.

"It is not what may be thought by others. I am not here for any specific purpose mentioned to me by the Holy Father. I am only to do what I can for the general good. His Holiness has no particular view of the New World but only wishes that the course of things would turn more firmly to the matter of winning souls to Christ. He felt my experience in other places should be of use. He sought from me an additional vow above and beyond the four taken by our Order.

The Superior could hardly believe what he was hearing.

"And, pray, what could such a fifth vow have been?"

"That if God revealed to me a way of winning native souls to Christ, it was to be followed by me independently of other instruction from the Church here or my Order, until such time as I could return to Rome and put this revelation directly to His Holiness himself."

The Superieur was shocked, but gathered enough control to emote,

"I do not even hear these words you speak. There can never be such a vow! Surely you must have not heard correctly or over-interpreted the Holy words. How can such a vow be given or taken? It is unprecedented for any Catholic, even clergy to be so enabled to act, even if temporarily, outside the structure of the Church! If you say otherwise, you are deluded! "

Laliber remained silent.

The Superior said, "What were His Holiness's exact words to you?"

"He spoke words of God that had come to him from his own Bible, from the Acts of the Prophets. His words were "Arise and go into the City and it shall be told thee what thou must do...But seeing ye put the Word of God from you, and judge yourselves unworthy of everlasting light, lo we turn to the Gentiles.""

"This is outrageous. He cannot have meant what you say. He must have meant you yourself had put aside the word of God. How could he think we have so strayed from our most devout beliefs and vows here in New France? We only serve Christ here. And, anyway, what is the wording of the vow itself?" the Superieur questioned, more pointedly.

"That is all he said. He merely uttered those passages and gave me his blessing, knowing I was already ordered by my Superieur to travel to the New World a second time. How can I say, why?"

The Superior could not believe such papal behaviour, let alone why.

But Laliber continued.

"I think the Holy Father saw me as a possible vessel of a new revelation of God's will in these countries, if and when it should be revealed unto me. He cannot have meant me as the one turned away from God, or he would not have given me his blessing."

The Superior continued, waving his hands in increasing desperation,

"So, have you had such a vision for this new world? "

"I have not. The Iroquois remain unknown to me. I see from afar that they calm their inner conflicts with a genius for government, not just the shifting trading and war-making alliances that keep all nations confused. Even so, I have had no contact yet with them in their villages. But, I can confirm what Rome suspected. Everything short of some direct intervention of God has been attempted here and still most of them resist true Christian belief or the Church's guidance in such belief. The wondrous but small exception is the few, including even some Mohawk, the most reviled of all, at their Christian village across from Montreal. What I cannot doubt is that turning the leading Iroquois more to Christ would be strategic for conversions of the other nations, all who fear them."

The Superior struggled not to accept the thought. He said,

"Any such attempt would be more futile than the saintly acts of our martyrs among the Huron. Our latest reports indicate the tide of the inland wars is turning against the Iroquois – they may not be as strong as you suppose.

"I know not of that, yet."

"You may not know a great deal yet. And, to validate any new approach of your own interpretation is not for you alone. I am your Superieur here and I deny that you have been given any authority to do so, until I hear directly otherwise. Remember: you have confessed your feverish state of mind to me as one of my obeying Jesuit priests."

The Superior was imagining how the other religious in Quebec would react to a clearly heretical Jesuit loose among the savages. He imagined it would actually please them. It could well lead to ridding the colony of all those from a difficult Jesuit Order with whom they competed every day.

"Before you abandon us, can we not together seek God's help in prayer?"

And then, after a pause, pleaded more to the point, "Must you ruin our Order, here?"

"It is my own soul for which I alone must now struggle. I am properly instructed by my fifth vow to His Holiness to go beyond my four vows as a Jesuit to work among these savage peoples. If I am to be damned by my Order and the Church when I serve God in such a way directly instructed by his Holiness, so be it. "

The Superieur was stricken.

"But surely this is not admissible, Laliber. You are professed to the Society of Jesus. How can you value so little the state you only attained with your four vows after labouring all you previous life and so much spiritual assistance from others and the blessings of God?"

The Superior raised his eyes and folded his hands. "Oh God, may you expel these heretical thoughts from your servant, Laliber. They will destroy his soul and our Order here and will unleash the Iroquois and the English all the more against New France's current weaknesses."

Laliber retorted, "There is no heresy here, Superior, unless it is in the form of that utterly closed minded monsignor. Report to him everything we have said. I am undeterred by any such prospect. Indeed, I anticipate quite another prospect when the end of this matter is upon us. In the meantime, I must leave for The Island of Eyes, for I have just heard the news that the de Merlots there lost a son to a Mohawk raiding party. Perhaps I can be of some comfort or help to that worthy family of Quebec's otherwise dreary and self-defeating officialdom."

The Superieur threw out his arms to try to prevent the priest from leaving, pleading with him to be reasonable and not to leave against direct orders to remain at Quebec from both himself and the Bishop's office.

Laliber pushed his Superior aside and hurried out.

Laliber looked out at the black night beyond the window. Then he noticed the window reflected the weak flickering candlelight inside the room which was illuminating the area at the cross, seeming to leave the Superior himself in darker shadows.

"I have heard your words Father, and will abide by them." He turned and was soon gone from the room.

"If you love Christ, you must, Laliber," The Superior called after Laliber.

But the priest had already vanished into the night.

Chapter 13

L'Isle des Yeux – The Island of Eyes – is a flat island in the middle of the River of Canada a few leagues west of the Quebec heights. Its flat surface was slightly tilted from higher northern shores to lower southern shores. By 1685, it had already lost some of its original forest to human needs and was now settled in a few scattered farms with their surrounding fields. The flatness was relieved by the view of a few distant mountains beyond the south shore, and by its great seigniorial house that had been built there by Emil, Sieur de Merlot. It had a steep roof, to void the winter snows and, as Kastler, already a visitor several times, noted in his diary, was a most pleasing and large log version of a French design that was then much favoured in Normandy.

The great house was closely surrounded by stands of tall bending red pine, which whished wonderfully in the winds, and from which the five daughters being raised by Emil and Antoinette de Merlot in good weather swung on swings to their hearts' delight.

The evening Laliber arrived for his visit gave a chilly hint of oncoming winter. A late October sundown still glowed in the western sky and gave a shimmering view up river. Here and there, small boats headed between the Island and the two main shores to the north and south making their way through the choppy waters and strong currents of the great river. Ice was already starting to form in some of the island's bays. Large rafts of migrating geese and duck bobbed about in the open water.

As he strode with wind flapped black robe from the landing up to the front porches of the de Merlot manor, Laliber was greeted warmly by Antoinette. She was wearing a becoming lavender frock, her fair face hidden and then gloriously revealed by her wind-tossed lustrous black hair. Laliber could not help notice her beauty had little diminished from university days.

Laliber was welcomed more guardedly by Emil, now a tough looking solidly-built man with greying hair who was had not changed out of his country clothes. Unlike his wife, he looked much older than in university days.

"Well, Father Paul, it is most kind of you to visit. We only met once in Quebec since you arrived there."

"Well, our duties do not bring us together. Perhaps absence makes the heart grow fonder, eh Emil?" replied Laliber, not hopefully.

"Just so," muttered Emil as he bowed slightly and waved Laliber inside the house.

At dinner, after having greeted, patted and been enchanted in turn by the five de Merlot daughters, all of whom were immediately sent off to bed, Laliber probed his sometime friendship with Emil.

Emil would have nothing of it.

Not caring to answer questions as to his own well-being, de Merlot only bothered to answer as to his family's present circumstances. He simply asserted, "We are down to "G." Those daughters you saw go from "A" to "E" and Francois we have just lost to those Iroquois devils, so G is our next, possibly Guy."

"Or maybe, "Antoinette said, "Georgette – after all we seem very successful with daughters. It is a gift from God, is it not Emil?"

She wanted to lighten what she knew was a difficult meeting between the men.

Laliber persisted, "I understand you lost your infant Francois to the Mohawk."

Emil's look darkened. "Yes, if you wish to know the specific devil. But please do not press me on something we carefully avoid. That boy is assuredly lost to us."

Both Laliber and Antoinette knew that look meant Emil was not only closed to further discussion on a matter, but would become ill-tempered in discussion of other matters. She now sensed that no intervention on her part could alter what was to come between the two men she valued most in her life.

"So," Emil said as he laid down his knife and fork carefully at the end of the meal, and waved Antoinette to arrange for more wine, "We have not shared our differences for a long time. From what I hear, you struggle here, even within that sweet divine grace given with your vows. "

"My struggle as an active soldier of Jesus has not been the sweet freedom of the angels or of a monk's order, Emil. Alas, it now more sourly languishes in the twisted reasons of state and your own government here in New France."

"Oh I think not the government primarily. It cannot escape the sometimes more twisted state of relations between your own Order and the other Orders here, the Bishop's cathedral and increasingly that sharp new monsignor, playing out locally the larger twists between Paris and Rome."

"Well, I disagree only in your exemption of the government. They each of those interests follow only their own way. The brandy trade is an obsession of each, whether for or against. It conveniently distracts from the real needs of the eager spirits of the native people hereabouts. We have new souls to win, here, even the laggard ones we should regain, among our own. Do you put pelts above that?"

Emil looked for more wine. Antoinette reappeared and it was brought to the table by a servant.

Laliber continued, "We argued this civil versus religious sort of thing in the old days. Neither of us won the other over. I suspect that cannot change."

"You are such a stiff one! You cannot bend in the wind. You never could. You do not see the value of good government."

"Oh, but I do: a government which is in good hands."

"You speak of my hands – I am the Assistant Intendant, for God's sake. Are you saying the French interests here are not in good hands! That the savage hereabouts has somehow better than us. Do you say these things, you foolish Jesuit!"

He stood up, and hurled his glass of wine at the table, soaking Laliber.

"I know not enough of what you are about here, Father Paul. Much is rumoured. I suspect much more than the rumours. I grant you all the conflicting French interests he re, that reflects our Mother civilization. But we others are at least constant in our own disciplined ways. Do you still know a disciplined way? You were always too taken by shifts of your own mind. I am told by your own Superior that you may have lost any disciplined way whatsoever and head to the savages with no certain plan."

"Better no plan yet than the forces from our own civilization acting on them with no good result for them."

"Help him go from us, Antoinette. Let him go to his ill-gotten savage souls and do what he will. I will not condone it. Never," he shouted

Emil left the room calling for his servants to bring his shore boat around, with his boxes of official papers and three blankets against the cold. He turned as he left,

"Be gone by the morrow, too tricky Jesuit. Look beyond our Island's shores, at the "Eyes" They are our growing French settlements that we govern here well enough that someone as you, seeking perfection cannot abide."

Laliber and Antoinette remained alone and quiet at the table for a long time.

A candle and then another candle gutted. They sat facing one another in a dim light.

Antoinette broke the silence. "I am truly sorry, Father. I dreaded this might happen.

"As did I."

"Perhaps we should go out into fresh air and for a walk.'

"Of course," replied Laliber.

"We may need more clothes," she said.

Feeling already too warm, he said, "Perhaps not."

Antoinette and Laliber stepped into a dark and cool moonless night.

The pair moved away from the manor and along the starlit path to the near shore. Neither spoke. It was an agreeable silence they shared. They each knew this might be the last time they would have to be alone together.

The priest thought, as she, of how Emil had always trusted the two of them to do nothing askance. He broke the silence.

"The evening is crystal, Antoinette. There is always now too much smoke around - after this summer's forest fires and then increasing home fires into the winter. Here, the night air is so sharp and pure. Would that it bring only pureness to this wondrous moment?"

"Yes," was also she spoke and in the chill drew his arm more closely to herself.

"And yet, I see the twinkle of fires on the far shore there – those are surely the eyes Emil mentioned giving this island its name?"

"It was such night fires for sure that did so name us here. It is said Champlain himself named the Island when he saw the evening fires of the savages along the mainland shore. He thought the more that he was being watched by the savages."

"I feel it unseemly to inject troubled thoughts into so pure a setting and with such purity of company. And yet, I fear I must. Emil was very angry with me at dinner. I fear we may have had a final falling out. It was not like that at La Fleche. We all argued until the next day dawned. Then, we made up. But, that time is gone."

"Emil had too much wine. I have seen him this way before, especially since the last Mohawk raids. He might not even remember this in the morning."

"I fear otherwise. Wine is not the only ruler this time. Like my Superior, whom he had just seen, he expressed unalterable opposition to my efforts to understand the strongest led savage folk as part of God's purpose for this wild country. He seems to believe only his view now that they are implacable heathen, and has no patience with any attempt to fathom what I still believe to be the unknown savage. Of course, it is understandable. He cannot now see beyond the cruel facts of the latest raids by the Iroquois- most assuredly, retaliating for our raids against them – and your lost son. Alas, it is likely this covers his inner feelings of failure to prevent these attacks in the first place "

Antoinette looked at Laliber more earnestly.

"I have not known Emil since the Mohawk stole our baby Francois from us. He was just two years old. Emil has waited years for a son and put such hopes on him. It was even as Emil was negotiating with them for some kind of peace. Ever since, Emil cannot accept anything can be good about the Iroquois, or that Francois was ever born, though I cry for our lost Francois every night.

As Laliber listened, her dress blew against him.

She continued, "And I have another confession to make. I have these past months tried to befriend myself to the praying Indians living along the south shore of Quebec. These help us sometimes with our corn and wheat planting and share other things of the woodland with us. It was my hope that greater familiarity with their ways would give me some answer to Emil's now unremitting hatred of the Iroquois and some reassurance that what happens to our precious Francois does not, as Emil thinks, damn him to the worst.

She wiped away tears.

"But I dare not share these things with Emil. I fear he is not ready to think more clearly about this. I fear that he would then despair over not only having lost his only son, but then his wife. It is this, more than his terrible anger that deters me from confronting him with my real thoughts."

She lowered her head.

"And, as a result, because we cannot tell the truth to each other, there is no peace between us, each of us concealing our inner thoughts.

She wept quietly.

"And then he wanted us to have another son, so much. It is so painful for us. We have tried, but we both have been told maybe he cannot make more children, even female."

Laliber had listened carefully to these sad words from Antoinette.

He tried to change the subject to something positive.

"Dear Antoinette, their towns are my destination. Whilst among them, I can seek to find out the fate of your son, and whether perhaps they would at least send him to those Christian Indians."

She looked "Some say even if he is alive among them, they would never return him. That they laugh at how strongly Emil has come to hate them.

But, surely you must conduct your own mission without endangering it further by these things about Emil and me."

"Be assured that nothing in either mission shall be in conflict, my dear Antoinette."

They gazed into each other's eyes, each remembering their youthful love.

Then giving in to the impulse, they kissed away each other's tears.

When they broke away from each other, he told her his own truth.

"My dear, sweet Antoinette, I have something to confess to you, too. I have taken a special vow to go among the Iroquois where I must find a way to join that unknown savage spirit to Jesus. This last vow was a rare vow above and beyond the four Jesuitical vows which priests of my Order make to the Church. It was a vow to his Holiness himself, in his presence. It was that I should find the truth of the savage spirit directly on his behalf, in my own way, and turn their way somehow closer to God's way."

She was astonished and looked at him so.

"It was a supreme test even for Pope Innocent himself. Had he denied my requested fifth vow, there would have been no more to it. But gloriously, he accepted my fifth vow. I was at first astonished and even terrified by the Pope's acceptance of my challenge. Yet, nothing I have experienced here makes me think otherwise. A renewed battle for souls here begins with the savage, for it has failed otherwise."

She looked at him and understood his torment. She embraced him even more lovingly.

"Paul, you must be tortured inside with these things"

"I am. But I melt in your arms as I did once before. That tortures me, too.

They pressed against each other, with passion neither dared imagine before. He could not avoid it. He spent himself quickly against her frock at that precious moment.

They knew their love was deep and only reluctantly did they separate, beginning to feel the cold air.

Laliber was red faced from the ecstatic moment.

Laliber whispered, "This must be as God intends. It is as close to manhood and womanhood as God will allow us. I can only say that I must now leave you. – I must be away before morning. I now see a paddle is being waved at me from the front porch. Let us hope Emil will forget his harsh words.

'I shall try to help Emil to take hope from your mission and chance to save Francois." she replied. "I would not delay you any longer. God watch over you. Would that my pretty Francois still out there somewhere if God has spared him, grows to be a good man.

"Let us pray that he will be so. Good bye, sweet and pure Antoinette."

He slipped away into the darkness.

As the canoe moved off the shore he asked that it be stopped for a moment.

He said to his companions that he wished to pray. But then, disgusted with his weakness, he made to himself a sixth vow, that he would find the truth in this new world in his own way, even as necessary outside the Church, outside even, the vow his Holiness himself.

He watched the twinkling eyes on the far shore of the St. Lawrence. He did not pray. He only thought bitterly that he had just almost admixed the evil surely within himself into the Ones he loved most. He knew this had sealed his departure from Christ's promise of divine Grace. He prayed to find a way back to Christ again.

As, Antoinette watched his canoe disappear, she shouted into the night,

"It was always you I loved, wondrous priest! It was you!"

Three months later, well into a hard winter, Laliber came abruptly awake one morning.

He had been awakened by the cackle of an old one. They had made him sleep beside her in her family's longhouse in the one stockaded Mohawk village that at this time accepted Jesuits living among them.

He had come to realize the woman used the device of feigned madness to chase away her relatives when they too often came to her with a foolish problem not worthy of her. He wondered that she had not tried the same thing to chase him away from her.

With the help of the resident Jesuit, Father Lamberville, he had learned some of the Iroquois ways, or at least the Mohawk ways, which often expressed their ironical sense of humour. It had been a far better education than he would have gained at the very proper Christian Mohawk villages across from Montreal.

Though known by their enemies as "man-eaters," and fierce in war, the Mohawks were known to themselves more modestly as "the possessors of the flint," which tipped Iroquois arrows from local slate rock. They were also known within the Iroquois Confederacy as the "Keepers of the Eastern Door." That status reflected prolonged wars with the Mahicans and other eastern tribes, and a century of treacherous contact with the new European colonies. It was their demanding role, with their central Iroquois Oneida and Onondaga brothers, to engage in a complicated on and off war back and forth along the frontier with the colonists and their native allies, while at the same actually or at least seeming to be suing for peace. It had bred a generation of great Iroquois diplomats and orators and several chiefs who were equally adept at war and peace.

The main Iroquois villages were surrounded by stockades beyond which were their fields, planted with maize, beans and squash. Within the stockade, the settlement contained several alignments of longhouses clustered in the Iroquois way.

During the cold winters, the nearly naked Mohawk of the summer wore buckskins and blankets. Except for occasional hunting sorties, most families stayed in their longhouses unless occasionally alerted of news to be told or other events at the central longhouse. Such news sometimes began with drums to summon an important meeting there or at the main Mohawk town or at the Iroquois Council Fire in the Onondaga hills. Depending on the precarious state of war and peace, such meetings might be called to warn of or organize retaliatory raids, by or against New France or new moves to be considered with or even against their putative allies in the fur trade - the Dutchers and lately the English New Yorkers, in Albany.

Laliber had chosen the right time to assess the spirit here. It was through the inactive winter season when the Mohawk and all the northern nations settled down in their smoky dwellings to hear the stories of their culture. As he began to learn the language, he listened carefully. He also watched the children. If they listened, he reckoned, the culture would go on. And they did.

And what stories!

His favourites were about the sky splitting and heroes falling through to the Earth below. Similar stories he had heard in the Abenaki villages near Quebec got subtly changed. There, of all the animals, the fish arrived last. Here, the water animals were the original animals existing in the waters below the land of the spirits. More importantly, there, the founding story heroes and the many spirits were recognized but while they could be warded off, the evil spirits could not otherwise be affected by humans. Here, among the Mohawk, the evil spirits could be converted to good spirits by feasts during which there was dancing behind grotesque false faces.

He had approached Lamberville several times about interesting differences among the native peoples. His brother Jesuit thought the native peoples all the same thing. The two priests had had a falling out about this careful differentiation of the tribes by Laliber.

"In Quebec, they would use such differences to divide these peoples," said Lamberville. "I try to report their universal character and emphasize their pureness of spirit."

Laliber had replied "Yet Lamberville, would you deny the differences among the myriad nations and principalities of the European world? The productive interaction of those differences is surely what gave us our own high culture."

Being a simpler man, Lamberville had little idea what Laliber was talking about.

The night of their biggest argument about this, Laliber had retired to his longhouse, exhausted from arguing with Lamberville.

The mad woman beside him now gave him a sharp poke. "You two – you argue about differences among nations. Maybe, I'll show you our differences, if you show me yours." She said this, chuckling.

He smiled and then marvelled at her challenge. Is this a 'fool,' he thought?

"You are a more interesting black robe than Lamberville. Let me tell you who I am," she said. "I am Dancing Pipes, for twenty seasons a good war captain of the Mohawk. I have won many battles for the League. I no longer take the war path and I choose to keep out of the silly village chatter that bid me take the war path in the first place."

"So, why am I interesting," Laliber said.

"Because of what you just said to Lamberville. The French, the English and the Dutchers are all different themselves. We ourselves make little of our differences, except to see it as a weakness. Except for you, you palefaces see us all the same. A lot of folks here are from different tribes now. Some don't even speak Mohawk! You are the first, father, to see our differences and see that mixing and stirring our differences in the right way could be a strength. "

They talked long about that before sleep overcame both of them that night.

Then the sickness had come.

It had been slow at first. A child here and there. And then whole families. Many were dying. Two false face feasts were held. Still more deaths.

Lamberville had come to him first.

"They see this as something we have brought upon them, something since you have come here. They blame you. Go now, when you can, back to Montreal.

"But then, they will blame you, Lamberville."

Laliber had stayed.

And then they came upon him. The angry ones.

They shouted at him and then they mocked him. Then they threatened him.

"You would learn our ways only to bring us this sickness. Let you be gone from us. We will take you into the winter. Make your way in our way, if you can. There is no other way to survive. If you return to us, we will accept you back." It was decided: the next day they were going to take him out far away from the village and leave him to die in the snow.

That was what Many Axes was told when he arrived at the Mohawk village late that day, on his way through to a parley with certain traders in New York.

Many Axes did not trust the judgement of the Mohawk about the black robes – some were useful, some not. Mostly not. He went to the Longhouse of Dancing Pipes which he always did when passing through her village. He had been told the new priest was also there, awaiting his fate.

He greeted Dancing Pipes. "Ho, my captain, I see the black robe there - I am told he is about to be sent into the snows to become white."

She chuckled. "Truly, he is seen as the bad spirit of our sickness. But, he is also seen equally as bad spirit by his own people. I think he is a true spirit. He actually sees things about us that seem of little benefit to anyone, but I think may be. Get him out of here, and see what you think of him."

Many Axes looked over at Laliber, who indeed lay silently awaiting his fate.

He knew a bit of French. "What do you think is happening here, Jesuit?"

Laliber rolled over to face Many Axes.

"A mix of peoples, all destined to die."

"Possibly so, but I mean about you."

"I too am a mix of peoples, but unlike me, those people I mix are not destined to die."

"We are all destined to die."

"Not yet, whole peoples: some yes, some no."

"Why do you care about my people, our people?"

"They are people. Christ gives all people his love and attention. All have a chance to find His light."

"So, everything is Christ?"

"No – a people has to know its own spirit, its own mind to flourish. Here I see your people distracted from that, even as we soldiers of Christ would seize that. It is not resolved here yet to Christ's liking."

"You alone can speak for your spirit?"

"I am so instructed by the leading servant of Christ, His Holiness, the Pope himself, across the big water, an even bigger chief than the English Crown."

Many Axes was surprised by this. He thought about the Iroquois device of the covenant chain that had enchained and delayed the English in their decisions by their fealty to the English Crown. He wondered about colonial ways. He began to sense a way of tying up the Catholic French in Canada in a covenant chain back to the Pope in Europe that might be as useful as the device that tied the English colonials back to their home country. Many Axes considered an option. He looked down at Dancing Pipes, who had been enjoying his exchange with the priest.

He said to her, "I see here some of the dream of Water Bear. What say you?"

"Oh I think we're close. Take this black robe to New York with you – see what difference he can make there, eh?"

"Just my thought, though I will never really trust a clever black robe."

"Chances are, he'll have you so mixed up that you will want to brain him. But don't, at least right away."

"Thank you good Mother."

Part Four:

Changing Winds

When the Strong Winds

Of history
Gain to a common gale
Are they perturbed
In their mighty flail

By mere eddies from below
Funneling up a tiny chance
To change those forces
Of immense probability?

Can a new thought
Sucked into that gusting flow
Like a bursting hybrid seed
Break and re-make ideas known
In the main winds wrought
With a new storied deed

To wreak new havoc
Upon all that old havoc
Long since fought?

Chapter 14

I was born on the Atlantic and so, I was born for a sea life. It is just as well. My life on land was, until lately, a mostly sour existence. Even after I owned a privateer fleet and became a wealthy man in New York, I was shunned by the very gentlemen with whom I made contracts –always unfavourable to me - for my considerable plunder from the Spanish Main. Before that, a promising life on land, a beautiful Narragansett princess to be my wife – that had all been cut short in the stupid King Philip's war along the Massachusetts frontier.

So it was, that I, Roger Smith, New Yorker, ended up seeing a new opportunity that could partly make up for what my people had already done and were set on doing even more of, much more of, to the sweet native people of this vast land.

It all began on a very cold night.

* * *

Few of New York's citizens were out of doors. It was the late afternoon of a crisp mid-winter day in 1686. Only the smokes and vapours that danced about the chimneys of the few score buildings that were clustered at the south end of its still mostly wooded peninsula, and the dozen seagoing ships at wharves or laying by in its near and far harbours, gave the town any sign of life.

The adjoined brick buildings told of the Dutchers who had built most of them – they were sensible yet imposing structures, many stepped upward on each side to a central peak, some to considerable heights.

For a moment, the setting sun burnished the brick buildings with a golden glow.

Then, the winter night fell quickly.

A large charcoal fire along a creek at the north edge of the town illuminated some of the nearby snowscape. Apart from that, the darkened peninsula now blended imperceptibly into the surrounding fields and forests.

Inside a tavern on one of the harbour streets, the men at several tables were beginning to drink seriously. The tavern was poorly candle-lit and stank of the tobacco smoke and sour gin of the Dutchers' place it had once been.

The rising shouts of laughter briefly stopped as the heavy outside door crashed open to admit three figures. Two were obviously dressed for the frontier in huge black bearskin coats. The third was clothed, if it could be said so, in a nondescript array of blankets.

Their entrance was greeted by angry shouts from those among the patrons who felt the blast of cold air.

This quieted to a few murmurs, as the newcomers made their way to the rear of the tavern where a single man sat alone at a long table, lit from several waxed over candled sconces on the wall behind. Even in the gloom of the tavern, the seated man's eyes were an astonishing blue. Though his other features and stature were average, these eyes gave him a strikingly handsome appearance.

"John Lonquil, you arrive with Many Axes. And you have brought us a priest," he said in greeting, the news having preceded the newcomers. Please join me."

Many Axes said in a fair English "It is I who brings the priest. We met Lonquil along the way."

"Aye that is fairer said, though he be silent for a black robed one," Lonquil replied.

Many Axes took corn from a hidden pouch and refused any food or drink offered.

He said, "You Smith, try to speak his name."

"Father…Lalisomething, is it?" The name seemed strange and was difficult for the seated Englishman to pronounce. The word that he repeated sounded like 'Laliver'.

The priest was silent.

When he says it, it sounds more like 'Laleebare,'" offered Jonquil, to fill the silence.

"Oh. Of course it must be short for 'la liberte,' a good word and meaning that." The blue-eyed man now spoke in clear French and looked as earnestly as he could at the priest, trying to encourage some talk.

But, getting no response, he ventured further, "My name is Roger Smith." He partly rose, tipped his hat and then swept it in introduction. "The Long Island beyond us is my base. It is a long finger pointing rudely at the sea, almost fifty leagues long, just across the eastern river on the other side of this too often wicked place. Quite an interesting country when you get to know it."

The priest had still not looked at him, let alone spoken.

"Take your time. No harm will come to you here. My French is adequate, unless your English is better. We may speak comfortably enough in your language. Many Axes knows each."

"Though not loudly here, please, or we risk censure." Lonquil warned, looking around.

The priest looked up at the blue-eyed Englishman. Laliber was haggard, but, his look seemed to study Smith with some interest. Smith caught this and again spoke to him, "Do you have any immediate need: Are you more tired and sick than hungry, or, possibly, more thirsty than any of those? Please let me know, so that I may decide what we are to do here."

The priest finally spoke.

"I have no immediate need, except to repair my soul. That need cannot likely be met in this place." He spoke in passable English.

It was Smith's turn to remain silent.

"It would seem that it is to you and Many Axes here, to whom I owe my recent survival, though my stay with the Mohawk had turned sour only at the last," said the priest.

Many Axes erupted, "Your 'stay' with the Mohawk was greeted as bad news all over the League. Winter is the season of sickness. It was the wrong time for a 'visit' by a new and suspect spirit." Even Laliber nodded in agreement.

"I could not stay in New France any longer. Anyway, I enjoyed the stories at the winter fires. I gained some respect for that."

Many Axes decided he would accept this. "Dancing Pipes told me as much. She also told me about your disagreements with the other black robe, there."

Laliber looked at Many Axes. "Your brother Mohawk are a people of many admirable qualities, though perhaps they have become too clever battling the excessive English and French influence from our respective colonies, is that not so, Smith? Certainly some of them can be rude and not always aware of their own best side."

Many Axes said, "I cannot these days defend any side. But, you had better speak your best side, priest."

There was another silence.

Laliber said, "In any event, I myself require only passage by any means back to Paris, or Rome. Whichever is the less loathsome to you English, Smith. I must take leave of these shores as soon as something can be arranged. Perhaps, you could arrange this? If so, I believe that I could eventually make it profitable to you."

But as he completed these words, weakness again overcame the priest. Lonquil caught him before he fell in a faint spell from the backless bench at which he had first been seated and helped prop him against the rear wall beside Smith.

Laliber finally accepted some reviving hot broth.

Smith said, "Indeed, I can arrange such a sea voyage for you. It would be my pleasure to do so. But let me tell you priest: If you have a purpose still in this world, you cannot take to the sea in your weak condition. You must remain on land for a time to regain the strength you need for such a voyage."

The priest responded slowly.

"It is not easy for me to see any value or purpose in my life as it has recently turned. Some the things I see here in this new world would diminish any true spirit. But, the broth does restore me. And, you are right: God's purpose may not be served by a mood too welcoming of death. Such a succession of excitement and depression of spirit must not make me seek to follow my dear martyred Jesuit brothers' ecstatic surrender."

He paused to sip more broth.

Many Axes thought about what the Jesuit said. What purpose would be served by having an interesting and sympathetic priest return home again? Here was a mirror to Smith – disaffected in his own colony. Could the priest be trusted as an ally against the French?

He said "I did not rescue you, priest to have you leave us. Though I distrust you, I am bid by my own spirits to want your powers here. I want you to help my people by influencing the French. I brought you here because this Englishman also has a desire to help us, and the wherewithal to do so. Tell him your story, Smith."

Laliber also turned to Smith. "Yes, now that my despondency is passing, why is it to you Smith that I ultimately owe my change in circumstance? Are not most people in this place even more opposed to Jesuits than they are to the French? What interest do you have?"

Smith settled himself in reply, "My life in the Long Island is sweet enough, though I am there alas, too briefly. My neighbours there, as here among Many Axes' nations provide some of my crew and even now supply one of my best captains. On Long Island they all are an Island tribe that has lived well in their time off the whales that could be found beached along the coasts. There are still some of their villages around my own settlement. We understand each other enough to have lived together in peace for the five years since I arrived on these shores. I am used to them and they are used to me. I keep them well supplied, and in return I gain knowledge of how the native man thinks."

Many Axes watched the priest take this in and nodded for Smith to continue.

Smith continued, "It is time that you knew that I am not quite what I may seem. I spend more of my time on land now than I do at sea, although not hereabouts. I spend only enough time at sea so that I may still be seen by my nine ships' captains and am still known for that. It also enables me to help pass on the skills required for a life aboard ships to those new folk who now sail for me. I must sometimes make sure a given crew is sea-going and is settled on the right relationships between my rollicking long-time mariners and those from the woods who have a more guarded mien. One time, my second mate hollered at some new native crew, 'Like your manner your blood must be thick.' It took a week for that to sink in and for a native sailor to say back to the second mate 'Like your mouths, your blood must be loose.' Everyone laughed at that one."

Laliber said, "So, the strange mix on your decks begins to be stirred."

Many Axes said, "The Iroquois I know of are like the others from these woodlands – they have accepted Smith's own idea that the wooden masts and the sails makes each of his ships a forested island, moving across the waters."

"They monkey the spars as well as any of my seaborne knaves."

"It is truly a conversion, though not what I seek," said the priest. "But, do your knaves learn something from them as well as they are equally capable of humour?"

Smith's eyes widened. "Do you know, I think some do! More than one has said to me they learn a kind of patience with life, less seized by their inner devils. Like Many Axes himself here, my native sailors can squat in contented silence for long periods at a time while the rest of my crew get too restless and begin to fill inaction with disruptive nonsense."

"So, again, a trade of strengths. That is my hope for conversion in this new world," said Laliber.

Many Axes muttered, "You and few others."

Smith returned to his own story. "Now much of my time is spent inland well beyond Fort Albany, among the nations around the Great Lakes with whom, when the market is good and in their favour, I must try to ensure a reliable commerce through New York in the beaver pelts. To cut out a trade that is not with the French, or with the wrong English, who would some years sell for better prices in Montreal, things in the woods must be delicately negotiated. In the course of my forays into the wilderness with Many Axes, I too have learned to respect the natural men who inhabit those countries. Indeed, that is where I first learned of your arrival here, Father Laliber – from a botanist and physician travelling far into the forests in search of new plants and new knowledge of the frontier."

"That would be Emil Kastler."

"Yes."

A new round of drinks arrived at the table. Laliber asked for a brandy, which quickly came.

Smith continued his story. "I am mostly a Providence man, from the newly recognized Rhode Island colony. I am from Puritan stock, but perhaps through my birth in a rough sea in my family's original passage here, and certainly through my most wilful father, a very strong man whether he was at sea or on land, I inherited a rebellious heart."

Many Axes laughed. Laliber nodded, accepting this admission.

"Did you know Laliber, that among these colonies, Rhode Island alone is tied to no one religion? It alone is free to all. And to one man alone, we owed this freedom – Roger Williams. I am myself named after that great man by my father who was one of his adherents. In the end he rejected any church as a path to God. This un-churched freedom of religious preference must be as alien to a popish priest as it was to the Boston Pilgrims. But, alas it is most true in Rhode Island."

Laliber looked at Smith. "I know little of these things, except very indirectly and perhaps falsely from the information in the propagations of my own Church. It seems that freedom in all its senses is to be a more natural thing in this new world. But, pray go on."

"And so I shall, for there is an ignorance in the home countries of the essentials of these northern English colonies—in fact, a country larger than all their Mother countries and yet only begrudgingly recognized by the ignorant colonial Lords in England as something more than a mere "north of Virginia." And it is a foolish misjudgement of the French, as well, who can, under their most glorious King Louis, imagine even less the existence of independent energies here, but simply tolerate them and seek to impose small numbers of Frenchmen in their scattered forts among them. And you have hinted that you yourself realize that just as the colonists are failed by their over-dependence on the corrupt home countries, so also, on this side of the sea, a too close relationship between these colonies and the native peoples may be failing the native peoples' and even the new peoples' best interests."

Laliber could no longer doubt he shared much the same understanding with Smith. He knew now why Many Axes had brought here.

Smith continued, "For my part, I have mixed well with these native peoples from my early childhood on the New Englanders' frontier. But later, this fair relationship was foully ended by several waves of cruelties and stupidities by my people and the native tribes in retaliation to one another during a war stupidly called King Phillip's War. That tragedy brought a bitter end to my innocence, and to all the family of my betrothed beauty, the daughter of a Narragansett chief. It drove me recklessly to sea."

The priest then spoke, "These things can try the soul."

"Ah yes, the soul" Smith began again, bitterly. "New England has a soul, a kind unknown to you. Believe me, I have seen it and it can be very pure and very ugly."

Many Axes listened carefully to this talk between the colonials. Let it bring them out more, he thought.

Laliber said, "Well, I speak only of the immortal soul possible through the great mystery of Jesus. But then I fear that I speak not for most of my compatriots these days, either in New France or in old France. Their joys in life are all lesser ones, taken up with service to an over-strong King and to the pleasures of trading low prices for high, and pleasing their bellies and their loins."

Smith was pleased at the strength of Laliber's seemingly anti-colonial words.

Laliber continued, "As I think of this, the foolish glories of the King's service and the temptations of office blind many a high borne man from the duties of his faith. The pleasures of this world consume most others in France and many a rude habitant living a sweet life along the River of Canada. Gone are the days of which I have been told, some forty years before now, when all in those rough new settlements at the edge of the world were truly seized with god's purpose and blessed with a natural piety in facing the dangers of this new world. But in none of their new and more settled ways can I see God's order advanced among those with a natural freedom!"

"Yes," replied Smith, "that kind of freedom is a great challenge to us palefaces."

Laliber slowly nodded. "I have spent time among the Indians near Quebec and north of Montreal. I found there a few French freed from the squalor and hypocrisy of their miserable lives back in France, seeing in them a joy of freedom to live their lives without much formal society amongst those simple-seeming savages. Though I am French, I cannot say they are in any way a worse or better people for this frontier than your English. I am pleased you speak to me honestly about your own people in this way."

Smith replied, "Freedom seems an elusive thing. What freedom is better, think you: the freedom with few restraints, as you say may exist in the bush, or the freedom within the strong restraints as we Europeans have, to break the restraints?

Laliber thought about this.

"The former gives happiness and sadness, I guess; the latter joy perhaps, which rises above happiness, but can plunge well beneath sadness, to a misery and despond perhaps even unknown to the savage."

Laliber said, "But surely you are alone here in these thoughts. Surely my presence will only invite incident and cannot but reflect badly upon you, sir."

"Well, you are right, in that I am not proposing you linger here in New York. That would indeed cause incident. But you may stay the rest of the winter at my remoter place toward the end of the Long Island, beyond the New England settlements there. It is a good distance from here. It is there that you will find the respite you need before embarking upon the voyage back across the great Ocean that I can then arrange for you. My plan is to return there this very night. I await the ebbing tide and then we shall be off in my little brigantine to a place sweeter than you have seen in many a month."

He looked at the priest. "Will you agree to this, for it is indeed retreat I offer?"

The priest was about to reply that he would agree, when a large man approached the table and began to speak gruffly to Smith.

"So, Smith, by the smell of it, this is a rare cargo you have taken on! Though he is wrapped in more clothes than my grandmother as she died, God rest her soul, anyone can see his black conspiring eye! What return will such a popish parcel fetch? I think little enough for the effort, eh? Take care, or the winds will blow you and your painted crew all the way to Rome itself."

The room had grown silent and all eyes were upon the rear table. And then the room erupted into laughter.

"Van Pammister, you old blasphemer!" shouted Smith above the brouhaha. "How can your words be answered without a greater blasphemy? You know that it is from my human compassion that I take on this French priest. Would you have him walk your plank?"

"Indeed I would, for at his last moment, we would see him rise to Heaven – but only methinks to see him plunge again into the sea from that greater height!"

An even louder roar of laughter erupted in the room.

"If I did not know you better, I would run you through for such Dutcher talk. Have no fear Laliber my priestly friend. This is Jean Van Pammister, my best ship's captain, and at times the meanest jokester. He is part French himself, but of mostly Dutch sausage, I think, and more anti-popish than anything else."

"Son of Huguenot, to be sure," said Van Pammister, switching to French. "But bearing no grudges toward even one such popish black bird as this, if, that is, he be a friend of my captain, Smith here."

With a massive smile, he bowed deeply in the direction of the priest. Getting little response, he continued,

"Then, let me apologize for my geste, for you did not know I was speaking lightly at your expense, nor did I know at first you would fathom the English. But, t'is the truth, you are fortunate indeed to be in this tavern, which your present benefactor has in his control. I fear your presence would draw a ruder welcome anywhere else in New York or amongst most of the English colonies along these coasts."

The priest appraised the man before him and having decided to take him at his word, he answered,

"I have said as much to monsieur Smith. You may be assured that, with his help so generously offered, I will be in this place no longer than I have to.

But tell me, I see here a kind of fraternity. Do you all serve the same master, or are you independents?"

Van Pammister laughed loudly.

"Among us, only the sea is master, my friend. " He turned to the other tables, "Though I daresay we all take to it in Smith's ships." At this, there was relieved laughter and many of the men about the crowded tavern raised their drinks in Smith's direction.

Smith acknowledged this and then began to get up from the table, saying as he did so,

"Yes, along with their smell, there are more than a few things that bind us together here. But, come, if you are now well enough, it is high time for us to depart, afore the Governor's men get wind of this."

As the still weak priest was helped back through the room toward the door, Van Pammister drew Smith back for a private word.

"What tricky business are you up to, Smith? It is dangerous enough to comport here with Many Axes. It will certainly not go down well if you are seen comporting with one of the French black robes. You know this one has an advance reputation as being even more treacherous than the others. Send him back to where he came, say I."

"That may well be his ultimate destination. Yet I would not deny him his intent to do mischief to those other French Catholics up yonder. Not just yet I think. These priests know a thing or two, which could be to our advantage in the beaver trade through the western country. But, I will make my reasons for this "business" clearer to you later.

Again weakening, the priest ahead of them had stumbled and needed to be taken more firmly in hand. As Smith moved to help, he quickly finished his reply to Van Pammister, "In the meantime, pray remind all the others to say nothing as they are bound, about who paid a visit to our tavern this night.

Chapter 15

Trade is an essential human thing. It has caused fruitful contact among nations everywhere on Earth, even while they may detest one another.

Just as the sun's energy irradiates the Earth and causes otherwise reluctant interactions of physical systems, so a hot desire for gain causes human contact in trade across deep cultural divides. Consider the attributes of the good trader: shrewdness in judging others, an ability to keep informed with wide and current knowledge of anything influencing the terms of trade, agility in sensing good value through tentative, twisty talk, and decisiveness at the last moment making the trade. That is the good trading man.

So it was with Water Bear. But he was a trader driven by an additional imperative to interpret his dream. And, so it was that he had devised a way of bringing together all the black and white elements of his dream into the northwest to a multi-sided trading parley in the fall of 1686.

He had arranged to meet Many Axes at a convergence of western rivers several leagues inland from the Green Bay to travel together for another few days to the appointed trading island. Magic Walk had remained at the Sault, though strongly against her will, because she was in mid-pregnancy.

He had already received news that travelling with Many Axes as anticipated was the New Yorker Roger Smith, but also, remarkably, a Jesuit priest from New France.

As he thought about it, Water Bear was at first doubtful that such an unlikely combination would help him in conducting trade with the western nations and the French traders. But he had come to see it as making up the symbolic mix in his dream. He was intrigued with the prospect of meeting the priest and hopeful that he might turn out to be a better representative of the dream's black robe influences than those who had so failed him in Montreal.

For his part, a day or so away from the meeting with Water Bear, Many Axes' face was glistening with sweat as he bent to the rhythm of the paddling against a steady west wind. He strengthened his stroke. The others in the party strengthened theirs.

The thick-set man was good at and insisted on paddling, though he was the senior Iroquois man among those in the three canoes making up the mostly Seneca trading party heading northwest.

Now in his early fifties, the skin was still tight and not much wrinkled on his large head. But it wrinkled a bit more as a troubling thought once again returned to him.

He looked back at his companions and saw the black robe alone struggling to keep up the paddling pace. Actually, he had been surprised at the Jesuit's determination to paddle – Smith, a stronger man, was content to let others do the work on this trip. For the first few days the priest had not talked much, explaining that he was in constant silent prayer. He seemed to be falling back under the spell of his Jesus. He dared to attribute to his God's purpose some new meaning that would be revealed at the forthcoming meeting at the trading island with Water Bear and the French traders.

Many Axes anticipated that he might have to work hard to dispel that source of anything new at the trading fires. It must not replace Iroquois and other native will. He still did not trust what he anticipated would be the competitive presence of this disruptive black robe. Laliber was not a truly turned man, as was Smith, who, never forgetting the loss of his own native betrothed, more simply waiting to fit into any good strategic ideas to assist the native peoples' survival along the frontier.

The party was approaching the convergence of rivers where they were to meet Water Bear. It would be two or three days beyond that to the trading island.

Many Axes frowned as he considered the situation they would face. They were now deep into the northwest, paddling the rivers and lakes well beyond Iroquois control. He looked back at the three Seneca accompanying him west. It had not been his choice that he and Smith, and now this priest paddled west with three Seneca.

He was angry with the Seneca. The whole situation in the west had been made weaker for any Iroquois by the Seneca's own latest war party. He had told the young hotheads to stay out of the northwest in the latest season of war, but they were used to summer battles. Battles they were no longer winning.

Somehow, they managed this time, both to lose a skirmish and to kill a famous enemy captain. It would likely be many more Seneca than just the Seneca captives who would eventually suffer for this. It was the sort of unnecessary thing by the younger warriors replacing the more seasoned ones who were being lost in increasing numbers in the northern wars that were reversing the fortunes of the once undefeatable Iroquois.

To stop it all, he knew he would have to rejoin the Grand Council. Use his mouth and if necessary his axes to talk the silly young braves out of their foolish belief that they were as strong as their ancestors. Get back to some peace talk in the north, where the great covenant chain of agreements with New York in the east meant nothing.

He scowled and was turning his thoughts to the trade prospects ahead, when he saw a column of smoke on a distant ridge. He shouted in passable English to the man not paddling behind him, the New Yorker, Roger Smith.

"Pirate, that smoke in the sky could be some foolish Seneca being burnt at an enemy fire."

"If so, the Frenchmen will be troubled by it and it could favour our side at the trading fires. But, I doubt any other nation in this country whomever they may be would waste a hapless Seneca. They would know about the temporary peace in the woods pending the big trading parley. As you say, it could give some kind of trading edge back to us. They would rather protect any Seneca left there to be displayed to us as a bargaining advantage."

"You speak truly. I wonder how you know these countries so? You have been here, maybe twice. You're a pirate! A buccaneer. Those were the words I was told for you - some thief upon the seas."

"The word is 'privateer', please. A most legitimate business. Though maybe here, you could call me a 'bushiness man'" He chuckled to himself at the alliteration in English. He tried in his child's ability with the Mohawk language, but thought he could not convey the low humour to his companion. It left Many Axes scowling even more darkly.

"Word magic is needed for more serious things," he said, in good English, learned, Smith knew, in many parleys with the New Yorkers.

Smith retorted, in a worse Iroquois, "Yes, I know your words make mischief with those whom you would persuade over to your way."

"That is different. Your word mischief was just play. Besides, there are too many English words for things that need one word and too few English words for things that need many."

"I could say the same about your language."

Recognizing the weak subjunctive, Many Axes said, "You could," and turned to look at him, "But you do not. Hah."

The exchange quieted Smith and made him think back over the past few frustrating weeks.

Earlier that month, after Water Bear had arranged for the all-sides early autumn trade meeting in the west below the Upper Lake, Smith was moving through the Seneca towns on his way to the meeting.

Smith had mixed thoughts about this trip to the western trading parley. It was his hope to enlist the great Iroquois chief, Many Axes into some scheme that would reduce the influence of the English and French colonies which he could clearly see eating away at the native peoples. He could not see a way to implement any such plot, without the lead of a renowned native Chief. Many Axes seemed ideally fit to the role. Many Axes was a man gifted in the ways of war and peace, revered by the Iroquois, though not at present sitting at

Onondaga with the great chiefs there, by his own desire for a time to remain aside from the official business of that great central council.

Not wanting to create negative feelings, Smith left Laliber camped outside of the last town he approached, where Many Axes was said to be in retreat. Smith wore his inland buckskins, as did the two of his Iroquois ship's crew members accompanying him, one an Onondaga, the other, a Seneca, both already known at sea for their fierce attitude in sea battles. His Seneca companion was warmly welcomed back to his home village.

Smith looked about as he entered the village. He had been there the season before, but this was not the busy town he had experienced the year before in the war months. He noticed that only half the corn had been harvested. He saw few children. He saw no women. He saw few men, and those only dawdling outside the longhouses. There was a palpable sense of gloom. It followed the news of a defeat in the west.

There were other chiefs here wanting to talk to Smith, but he sought out Many Axes. When he found him, he was drinking a large draught of water.

As Smith entered the longhouse, Many Axes, having been told Smith approached, simply said, "Much water is good for the bowels. What do you think? But I guess the water you know most, with some of our brothers, is salt water."

Many Axes grasped Smith's arm and became serious.

"Welcome to this Seneca village, though right now it is a mostly defeated village. Those Ojibwa have learned from many wars with us. They carefully outnumbered us and the Seneca suffered a large defeat in the north this past season. Many warriors were lost."

He backed away and studied Smith.

"So Smith of New York, you remain the man who bewitches us and steals us to your wooden ships which you say are simply the forest, in another way. Indeed, I see the two Iroquois braves who have brought you here walk proudly."

"So, you encourage your people to do the best European things and try to do it better than they."

"Well, I do not discourage anyone here so strangely inclined to try your fleet. Something like that might be handy in our big lakes – the French have already tried it once but the ship was lost somewhere on the upper lakes. But I do not encourage my people to do everything European. I find the white spirits more than a little strange, especially, those black robed ones. The white and the black do not well mix even among your own people."

Smith smiled. "The Catholic priests are hardly our English spirits. You know well that we English differ greatly from them. Except perhaps for the one among them we bring with us in this trade mission, who says he seeks the same truth as Water Bear, the giver of dreams."

Many Axes shrugged. "Water Bear now starts and ends the fur trades in the west each season. He often betters the price first offered by either French or English traders. He converts the goods in exchange to the livres that would buy them in Montreal. It helps our people think about the trade. I like the man. But I do not like that he is being sought by that black robe, Laliber, even if the priest says he is on our side. Hah. When they are among us, they all say they are on our side."

"You speak from experience, Many Axes?

"The one named Lamberville has been among the Mohawk for many seasons. He knows and lives well the Mohawk ways – I guess that's why he lasted among them. But when I talked to him, he was most confused about any interests we might have in common. That new one Laliber had a sharper mind. "

Many Axes threw a rug aside and crossed his legs, forgetting why he was covered in the rug. He looked down at a big toe coming through one of his torn moccasins.

Smith looked away, and then, looking back, said, "A chief with torn moccasins is not a good sign."

Many Axes answered bitterly, "You are rude to point it out, but you are right. I have been brooding too long and must change my spirit." He angrily kicked out of his way a heavy carved turtle shaped wooden box in front of him. The pain surged through his big toe. "Fucking Turtle: give us something more than mud to live on!" he uttered. He stood and punched a black and yellow mask hanging from a pole grotesquely staring out at them. It fell on the dirt floor looking up at him. He jeered at it, "Ya, ya, ya!"

He took a moment to regain some composure, and concluded his answer to Smith's earlier question, "Yes, I speak from experience- it should not be hard for anyone breathing to know these things."

He strode further into the longhouse and got new moccasins, put them on, throwing the old ones into the smouldering fire. He returned to Smith, reshaped the false face carefully, put it back on the pole, sat down again, put a placating hand momentarily on the wooden turtle and changed the subject.

"You are English. You always know things to your advantage."

Smith thought it important that Many Axes had put on new moccasins. He said nothing of it. "Yes. But, not just to my own advantage. Water Bear and that black robe, Laliber, could find a useful new way from the dream."

"You think that those two might interest us Iroquois in some new way. Ha!"

"Well, since you were there, you know that Water Bear has promised to Dancing Pipes, your Aunt, to give his dream when it is fully interpreted, first to the Iroquois fires."

"Oh you pale faces make friends with us to catch us in our own traps," Many Axes said, raising his voice, looking up to the smoke hole of his Longhouse as his old moccasins began to burn, "I am told that dream too many times. I helped Dancing Pipes with the idea for Water Bear to escape, just after he first had that dream. I think the dream of Water Bear if it survives at all may be nothing for Iroquois listening. But, you are telling the truth that the dream, whatever Water Bear finally decides it speaks, must be first be brought to our

Iroquois fires. I suppose that alone means it must have some meaning to us. But I was told by those returning from the western countries there was no interpretation even now, several seasons later. I say a dream so long un-interpreted is the nonsense of the bad spirits. But most do not agree. They say that such a long time for its interpretation makes it more important. As often I have done before, I paddle against a powerful current."

"Well I say it is for Iroquois listening, and that you are, above all, the right listener."

"Ho. You are right in that, Smith: if there is something new in this country, I can say that it is so. I have brought the Iroquois strengths to all the nations in all the directions." He spit into the fire. "There are now many 'confederations' who fight us to the north, south and east."

"You have tried to spread the middle tree, to be sure. And you know war alone, without an idea even more powerful than the covenant chain, cannot win this too conflicted world over to the original Iroquois idea of a tree of peace."

Many Axes opened his hands in disgust.

"I had to save our confederacy from many threats, even before I was accepted as a chief. Despite being the nephew of Dancing Pipes, I was laughed at. Why? Sometimes, it was because of my big head! But I finally took them all to the ground until they said I was their chief. And then, only as a War Chief, I took our parties as far west as they had ever been. Too far, maybe. But, then I saw how to parley with defeated peoples. You don't push them into the dust. You can learn from them, take in some of them, and then you give them stones to throw at your next enemies. So, I am now the Peace Chief as well as War Chief. And then I saw that the same strategy was being used on us by the English – not so much the French or the Dutchers. I think something must be made of our recent defeats as well as our victories. Something must be made different before we again must truly and strongly make war."

Smith nodded. He asked, "Do you know of the Rabbit's power in Water Bear's dream? It controls the power of Bear himself!"

"Yes I know the dream. I have heard it at too many fires. And, it is true: Maybe I am the Iroquois leader who can control both the strong powers and the soft powers, the black and the white even in a time of Iroquois weakness, to make new things happen."

He went over and stoked the moccasin fire.

"It is not just our latest defeat in the north. The new confederacies there are as strong as our own. To the South, we now meet such a tangled set of alliances between the Lenape and Susquehannock and the English there, too, that we could not make any final victory. Many Seneca have been lost there, but we have at last a peace of sorts. To the west, we know no one nation who can defeat us, because they fade away farther west. To the east, there are again so many twistings and turnings with and between the colonies of your peoples. The Mohawk towns refuse to break the Covenant Chain with the English. But, I say it now enchains them more tightly than the English, and they know not how to shake off that chain of their own making. Where once they welcomed my combination of peace and war powers, I now have little influence there. So, Smith, what is it that your subtler spirit would wish me to do next? I have unused powers. I may give it consideration."

"Again, simply this: Go with me to the north-western trade meeting and listen to what you hear."

"I suppose I too sense that I should do that, if you will do one thing."

"What is that?"

"If I do not like what I hear, and it is not right for my people, all the schemers will die."

"What gives you the notion you would have such power so far away from here?"

"Hah. I have made a pact with some chiefs of those northern nations. It is that any who possess the dream are not to be suffered alive unless the dream gives them life. It is too much dark mischief otherwise."

Smith considered this surprising news.

"I hear you, Many Axes. Yet, I'll take my chances. As I see things, the dream may be all that is left for your people. The pale face waves from across the great ocean will wash over you otherwise. What I know most, is that, if there is to be plot, you and the Iroquois must be part of it, or we all die, not just the dreamers."

"Good. Then let us go to that trading island. "

Chapter 16

As they approached the last river between lakes to the lake of the trading island, both men came out of their inner thoughts of what had led him to go to this place. Smith started to explain some of whom they would meet at the trades. But, Many Axes broke in.

"You tell me things you cannot know for sure."

"I keep telling you, Many Axes, I have contacts here. They know by keeping me informed they will not lose their advantage from my knowledge."

"Ha. I still say a man must be there, to know much about anywhere. Water Bear alone seems to know all. That's because he travels in trade everywhere, like his dreaming father did. You know everything from someone else. But, the bait is not the catch, you will see."

"You are in a grumpy mood. How many treaties have you talked others into with knowledge you learned from other informants?"

Many Axes shrugged. He felt his own sour mood. It wasn't just the latest Seneca foolhardiness. It was everything going wrong. He spat into the water, and partly changed the subject.

"I sometimes think you are one of us dressed up in paleface skin and clothes."

"Ha. Maybe I do have one of your other faces. Maybe you think I have one of those ugly False Faces that tell so much without saying anything. Just as over a hundred of your best braves now man my ships, monkeying, nay cooning about the spars, riding out the storms, seeing land and ships first, staying out of trouble in port, better for my fleet most times even than the best whites."

"Hmpff!" muttered Many Axes. He thought of his sometime champions, the Mothers. They were right. Leave it all alone they said. Let it all blow past. Keep to peace making. Give away all the others' land. Tell them it is far richer than ours. Make an agreement. Make it over and over again. When blood flows from us, we are fewer, but when blood flows from the palefaces, there are yet more of them. It is not our thing yet. Make it our thing.

That is what they confusedly advised him, because he was their favourite in every village and town.

But he had tried that long ago, over and over again. Too many times – every time – it always led back to war. And then the chiefs and the warriors again wanted him to be the War Chief. What he wanted was something that he wanted to do, not their story for him. It would be maybe some war; maybe some peace, maybe some both. It would be his own timing; on his own; his decisions, maybe in an empty Longhouse. No mothers, no clans, no warriors, no other chiefs messing up some kind of plan - well, he had to admit, it too might be a mess. But, something he could just straight out tell them. With such force they would all agree. And then he would do it. But then they would push back.

During these frustrating thoughts Many Axes had increased his paddle stroke, to the point that Smith said, "If you're going to paddle that strong, I can't do much up here. I'll just relax up here with my paddle athwart. You can do it all."

That helped Many Axes break out of his thoughts.

"Sorry, I got lost in some sour thoughts about Longhouse politics. Here, as there, I must resist trying to do it all."

"You are very strong, Many Axes, but even the strongest leader must work with others. That's always the trick. Makes it easier all around."

"Yes. Good words. Now get your paddle back in the water. We will resume the best pace together."

Later, their canoes approached a river outlet where Water Bear's small party awaited them. Water Bear had seen them and headed out alone to meet them.

"Ho, Many Axes, you did not make me wait."

"No. And we have extra baggage. Take this black robe into your canoe. He has been silent with us, but he weighs ours down with his Jesuit thoughts. Let him weigh yours down. It is your turn."

They made the exchange on the shore. Laliber knew the man who now shook his hand was Water Bear because of the jagged slash of white paint on his right cheek, now always worn by the man as a symbol of his great dream. Laliber had listened when Many Axes had explained to Smith that Water Bear would add a black slash to his right cheek when the dream was finally interpreted as a basis for some intertribal action.

As the canoes now headed down the river that would lead them to the lake of the trading island, Many Axes called over to Water Bear, "You are the chief he seeks: make sure he passes your test."

Water Bear said, "What test?"

Many Axes spit in the water.

"Make one."

Water Bear deliberately lagged behind Many Axes' canoes. He was considering Many Axes' challenge: make a test for the Jesuit to pass while you paddle with him. He began to strengthen his stroke to see up to what point the priest would try to match it.

As they paddled through the morning, Laliber tried to match the increasing power of Water Bear's paddle strokes. He began to sense that this was Water Bear's test. If so, it was also God's test. He was failing both.

Mocking his own weak stroke he said, "This river seems atilt - whenever you strengthen your stroke and I try to match it, we turn shoreward."

Water Bear laughed at the indirectness of the priest's first words on being so tested by Water Bear's far stronger stroke.

"There are many rivers and lakes atilt where I paddle with others, my friend." He dug his stern paddle deep. "Though always, as I look back, the waters seemed to have righted themselves."

They shared the humour for a time, but gradually, their expressions changed as they began to talk of more serious things.

Laliber was the first to speak in this changed mood.

"Talking of waters atilt, is it not also true about the affairs of your peoples on the land? Are not nations everywhere in this woodland all atilt? Caught in a vast conflict leaving peoples so twisted they begin to consume themselves as a ball of snakes, many devouring themselves thinking they are devouring another? Can your great spirits be pleased with this - the energy they give to the people being wasted this way? What is surely best a life of freedom seems lost to wars and vengeance instead of saving your energy to struggle with the white man's deceptions and diseases."

"If our affairs are so atilt that my people fall against one another, it is indeed you white men who have tilted our world. What we had before you came worked on a more level surface. Besides, I know your side, too. The colonial people are caught in treacheries of their own from too meanly and tightly held a supply of their money, goods and authority. They are only truly superior in their sciences. They make too easy an assumption of a whole superiority they call civilized."

Laliber pondered this insight. "It is true. God is not well served either in my peoples' colonies either. The fever of the fur trade and the hatred between our French in Quebec and the English in New York fuels all kinds of mischief among their respective native allies. It is a time of war in all places. God surely cannot mean war to be his only instrument? "

Receiving no answer to this, Laliber admitted more. "Those of my Jesuit Order here are even taking sides. The western and northern brothers urge the French to make the war waged by your nations on the Iroquois into a final defeat. Yet, some Jesuits who have spent time in the Iroquois villagers defend those nations. They and those now living among them are the most Christianized, though that is not a great number to be sure."

Water Bear listened but said nothing.

Laliber continued. "I myself cannot but help admire the Iroquois who have held all the Europeans in check for a time. But, they have been blinded by their own previous success. Not enough of their statesmen see the truly lasting strengths and weaknesses of their own position. Your people rush too unplanned at success in war under our influence and then suffer too bitterly from defeat – I have heard it called a "mourning war." If there is to be a good war, methinks it must bring a lasting peace so that peoples may serve the purer lives that we owe to each other and to God and the spirits."

Water Bear noticed that the Jesuit's weak stroke got stronger as he spoke these strongly felt thoughts. This was the test he had set. If the man had true spirit, he would express that in a stronger stroke when he spoke his most heartfelt words.

He said, "Who knows what could improve this world? Some of my brothers say our human world is held in the web of a spider, whose eye is the moon. The web can be seen only in the jagged flashes of a storm at night,"

"It is a marvelous metaphor," delighted Laliber.

"I say nothing of this. It may be true. It is possible too, that my brothers sense we are caught in webs of our own making. Either way, the spider is a terrible spirit and has got us nearly caught. My dream foresaw that we need a power to break through the web."

"Or perhaps to make a different web," Laliber offered.

"Yes, that would require a different spider."

Neither man paddled for a time. They had been distracted by their talk, and had not given enough attention to the quickening current as the river made a gradual descent. Shouts of warning came from the canoe behind them now headed toward shore, where Many Axes awaited them. The canoe behind them was too far away for the shouts to be heard,

Water Bear saw his error. "Hold tight! We have come to the most treacherous of the rapids along this river. I had thought they would be manageable at this time of year, but it has been rainy. I have paddled like a boy, heedless in our talk. I fear we must struggle hard if we are to escape an upset at its rapids which await us there. Bend down, Laliber, so that I may see ahead."

As he spoke these words, Water Bear began a mighty stroke to redirect their canoe to the shore. The priest crouched in fear as he saw the raging waters ahead.

Even with Water Bear's strength, by the first rocks the canoe was out of control. He no longer could gain shore and tried to move back toward the middle of the river where the water was deeper and the rocks smoother. For a time he just managed to propel them around the rocks and then spotted a group of rocks forming a small island ahead that he knew was the only hope to save them from being tossed to their death among the killer rocks beyond.

Within moments the canoe was hurtling through the air and its human contents were swept into the foaming waters. Water Bear grabbed Laliber by his sash, took a rock on his free forearm then shunted from it onto the island, gaining enough ground for the priest to grab a bush which went full in his face. But the slowing had been enough for Water Bear to struggle up onto ashore, with Laliber holding onto the bush, until he was pulled onto the island by Water Bear.

They collapsed together on the stony ground. Laliber brushed blood from the scrapes on his face. Water Bear held limply at his side his badly bruised forearm. He moved it to see if it might be broken and was relieved that it was not.

As they regained their breath, Water Bear explained their situation.

"I paddled like a child – I failed us badly not to notice the danger. It will be a cold night, but we are safe enough here until these swollen rapids lessen or those from the other canoe can get to us. That is not likely until the storm waters recede - not until tomorrow. If we cannot gain the shore, they will fashion something to get to us"

He now stood.

"I see them there on the shore." He waved to them and then exclaimed, "Our canoe danced madly along the far rapids and awaits us down-river. One of my brothers is heading for it already."

"It will be a cold night. We must get out of these wet clothes. We can roll in the dirt over there. There is not much to make any shelter. What otherwise might be dry up here is kept damp from the spray. There is no chance of a fire. We can sit close together, and then after night fall if it is too cold we will have to lie together for each other's warmth."

"We are naked. It is not a thing I would do," said Laliber.

"You will want to do it if you get cold enough."

And shortly after nightfall, Laliber shivered from the cold and went to lie with Water Bear

"Here. Put these few branches between us. But we must otherwise make like lovers."

Laliber reluctantly joined in the embrace Water Bear offered, their legs tightly interlaced.

He felt the new warmth thankfully.

For a time, he marveled at what they were doing. And, then impossible to imagine, he felt himself harden. As Water Bear pressed closer, he felt the priest's alarming problem.

"Ho, this happens sometimes. Turn aside for the moment."

"I... I am afraid it's too late. It is already done."

Water Bear could hear the shame in the priest's voice.

Laliber rolled aside to clean himself and threw away some leaves.

"I am mortified. This is a terrible thing. Please forgive me. I had no control, no thoughts of you like that...

"Of course not," Water Bear broke in. "I told you, it happens. The Trickster makes fun of you. But come close again, we must give each other warmth for the night grows even colder "

By the middle of the night the torrent around them had lessened to passable waters.

Water Bear rolled away from the priest and got up.

"Come Laliber, we can now make it the shore. Do not worry – I will be the only one tormented by the others for being a boy this past day. For your part, Many Axes should be pleased that you met my test of a healthy spirit. Had not your stroke increased this day as you told me your most deeply felt things, I would have had to lay my axe to your head. In these woods, we people fear most an idle madness. Nothing else of our time together along the river will ever be known."

By the light of a full moon, the two made their way across a now gentle river from the tiny island of stones to the shore and slept the rest of the night by the warming fires of the encampment.

The next day required a portage along another rapids through the middle day. Water Bear and the priest had made this trek together with their canoe hoisted on their shoulders along a well-used forest path beneath towering evergreens

As they crossed a gurgling creek at the bottom of one shallow ravine, a white rabbit darted out in front of them.

Water Bear could not resist saying, "Perhaps that is the white rabbit from the dream, following us, eh, Water Bear?"

"That is how wrong stories start," muttered Water Bear, "They draw wrong spirits. Say nothing of this." He kicked leaves and sticks underfoot to chase the mythic creature from his dream away from him.

The mid-autumn sun was no longer warm in the western sky, but it lit up this wondrously mixed woods. It seemed to Laliber that they moved within a vast cathedral. The sunlight ignited the deciduous foliage above them with the season's pallet of dazzling yellow, orange and red leaves, as if they were great colorful windows among the soaring evergreen columns.

After a short while, they emerged again along a now quietly flowing river. Laliber was tired from the portage but exhilarated at the site of the trading lake at the end of the river. There, along the shore was a much used campsite where Water Bear had said they would spend the night.

Laliber had hoped Many Axes might initiate some talk or give him some recognition, but there remained a cool silence between them that neither would break. The freshness of the west wind gave Laliber new vigor. The smoke of the cooking fire whirled about Laliber, who had before been too tired to eat, though he was now as hungry as he could ever remember. During their meal, the wind suddenly died, and by the time the last red of the sunset had bled over their west-facing shores, all the tired men in the camp were in a deep sleep, beyond dreams.

Early the next morning, the canoe flotilla set out across the large lake.

Water Bear pointed ahead. "We head for that island. It is more distant than it seems. It will take much of the day to get to it. There, the other traders will come. Your paddle stroke has been good this morning and it is well we were not visited by the killing frosts. Let us welcome such a mild day."

But after paddling for a while, Laliber felt some dizziness and he began to lose his paddle stroke.

Noticing this, Water Bear said, "I see you lose strength – we will arrive at the island behind the others."

"Yes, I confess I feel some weakness. It besets me from time to time."

"Take in your paddle and I will get us there," Water Bear said, "As you rest, perhaps this moment is right for me to make my thoughts known to you about my dream."

Although he had heard it related by others, Laliber listened to Water Bear's own version.

"Such a vivid dream – and yet you have not fully interpreted it. Indeed my mission to this new world is to help you do so. All are in wonder of it. What in it blocks you?"

"The first part is all black and white – that is our world now. I even see the soft power as something that my brothers and I must learn more of. But what of the snakes I had to swallow, even when surrounded by the friendly fish spirit? Some kind of separation from the paleface even though we take the paleface into ourselves must be meant. But what form could it take? Many Axes has told me from his information, that even if we defeat some of his colonies, the pale face will return again and again to our shores in even greater numbers."

Laliber thought for a moment, "Well the fish is a symbol of our Christ as well – it means peace and plenty. I too see it as a friendly spirit."

"But what of the engorgement of snakes? I made peace with our shaman and we sought a medicine bundle to help us interpret the dream. Leaping River still could not help me on that part, though he found the talk to persuade other powerful shaman in the neighboring tribes that the dream held an important truth with a meaning soon to be fully revealed. They all believe him and await that meaning along the shaman trail. My good wife Magic Walk is as smart as the smartest man, yet even she has no idea for the meaning of the snakes."

Laliber bade Water Bear continue.

"I have awaited some new event to reveal all the dream's meaning to me. Perhaps it is you. You met my test. And you have put your paddle in the water again."

Laliber was inwardly pleased.

They had paddled more than half the distance to the trading island, though, as Water Bear had warned, it seemed no closer to them. Laliber again needed a rest. He again pulled his paddle from the water, rested it athwart and turned to Water Bear.

"Who should we expect to see at the trading island?"

"Our Ojibwa party from the Sault will be there. So too will be several other western nations. There will also be the French traders in the area, probably headed by the Sieur de Lut. I am heartened that Many Axes brings with him an Iroquois trade confirming belt."

Laliber asked, "Language and interpretation must be very important for the success of trade and meetings between so many peoples."

"Yes, usually now I have along Magic Walk. She seems to know all the languages of any Nations with whom she has had even a brief contact. But she is pregnant so she remains at the Sault."

"I know too, that there is a limiting prophecy among some of your people that they will be overcome by the pale face spirit unless the old ways are strongly kept."

"My dream may have an answer to that difficult prophesy - we are at its worst time, a time when the old ways, alone, seem to fail the people and we are not yet up to the new spirit in our midst, the paleface spirit."

"So it seems, yet I am not alone among the palefaces who see value in your ways – there is a welcome freedom and sharing in your life lacking in ours. Many of our French traders of the woods seek it out."

"We need somehow to keep that old way, and yet it is threatened by your people's more entangling ways unless we can resist."

"It will be a close thing. Are there brothers in the other Nations who know the truth that the old ways alone cannot stir the people enough against the approaching paleface?"

"Leaping River says this new foretelling dream of our own does not just foretell an old one from an old crow like him. Neither can it be the Christ dream of those new crows."

"I am sure he refers to us Jesuits. I alone among my brothers would agree with Leaping River. You must find your own meaning of your dream."

"I am pleased that you see the direction of the dream is beyond a thing only of Europe, just as it is beyond a thing only of my own countries. My interpreted dream must be told very soon to the Iroquois fires, or it will become a thing mocked and to be let go. I will be judged as taken by a bad spirit."

Laliber looked ahead and could make out that a considerable number of canoes had already arrived at the trading island. Flocks of ducks kept rising up from the surrounding waters. It reminded him of the flocks of pigeons in the Cathedral squares of France and the old women calling for scraps to feed the pigeons, then, stealing them from the birds. Swallowing any scrap to survive.

Laliber said, "I think something is about to happen. I am sensing it. But my head has begun to pound. I am feverish from all this powerful talk. I fear I must become but your cargo – I must sleep for a time."

Water Bear looked with concern as the distressed Laliber indeed fell into sleep.

The priest dreamed only a moment and then came awake, feeling the joy of God's touch. His short dream had been vivid - as the birds fought over the scraps, the old woman steals the scraps. Then he somehow jumped to the thought that, for Water Bear's dream, it meant we need to steal them even as they are fighting. Yes.

He turned to Water Bear. "As you always thought, your dream is surely a reverse. I see it now as a reverse of our Jesuit plan for the Southern America – there we tried to take the native people away from the colonists. Here your dream tells that we must take the colonists into the wilderness under control of the native people. It foretells a great hostaging of some of the colonists, perhaps when they too become weak from their own wars against each other."

Water Bear whacked his paddle on the water. He had been given the final key to his dream.

He cried out, "The snakes, Laliber. Yes, let the snakes swallow each other and then let the snakes be swallowed," and then, he shouted to the sky, "And let it all be spit out again somewhere else, where we have enough control and are surrounded by the friendly fish. And, only enough control is needed, not control of everything! It is indeed the full hard and soft truth of my dream!"

Water Bear looked excitedly at Laliber.

"Priest, I see what you have helped me to see. God and all the Spirits have spoken to us! The dream is interpreted."

He preciously touched Laliber's still feverish brow.

Laliber looked up and saw Water Bear's triumphant manner. Then, even amid a bout of nausea, he slowly nodded, then smiled, and then broke into a rapturous laugh.

"Ha! Oh, blessed Lord Jesus, your soldier has helped make this miracle happen!" he shouted, as they neared the shore of the trading island.

Chapter 17

Many Axes looked displeasingly around the trading island. He was in his own encampment, with three Seneca he didn't trust, a little ways from the main fire. Smith and his two attendant Iroquois were at theirs. There were at least a dozen other encampments. He figured his party was unnumbered seven to one. The whole thing was under a peace belt. But the reckless Seneca war parties had given new reason for anger against the Iroquois. And it was not only about a trading pact here. Some larger scheme was afoot. He was committed to some large scheme, but only if he could lead it himself. Dancing Pipes told him no-one else could, in his own nation or any other. He believed her. But he would have to be careful.

Smith had come over. "Water Bear arrives, with the priest. But he stands on the shore."

Many Axes turned away and then turned back to look when Smith continued, "A warrior is bringing him something from the fire. My God, Howling makes a black slash on his cheek, above the white slash of his dream. It means he has interpreted his dream."

As Smith and Many Axes saw this, a shout went up along the shore from among the various tribal groups there.

Many Axes said, "I see it is so. The spirits must have changed. They have made me too think strange new thoughts this past moon. Yet, even if he has now fully interpreted the dream, I will hold him to his promise. He must tell it first, at the Onondaga fires."

Water Bear was pleased with the shout that went up around him. Many Axes approached him.

"Water Bear do you now see a way to swallow snakes, as foretold in your dream? I am not the only one who thinks it is too long we have waited for this dream to tell us something."

"I do see such a way – the dream now speaks clearly to me. But I know my promise that its final interpretation must be told first at your fires to you and Dancing Pipes."

"She is an old woman now. But as there seems some agreement on this, and I see other nations represented here continue to give you much respect, you may tell this to me, here without her. Then I will decide if I you can take it to Onondaga, where indeed it must be told to the people first before our fires. But, if it does not please me, I will leave, alone. Do you hear this, Water Bear?"

"We all hear Many Axes when he speaks. But the trade comes first. I will talk with you tonight."

"Good," replied Many Axes, feeling another sour mood leave him.

Water Bear had not yet taken in the full presence at the trade encampment. He knew there would soon be Frenchmen. But as he took his first thorough look around he saw something that made his stomach turn. Only now did he see toward the back of the camp, standing apart, Magic Walk and Copper Star.

He strode toward them.

"How can this be, Magic Walk? I left you at the Sault. We had agreed you would not come on this trip. I now care not of your skills in language and of all the tribes. You are expecting our child."

Though his words had been spoken sharply, he held her to him.

"My husband, you will have to accept what I tell. What happened, we cannot make it different."

Water Bear felt dread. He had not felt anything in her abdomen.

He pushed her back. "Tell me."

"The night of your departure, I could not resist my need to be with you, as on all your trade missions. I thought was still early enough with child and felt no problem walking or would have trouble paddling, even a great distance. I would simply paddle down the big lake, which was calm in this warm autumn spell, and take the shorter route to this lake I would be at the trading island even before you, who had to meet Many Axes coming across the rivers. I went for a canoe, when Copper Star called me to stop."

Copper Star gave Water Bear a grim look.

Magic Walk began to weep. "When I refused, he tried to stop me from disobeying your command. He took a fish net and threw it over me. I struggled furiously to get out from under but finally dropped exhausted from my attempts to free myself and then felt a stabbing pain. Copper Star took me to the birthing mothers, but it was too late. Our baby was lost that night. In the morning, though deeply saddened and disgusted with myself, I felt only the same longing to be with you. Copper Star agreed to paddle with me, to be with you."

As Water Bear heard this, he slapped his forehead repeatedly and moaned. When the weeping Magic Walk had finished the story, he looked long at her and then at Copper Star who was himself remorseful with tears. He brought both of them to his side and looked toward the sky.

"Let me find words…This is a terrible trade here: to lose a child in exchange for gaining a dream. But, I cannot blame either of you. It is a thing of the spirits. They play with us. Copper Star: leave me alone with Magic Walk. Tell the others I will be with them later. I must be alone with Magic Walk for a time."

When Copper Star had moved away from the pair, Water Bear led his wife into the woods where they found a clearing and sat together for long time in silence.

He spoke the first words.

"You see by the black streak on my face that the dream is interpreted. The swallowing of snakes – that will put us all on a terrible course. But the spirits, by this thing they have done to you, they leave me now with only the course of the dream to repair what offends them and what is out of balance."

She wept quietly.

A thought came to him that would comfort his wife.

"Let us name him who was once to be. Let him be named, so he is among the spirits. Let him be named, Magic Wolf."

Magic Walk whispered to him, "Yes, good husband. That is a good name."

She waited a time, and then said, "With that name he will be with us. Our son, now named, looks from the spirit world. As I, he wishes future brothers and sisters."

She managed to smile up at him. Then she rose with him and said strongly, "But now, I am here with you, and can again be the best interpreter among all the Nations."

They embraced as warmly as their dark mood permitted.

Even as they did, throughout the rest of the encampment, trade was in the air.

Water Bear prepared himself for trade on behalf of his Ojibwa nations and the other western nations represented there - the Pottawatomi, Menomenee, Mascouten, and the host Sauk and Fox Nations. All were directed by his ability to face the facts of the time. All respected his lead in the exchange between them and the European peoples. They knew that without him, they would eagerly trade at worse terms than could be gotten with one wily trade by Water Bear, a trade that would set a fair price for all the others.

By late afternoon, Water Bear and Magic Walk approached the trading fires.

There, they were joined by three Frenchmen who had just arrived at the island in their large freight canoe. They were led by Daniel Greysolon, the Sieur Du Lut.

Duluth was a tall man, with a striking moustache and pointed beard. While the others beside him were squat buck-skinned couriers-de-bois, he was wearing the clothes of the French lesser nobility: a fine brocaded coat, silk embroidery at his neck, a rapier at his side, and a sweeping broad brimmed hat with feathered edges, all of which served to enlarge his presence.

He was a man Water Bear had encountered before. Though he was known as a good friend of the northwest nations, Water Bear also knew for a fact that Duluth, in some seasons, would resell furs supposedly destined for Montreal to the English for much higher prices than the his original trades for goods with the western Nations. Indeed, though he had traded as if he would return with the furs to Montreal, in recent seasons he would have been arrested in Montreal for trading without a license and as an elusive middle man sought after but operating well beyond the French regulated trading areas.

The renowned French trader moved toward Water Bear with a noticeable limp. He greeted Water Bear warmly, in French he knew would be translated by Magic Walk than his own poor Ojibwa. The greeting was as if he were a good friend, speaking confidently, as though nothing had been changed by Water Bear's presence, which would likely mean a lesser trade for the French than he would have gained otherwise.

"But I see I am not the only one with a wandering leg. I see too, Magic Walk. I wish she could teach me to move as lithely as she does. "

"I prefer to let Water Bear teach you about trade," said Magic Walk in good French.

Seeing from Water Bear's frown that his familiarity had gone too far, Duluth quickly turned toward Laliber, now standing on the edge of the group. He pointed to the Jesuit and said, "So, we behold the far traveling Father Laliber. I trust this man's presence means we have a French trade today. Pray, let his dark presence not prevent a trade at all."

He looked equally sharply at the Iroquois contingent.

"And I see also we have an Englishman with his Seneca allies.

Smith said, "Many Axes is Onondaga, Duluth. Do you understand that? You made that same mistake last season. I repeat, he is Onondaga!"

Many Axes crossed his arms, aware of and annoyed at Duluth's mistake, not so much at the tribal mistake, but at having been identified as simply an ally.

Speaking through Magic Walk, who was now near enough to interpret, he warned, "We are not heartened that you begin this trading with these mistakes."

Duluth shrugged.

"Well, I was wrongly advised, Many Axes. Yet, I have heard much good of you. I am pleased to make your acquaintance. Please accept my apologies for my error." He swept his hat and bowed toward Many Axes. "But pray, remind me who is this Englishman? "

Many Axes spit. Smith presented himself, un-bowing, knowing Duluth knew all about him, "We met last season – Again, I am Roger Smith, of New York."

As he replied thus, the various personages and those accompanying them at the trade camp began to seat themselves. Many Axes remained standing, with his arms crossed.

Smith looked over the pretty island Water Bear had chosen for the trading. It was small enough easily to prevent any side making a secret attempt to bring larger forces to bear. It was still draped in golden leaves shimmering in the afternoon sunlight.

Smith thought of his brief talk earlier with Water Bear. He had told Water Bear what he had earlier told Many Axes.

"You know very well, Water Bear, how your appearances usually stop all other trading so that you can work your own terms and thus bid up the rest in favour of your companions from the woods. Well it is such that this year there is little room for tricks of the trade. There is a loss of prices. It is as simple as that, my man. Yet it is also more complicated. It seems a poor financial wind has blown upon the wealthy in those countries back across the great Ocean. There is an overabundance of the highest quality fur in Paris, which sell not at all and are held from trade to avoid the sharp price adjustment that has furs of average or lesser quality selling for almost nothing. Good quality pelts such as these brought here in the best season must be withheld for a time. It will not take long methinks, for the market to right itself. Then, we can expect higher prices soon again; especially, I think, now that the beaver has all but vanished from the lands to the east. Higher prices must in the end be fetched by scarcer better quality furs borne from the more distant places hereabouts. What think you, Water Bear?"

Water Bear had taken in this disturbing news and replied, "You foretell the trade. I know you to speak truly of the market for furs, and to be fair to us who trap them and trade them first. Pray let foolish and fabulous fashion continue in Europe. Without the European demand for Indian goods, the whole fur trade will collapse, regardless of our supply."

As aware of most of the trade facts as Smith, Duluth now challenged:

"So, Smith, you and Many Axes are both bold indeed to join us here. This is an area where we French are well known, but not you English. And the Iroquois are the enemy of the Nations hereabouts. This surely does not make for good trade."

Water Bear intervened.

"Sir, this meeting was arranged long ago with your own knowledge. All here are from many nations, including both the French and the English, precisely so that we can repair the damaged trade pattern when too much traded peltry ends up with the party not traded with by our nations. Many Axes is known for counselling peace among the Nations. Smith does nothing but wish for a trade to everyone's benefit. We are none of us here to be preached at by anyone."

Water Bear immediately regretted his choice of words.

"Only one man among us preaches, or used to do so." Duluth looked severely toward Laliber.

Laliber spoke for the first time, "We army of Christ prefer to teach, not preach."

"Well. No matter. But, now I remember more of you, Smith: are you not a well-known privateer on the oceans; a man of illicit reputation, depending on which King is warring against which other King?"

"I am indeed a man of the seas where I challenge unfair monopolies, licit or otherwise."

"Well then, since there are no such unfair monopolies here, perhaps we have smoothed a rough beginning. By all means, let us begin the trade. But, I do not see much peltry before us."

Water Bear spread his arms. "There are furs enough in the western canoes."

Duluth looked about. "Yet, again this season, you have only a few skins which you say must set the price." Duluth seemed to look searchingly at his sometime allies among the Pottawatomi for their piles.

Water Bear replied,

"It does my brothers good to see the talk of the trade and how and why the final terms are made. This way they see from a first trade how things are valued. They can work it better in later trades How say you, captains of the Pottawatomi? And you, the far Mascouten?"

Magic Walk helped out Water Bear's words, putting them in every language of the Nations represented.

A majority of heads nodded. Hearing and understanding this in their own language much pleased them.

Duluth was clearly irritated by this sympathetic exchange between Water Bear, as usual the mediator of trade, Magic Walk and those chiefs he had supposed were among his own strongest trading allies simply awaiting his own lead.

"Pray, let the skins be piled."

Water Bear now moved with a powerful stride to his own nation's first small pile. Duluth had seen enough. "These are all summer skins, Water Bear. The felt is better from fur later in the season".

"Well, I say they are the best peltrie, as good underneath for felt, but perhaps not as thick as winter skins for the fur itself."

"Then, let us all get this minor transaction out of the way, so that the large part of the trade may happen."

Water Bear pointed to the small pile.

"Now that we have all learned the use of a "price," he looked around at the nodding chiefs, "last season, these would have fetched 100 livres worth of goods in Montreal, but the trade from this area gave less than half that to my people and the Pottawatomi and their sources."

Duluth quickly replied, "There were carrying costs and still risks from Iroquois ambushes last season and on top of that only a modest mark-up for our runners. Besides that, my companions here come only in the past month from Montreal. They bear tidings that discourage us all at the terms of trade this year. Three bateaux of winter furs received in the summer obtained half of what they would have fetched at last year's Montreal fur fair and we are told they could not even be sold for as much at Albany."

Water Bear looked about.

Smith offered further information.

"Let my untold information turn your told information to a lie."

Some heard what he said and marveled at the tough talk. But Many Axes laughed to ease the tension Smith's words brought.

"It is true the demand in the Mother countries has declined for this season. But this is only a season when the bear has more salmon than he can devour. And they are distracted there by a war. I expect prices to recover for next season. So, this season, I can offer the best price and, with Many Axes' word, quick movement through the Iroquois castles on to New York."

"And," Many Axes continued, speaking louder to the noisy talk that had been excited, "Only Smith is in a position to keep large fur stores in his ships for fast delivery across the big water when the demand has recovered. Let it be three-quarters of the Montreal price last year and we shall be through this trade. "

Duluth and Water Bear turned to the Ojibwa and Pottawatomi captains and took turns discussing this offer.

Water Bear then turned, shrugging.

"When you Frenchmen and the English come again, you will then have to pay much higher prices. Now you would be wise to keep the trade with only a small discount from last season's price. Otherwise, Smith could take the whole of this year's peltry and market it directly from his ships when the time is right, without Montreal or New York."

When they understood what Water Bear was saying, all the nations represented showed strong agreement.

Duluth stepped forward again. "You shall never have all the fur trade, Smith. I call your English bluff and offer the same price as last year at Montreal for half the skins to be piled here. Smith or New York can have the other half, at the same price."

This was met with some "ho ho's" of native agreement.

Water Bear looked sharply at Duluth.

"I accept your price. But if we hear that our skins, once taken by you French, are next found in Albany at an even higher price then we will not trade with you again."

All the tribal representatives listened closely as Magic Walk helped them understand this strong talk. There were more

Water Bear concluded the deal. The 'ho, ho's" of native agreement were stronger this time.

"So an equal trade of half of my skins to each of the French and to Smith, of the English at the same last year's price and then of the others at the same price, adjusted for lesser quality alone. We accept this trade. Let the trade goods be brought forth".

The French traders brought forth much iron ware, axes, mirrors, blankets and cloth. Water Bear gave a fair price of those goods in Montreal livres. Smith produced the same, with better woolens. Water Bear gave a higher price in Montreal livres. Smith then reluctantly added ten cases of rum. Laliber withdrew from the fire. Duluth added from somewhere ten more cases of brandy. He could not have done so with Quebec's approval. Smith added two more cases – actually cases of muskets and ammunition, but labelled Island Rum for Duluth's benefit.

Water Bear replied,

"I see an equal trade each way, but seeing Laliber's disquiet, he put back two cases each of the fire water," carefully pointing to cases that were not masquerading as such.

There was some disappointment among the native traders.

Water Bear commented with a severe glance at all his brothers, asking Magic Walk to interpret his words even more clearly, "And let not my brothers overvalue the rum, or the brandy, in their own trades!"

Many Axes, who hated the effects of rum on his fellows, nodded and put an axe through one of the withdrawn cases, breaking a bottle."

"Let that spill into the lake. Let it be a bleeding bottle, not a bleeding brave."

He looked sharply around, and some braves nodded and some braves turned away.

Chapter 18

Duluth's party had left quickly in the late afternoon following the final trades.

The fires at the trading island burned high into the night, illuminating half the inner bay. The sky was without a moon and vividly starlit.

Many Axes watched as a few others began to join him at a small fire apart from the main encampment. Though the deer meat at the meal provided earlier by the western tribes had been choice, he scowled as he heard loud hoots and screeches at some of their fires where the alcohol had been opened.

He had started his feathered red-stone pipe and remained silently smoking it as Smith and Laliber sat down. Magic Walk should have remained in the background, to interpret as necessary. Instead, she sat in the place saved for Water Bear in the circle of men, pushing against Many Axes, until he gave way.

They all accepted the pipe and it was passed it back to him.

Many Axes eyed Laliber. "We have this black robe, here. He sits opposite me. That is a natural thing for two opposing spirits. That way we best see each other."

Laliber wiped his nose and said nothing.

Many Axes turned to Smith, nodding at Magic Walk, to help him with his English. "Do we really know this man? I know of him to be an even sharper talker than his fellows from his time earlier in the Mohawk villages. Smith, you devil yourself. You vouch for him but knew him not before I did. Water Bear paddled here with the priest, and escaped harm, unless it be he now has a wrong interpretation of his dream."

Mire pipes were lit and traded around.

"Perhaps I would not think so much of his powers, if I but knew them." Many Axes looked about. "Where is Water Bear?"

Magic Walk said in passable Onondagan, "He is telling the Pottawatomi and the other western chiefs that he will come back north from your Iroquois fires after he has related the dream there first. It is not an easy discussion."

Many Axes had not yet himself explained the arrangement to the northern chiefs. He said, "Has he told his own people that I do not want any Ojibwa but him traveling to my country?"

"You can ask him. Here he is."

"Ask me what?" said Water Bear as he took his seat, careful to sit between Magic Walk and Many Axes.

Many Axes asked him directly, "Do your brothers know that the Ojibwa warriors here must all return to your country without you?"

They are well aware of the promise made to you and Dancing Pipes. None, but my wife would be of any use at Onondaga. You must make an exception for her. You only said 'no warriors.'"

For a moment, Many Axes looked irritated at Water Bear.

"So, if I did say that, she only may come along. As I think about it, it will only make you look weaker."

"Good," replied Water Bear, ignoring the taunt. "Let us get to the things we must consider. Many Axes questions Father Laliber's presence here. The fact is, Many Axes, the priest wishes us to make more of our own powers. I can tell you that we Ojibwa welcome his talk. The church in Quebec wants no more of him. But now I have traveled with him. I know him otherwise. He has shared a new truth with me that will help us see a better way ahead with these pale faces in our midst."

Many Axes scowled. "So he knows no friend. Does he then tell us a friendless truth?"

"He is my friend. If you will listen, I will tell you why he is still among us. He is here at the trading fires and knows the French peoples with whom we trade and must somehow challenge."

This angered Many Axes. "What can he know of the true story here?

"We also must challenge that evil spirit New York, and we have accepted Smith's help for that purpose. Together they give us knowledge of the white Fathers across the great water."

Many Axes shrugged this off. "All of them across the great water know little of even the story of their own people in New France and New York. Our covenant chain is a rotten rope."

Smith, was silent through this exchange. He was pleased that the trading had been at a favourable price, and had for the first time introduced the possibility he could within his own means control it back to Europe, and he was in a jocular mood. He dipped into an unbroken bottle of the trade brandy left at the camp. As he wiped the brandy from his mouth, he wanted to change the subject for a moment. He said, "There are many stars in that black vault above us. Water Bear: beguile us with a tale of this night sky."

Water Bear agreeably said,

"It is a good time for a story. You see, just there, above us in the night sky. That little smudge of stars is the seven sisters. There was once one more. She was the brightest of them all, but she now lives in another part of the sky, with her lover. For it is told, that long ago, the sisters would once each year come to Earth to sing and dance. Then a great warrior chanced upon them and took the most beautiful as his wife, and rose to the sky with her. Those two now dance together in a different part of the sky. There!" He pointed almost straight above them.

Laliber spoke to this. "I too learned a story of the twin stars once, on the seas far to the south. Those brightest two stars over there are called the Twins. In our ancient myths, the twins shared the same mother but had different fathers which meant that Pollux was immortal and Castor was mortal.

When Castor died, Pollux asked Zeus, their King of Gods of the ancient peoples before Christ brought us to the true God, to let him share his own immortality with his twin to keep them together. Zeus granted this. Those twins are now regarded as the patrons of sailors, to whom they appear, sometimes keeping lightning bolts hurled by the other gods from hitting the ships' spars. Is it not true, Smith?"

Smith laughed and nodded.

There was again an appreciative silence at the fires, as the pipes were passed around.

Smith broke the silence, "Laliber is right about that pale face story. Yet I think those seven sisters in the Ojibwa story must be jealous of the eighth – how is it the other seven never found such a warrior?"

Water Bear said, "They did try for a while, but the spirits decided to keep them jealous. It made the sky more interesting. That tension between the sisters - it was a better story."

Laliber said, "You give me an intriguing idea – does that tension help hold up the sky?"

The others were surprised at Laliber's idea.

Water Bear, especially appreciative said, "Laliber tells us a story and brings forth a question of his science at the same time."

Many Axes said, "That tension may be true of the role of the Sky Sisters and their one husband, Laliber - though if he wore a black robe, no one would see him up there."

"They would, if he passed in front of them."

"Yes, and hide their true light."

"The better to appreciate it!"

All around the fire enjoyed this repartee.

Smith said, "That was as good an exchange between your people, Many Axes, and my people –though he be a Jesuit - as I have ever witnessed.

But, now, what is the final meaning of Water Bear's good dream told in so many countries and even along the once resisting medicine trail?"

Water Bear replied, "Let the priest begin. He helped me give it the final interpretation."

"What say you, then, priest," said Many Axes?

"I only knew before there was a strange dream disturbing these countries. Like all who hear it, I too was astonished by its strange turnings. I cannot deny the black of the dream must in part be the troubling influence we black robes have had on the affairs of your nations and their relations with my own peoples. But what of the white power flowing through all of the spirit creatures and controlled by Rabbit, the least fearsome of creatures? It was a mystery, unless and until you see truly the last spirit, Snake. Its coils make the white even more brilliant before twisting among themselves and then into and out of Water Bear's throat."

Water Bear now took over.

"That is the key to the dream. It means we must capture some part of the pale face spirit at a time when it coils self-destructively in on itself, like the coil of the snakes, and draw some of that we can use into us and spit out the rest."

Many Axes interjected his own revulsed thoughts, "A snake cannot get to any hero's mouth, let alone inside and out of it. What strange meaning is this?"

Magic Walk said, "Could that mean the French of New France and English of New York fight each other to a fatally weakened draw, like the self-devouring snakes, and that far from helpless, Water Bear swallows them and spits them out by his own power? We always thought it was the snakes taking over Water Bear. That blocked the true interpretation of the dream."

Smith exclaimed, "Perhaps it is like a hostaging. I mean, if it is strong and soft power at once, it must mean those people in those places aren't just to be destroyed by us."

Nodding slowly, Water Bear added, "Maybe it would be a hostaging far inland, as if they are swallowed."

Many Axes was getting interested. "By what means would this 'hostaging' be done?"

Magic Walk now offered, "Does the snake not also mean there is much twisting yet in the story? I have thought that among Rabbit's soft powers is the power of deception we all know among ourselves and sometime use well with those colonists as they do with us."

Smith uttered, "Yes, of course! Now I see that, too. The dream is brilliant. I can tell you that the time is at hand when they in New France and in New York will both want to go against each other, if we, their sometime allies, can help make them do so."

Many Axes was more interested. "So, how does that happen?"

Smith answered, "It is the present circumstances of those two colonies that they face each other with equal hatred and fear. They have equally haughty and sometimes reckless leadership and temporarily at least, roughly equal forces, if New England can be made to reinforce them too late because of their own current wars, and we add to each side a balance of many native allies. It would take only a little nudging of each side – reports or intercepted falsely planted messages about this and that additional menacing move by the other side, to bring both sides to a fever pitch and ignite a mutually destructive war between them. "

Many Axes considered this, and again slowly nodded.

Water Bear, seeing Magic Walk's slight motion, wanted to end the talk in the way she had suggested.

"So, let me help us conclude on what we have considered here. It seems this would be four matters of a large scheme, upon which we must be all agreed. I have here two white shells and two dark purple – what we call black shells. The first white shell tells us we are all in rough agreement that some large change is near throughout all our countries."

There were nods of agreement.

"The second white shell reminds us this truth must be given first to all the Iroquois towns at its central fire. For that, we shall depart with Many Axes tomorrow. And then, that great truth must be shared by all Nations about the Great Lakes."

Again, there were nods of agreement.

"The first black shell tells us to prepare for a dark and deceptive time ahead of us. It is first necessary to tell and hold the truth among all the nations, so that we all may hold our unity and not let the plot behind our deceptions find its way to any ears in New York or New France. I have thought of this before, and propose we use the Shaman path for the telling of the dream and what it now requires of the peoples. It will be like the Iroquois wampum belt and use its own code of white and black shells."

Many Axes said, "What is this word 'code'?"

Water Bear saw some doubtful looks.

"A code is a way to talk and pass on the talk that only those knowing the code can understand. Many nations use images standing for different spirits in us and around us to pass on messages about important things. Some are painted on rocks, or put on our clothes or banners or masks. The colours used also can have special meanings to us. Any of those settlers would not understand these meanings. A code is like that. It is a language that hides our normal way of speaking. Say, a pattern of different coloured black and white shells, representing a story or agreement of some kind, laid out in a belt, but in a code only those who know the code could use to understand the story. How to use the code to interpret the shell pattern into a story is passed on separately. Otherwise, it is not obvious as say, attempts to make our language into written words or use images of things, like a gun or an arrow. "

He received more doubtful looks.

"The shaman of each tribe would receive and understand the story told in the shells with a separate explanation passed along of how to decode the shell pattern and send the shells to the next tribe's shaman. Here, look at the shell belt Magic Walk just made."

Passing Magic Walk's shell collar around and letting everyone take a turn to see and feel the sequence of the shells made the use of a code easier to grasp and the others could readily see the complex message in a disguised form that it began to much please everyone.

Many Axes now spoke strongly. "Well, a shell belt in such a code is a quick and secret way of passing on the plan. That is good. And the idea is worthy of uniting all our peoples. But, code or no code to keep it a secret, we must come up with the plot itself that will make the colonials' defeat of each other thus allowing our forces to then take hostages from those two colonies somewhere far inland."

Water Bear turned to Laliber. "We see Many Axes and Smith in agreement. What say you, priest?"

"Well, even I, who, with God's help, helped Water Bear unlock this last part of the dream, must wonder how and for how long we can so deceive so many in those colonies."

Water Bear answered, "We will need a careful plan."

Smith added, "As I said, the possibility for this kind of deception is very good now. I think it might only take a little extra goading of each side on our part over a month or so of deception, at the right time of year. Their land forces are already on alert and mostly prepared to move against one another. They are roughly equal, if the Boston colonies are still pre-occupied with their own border wars and cannot get there soon enough to reinforce the New Yorkers in time. And, both Mother countries ignore their colonies across the sea. As it was between Kings in England across the great sea, it is still a time between Governors in New York. Because of other wars and threats, even a new Governor will not bring more than one or two big ships. Even if they are sixty gunners, I have more than one way to deal with that threat from the water."

"But what of Quebec," asked Laliber? "Frontenac is back as Governor and he is formidable."

Smith replied, "At this point, I may know as much as you of New France. France still gives little even to Frontenac in Quebec, though I give you he is a bold leader. His only strength at sea is d'Iberville's fast but not very well gunned ships. That man's tactics are clever. Even so, I can bring a fleet of my own near enough to deal with him, if necessary. France and England cannot make a serious new landing of additional troops in New York or Quebec and Montreal early enough to save those places from the temporary control we need for the hostaging plan."

The others around the fire nodded.

"So, if they are truly led by our plot to believe the other side moves a strong force against them, they will be an equal enough match to nearly destroy each other in a full and bitter engagement. If enough of our allies on both sides are ready to join us and turn on all the palefaces, we can clean up the battle field and take the undefended colonies that will then lay exposed to us.

Laliber was not satisfied.

"I too accept that part, if it is a good detailed plan and works on this side. But, the main question I asked is how we can maintain the deception – if they realize on their side what we are up to against both their sides - they may not attack each other with full forces or withdraw, and then the whole plan fails."

Smith replied, "I think it unlikely in their current state of enmity."

Laliber persisted with a last concern.

"Would it not also be likely for someone from our own native side to betray our plan to either or both of them?"

Many Axes said, "You have the best point there, priest: those who turn on their own are our worst enemy. You would know that well from your own example!"

Laliber turned away.

Magic Walk was distressed. "Great Chief, I think we must not lose the value of having the priest on our side unless there is cause. You will drive him from us unnecessarily if you keep using your mouth at him as one of your axes."

Many Axes was surprised at the force of Magic Walk's words to him. But he backed off. He glared at her for a moment.

"You too must resist turning an axe on me, interpreter. No one would dare do that twice."

Water Bear took hold of her arm.

"You are very strong, Magic Walk. Give Many Axes time to learn that. But, let us concentrate on present necessary things."

As they discussed Laliber's concern about traitors, Many Axes agreed the French allies could only be approached late in the plot and that in the meantime the main source of such a betrayal could be among those of his own Iroquois who were closest to the English alliance and among whom some had betrayed the League's policies before.

Water Bear offered some reassurance. "Revealing the interpreted dream first to the Longhouse fires surely will persuade all in the Longhouse that the dream is of crucial importance for them."

Many Axes nodded his agreement. "And I know where the potential traitors lie."

Water Bear continued.

"Somehow my presentation of the dream at Onondaga should include fear of betraying the specific meanings of the dream, even though the specific plan we have mentioned here will only be discussed with the Council of Chiefs at Onondaga. Certainly our detailed plan will itself not be widely known until the time is near."

Many Axes said, "I need to step aside a moment to think on this."

He began to walk away from the fire, when his three Seneca companions approached from a distance away. The closest, Singing Red Bird, went to stop Many Axes, while the other three drew back their bows.

The leading brave fearfully said, "We have been instructed Many Axes that little of your direction works anymore in the West and that you must leave here with a new agreement to our advantage or you too must die. We now see you leave without agreements, I cannot say more." The outer three aimed their arrows at Many Axes, all thinking too quickly that Many Axes had failed to reach an agreement.

"What! Who dares?" shouted Many Axes. As he uttered this, he grabbed the man who had stopped him, and made of him a shield. He spoke angrily to him,

"Tell those other foolish Seneca I am far from through here at these fires. We are near an important agreement for all of us. Tell them they are from the town that defeated itself. You and they have been tricked by some chiefs there. I will deal with this later. You are lucky even now to keep your skin from my axe. This whole camp is ready for something stupid by you Seneca. For every arrow sticking in you and me from those other two, there will be ten-fold back into them! "

As Many Axes edged back toward the fire, he pointed slowly to more than a score of western warriors on the other side of the camp moving forward, with their bows taught with arrows, aimed at the Seneca.

The fearful man cried out "hold!" and tried to convey Many Axes' words back to his companions. The two other Iroquois realized their mistake in having taken too hasty an action and lowered their bows.

"I will now walk back to my seat at this great fire. It seems this insult leaves me no choice but to make an agreement, unless I want all three of you killed. When I am finished, I alone will bring to Onondaga an agreement so important to us that it will cause more wampum belts and shell necklaces to be made than even in the time when the Longhouse League was created."

His captive moved carefully away. Many Axes kicked him. "Do you hear me?" This drove Singing Red Bird more quickly back to his fellow braves, who had now put aside their bows, all in awe of the great Chief.

Many Axes moved the rest of the way back toward the fire

Water Bear waved off the advancing phalanx of western warriors.

Many Axes settled back at the fire and spoke again to his companions.

"Even with this insult, which shows the treachery possible within our own side, for which I ask your forgiveness, I have listened enough to what has been said about this dream of a swallowing up the palefaces. I agree we are all now set upon its path. We all must depend upon the truth of Water Bear's dream becoming a living thing."

Tears formed in Water Bear's eyes as they all shook hands upon this acceptance of his dream, Many Axes making sure Magic Walk was part of the hand shake. The fires at the encampment burned late into the night with more talk of the details of the plan needed to make the dream a living thing.

When finally the meeting broke up, Many Axes stomped back to his sleeping place. For a long time afterward, he could be heard berating his Seneca companions for what they had done; still angry at their near betrayal; still furious at those who had made them do it, still muttering as he took to his blanket, though they now obeyed him even more than before. Then, getting up again and berating them some more; still angry as he eyed them menacingly, still Many Axes.

At the other end of the camp, others were settling for the night. Behind them, near the edge of the forest, Laliber was restless beneath his blanket, and then arose quickly as he heard someone approaching.

It was Magic Walk.

"Shhh," she shushed him. "I come from talking to Water Bear. We must find a way for you to win over Many Axes to you. He will remain your enemy otherwise, at least in spirit. Do you not think so, Father?"

He was surprised at her reference to his priestly status.

"And, Magic Walk, do you have a way to suggest?"

"Not yet, Father, but we must all be wary. We care much for your role already and sense there is a future role for you. You shall be a true French witness of what is to come. Many Axes has not yet seen that true value you give us."

She looked earnestly at the priest.

"Many Axes is a very strong presence, but I still must await the equal strength and words God will give me. I have not felt that fully yet at this camp, except in the questions I know need to be asked about the plot. But, I pray God's light will shine again upon me and Many Axes, as it seems now to shine upon you."

"Let me pray with you. Do you know Father, that I am drawn to your faith, as are some of us in the north?"

"God bless you, Magic Walk. Let me kneel with you and pray to God."

"Oh God, through Christ, and Mary," he pleaded, "let me help undo the wrongs done here and make the right path to return to your love for the many peoples of the woodland. And accept my special blessing upon the shoulders of this marvellous Magic Walk, that she may aid your cause and the just cause of the dream of Water Bear."

After he said amen, he placed his hands upon Magic Walk's shoulders. She felt as if a force had flowed into her.

"Thank you, Father. We shall be at your side, as you are at ours in this next difficult time."

She stole away into the night.

Laliber lay down again, but could not sleep.

The faith he had all but lost had returned to him just as it had been most mightily challenged by the native peoples' resistance to it. And now, if he could believe Magic Walk, faith in the Christ may be spreading. It was a miracle. But what did it prompt him to do? Many Axes' seemed already an implacable enemy. Yet Many Axes alone, he sensed, had the strength to see the whole plot through. But it was a terrible plot – it would mean the blood of many of his own kind. He could not feel a final sense of commitment.

He was sweating badly and rolled to one side. And then, sensing the on-set of another headache, rolled to the other side. He got up, wrapping himself in the blanket and began a walk through the thin woods. The mid-autumn air was sweet. He methodically breathed it in, and out, again and again.

Why had God made for him such travail in this world? But he knew the answer before he had finished the question in his mind: to test me; to test my faith.

A screech owl hooted.

How could God give him such a test: a tortuous path veering away from Him and now back to Him? Should he suppose from that again his path could again veer away? He had paced well into the woods. The half-moon was brilliant this night. One of the brightest planets was almost nestled by it.

He thought that those astral bodies seem as to care about each other; yet, they are both set on their nearly perfect separate courses, as the Europeans now understand the heavens.

He wandered and wondered further into the woods.

He listened to the late night sounds, until they went quiet as the night air cooled.

He thought, if that sudden silence counsels his own silence, if that is God's will, so be it. Let that be his own will at this moment. Let more silence somehow win him Many Axes' trust. But it was still short of his final commitment.

Then a figure approached. It was Water Bear.

"Laliber, what are you doing here?"

"Here?"

Yes, this is where Magic Walk and I are camped."

Laliber realized he had walked in a circle and somehow ended up back at the encampment, at Water Bear's lean-to. Something clicked. Laliber felt his final commitment was made.

"Oh, I was on a path."

"What path?"

"The path God intends me to be on. Good night."

Early the following morning, Many Axes pronounced, with a fresh voice,

"Well, we all seem still to be alive, so let us all five web weavers go to Onondaga."

Water Bear now concentrated on the Pottawatomi and the western traders.

He turned to the senior Chief among the Pottawatomi.

"Do you agree, White Cloud that you shall see all our northern nations will triumph with the new way dreamed first in these woods by my father of the Odawa? We will together, with our shaman seek the help of the People of the Longhouse and find a new way for all of us. For those pale face people will be resettled among us down the Great River near its middle. That is where we can control them, and not have them control us. We should all welcome this."

The Pottawatomi chief nodded his agreement. "I will tell my shaman to await the shells and hearing the details of what needs to be done so that we may help find something truly new to build the old way."

His group and then the others from the western nations at the morning fire nodded in agreement. Something new was in the wind. Something that could destroy the eastern menace and win peace for the western tribes too, and yet continue the trade for the white man's goods, if the spirits who seemed to favour Water Bear and Many Axes, wanted it so.

Water Bear was pleased.

But, Many Axes looked again sharply at Water Bear with a warning.

"You think you will have my Aunt's protection passing through the Iroquois towns. I warn you, despite this old bracelet you have shown me, her protection cannot be. You must have my protection alone."

He waved aside Water Bear's attempt to answer.

"I will give it. But, I will see no wrong is done to my longhouses by it. My Aunt knew many things and gave us many stories. But, she told me herself, she trusted but did not quite enough know you northern people. I trust even this Smith, from New York, more than I can trust you Water Bear, because you may be full of more dreams than we cannot do."

The Iroquois chief continued, "I have no experience with this black robe here, except that he betrays his own. It will be all our blood, if this is not a sound truth you bring from the woods to our Iroquois fires and only if, as you have said, you and Magic Walk can find the right way to present it so that we are not betrayed by the very next morning."

Then he looked even more darkly at Laliber.

"I tell you, I see yet no role for this black robe. Why would he betray his own people, his own god? No one should trust him. I do not."

"But, he helped me interpret the dream," replied Water Bear, prepared from the previous evening for this reservation about the priest. "He is clearly one of us, seeing things from our point of view, because he understands the French and understands the declining state of our own people. He has already had a most crucial role."

"That may be his last," Many Axes muttered as he stomped away to his canoes.

Chapter 19

Seigneury of the White Goose
Trois Rivieres
New France

October 12, 1690

Moreau,
Le Comte d'Amboise,
Le Fort d'Amboise,
Tours Nord 2eme, France.

Most Esteemed Sir:

The summer has come and gone before I have had a chance to pen a reply to your last enquiring as to affairs here. I hope most desperately that this will make the last ship back to France, so that you may not complain too much of my tardiness. I can only say that is not that I am negligent or lack a desire to correspond, most dear Sir. It is rather the feverish pace of events that has kept us all fearful here and much preoccupied in Quebec.

We have a strong Governor here again, in Frontenac, and a surprisingly good naval force under d'Iberville, whose ships dart all over the vast seas and coasts hereabout to keep the English out of our Northern Bay and our great River of Canada. The officials are not as bad as they were, since your friend, de Merleau, became a most diligent sub-Intendant.

The war with the Iroquois has resumed and even some of our own native alliances are apparently in some doubt. Since I arrived here, the English in New York have changed governors three times making and then reversing laws and reforms there. All have had in common their usual treacherous tricks on our frontiers.

Now the leveller Leisler, controls New York, himself Dutcher and anti-Catholic and against the too near-papist English church. He is causing riots, they say falsely as some are incited against him by the rich merchants there, awaiting the change back to Protestantism in the new English Crown with William of Orange, and Mary. Leisler mounted forces against us, though they had to fall back.

There are rumours in Quebec that we shall have to muster our best land forces soon to head south before the English in hated New York march successfully north. It will be difficult for us here so outnumbered by the entire English colonies to find a favourable ground on which to confront any such force moving north from New York. Perhaps we can turn some more tribes toward an alliance with us, through the winter.

But enough on the general plight hereabouts. What you must know and what I am still trying to reconcile is the news that our own dear friend, Laliber may have entered a dangerous path here. After a terrible row with his Superieur, he took to the Mohawk villages and reports have it that he now travels west with some Iroquois to meet the Odawa fur trader known as Water Bear. This is the man whose dream of changing his world from the sway of the European colonies, somehow reversing who gives what to whom, has, increasingly excited much of the savage world.. It is this dream that I believe was the reason for Laliber's instruction from Rome to come to this land.

To add to my foreboding, Antoinette de Merleau has recently admitted to me that Laliber was much tormented in his mind when he visited them. He and Emil argued and parted badly. What she told me suggests Laliber is set on a dangerous, possibly even heretical course. I am frankly just now confounded as to what my duty is, but intend to have resolved it all by the next letter to you.

In the meantime, I am hoping that Father Laliber will send me some message of reassurance from the wilderness. But if, as you friends of his always said, he was the kind of Jesuit more mind than soul, I fear we need to be prepared to face the fact we may never again hear from him, only alas, possibly horribly, about him.

Let me close on a pleasant note: the botany work proceeds well. I have enclosed with this letter examples of several astonishing species I have found in the mountains to the south of Montreal and around the great lakes to the west. My medical work also proceeds as I have wished it to: I am trying to discover any reasons in science that the savage people, as indeed we Europeans did, so suffer from our European diseases. I have tried to conduct an enquiry in two of the Mohawk villages, one where there is a mix of native peoples, the other where there are still mostly Iroquoian Mohawk, to see what this might tell me. Against Emil's strong wishes, Antoinette accompanied me on one short trip as I try to establish the conditions at the onset of these terrible scourges to the Mohawk and other native villages. She did so, alas, to gain any news of her infant son, lost to the Iroquois last year. I hope I will be able to report sufficiently more to interest your own scientific mind, with my next letters,

> *Humbly,*
> *Johannes Kastler*

Kastler thought that maybe he should amend it to more please Emil de Merleau, the sub-Intendant's eyes (which it would not escape), or simply not send it. He threw the letter aside.

It said some but far from all of what he really felt. But to not send anything, would weaken his ties to a powerful and sympathetic group back in France.

The facts were simple. Antoinette had been abandoned by Emil after the visit from Laliber. When she had come to Montreal to apologize to Emil, and he had again rejected her, Kastler had met her wandering the lower city streets before her boat left for the Island of Eyes. He had befriended her. And then, most damnably, he too had fallen in love with her.

When she was satisfied he was a good friend of Laliber, she had explained to him her dilemma: "My Emil has become someone else, yet what can I do? He leaves me thus, to stay on the Island. When I come to him in Quebec, he leaves me to wander the streets while he does his administrative work, which when done for Frontenac, who overrides every proposal, means little. That man cares nothing for what a good sub-Intendant does. Emil cares of little else, except his hatred for the Iroquois who have stolen our son. But he does nothing about that either."

She had stopped, sobbing.

The afternoon wind had come up. He wrapped her with his cloak and offered some consolation,

"If it comes to it, I will go again to their towns to find your son. I have not collected there for a while now, and they will not be surprised to see me. But I see your boat…

He had taken her and helped her aboard and said a simple good bye.

He had hardly thought of anything else since.

But a letter to Moreau was overdue, so he picked up the discarded letter, reviewed it and decided to make no significant changes. He bundled up and took it directly to the next ship leaving for France, hoping it would escape the sub-Intendant's eyes. He found a willing first mate whom he had paid well to care for a previous botanical shipment, paid him well again, and the letter was transported to France.

Part Five

Heno's Plot

When the Map is Re-drawn

Who says those new lines, there,
Apportioning those shores
Or following a new inland mark
Just now carved on tree bark
Do more than stupid witness bare
To the messy gore
Of only the latest war?

They replace vague jottings before
Upon this map
Now made up once more
Into still more foolish scrap
Only again to celebrate
Some new Nation's favoured fate
And then its vanishing gloire.

Chapter 20

Many people want to know about Many Axes. This is the story of what I did, in the time of Heno's Plot.

Much of it was given me to do: the dream of an enemy chief, the collaboration of a few shit-causing palefaces, ahead of their world as I was of mine, and only then the plot for all the chiefs, to mix the peoples.

They needed someone to do it.

I know why I did it.

I hardly knew youth before I was down on the ground with an Erie axe in my shoulder. After that, my younger brother helped me learn to throw the axe better than anyone. I was an early war chief, and then because of my visions ahead, a chief equally good at peace. Nearly everyone's favorite, sorting out when war and when peace. But then mostly ignored in decisions of the great counsel at Onondaga, from whose duty I have escaped for a time.

I knew of the dream for some years because the dreamer, Water Bear, a once captured enemy, had promised to bring it back to our fires when it was interpreted. I had not thought about it after the first seasons, although I knew it was still being told in the north and in the western countries beyond my League's control. The dreamer then called an all-sides trading parley and, as we arrived he announced that he had interpreted his dream. He laid it before me and a few others. I am not sure I am right, but he persuaded me to take him back to Onondaga for him to present its interpretation first to our Iroquois central fire.

But, I agree with Water Bear - I will give it to the story teller to tell it best.

* * *

In the early morning of an unusually warm November day, Many Axes led a small party southeast of Niagara Falls toward the central Iroquois towns. It included Water Bear, Magic Walk, Roger Smith and Father Laliber, along with a Seneca escort.

Water Bear and Magic Walk sensed a nearness to each other beyond anything they had experienced before. The previous night began with a crisis between the two. Magic Walk had been quietly pestering him the whole journey from the country of the Sauk.

She wanted him to think through what he would do at Onondaga, not only to tell the interpreted Dream, but somehow dramatize it and plant it into the minds of and hearts of the Iroquois. He had nodded and nodded, and nodded again. But he knew he had no plan, other than talk about it at the fire and then at his turn at the Great Council meeting Many Axes was to arrange.

Magic Walk laughed. "Yes, if anyone listens to the thirtieth on the speaking list. You can be a fool, you Odawa Indian," she had laughed, instantly regretting her mistake.

Water Bear was irritated with her, the more so to hide his uncertainty about how to face things at Onondaga.

She backed off and went to the end of the group of travelers, leaving Water Bear to steam off his anger, mostly at himself she hoped, up front with Smith and Many Axes.

At the end of that afternoon, as the sun set, he too had taken a position again beside her at the back of the column.

He looked his wife and then held her to him.

"How can a woman be so hard and so soft? Tell me what I need to do, hard wife, and laughed as he kissed her strongly and felt her good breasts.

That night they made better and deeper and longer love than any time since he or she could remember.

As they lay together looking at the stars, he finally asked her, "It seems you don't think just some talk at the Great Council meeting about the Dream is enough to turn things toward it?"

"Ordinary talk will not do it. My adopted Ojibwa father at the Sault once told me the salmon does not leap the chutes backwards. Show not a twisting tail and hope it will gain the purpose – let those grand chiefs, like Bear, have to catch the fish coming with its head full force at them."

"Stirring words, but by what means?"

"Make use of their means. I have talked to the Seneca. Those Iroquois like to dance, sometimes with false faces. Dance the Dream at their open to all fires on the first night. Let all present sense and fear its main force. The following day, you will be less likely to be smacked by the twisting tail of the Dream by those who resist it. Do you see?"

"Not yet."

He was still playing his fingers in the still wet place between her legs. Then he scooped from her a sample of the sweet liquid, reached up and caught a whining mosquito.

"Lucky bug," he said and smiled down at her.

She took him to her and knew he was ready to listen.

"Let me imagine a different thing, or at least something you need to bring off at the public fire before the great Council meets. Something you must insist upon with Many Axes, who trusts you, as they do him, since they are the first receiver of the interpreted Dream, and it will be in their own way.

She had given him her idea and then, together they had perfected it.

The following day, as they proceeded south-easterly, without much notice, Many Axes had slipped ahead, and was not with them to intercede when they encountered a Cayuga war party heading in the opposite direction. The war party confronted them belligerently.

The head of the party, Stonemark, a handsome man, only slightly marred by a birthmark along the right side of his forehead which had gained him his name, was confused. He addressed the Seneca warriors accompanying the strangers "I am Stonemark, war chief of the Cayuga. Are you the remnant of Many Axes' party? Are these your captives? Why are they here when it is still a time of war? "

He was met with silence. Recognizing the widely reputed Stonemark, the Seneca he addressed were uncertain what to say.

"I would have their scalps and throw them all in that ravine before I even hear your answer." Stonemark was very angry, knowing the Iroquois were challenged all over.

The Seneca accompanying the others still could not organize a sensible reply.

Water Bear intervened, speaking as correctly as he could, through Magic Walk.

"You are right to be angry. Many Axes is bringing us to your towns. Here, you must now take this wrist band. It should be recognized by your most senior chiefs as a pass from the famous Mohawk Grandmother, Dancing Pipes. I am Water Bear of the Odawa. I come as Water Bear, the man of the Dream, with Many Axes. He has gone on ahead.

"It is more meaningful to take you as miserable captives to Many Axes."

"But, I see him now returning," Water Bear broke in.

Indeed, the great chief had come into the clearing and strode toward them.

"Talk not yet of captives, Stonemark. These people bring us important news. Return to your own towns and tell the chiefs to head for Onondaga, not for more fruitless war in the northwest. Then make runners of yourselves. Run the trails to the Eastern Door to tell the chiefs at all the towns of the Onondaga, the Oneida and the Mohawk castles. There will be a meeting of the Great Council at the full moon. Do that now. We ourselves head directly to Onondaga."

Stonemark was startled at this but he could not disobey Many Axes, who could wear a head-full of feathers if he so chose.

When his party had disappeared into the woodland margin, Water Bear questioned Many Axes temporary absence that had nearly caused them harm.

Many Axes replied, "That was a warning to you. I have told you that Dancing Pipes has no current reputation hereabouts save that some say she has gone mad. Her bracelet was a pass of long ago. It now has no meaning, except to me. You are under my protection alone."

As they again headed east, Water Bear thought Many Axes told less than the truth. He thought Many Axes had been aware of Stonemark's approach and had engineered a more dramatic meeting with Stonemark by reappearing alone to drive home his importance to the others in Water Bear's group. He thought he should be even more careful of Many Axes' clever ways.

The central town of the Onondaga was situated among the rounded and prettily treed hills held in the eastern most fingers of long lakes below the lower of the great lakes. Its many longhouses fit pleasingly into the gentle space formed by the palisaded town and surrounding fields. Near the centre of the broad avenues between the longhouses, the largest structure stood, fronted by large fire pits.

Gathered there now, five days later, just after sundown, with the fires beginning to roar high, were all the senior chiefs of the five nations of the Iroquois Longhouse Confederacy, surrounded by many of the people.

They awaited the public interpretation of the Dream of Water Bear. The Mohawk leadership most especially, bidden to listen carefully by the aging Dancing Pipes herself, who had travelled in difficulty from the most distant Mohawk town in an apparently lucid moment.

At Magic Walk's insistence, Water Bear insisted that on the first night of the full moon, all the people must experience the Dream, and only then would he meet with the Chiefs the next day on its details.

Much talk was occurring, until a hush fell over the crowd.

Water Bear emerged from the central Longhouse, naked but for a black and white loin cloth. He was painted black and white. Though it gave each of his head, heart and loins some of each, it was not a simple bifurcation. Much more dramatically, the black paint had made him into an Iroquoian balled club – most of his head blackened as the wooden ball, curling around some white at his mouth and neck; the black club handle ran across his otherwise white right side down to the thigh and leg.

His astonishing appearance silenced the crowd. The chiefs and hundreds of people around the fire were all now looking at him and moving toward him.

He made a shuffling dance toward the fires. He pointed to the Mohawk drummers and they began a beat that accompanied his strange movements as well as the drummers could manage.

He motioned to his wife Magic Walk to make the correct interpretation in central Iroquoian.

"Louder than Heno, Orenda the spirit of all our energies now speaks. Louder! Louder!" he bid the drums.

The drumbeat strengthened, as the drummers learned Water Bear's strangely syncopated gate. It had been his own idea to follow the rhythm of Magic Walk's strange gate.

Water Bear held on one arm four shell belts. He began to swing them and to begin his accompanying chant, speaking through Magic Walk, who swayed with the music but in one place.

"Each of these four black and white shell collars tells a story from my sacred dream. They are different stories of the actions all we woodland peoples must take. We must intertwine them in a way that finds the truth they together tell." He twirled all four collars around his arm in different ways making different curved geometries.

The chiefs moved back. The people stared.

"As all our peoples, you Longhouse people love the dance. I choose the dance to tell these stories from Water Bear's dream, and how they must be brought into one story."

He rose to his full height and said more loudly, "The details of making the dream live amongst us will be the task of the Grand Council, beginning tomorrow." He pointed to all the members of the Grand Council.

He swung the first belt onto his other arm.

"The First Belt is much white and only a little black. It is the Heroes and our peoples – it is the old way. In all the first stories of your people, this world is formed of Heno's imaginings, whose powerful brooding spirit behind the great falls at Niagara, feeds the energetic spirit who is the centre of us all. Orenda is your name for the Great Spirit among all our peoples. We live on the Turtle's back, rising from above and below this world, and we try to return to those worlds forgetting we must live in our own world first, even if we all must take a walk to the spirits in the end."

"This world is not with the Spirits until they call it back. It is for all of us to live in it and make good lives in it, a place along the way. The Dream says it is a changing place, needing a changing way, even while traditions must be preserved. And even beyond the world we have known is a world far beyond us we must traverse that we did not know before the dream. Let our spirits speak to us about the future we face I our world. We must find a way to help them continue to do that."

Water Bear then swayed back and forth in a way different than, but yet building upon the same rhythms as the Iroquois at Onondaga had long known. Some around the fire began joining him. He welcomed them.

"And so small are we in that larger future world that we must move as a whole village even as a whole league, even as a league of all our leagues knowing our own world wants to change, just as the drummers have learned a new beat from the old."

He moved and swayed more smoothly, now that the drummers had learned the new rhythm.

He swung the second belt to his other arm.

"The Second Belt has an uneven pattern of black and white. The black shells, rising up from both ends, are the black spirit of the new white people who begin to flank and surround us white shells in the middle. All our peoples are in contact with the new people, who could know us, but choose to know us not. There is no balance in this. They separate us. Their way is not our way. Our way is not their way. But we become more and more dependent on their way. Water Bear dreamed for all of us: is there, another way? Who is Black? Who is White? Can there be both ways?

These words he shouted out. "Is there both ways? Who controls both ways?" Again and again, he shouted out these questions.

"The Third Belt is equal black and white, but the black begins it. The Dream of a new way travels along all the rivers is now interpreted and, by my command, though I am Odawa and from long before but not always before, your enemy, the dream by my promise to Dancing Pipes, must now and is first being told here at the Iroquois fires, as sworn to Dancing Pipes."

These words he growled loudly and glared at the next row of chiefs until they backed off more.

"The Fourth Belt is the greatest of these. It tells, by the white rows surrounding the black and white that it is our white swallowing the black, making our own new way with the black energies, from our own old way with the white energies Orenda has given us from the new people."

These words he said with a triumphant roar, startling all.

"From this truth, flows another truth: a new way even closer to the Heroes can be found in the two old ways, our own best ways and the best ways of the newcomers. Many Axes will make this known to the Council tomorrow."

Many around the fires, but were then startled anew.

"But hear more! We know that, because we know this world has so many things that might be perfect, but are not. We people, just as those we face in such large numbers, are never rid of Mischief who dwells with us. He is the Wendigo with us Ojibwa. He is Heno with Many Axes and the Longhouse. He is the anti-Christ to Laliber. He is New England and the English Admiralty across the seas to Smith."

Water Bear saw that everyone listened intently. He continued.

"But Water Bear tells us Orenda and the Great Spirit of all of us is more than Mischief: No energy is lost to Mischief, when he appears in the stories that give us warning and tell us how to live. And no story is lost, as long as we people remember and tell them. One after another story tells us that Mischief blocks Orenda's strength in this new mixed world of ours. So, let my story say: To trip Mischief, no story tells all the wisdom. However to be honoured and remembered our past world here, we must see ahead to an equally great future world here. Mischief is confused by the many stories of the people from which we learn each part of wisdom, as we have different colours of our corn in the dish that nourishes us and the different colours of the shells in our wampum belts that keep our best stories. And we fool Mischief most when we make careful use of him and then make our own way. Then no energy is lost."

"No energy is lost," he repeated. Water Bear had found a mantra.

Water Bear leapt an astonishing height and then he spoke more, as he was surprised as he saw the growing power of his own words, though they had only been roughly made up with Magic Walk in the past day and depended upon her translation. He was pleased her interpretations made exactly the impact around the fires that he had wanted.

He shouted loudly again at them and again glared at the front row of chiefs until they again backed away.

"How can this mix of two ways be, and not destroy those living and choosing the old ways? "

He glared to all sides.

"This is because two parts of two mingled goods can equal a greater good than either one."

"Is not our place always at the middle of winds blowing in all the four directions, though each direction is perfect, between north and south; east and west?"

There were nods of agreement.

"By the fallen spirits, are we not all on the Turtle's back, between the sky above and the mud below?"

There were many more nods.

"Through those mixes of perfection and our own near perfection we become, as a league of leagues a new and more perfect unity, mixed though it is. It is you, the Longhouse confederation who are now so mixed of all people under the Great Spirit and yet still seen as strong by the new people. So the Dream of Water Bear speaks of a new perfection that must surpass, but never destroy the perfection of the old ways as it blends them into one greater perfection, taking only to us what is good and meant to be from the new people..

He gave a burning look.

"And Orenda tells us in the dream: Orenda remains; no energy is lost."

Here he made two astonishing leaps. But yet again did not finish

He danced his shuffling and bending dance over to Many Axes and draped upon him all the four collars.

"Speak well to the Grand Council, Many Axes. The truth is now with you, reluctant chief of war, reluctant chief of peace."

And then to all he spoke. "Listen!

"Do you hear the drummers have found an even newer beat? "

It was true - a new drum beat had emerged.

"Come join me and we shall all dance to it and bid wisdom to the Grand Council, beginning tomorrow. Take up these energies. Be very wise and find a new way from the old way."

Water Bear was sweating profusely in the fetid pre-storm air that a late season warm front had brought to the rounded hills. He had moved his hand to wipe sweat from his brow, when there was a blinding flash.

An enormous thunder clap shook the village.

Many screamed in fright.

Water Bear took advantage of this natural intervention.

"Stay here! The Spirits talk to us. They are telling us to let those of you who would trade the news of this meeting with the palefaces tell only that the peoples were divided, as they always have been. If you tell otherwise, your families in your houses too will be spit out as the snakes of the dream."

Two new flashes and sharp cracks followed and emphasized his words.

"The warning Spirits tell you to listen. You cannot escape the bidding truths of the Dream of Water Bear. You cannot escape what is willed by the spirits."

And here, another sizzling bolt laid everyone low.

But, in the next moment, a fresh wind blew through the remaining cowering throng of people. Water Bear danced along the lines of the people and then disappeared.

Only when Many Axes, opening his arms and shaking his head in wonder, arose and departed, did the people quickly disappear.

Only the drummers remained, pounding out the new beat that Water Bear had led them to discover. They drummed through the night.

The same new drum beat announced the convening of the Great Council the next day, as the sun finally broke through departing rain clouds. The Council members had earlier sought shelter from a cold rain and had crowded into the main longhouse.

Many Axes was given a respectful welcome by the principal chiefs of the five nations of the Longhouse. The Onondaga first chief, Cloud on the Hill, then recited the law of the Longhouse people to convene the meeting of the Grand Council. He noted the point of the meeting: to convert the interpreted dream of Water Bear into action that could be taken by all the peoples.

He bid Many Axes speak.

Many Axes began his talk by formally introducing Water Bear, Magic Walk, the interpreter, Laliber the priest and Smith the white trader, as strong allies in the need for the League to understand and follow the dream of Water Bear.

"Water Bear last night danced the dream and its meaning first to all our people. He thereby fulfilled that ancient promise that it would be first interpreted to an Iroquois fire. That means we must give it most serious attention here at Onondaga. The Longhouse people heard what Water Bear respectfully danced and said to them with the new drum beat, and they were much pleased."

The chiefs all nodded.

"That dream brings us the truth and the challenge of gaining control over the new peoples among us and allowing their good side to mix with our own in a way that we control. Perhaps that even leads to a new people forming of us – a people we help create and that are still ourselves."

Many of the chiefs gave ho ho's.

"We are losing the old way to the manipulation of our peoples by the palefaces. Nothing good is truly mixed in us now, because the palefaces bring Mischief among us and we have lost control of Mischief. But I say to you, the old way can be saved and it can begin anew in our own controlled mixed way. The Middle Tree shall still be our strength. It will always spread, if we all find a new way to protect it. The dream speaks of this."

The Chiefs were listening carefully. Like the spirits, Many Axes liked good listeners.

Chapter 21

Many Axes pushed on.

"The plot called for is simple. First, we unite the nations around the Lakes to make a mischief of our own on New York and New France, one that will turn those places against each other. And then in their divided and weakened state, we defeat them."

The chiefs were audibly uneasy with this, but they waited for Many Axes to become more specific.

"Now listen to Heno's plot. As with that angry spirit of Niagara, it hides behind a veil. Listen to how the plot makes the dream of Water Bear live among us to the advantage of every native country.

Smith tells us each paleface side now strongly fears the other will soon send strong forces against the other. We shall tell the French, the New Yorkers come. We shall tell the New Yorkers, the French come. They will make as large force as they can against each other. Each side will call upon their allies among our peoples to make the difference. We shall do so. As they slay each other, we shall be the difference, to ensure enough of each side is destroyed so that they both lose. And then we shall sweep them both into our woods. We shall swallow them entirely, as the dream foretells, so that there is no doubt."

"What does this 'swallow' mean?" some chiefs asked.

"We shall take those then defenceless pale faces from those towns and bring them into ourselves, far from their towns, and settle them in a far town only we control. That is the regurgitation. Then take their strengths, so that they may be ours. We shall let them live with their own powers in that town but we shall control them and we shall dare to take their powers and make them us."

"Where is that town?" several chiefs asked at once.

"I agree with Smith: that town shall have to be as far west as the Michissippi, where the biggest western river and the biggest eastern river both flow into it. It is an important place of western and eastern tribes, and a place passed thrice now and noticed as a place as important even in their eyes as it is remote, by the Frenchmen who have travelled up and down the great river."

Stonemark of the Cayuga whispered to the leading Seneca chief, Hunts by the Big Hill. The latter signalled he would speak.

"All this last night and from you today is from the dream. Let our principal medicine man, Barred Feather, tell us if he accepts this dream from another Nation."

"That is as it should be."

An old man moved slowly to stand beside Water Bear. In all aspects, he was a very old man, but his eyes flashed as he looked the Odawa up and down and then looked directly at him.

"I have heard your dream told many times. It told me nothing and offended our sense that dreams are personal things, only to be interpreted with the help of those who know the right things that are the keys to dreams. Dreams are not for public display. But, you have so offended the medicine of dreams as to dance the dream to our people, even before taking it to the medicine men here, even before taking it to our Chiefs. How can you so offend the long accepted ways? Yet, I cannot the meaning you see in it, or that it seems beyond my powers."

Many Axes permitted Water Bear to speak.

He looked at the old one.

"I have not offended the long accepted ways. I long faced the same disdain from our shaman, but in the end, he was won over, so powerful was the Dream, though public in meaning. All northern Shamans now accept it."

Barred Feather nodded slowly.

Water Bear more softly continued. "It is now told along the northern shaman trail, everywhere above and to the west of the Lakes by fully ten of the shamans of all the nations there who take Leaping River's promise not to repeat his own long opposition to the dream."

He named the ten shamans.

"They all pass along the dream, with the passing of the medicine bundle found in the blueberry country with the help of Magic Walk, who knows the medicine of so many nations even more than did Leaping River and Water Bear. They all await the dream's interpretation."

"There is no such trail in this country," said Barred Feather.

Many Axes intervened.

"There is one now. I have made sure a runner has taken one of the dream's medicine bundles along the great trail connecting all the Iroquois nations. The medicine society from Onondaga supports me in this. This is not just an Ojibwa thing,"

Stonemark again whispered to Hunts by the Big Hill, who spoke next.

"But Barred Feather is not satisfied. Let him speak again."

There was a long silence.

Barred Feather finally said quietly, "I saw the spirit power of the dream as Water Bear danced it last night. I am not a fool. I do not make small of it. I too feel the new beat of the drums. It may well be Heno's plot. It would make us bold and smart, like the crow. Bring me one of your shamans, Water Bear, and let him speak to me. I have nothing to stop the way of the Great Council as it sees fit on this matter, as long as the traditional medicine is not lost."

Water Bear answered, softly,

"I will do so. The dream assures us that no energy is lost."

No Chief spoke against advancing Heno's Plot. The decision was taken, but required the traditional process. The Little Brothers- the Oneida and Cayuga - would bring their consensus to the Big Brothers – the Mohawk and the Seneca - who would bring the agreed upon course to the Onondaga fire for the Grand Chief and all to approve.

The traditional process of approval had taken place over the remainder of that moon. The chiefs deputed by the Grand Council at Onondaga to work out the details of the Orendan plot against the New York and French colonies met with Water Bear and Many Axes. As this process wound its way along, Magic Walk became increasingly important in her interpretations, as they explained its details at a further meeting at Onondaga.

Smith, when asked, made the occasional comment.

Laliber, not wanting to fuel Many Axes' remaining suspicions, much less attract the attention of those chiefs who suspected him even more, said nothing. That they accepted his silent witness was victory enough for God's plan in this wilderness.

Many Axes looked around at the nine chiefs at the Counsel. They were a mix of Mohawk, middle Iroquois, Seneca and Ojibwa Grand Chief White Fish who had been summoned "in peace" and spoke for several nations around the upper Lakes. "Is this to your liking?" he said, looking at each chief in turn.

All but the Seneca Hunts by the Big Hill replied with assenting Ho Ho's. The Seneca chief said, "We are eager to hear more." The senior Mohawk chief. Lightning Throat said "I know the Abenaki war chief most allied to the French, Red Bird Moving Slowly. He is proud, but he is indecisive. That combination of stubborn pride and indecisiveness gave us Mohawk a victory over those people two seasons ago."

The other Mohawk chiefs laughed and nodded in agreement.

Many Axes summarized: "If he does not understand the field, but he would not run from it; this may be our answer to him, too closely aligned as he still is to the French alone."

Lightning Throat quieted some of his fellows who were concerned.

Hunts by the Big Hill again pressed, "So, what is your detailed proposal, Many Axes?"

"It is this. Smith and I are agreed that it is probable that the English will bring greater forces to bear up from New York and especially any who come across from New England. But, we think the New Englanders will be slow and not send their main force because of their own renewed border conflicts. With the help of the Mohawk who would normally be with them, the New Yorkers will at some point begin to achieve an apparent victory in any set battle over the French, however reinforced by the northern and eastern Algonquin tribes, coming down from Montreal. That such a battle will occur along or just to the south of the big lakes coming down the river from Montreal is likely, but it must happen far enough south, to prevent any effective retreat of the French forces."

All nodded, understanding a need for both those sides to stay the field, if they were to all but annihilate each other militarily.

"It is just at this point in the coming battle, that we would then seek out Red Bird Moving Slowly and offer him an alternative to having his own force destroyed. I will have the last matching belt in the Shamans' code passed to him from the Ojibwa by his main shaman, telling of the new alliance among many nations. If Red Bird does not accept the belt, then we must defeat him first. But, I think that defeat would be quick, if he lacks his own shaman's support and remains indecisive, as you say he usually is."

"If he takes the belt, we will all turn on the English forces from two directions, with the remaining French facing them straight on. Together, with Smith's mischief by sea around New York itself, should there be any English or even French naval presence, we shall decisively defeat those two colonies and can hold them for a time."

Water Bear nodded his strong support of this plan as the detailed interpretation of the meaning of his dream. The other chiefs conferred among themselves for a time.

Hunts by the Big Hill continued to speak everyone's concerns

He said, "How can we stop them invading our traditional countries here in the east, just by taking some of them further west?"

Many Axes said, "We think we know the English plans for us, to take from us our lands which give us our way of life. The French want mainly the lands they now have. Yet they would still build their trading forts among us – we think those French who would win us that way are not strong enough to withstand the far greater numbers of English. We think they have root beliefs that would be the same as the English. We know they both will try again and again. If we stay solely in the old way, we continue only to live near them, make wars for them, and destroy ourselves for them. We know their brothers will be returning to these shores, again and again, only to pretend to trade again, but really to destroy us. I am afraid that because of their great numbers we may even at some point have to withdraw from our traditional lands nearer the pale face colonies if we wish to continue our traditional ways. We may have no choice."

Several chiefs expressed anger.

Many Axes raised his arms. "I am not saying that is part of the plan. For as long as we Iroquois and other nations can survive here, we will do so. The plan only gives us a western option, one that makes use of the paleface's strengths under our control and transfers the best of them to us and our cousins everywhere."

This temporarily quieted the circle of chiefs.

Lightning Throat spoke. ""Many Axes, we must know better how trade with the palefaces is affected by any such victory. Would we then any longer be able to continue the fur trade with the remaining English colonies? They will surely mass their forces from the other colonies and also come again across the sea to retake New York, if not Quebec and Montreal. We would have to withdraw inland and there is no guarantee that the trade that gives us their useful goods would be resumed through any of the participating tribes at least until after many seasons."

Many Axes smiled grimly. "Yes," he said, sweeping his hand before them. "This is the very point of the plan. The fur market has shown itself to collapse, more than once. We will be taking as many of the English and French as possible to hostage them in new towns far inland we will bring them to. That is the dream's engorgement! They will be forced to make and trade all their own goods, but with us in control this time."

The Chiefs glanced at one another, finally with more understanding.

Hunts by the Big Hill said, "We will have to ensure the Illini and other western nations are with us – we will have to well outnumber the pale face hostages. They can be devils."

Many Axes continued relentlessly, "It is the truth you speak. All here must listen. Those palefaces will come again, even with our plan, to rescue their hostaged populations, even though they would fear their many hostages we have taken west would be put to death before they could reach them. But as time passes, they will want to enter a peace with us, if the hostaging remains out of their reach."

Smith added, "As the dream foretells the hostage towns must and will be far enough inland to make a long delay for them. By then, my own ships, already well manned by some of your own, as I have taught them, will have enough upper hand to make the better trade for your goods on the great Gulf seas along these coasts and up the Michissippi to the new settlements we will control. With the many hostages there, this time we will have, to offer them, some of their own goods to their own colonies. They would be made well, as many of you and the hostages mix both your ways in the new towns. And we will all learn to trade better down and up the Michissippi. A port there, at its mouth, to better effect, with the Spanish, if necessary, will be the place where our goods and their goods can be best traded to everyone's advantage. A port I think we can hold for a time, until and perhaps beyond when it does not matter to others who controls it, as long as it functions to everyone's trade advantage. That continuation of trade is a good interpretation of the dream's surrounding friendly fish."

Many Axes looked at the chiefs. "Do you see the reversing nature of the great dream that will make the new Orendan way?

There were again some ho ho's, but further questions were still raised.

This time the leading Mohawk chief, Lightning Throat, spoke the concern. "How many of those hostaged people are you talking about?"

Smith replied, "Oh, we estimate that at least 10,000 would be necessary to give us a good new kind of Orendan mix and give other Europeans pause before warring with us again."

The chiefs were astonished.

"That would surely far outnumber our people guarding them!" cried one chief. Lightning Throat nodded his agreement with the concern.

"Good point!" replied Many Axes. "Our answer is to take them west in the midst of winter when no paleface escape is possible. Then we also do this: the armouries from all the guns and ammunition to be captured from New York and New France will be transported and kept at a distance from the Michissippi town of the captives, and a much smaller number of our well-armed peoples can then oversee them."

There were a few still doubting looks.

Water Bear said, "Perhaps, in time, they will simply blend together with our nations and have no hostage value. That is the final stage of the dream which we can fully call "Orenda.". And those people would then help us make an industrious new nation and would be used to mixing well with us in the middle of our great continent, without them warring against our nations."

"Yes, as the dream foretells, an industrious new nation," repeated Many Axes, who liked the word and was again showing others his own strong support for the plan.

Magic Walk had not needed to help much in interpreting the talk thus far. But she saw the word "industrious" was not understood by the other chiefs.

"That word 'industrious' needs some interpreting. It means making man-made things from natural things with all kinds of energies, such as their water wheel, for ourselves and for trade – that is industry and being "industrious." We do it now, but with a mix of those French and English, we would do it more in that new town along the Michissippi. It is the deepest talk of Water Bear's dream At the same time as affording us protection against any immediate new European foray into our lands, we will be deliberately intermixing with this hostage European population so that we ourselves may gain and begin to use their subtle Rabbit powers, even while protecting our own people with the power of Bear. That is the message of Water Bear's dream. It is as Water Bear told it at these fires the last few nights. It is what "the swallowing" means."

Water Bear nodded with the other chiefs at this talk.

Magic Walk continued, "It is the message to all peoples that even the western tribes now wish to relay in this belt which speaks of our great Plot. They too will see their own Heno in it, and that Orenda who some of those western nations call Wakunda and is the Great Manitou of the north, and their spirit cousins in all the directions will be stirred by it. In this way, we will swallow the snakes and make them one of our people."

Many Axes said, "When the Grand Council has decided to go ahead with the Plot, we will make four belts, each showing the black and white shell code of the Plot. One belt, Water Bear will take to the Shaman and White Fish of the Ojibwa, who will then, with the agreement of his peoples, relay it around many towns, finally, even finally to the shaman of the Abenaki near Quebec. We will keep two in reserve. One in case a belt is lost. The other we will keep aside for the battle field, as we discussed, which we will encourage and expect to come to a war on the lakes below Quebec."

Hunts by the Big Hill nodded. He conferred with the other chiefs.

"We agree to begin the process to approve Heno's Plot and its stratagems. We understand we must do so at first in utmost secrecy to avoid giving away of the plan to the palefaces of either colony."

He looked about at the other Chiefs from the Longhouse League.

Many Axes concluded, "When the Little Brothers and then the Big Brothers bring their agreement to the Onondaga fire for the final decision of the Grand Chief, it will be decided and it will be done."

He looked around at all the Longhouse Chiefs. They all nodded in agreement.

Chapter 22

One early spring day of 1691, the now aged Mohawk chieftain, Dancing Pipes, covered in an English woolen blanket, shuffled through the huge carved wooden doorway of the great spired church in Quebec and sat quietly in the back row of benches.

After a time, she painfully arose and slowly made her way to the double wooden booth where confessions were heard. She was an occasional visitor these days and knew she would soon hear the steps of the approaching priest.

It made her smile, when she heard those steps again coming toward the confessional booth.

The priest's voice welcomed her. "Ah, do I listen to my special child."

She chuckled inwardly at the reference to "child": she was probably old enough to maybe be his grandmother. His voice bid her say the prayers to the Queen of the World, Mary. It was a soothing, but firm voice. She was indeed in some awe of Mary. She felt almost compelled by his soothing voice to actually confess something. Again she smiled to herself.

What she told the priest, falsely, about her lithesome granddaughters she knew would at first arouse him. She knew her stories of them could do so. He sometimes asked for details.

But, then she seemingly strayed onto a subject that changed his priestly voice.

"You must please tell me more, Dancing Pipes," he said, urgently. She was no longer his "special child," she noted.

She waited and then said, "You see, the New Yorkers hate you French especially, but us praying Indians too. Word has come to us from one of my wandering family that those New Yorkers are making a large force with my people and other numerous allies to come here and destroy Montreal and all of New France. Your great Frontenac cannot stop them. They are too strong."

Her confessor was silent, but she sensed he listened raptly.

"We say that Christ must surely intervene. Our Lady, Mary must plead with Christ. Christ must make you French bring your strongest force against the English from New York before they are fully prepared. That's what a Mohawk Chief tells me. If you do not do this, we are all lost along the great river."

She expected some reply, but got none.

The priest had already left the church was hurrying to the new Governor's house. It was close enough, though through a sea of mud from recent rains, for the priest to make in a short run. Thank God, he muttered to himself, already badly winded and mud splattered, Governor Frontenac is again here in New France.

The large flowing white haired countenance of the seated figure of Frontenac stared at the priest as he brushed aside attendants and entered the Governor's office in the Chateau St Louis, a large grey stone edifice overlooking the St Lawrence from the heights of Quebec

The Governor spoke severely to the breathless priest.

"It is neither at my request for you," for the priest was the Governor's new confessor, "nor, I judge from your own filthy state of dress, but your own will that makes you appear so boldly here, Father Leclaire. Alas, what news do you bring?

Leclaire managed to relay what Dancing Pipes had told him.

"Surely you cannot trust that old woman?"

"She is one of the sharpest informants about New York we have, since our best spy in New York was recently lost at sea.

"Why do you Jesuits know so much? Anyway, we have yet more evidence of a devilish plot coming at us from New York. But it is surely a helpless colony as it awaits its new Governor. What can have changed so at this time?

"The woman told me apparently a rebel, Jacob Liesler, has taken the place in his grip and ignores the cautious voices there. Hr declares himself their military leader as well as their civil leader. He has ordered New France destroyed!"

Frontenac's complexion was florid. He stood and paced to the huge window, overlooking a sunset casting its last light upon the St Lawrence.

"How dare they challenge me so? I have more field canon and ball abandoned here by that stupid New Englander Phipps trying to come at us up the River than they can imagine. And our explosives are now better, thanks to the French armourers I returned here with. We are now disciplined here, thank the Lord. If they are taken by a madness, so much the better!"

He crossed himself, as did Leclaire.

"I shall summon my Council for tomorrow latest. Tell the Intendant and sub-intendant out there when you pass them to come in here immediately. Tell the Bishop that he, and St Vallier, and the Superiors of the Orders must all attend on the morrow. The entire colony must rise to this supreme challenge. Tell them that is my summons. Go!"

* * *

Smith was in Albany at about the same time as Dancing Pipes had given her false news to Father Leclaire in Quebec.

He had always thought Albany was a very strange place, and he had seen his share of strange places. Its buildings were rough Dutcher structures, one or two almost as high as the tallest in New York with stockades around a modest fort. Everything about it was Dutcher, really, except that even more than in New York, the established people here were themselves bitterly divided, a few pro English and tolerating New York's port advantages, many more not. And the town in turn was increasingly alienated from its farming hinterland and the free trading villages with the Iroquois people along the river of the Mohawk.

Smith finally found a Governor's Council member he knew from New York, a wealthy man known as Van Cortland who was visiting the Patroon of Rensselaerwyck, Killain Van Rensselaer, at the beguiling white washed manor house of that estate along the upper Hudson.

He was coolly welcomed to the Patroon's table. Smith's movements and affiliations were not understood by anyone in the Fort Orange community, though he was accepted here as a connected and informative man to whom some could talk, if they understood enough of each other's language.

Van Rensselaer spoke little as they dined and finally Smith addressed Van Cortland. "I have been told an expeditionary force was organized and sent north from here."

"That may be so, Smith. Leisler cannot be stopped in his foolishness at taking over temporary authority between English Governors. Yet he speaks of his betters with calumny and his ill equipped soldiers went into the northern woods under a stupid commander and came back again diseased and totally disorganized. But, what business do you have with that?"

"Just this: because of Leisler's ill-advised attempt northward, now aware of both his provocation and his weakness, I hear that a large force has being organized in New France and will march southward any day now. Should it meet any forces of ours, poorly led and poorly supplied as I have heard, our forces will be destroyed and not only will all those men and arms lost to the French, so too could the entire New York colony. I have too much at stake to have that put at risk by unnecessary military weakness against a smaller colony. Can you do something about this?"

"Oh, my God," Van Cortland answered, clearly upset at this news and conveying it in Dutch to Van Rensselaer, who was also upset. "We would be the first to fall, the Patroon says, and that New York must send forces here."

"Indeed. So, I put to you: how can the expedition against New France be properly reorganized into a more formidable one so as to properly defend our currently disorganized colony?"

"Well," replied Van Cortland, "I think the leader of that currently failed expedition would have to hand back his command – he is a most indecisive man and his men already suffer bad fevers, from what I hear. I will have to pass the word to Leisler, though – he runs the colony for better or worse at this stage – to organize immediately a much stronger military thrust to the north. As it happens, he and his brother-in-law arrive here tomorrow."

"Good. You must do so with the greatest urgency," said Smith. "I will do what I can in New York itself, but I have little influence outside my own circle."

* * *

In the late spring months of 1691, all the first nations around the Great Lakes and along the Shaman' Trail successively received, had interpreted to them, adopted by their own means, sometimes by their own arrangement of shells, sticks or stones - some only by the amazing memory of a story-teller alone - and handed on the black and white shell collar telling in a general way of how Water Bear's dream had been interpreted into Heno's Plot for the ascension of Orenda, to become the shield of all the native peoples.

The peoples had been made ready for something new. Even some strong actions against the French colony had been forestalled by this – some Mohawk leaders had wanted to again attack Lachine, still retaliating for the recent burning of Schenectady by a French force, but held back, not wanting to unsettle the balance of colonial forces the plot required.

The essential call to action in Heno's Plot for the New York and New France colonies to send their strongest forces against each other was concealed in the now widely circulating coded message and premised upon war being inevitable between the two European colonies, with a massing of large numbers of allies from their own nations. Indeed, that was the openly know subject of the coded message: New France and New England prepare for war: determine your initial alliances with the. That, in turn, helped feed the war expectations of each colonial side.

The key military idea of the plot was that, upon pre-arranged signals, their own war chiefs would quickly parley near the ultimate battlefield and determine the best way to take full advantage of the near self-destruction of the paleface forces. The specific instructions would be shared among Nations only when the New France and New York forces were in fact set irreversibly against each other.

In Quebec, Governor Frontenac strode back and forth along the balustrade of his chateau. He issued orders and commanded resources well beyond the means of his colony, but somehow commandeered a formidable strike force against New York. Frontenac commanded enough obedience that all things were done as he ordered. All available military and civil manpower, not just the remnants of the French brigades would be ready and would march down the Richelieu Valley to meet the New Yorker force expected there to be advancing toward New France. Only the skeptical Emil de Merleau, the French sub-Intendant, would remain behind in Quebec to take care of things in an undefended colony. All would march south to an assured triumph over the enemy colony.

In New York, the situation was more complicated.

Jacob Leisler, the head of the New York militia, had decided perhaps impulsively, that dispatches to the colony and its Governor-less Council from the new king, William III, during the period before a new Governor would arrive, "to take care to keep the peace and administer the laws of New York" in the Governor's absence, spoke directly to the extant holder of military power, namely himself.

Leisler had so far asserted his power over the colony as much to defend it militarily as anything else. But, that had at first assumed secondary importance to re-ordering the place. He had issued writs even to call forth a new assembly better representing all New Yorkers, not just the wealthy merchants and other powerful families and the now ascendant Anglican Church there. In this, Leisler had been backed by the large majority of Dutch laborers and artisans who resented the English or English-allied ruling elite, and this was even weakly supported by many outlying English colonists in the Long Island settlements who resented New York's commercial advantages and who thought they had won rights earlier answering only to the English Crown.

Leisler had begun a process of enacting a government of direct popular representation, and even held forth the possibility of land and property redistribution.

Then, Major Richard Ingoldesby arrived in New York in February 1691, He was an able aid of New Governor and had arrived ahead of him. He insisted Leisler surrender to him.

Leisler had delayed transferring his usurped powers until his name became synonymous with rebellion. But, because Leisler was now more acutely aware of the French threat from the north, and had been preparing for that menace, Ingoldesby, surprisingly to New York's elite, not only excused the man from imprisonment as a traitor, but began to rely heavily upon him for organizing the large counter-thrust with new militia and his own just arrived forces up from New York for the next few months.

Indeed, Leisler thought that not only he personally, but the colony itself was in dire trouble, and with his military authority thus renewed, sought out a new cooperation with his rich merchant enemies, through among others, Smith's gracious intercession with them, prior to the arrival of the new Governor.

By Late August, 1691, a strong French Canadian force of 1500 men, organized by a now enraged Governor Frontenac, reinforced by a regiment of 500 additional men and arms he had managed to plead from a disinterested France two years' before, with their almost 1500 Algonquin allies, not all of whom he himself even trusted, moved south from Montreal.

A small but powerful fleet of ships, led by the frigate of its commander, the daring Pierre Le Moyne d'Iberville, recently arrived back at Quebec from playing havoc with the English ports in Hudson Bay, was now also headed out to the mouth of the St. Lawrence to discourage any new New-Englander attacks from that direction.

In response to messages of the approaching strong French land force reaching New York, a force of nearly 3000 headed by Ingoldsby, Leisler himself, and his brother-in-law, Jacob Millburn, and three of Ingoldsby's best captains, moved north from New York, with word of reinforcements moving west from New England. They cared little of exposing their colony: a fleet with two frigates, HMS Provenance and HMS Duke of York, the latter with 60 guns, had just arrived at Graves End to bring the new Governor to New York.

As the new Governor of New York was warned, the French would move south against the still disorganized New York colony to pre-empt any further strengthening of the English forces against them from England, or more immediately, such forces as might come from Boston and the New England colonies, with their large militias.

In order to draw the French too far south for any easy retreat back north, the Mohawk chiefs most recently allied with New York suggested as the desirable place for the expected great battle between the French forces from Quebec and Montreal and the greater English forces from New York, to be the Cohoes Falls. This was once Mohawk territory but in an agreement with the Dutchers in 1630 it became part of the huge Rennselaerwyck manor at the confluence of the Mohawk and Hudson Rivers.

This place also impeded easy large movement further up river by the New Yorkers and was well enough away from New England to overly excite those colonies, who Smith predicted would rally to their New York ally, but only with too little force, too late.

It was the physician Kastler in Quebec who had supplied a final key to a successful plot against the European colonies. Already driven by his promise to Antoinette de Merleau to find her only son stolen by the Iroquois, he had secretly met with Laliber and had been won over to the Orendan plot, in part because he had long thought a mixing of peoples makes a stronger people, and in this case perhaps would give the native side more resistance to European disease. Even before the army of New France marched, Kastler had helped re-make twelve operative canons out of the poorly spiked field pieces left by the invading New Englander Phipps' land forces the year before. These field canon could counter any New York battlefield advantage if deployed at the right tactical moment.

* * *

Twisting Trails, a fast Mohawk runner, ran at top speed through the woods to deliver the news up to an east-facing hill near the Cohoes Falls French and English battlefield, where there was to be a meeting of all the war chiefs.

He was climbing a path of sharp stones. He had thrown off his torn moccasins. His feet were now bruised and bloodied. He had come down with a fever that morning even before he started. He cursed himself for getting sick and now beginning to become winded.

Then he saw before him the promontory only the Mohawk knew that so perfectly overlooked the Cohoes Falls. His running force nearly ran him through the chiefs now assembled there and over the edge before one of them managed to stop him.

He gasped at bringing the news. "The Plot has worked. The French and the English terribly defeat each other. Many Axes will soon come here, with Water Bear."

"We can see much of this," commented Hunts by the Big Hill... "But the Plot must be wrong - the English now seem easily to prevail."

"Not enough. That is my report from Many Axes. The Plot expected this and can reverse it"

He gasped again. This time he gasped blood.

The chiefs looked down doubtfully from the heights. They could see the converging movement of the English and French forces on the level grounds on the far side of the river narrows before them. The New Yorker forces looked as if they had started a charge all along their line.

In the near ground, several lines of opposing musketry were re-forming for likely the last and the most intense stage of the battle. The Frenchmen, knowing the English fusillade would be far more intense than their own, had begun to deploy more extensively into several groups before the English lines. This was designed to spread the British aim, while their aim would be focused on a larger but denser target. It was also designed to make room for the sudden appearance from behind log camouflage of the twelve field guns the French had saved until the last stage of battle.

Even before the exchanges of volleys between the enjoined inner forces began to take their murderous toll, along the outer edges of the battle ground, faster moving forces from both sides, some on horseback, others knowing and running the wilderness, moved in and through one another with much yelling and shooting. The shooting was into the air.

This outer battle was hoped by the conspirators to form a kind of tamper of confusion designed to contain the inner battle – the inner and more disciplined troops thought that few of their own nucleus would survive or could retreat fast enough through the outer battle between the Indian allies – which had now seemingly so admixed the opposing tribes that paleface retreat through them would be as dangerous as remaining in their lines. Even so, a few paleface soldiers had sought hasty retreat, and had been cut down by volleys of arrows or musketry as they tried to escape through the outer swirl of native allies.

Many Axes, positioned a little back from the main action noticed this and commented to the Mohawk chief, Lightning Throat, at his side, "those fools retreating do so too fast – they are easily spotted. Look though, a group of French there – he pointed - move slowly back into that woods, as if they were still in the main action. That slow way is the smarter way to retreat through our outer forces, at least for a small group.

Lightning Throat was pleased with Many Axes' acute observation. He summoned a chief on horse-back and ordered, "Go there and stop that crafty retreat," pointing to the group Many Axes had noticed.

Many Axes then shouted, "But spare their leader – he could be a smart one if he turned to our side."

Across the battlefield, just behind the well-defined New York front line, Captain John Jolie, an ex-patriot French Huguenot New Yorker via Ireland, turned to his lieutenant and spoke almost admiringly of the tactics of his former French countrymen: "Those outnumbered French have spread our fire cleverly and withstand it well, while they find us an easier target. We cannot outflank them from where we stand. We most charge through their middle and break away and try to scatter each of the groups."

"But look there sir!" shouted a lieutenant.

"Hell, man, they have brought out new canon from behind that knoll ahead of us. We must continue the charge. We must capture them! "He desperately waved his two squads along.

As Jolie spoke, though, many in the charging line in front of him had just fallen from the point blank fire of the suddenly appearing French field gunnery. He then realized that he was speaking to a collapsing headless body of his lieutenant whose head had just been ripped by a cannon ball from its now crimson flowered neck in a blood spattering, "poof!" just before the canon ball exploded behind them. Jolie had automatically kept on giving orders to the collapsing headless body of his lieutenant until an instant later he felt a searing pain in his shoulder and was also felled. He shouted from the smoky ground, "Charge those guns, men! Capture those guns at all costs!"

Chapter 23

The chiefs watching the bloody battle below realized the deadly enormity of the now equal carnage.

Twisting Trails spoke up brokenly, "Many Axes has said to me for you all to be sure to wait until his signal that each side has equally murdered the other – only then do we have them under our control and finish the business with captives."

"And, where is Many Axes?" Hunts by the Big Hill demanded.

"He will come after his final order. He sent me ahead."

Twisting Trails fell at these last words. His fever was already likely fatal and he had run too hard. As he fell, he passed on the collar of black and white shells that was counted on to secure the Allied Chiefs' victory. His head smashed bloodily against a rock, despite attempts to stop his fall. The chiefs knew that Twisting Trails was among the bravest of this day and they stood for a while in silence.

After a time, it was decided that Twisting Trails be taken to the highest tree in that place where his body would dry to sweet bones and overlook forever, the unfolding Orendan plot.

Besides the Iroquois and Ojibwa chiefs, there were also chiefs from the Northern nations assembled at the heights above the Cohoes Falls. They felt wrong about abandoning their French allies and they watched their braves below who now moved in seemingly weakly engaged confusion but blocking a retreat by the surviving French.

Among the two Abenaki chiefs on the lookout, the senior Chief was Red Bird Moving Slowly. He now pressed Hunts by the Big Hill, "You Longhouse people lead here. We must, bid by our own nations who have received the belt, follow you. But where is Many Axes? And, we even begin to wonder: why we should follow you? The French seem to have an advantage now. They were our friends." The other Abenaki chief nodded hat this direct challenge.

Hunts by the Big Hill searched for time. He saw a small flock of crows land in a nearby tree.

"Well now, do you not know the crows?" He paused and looked carefully at each of the other chiefs.

"Those smart crows consider things from different points of view. They see it's a question of seeing through the eyes of others. That's a skill that crows share with the cleverest of us. Sometimes, when one crow has lost out in an argument, the other runs its beak between the loser's feathers? A true victory must be a subtle thing. Look there." He pointed to the tree nearby. There indeed were several crows watching them. The Abenaki chiefs were satisfied that Hunts by the Big Hill was as strong as their own medicine.

They and the other eastern chiefs looking over the falls calmed themselves until a short time later Many Axes arrived.

He brought the news that the allied nations were now positioned to make the final difference in the battle fields spread out below. He was accompanied by Water Bear, who still wore his black and white striped face paint and who gave great credibility to what the once enemy of the Abenaki nation said, for it followed the dream of Water Bear.

Many Axes went straight to Red Bird Moving Slowly.

"As I just overheard Hunts by the Big Hill say to you, we must all now go below and preen the defeated crows.

Later a circle of native fires surrounded the hundreds of disarmed and many wounded paleface prisoners, Water Bear summed up the day in terms of Water Bear's dream, with the help of Magic Walk who interpreted so that all would know the course ahead in their own language.

As he looked out at his audience he saw many of the captured French and New Yorkers staring back at him.

He began, 'What has happened here today and will take place in the next weeks and months is foretold in the dream of Water Bear. We are all, the Nations here first and the colonies of New France and New York now bound to follow that path, paleface and native people alike, to ensure the final meaning of the dream is realized: a people in our midst, neither replacing the first Nations, nor all of the second colonies, with their peoples pressing upon us in too great numbers, that will give us a mix of our different powers that takes and builds the best from each way, but which we first Nations control."

An affirming buzz was begun in some of the crowd, some even of the defeated palefaces.

"Each of us native tribes and leagues had our alliances and chains of commitment to these French and English. But what did they do to us? These chains caught us up more than we, them. Now, we dare to reverse that."

"New York itself will be captured both by our forces on land and by sea by Smith and his ships. He is a man who knows and loves our new spirit. After taking New York and its many undefended people there, we march to the undefended towns of New France and we will capture that colony too."

"Having done those things, we shall march most of you and all of those people through our countries in winter when there is no escape, where they will finally settle among us in a town we will share. And we shall take your strengths and give you ours so that the people in our countries are the strongest anywhere, just as my people and other Native people now mix our own peoples."

Red Bird Walking Slowly, after conferring with his other chiefs, now stepped forward. He repeated on the key questions facing the plot.

"With whom then, shall we trade to gain the European goods? "

"You listen well and yet poorly. We shall learn to make some of those goods and because so many of those colonists will be hostaged inland to our own towns, the New Englanders and in the Philadelphia and Baltimore colonies and those further south and their home country will learn the new trade with us."

"But, will not many others come across the waters to take back their colonies and war with us with their powers?"

"Yes. They will try to challenge our plot. But by then, we will not be on the coasts which they may storm again and we will be ready along the Lakes and along the Great Michissippi to defend ourselves, with Smith's protection in the southern sea. Do you see the dream of Water Bear? It can be no other way. It has been told along all the rivers in all our countries for too many seasons now to count. It tells us to be ourselves in a new way that is the old way."

Red Bird Walking Slowly was given an even more searching question by his chiefs. He saw Water Bear himself moving into the fire light.

"Water Bear, what your dream seems to say is that we should no longer be ourselves – must we become these new palefaces?"

"The best question so far. The answer is that we must dare to be ourselves and know and trust ourselves strongly, to be able add to our own strengths, the strengths of others through this new truly mixed people among us that we will make. We need a mixed people under our control to help keep the rest of our own people from sinking in the mud. Do you see this truth from the dream?"

"I think so."

Then the famously indecisive Abenaki Chief said firmly, "Yes. We do," making many heads in his own camp turn and begin to nod.

Water Bear watched carefully as the chiefs were persuaded and realized the moment to turn ideas into action.

He checked with Magic Walk. She nodded.

He said,

"Now, this is enough for us here. We know the truth of this day and many days to follow. Tomorrow, we all march to New York."

* * *

Two days before the battles were joined at Cohoes Falls, Many Axes had ordered Laliber to leave the area, saying the appearance of the Jesuit conspirator surely would tell of some sort of conspiracy which could deflate the will to fight on both paleface sides. The presence of the controversial priest would, he concluded, "bring more uncertainties to an already uncertain situation." Everyone had agreed, including Laliber, who had not expected a role at this stage of the plot.

After his banishment, Laliber headed to the Mohawk castle several leagues west of the now largely destroyed Schenectady. He hoped there to see Dancing Pipes, whom he now knew to be a very wise Iroquois leader.

As he approached the stockade, he saw instead, hurrying out to greet him, his blond hair flying behind him, the physician from Quebec, Kastler.

"Father Laliber! What news from the battles?"

"You will get very little news from me. It was decided that I should not be seen in the area, though before I left the forces of each colony were moving toward each other as the plot predicts.

"You look tired from your trip. Let me help you."

"Take me only to Dancing Pipes."

"She is here. I can take you to her. But she speaks little."

"She will speak to me."

They approached a small Longhouse near the centre of a longer straight street of facing houses.

Kastler explained, "This Longhouse is for someone special. It now is where Dancing Pipes may be found. She can no longer play the mad old woman. They all know she helped make the French half of what is happening, with her cleverness."

"It is that cleverness that I now seek," muttered Laliber.

Several senior Mothers barred the door.

"You have been among us before," said the lead woman. "Why, then, do you again bother our Grandmother?"

Laliber answered in increasingly adequate Mohawk, "Because she is the only Chief I wish to bother. Tell her it is Laliber come to bother her. "

A cackle of laughter could be heard within.

"Bring him to me. I shall let him confess to me."

"Yes, she is whom I wish to see."

Laliber entered the house.

He saw that Dancing Pipes was sitting against a large folded red blanket, in front of the sleeping beds along a wall, inspecting her hands, still chuckling.

"Welcome Father Laliber, but I sometimes think you are Christ's fool, maybe even the Devil's fool. Why seek me out, now?"

"You were a friend in my captivity here. You have helped cause some of the big new events east of us. You are a sometimes praying Iroquois. Why should I not seek you out, when more meaning is to be had?"

"Well, all those things may be true, but what meaning could be added."

"Oh, much meaning is still needed, my dear ancient captain. It is this: Any resulting mix of peoples from this great plot must not be denied the right to seek and follow Christ. I can no longer guarantee that. Nor can anyone but Many Axes, over whom you remain captain. And under whom I remain a black dust mat at best"

She chortled. "Well, well. He is a very strong chieftain, is he not? You others have straightened out his tangled thoughts of many years. Even I sometimes hoped they would remain tangled. But, alas, he now knows his mind. What he will do, will be done, you will see."

Laliber looked carefully at her.

"I fear he disregards some of us who have helped build the thing to this point. We may be no longer in his plan. He could therefore put us out of his plan."

"Yes he could. You are right to fear that. I have no answer to what he may do, especially to you. He and I know that no black robe must be seen as a power in this. It is for our spirits to prevail, in his mind, even though he talks of a mix. But he talks that way, only because he makes a test for our spirits: he hates them too, you know."

Neither spoke for a moment.

"Yet, I think you deserve a good place in this. Not just your help in interpreting the dream of Water Bear. Water Bear has told us of that. Driven by your own, and sometimes my own Christian God. Indeed, as I think of it. It is a perfect story that no spirit is denied among the new people in that far away new place."

She wanted to go into more thought about it. "Let me think. Sit before me, and the physician out there may join us also. He has much thought for the people and we have even talked his science a few times."

Laliber wanted to say more, but thought the better. "Let her at least partly Christian thoughts work it out," he whispered to Kastler who had now entered the longhouse.

They waited until a candle guttered.

"Yes. I see now. It is not to require this Christianity, but for him, simply to allow it. For those who wish to seek it. I will tell this to Many Axes. In a way, I will get him to agree. I can still do this. I will. But I am very tired of all this. I cannot any longer "keep moving," as you two shall have to do. Do you know, I was once told that wisdom of surviving in the woods by one of your own, he called himself Radisson, and until he said that to me, I thought I would have him killed? Anyway, please be careful, both of you. And keep moving on a good trail, if you can find one."

She fell asleep.

The two men removed themselves without another word.

"Will you go with me to Montreal?" Kastler questioned Laliber as they left Dancing Pipes' house.

"No. I cannot yet be seen there, yet. But I would have a word. Stay here this night, if you can."

"Yes. Yes, of course. I am here only on a botanical visit. I have more botanical specimens for the Court, one that opens its leaves in a miraculous fashion, though I wonder if the specimens will now reach France."

"Why would they not? You have the highest connections in France."

"Oh yes, in France. But the ships taking these back are never trustworthy. Smith has told me, some specimens even reach the Sultan first."

"I wish you could safely transport to the Court the true stories of this new world, and not just the plants."

"Eighty barrels of stories, perhaps. But alas, as plants wilt, unless there are good stories, well written down, memory fades. "

"Well, these peoples remember and tell in their talk vivid stories generation after generation. Though they are much the same, they yet differ wonderfully, even from town to town of the same tribe."

They sniffed the smoke from the cooking fires.

"Ah, memory, I agree on its importance. In the last century, the French Court was told of a memory machine, but it was never built. I think it drove the maker, mad!"

"Well then, what is this century's memory machine?

"In France, the latest, in words that is, is The Encyclopedia, I suppose. Yes, that would be it. Though, I already told you of the Pascalini machina. Now that was a memory holding machine, but for numbers. Imagine it, among these peoples. What would they think of it?"

"Who knows? But it may interest you, that when I returned here to New France this last time, I happened to have brought with me that very Pascalini."

"What! What is it you say?"

"Well, I returned here to these countries via Paris, and it was right where you said, mouldering and of no use to anyone there, along with his notes on such machines. So, I took the liberty to return it to you. It is in good hands in Quebec and will be given back to you to share at the new Orendan settlement, if you join us there.

"That is astonishing, Father. I am most pleased."

"Yes, I think it is astonishing – it only occurs because of our friendship. But wait until I add to it, my good physician. As an educator sometimes in mathematics, I looked more widely about those subterranean depths and, what did I find, close against many casks of wine, but, a manuscript of the German, Leibnitz, with his own ideas about such rapid calculation."

"I know little of this Leibnitz."

"The manuscript tells of his early idea of a binary numeral system with a base two, not ten, and how he kept thinking about that throughout his life. He came up with a thing he eventually called a "stepped reckoner." It could execute all four arithmetical operations, which the Pascalina could not. Several such machines were made but they still did not fully mechanize the operation of carrying. He wrote later notes about it, even adapting it to do algebra and finally he imagined a machine in which binary numbers were represented by marbles as governed by cards with punched holes. I cannot myself imagine what this means. But, it somehow solved the problem of carrying. I have brought all those notes here to you, imagining it teachable, and you must help make it part of Orenda. They must be made to think of things about numbers at the level of our science – who knows, the new people may advance such calculating machines and make better use of them as both Pascal and Leibnitz showed was possible."

"I am overwhelmed by your daring act, Laliber. Once again you astonish me, my wondrous Jesuit friend.

"Since you are the scientist, Kastler, I rely on you to share these excellent European ideas in the place where these Orendan events settle."

"Just so! It is my promise. Just as I am promised to seek the lost child of dear Antoinette, somewhere we hear among these Iroquois, or as I now believe, passed farther west. Indeed, as a physician, I am most anxious to find out what the new possible mix of peoples whom you have helped conjure up, does with our understanding of diseases as well as other science."

"Well then, I shall also expect you to join me in writing to my high friends back in France more rich stories from Orenda. As you have suggested, I think it must be material they can convert into an Encyclopedia. Stories from here that will astonish them, as those stories astonish us.

Kastler replied excitedly, "I will do that! They will have the first and all the next stories of this new people. So astonishing all this will be to Paris and Rome."

He flung his arms up, "We shall call it "The Encyclopaedia of Astonishment."

They laughed and hugged each other.

What ideas, they thought, and to have them especially in these wild woods.

Chapter 24

The sunset seemed to pour rich red blood over little New York. So it seemed to those among the conspirators who took in the view through their spyglasses. They stood on a hill above the narrows near the bottom of the newly named Hudson River. The incarnate New York sunset and the few remote fires they could make out north of the town symbolized the advance of the Orendan forces. That excited all the viewers gathered on the hill. But, they could not stay long. They moved down the hill to the beaches across from Graves End where a strange business was unfolding.

Already word had been received in New York itself of the military disaster to the north. Those few outlying New Yorkers who resisted the rapid Orendan advance southward were being forced to their undefended fate. Here and there a farmhouse or barn was burning - but, on Smith's advice, crops and livestock were not destroyed and as many people as possible were being herded toward the town at the tip of the peninsula.

Water Bear stood on the hill, beside Many Axes' deputies: several chiefs selected from the Iroquois and the north to witness and take part in the New York episode of Heno's Plot. Many Axes was delayed at the Cohoes Falls, selecting a leadership from among the prisoners who would be forced to cooperate with the Mohawk Chiefs and their other captors on their ultimate disposition, the hope being they would agree to the full Orendan plot and accompany other colonists on the forthcoming hostage treks to the Michissippi.

Water Bear had said even before he had received the final reports of the battles farther north. "If we have succeeded in the north, this thing at night that only Smith can arrange will be decisive. Now he asked Copper Star just returned on a fast river boat commandeered from the New York invasion force, "What news from the north?"

"It has gone as the Plot said it would. Much blood spills below the Cohoes Falls from both armies. Of the original three thousand on each side, we counted less than three thousand in total left roughly the same from each side who are without spirit in our own now larger force's custody. Waiting to be scalped or worse, they believe. There are indeed no more than that left, even the force that came from New England, which was too small as Smith predicted. On his advice they would not mix well and their capture would give New England more urgent retaliatory cause, they were chased well away, by our now willing Abenaki allies alone."

"So," said Water Bear, "it is now the time for Smith to do his worst against the two big English ships lying across there at Graves End. Let us hurry to him down on the shore."

On that shore, within sight of the lower New York at Gravesend, Smith stood thinking through his plan a final time. Though he had contributed to the planning of the land battle, it was necessary for Smith to give a lot more thought to the naval situation in New York should there be the hoped for Orendan conspiratorial victory over the New York and New France land forces at Cohoes Falls, that defeat was too far north for any survivors to deliver quick reinforcement back to any engagement with the two British frigates that had accompanied the new Governor, lying off New York's outer harbour at Graves End.

The fact was, those two ships were already largely emptied of the five hundred musket men along with some of their canon, all sent up the Hudson on flat boats to aid the colonial forces engaging the French at Cohoes Falls. The majority of those left on-board had reportedly been left manning the off-shore facing decks, since the British hardly expected to need to bombard New York itself at this point after Leisler had yielded to the new Governor and such a powerful army had been sent far to the north.

Smith reckoned that his own available ships awaiting concealed, a little further up the Long Island coast – Van Pammister's own 30 gun frigate, two smaller 8 canon brigantines on each side, plus guns aft, and four large sloops, one with eight canon, the other three with six canon. This fleet, partly manned by his Native American sailors - could come in and have a good chance against the two much bigger, but crew- and canon- depleted English ships.

He again cursed the two of his often rebellious captains who had chosen to remain with their powerful frigates back in the Caribbean, awaiting an expected Spanish silver fleet. They would share the wealth and he would regain them in the long run, but they should have been here when they were needed in New York. He recalled the exchange he had with them. "I am taking much more than silver up North," he had said. "What could possibly be worth more than silver, although gold comes to mind?" they replied, laughing uproariously and hugging him, so that he knew he was still their leader in more sensible immediate things in Caribbee. They would pay for that, he thought. He knew the moment those captains heard of a success in New York, they would not hesitate to come north in their big ships to help commandeer New York's goods. But, he would establish Van Pammister more clearly now as his second in command over them.

As he thought through the New York naval situation, Smith hesitated, though: to waste his own available fleet in any equal battle with the British, even if the conditions were right, might not be wise because there was also a threat of d'Iberville's bold little French Canadian fleet, whose approach had been rumoured. For the same reason, the British ships' captains had left their seaward side more actively gunned in case they were approached by sea by any French naval forces.

Pierre Le Moyne d'Iberville, and his brothers, having mastered the English in Hudson Bay with his dashing ships, was even more Frontenac's darling since he and one of his younger brothers' helped in the previous summer's raid on Schenectady. The younger brother had been killed when the New Englander Phipps had foolishly challenged Quebec with sea forces also in the previous year. Pierre had then been back at the great northern Bay. The man and his remaining brother vowed revenge against the English, and Smith knew they would be a formidable match at sea, with too much of his own fleet still back in the Caribbean.

Fortunately, any such French naval threat had not yet materialized, if Smith could believe reports from his eyes all along the Long Island and a few fast reconnaissance craft he had left at sea far enough out to be able to report any approaching fleet from New France or old France or New England or old England, such being the various possibilities.

But Smith also knew d'Iberville, the most likely to approach so soon, could not move quickly against his more numerous ships – he knew d'Iberville had but three. With the good captains Smith had found, who were at their best as bold as Lemoyne d'Iberville's own, with a variety of ships some as well or better gunned and who had passed through these tricky New York waters which d'Iberville knew not, many times before.

With the arrival of Water Bear and his decisive news that things had gone well and were a great success inland, Smith still knew that his plan against the British naval force must be guaranteed to succeed in order to secure New York and leave his own fleet unharmed, should d'Iberville's fleet arrive. His fleet would have to survive in order to move confiscated New York goods via the southern Gulf to and up the Michissippi.

So, when he received the final news of the success of Heno's Plot on land, Smith decided, given increasing off-shore winds, to go ahead that very night with a tactic that had been used in history many times against an anchored wooden and tar-seamed fleet: launch fire ships against it.

In this case it would be large war canoes, in the last few days piled high with brush by numerous members of the now excitedly cooperating Eastern tribes. The covered fire canoes launched from the eastern shore of the Staten Island at night would quietly approach the British ships anchored off Graves End. Those fire canoes would be set afire, with their crews escaping to many smaller accompanying canoes.

The conditions were right. The strong off-shore winds riding after a cold front moving diagonally through the area were very favourable for Smith's tactic. The British ships would batten down against the winds, leaving them slow to weigh anchor against any danger and leaving their weakly gunned side, the side on which the English captains would expect no danger, exposed to Smith's fire canoes.

Equally important to Smith's plan, there was no moon this night. This was the only night that nearly guaranteed the result Smith desired and his co-conspirators required and expected of him.

Smith waited until well after midnight and then gave the order. The thirty-canoe flotilla moved away from shore rapidly and silently. The ignition torches were borne within barrels behind a screen of dark wet blankets to conceal their light. Smith himself now moved into the moonless darkness in the leading canoe accompanying the fire canoes. They had finally decided that a mix of pine gum spirits and bear and whale oils could ignite piles of light pine brush on the war canoes to achieve a conflagration large enough for its intended effect.

Ten large freight canoes were used, five for each targeted British ship. They had waited until the few sailors and soldiers still remaining with the fleet had returned by tenders from the City to the two big ships at Graves End.

Smith alone knew how crucial this step was in the overall Orendan Plot. It would be a powerful symbol at sea of what was also happening on land and it would render New York, already emptied of most of its able-bodied men, defenceless to the victorious Orendan land forces that would soon be approaching from the North.

The big English ships at anchor were protected the previous nights by fog before the cold front had arrived. No further delay was possible. As soon as word was received of the destruction of their inland forces, the British captains would be tempted to lift anchor and depart New York awaiting new orders and to ward off any approaching French fleet.

As the fire fleet came close to the British ships, Smith gave his order "We move, now! Ignite the fire canoes!"

Within minutes, the British captains and seamen were horrified to see the large war canoes carrying raging fires approaching their ships at a speed which could not be stopped or avoided.

All of Graves End was soon filled with wildly dancing light as the ten fired war canoes rammed the two big frigates. Fire leaped up the tarred sides of the ships.

The final stage of the Plot worked more quickly than Smith dared hope.

There was so much fire on one of the great ships, it soon became a raging inferno with its men leaping from its decks, no longer able to escape. The other surviving ship, also afire, turned about and tried to leave the Graves End, but, as Smith had expected with its under-gunned side now exposed ocean-ward.

It soon came into range of Smith's ships' advancing in a line on the scene. Their blazing guns put that ship beyond help. It too would burn fiercely for a time and end up disabled in the outer New York harbour, where Smith's men readily boarded and secured it and brought it haplessly back to anchor in good view of New York's fort, flying a different flag, the final stage of Smith's plan.

Part Six

Heno's Test

When a Bruised Sunset

Ripped by lightning
From a frontal wind
Spills backlit blood out of
And back into
A storm-cloud engine

When a whoosh of surface heat
Gives fecund air a twisted cleat
The hammer of hail coming on

Thank those spirits
Wanting Earth to learn
In such a violent churn
From those people
Only eagerly awaiting
The next day's dawn!

Chapter 25

It took a long story to make Orenda rise. It sure took all five heroes, and many others.

You might wonder if it was up to this point told by me. You might be mostly right. I am the hero who is the best at words.

As Orenda grew from a dream, to a plot, to a dance, to a grand battle and its aftermath, to a place we will now settle, I have learned and translated many languages and ways to help make it all happen, with countless nations, many lives and much blood – though mercifully much less than might have been the case - and half a continent at stake. It often took my words, back and forth.

Only then did I become a story teller. Not just the stories, but the right ways to tell them and the ways behind them. If you really want to tell a story, don't let anyone tell you how. Just tell it. And tell it right through to the end.

So, now I think I am ready to tell the rest of the founding story right to the end.

Anyway, it's a long winter's day, just wanting a good end to a good story.

* * *

In August 1691, the largest indoor meeting place in New York was within one of its tallest buildings. The Dutch built Stadt Huys that served as the New York city hall was a well-proportioned stepped and gabled five story building in cream-colored brick. Its long axis ran along the shore of the lower East River. There was a walled circular garden in front within which seven field cannons lurked, "enough to keep the drunks away," an early Dutch Governor had said about one of his main problems. The building rose from a strong 120' by 50' stone foundation designed to cellar the beer, wine and Dutch gin which supplied its original purpose as an entertainment place taking the pressure for that purpose off of the former Dutch Governor's own house.

The building's pleasing rows of windows admitted shafts of changing sunlight on this late summer day in 1691, the second day following the Orendan naval victory at New York, as clouds in the post-front sky rapidly passed over.

The main room was presently filled to capacity with an audience of nearly three hundred New Yorkers. They exchanged fearful thoughts on the purpose of the meeting. The first anxious chatter inevitably grew to a steady roar.

Half of these were important people – wealthy merchants, the senior clerics from the three main Dutch, Presbyterian and Anglican congregations of the town, a few elected local town councilmen and appointed officials, some Huguenot and English from Brooklyn and the Long Island, two of the prospering Sephardic Jews, some otherwise wealthy land owners from the small villages and towns north of New York to Fort Orange, several of the Colony's ruling Council, three senior English naval personnel and other key officials serving the whole New York colony. All of these seemed in varying degrees bewildered or flushed with outrage.

The rest were mostly lower status Dutch citizens, artisans and others, but included five black men representing the few hundred slaves and one of the half dozen African freedmen in the town.

All of the three hundred however, had been named as "influentials" among their kind or in their part of New York by others in a quick canvas of the town arranged by Smith.

Among this noisy lower class mostly Dutch part of the crowd, were several of Smith's people, more foul mouthed and foul breathed than the others, including Van Pammister himself, dressed as the buxom grand dame of a group of surrounding ladies of the night, to provide a disguised back-up security in the crowd and all serving as a claque, ready to do their part to add support to the Orendan direction of events that would soon unfold.

Surrounding the audience along the edges of the room and controlling security at its front door, was a line of fifty stern looking warriors from several nations, most never seen in New York itself before, each warrior holding a loaded musket. Many of the seated three hundred stole glances at this menacing guard.

In the middle of the platform at the end of the room there stood in deep talk Water Bear, Magic Walk, Copper Star and a few close advisors. They were dressed in their full Ojibwa ceremonial clothes.

Magic Walk looked about. She was the main organizer of the event. She now knew English from Smith and, though she did not know the language of the Flemish Dutchers, she liked the sounds of the language they spoke and the few Walloons present spoke close to the French. She could already make out the meaning of some of what she heard from the excited talk of the fearful and excited crowd.

On the left side of the stage was sitting, arms tightly folded and staring straight ahead, Henry Sloughter, the sickly new Governor of New York, trying to look very angry, and at his side, Jacob Leisler, leader of the late rebellion prior to Sloughter's arrival against the New York establishment during the interregnum between James II and William and Mary.

Leisler had been awaiting the foulest death as a traitor. He sat on the Stadt Huys stage within less than an hour of his release from his prison cell in Fort James. Leisler was almost unrecognizable to the crowd because of the unruly growth of his mustaches and once pointed beard, though there was shout from his lower class supporters when he faced the audience to make himself known to them by pinching his beard to show the tight triangle it once was.

On the other side of the stage were six empty chairs.

The growing noise in the great room was interrupted by a loud booming at the front door.

As the booming continued, the room fell quiet.

The door was flung open.

Six great chiefs entered, led by Many Axes, dressed only in moccasins and a summer breach clout and wearing his two head feathers. Three axes hung ominously from his belt. He was followed by a chief from the Iroquois, Ojibwa, Pottawatomi, Illini, and the Abenaki, each wearing their full ceremonial feathered headdresses. The contrast between Many Axes and the other chiefs had the desired unsettling effect on the crowd, which quickly parted in the aisles to let the chiefs' advance to the stage, where they took the empty chairs.

Many Axes was the last to be seated and, as it had been arranged, bid Water Bear to begin. He now spoke in a tolerably good English Smith had helped him with.

Water Bear said, "This is a fine town hall of a busy town, just enough room as it turns out to seat all you influential New Yorkers at all levels to understand and then embrace your fate, and pass that news to the rest."

Water Bear said this, recognizing by a slight bow toward each of the higher and lower status groups in the room.

There was a ripple of grumbling and even a few shouts of derision, until the surrounding braves raised their guns and Many Axes arose. He took out one of his three axes and hurled it through the nearest window which smashed loudly and rained shards over some in the audience, drawing blood from one or two.

After a few shrieks and frightened sounds, the audience was again silent. Many Axes stared the crowd down and resumed his seat.

Water Bear continued.

"Thank you, Many Axes, for reminding us it is Heno's test this day for those new Yorkers seated here: they should listen most carefully. Before any more foolishness, let me briefly explain what has happened to you, and what will be happening to you. It is as simple as this: our combined forces have easily triumphed over New York on land and at sea. You are surrounded, disarmed and overwhelmed by the forces of the Orendan alliance. We are an alliance consisting of the Nations in all the surrounding woodland countries that you have not yet had time to destroy, in your carelessness about our nations."

"Why?" or "Who are you?" These questions came from here and there in the audience, until Water Bear raised his hand.

"Let me answer the "Who are we?" first," said Water Bear.

"We are the Nations around the Great Lakes north and west of you, and even some of your allies to the east of you whom you found here when your peoples arrived. We are many angry tribes – he pointed to just those represented in the room, either by the platform party or the warriors standing along the walls. In all, he named thirteen nations." At each name at least one warrior raised his musket.

"We are also some Europeans who have in varying degrees mixed our lives with these native peoples enough to see that a new order among the old and the new Nations is needed here."

"Nonsense," and "Why?" were again shouted from the crowd.

Water Bear again raised his hand. Many Axes prepared to rise. There was immediate silence.

"'Why' is a good question. The answer is that we conquerors wish no more, or no less that you accompany us to the middle of this vast continent where you will be expected to resume your own ways, surrounded by we First Nation guardians, in a new settlement along the Great River leading to the southern Sea. Instead of you forcing us to change to your ways, we will force you to change with us, as we may choose to change, and then we will both become stronger, together."

The audience was already divided. Most had feared a fate much worse. Now many, mostly the poorer folk responded with a slowly understanding "Oh." The better folk still shouted such things as "Can you possibly mean this? Do you want us to be savages like you! We will lose our enlightenment, our goods!" Some of the fine women clutched their husbands. Some of their fine husbands clutched back.

Many Axes stood up.

Again, there was immediate silence.

Water Bear continued.

"That trek will take over two months in winter. Not all of you will survive. But, you will learn to live a life of survival through a winter among your native captors. They, and you, will welcome the next spring."

The prospect actually intrigued some of the room. Not the wealthy and powerful, some of whom spat at Water Bear's words.

"The purpose in this, is for you to learn to mix respectfully with the people who were here long before you who live in a more easy way."

There were again mutters in the crowd, most still angry, but some now more appreciative.

"The leader in all of this, both here, along the way and then there, is the great Chief of War and great Chief of Peace of the Middle Iroquois, Many Axes. " He bowed towards Many Axes.

Many Axes remained motionless. Not a sound arose in the room.

Then someone shouted,

"If you have defeated us, why can't we go to Boston, or the other colonies? Or why not just let us go home," he looked around, "to England?"

Water Bear answered smoothly, "Well, certainly not to Boston. It is in disarray itself and does not love New Yorkers. Why give them more reason to hate our kind. But we will provide you a choice. Some may foolishly want to return on that one remaining broken ship out there and the few other smaller merchantmen at the wharves here back to England, assuming they will accommodate even a small part of your population. They will be accompanied half way by some of our ships, to ensure you do not try to return to these shores."

He looked sternly at his audience.

"Those few surviving would return as a defeated people, to live again in your homelands as free as you may be there. But the greater part of you, even if you wished to return there, cannot fit into those overcrowded sick-making ships in defeat and scorn that will return to the old shores. Better by far the fate of those in the majority who will choose and be given a new life along the great Michissippi."

There was again silence in the room. It was then broken by a shouting question in Dutch, "Will there be whores permitted there?" It was Van Pammister, in a question asked flouncingly and deliberately planned beforehand to relieve the tension.

Laughter rippled throughout the crowd, almost stilling those repulsed by his question. It had the intended effect – an earthy reassurance that normal life in the former colony might be possible in the new place.

"Well perhaps, madam. You see: it is the entire life of this ended town of yours we will permit you to reproduce there. After that, who knows what might happen? But our people know it will be better than what has been happening, because they will be controlling the influence of your colony on us, not you controlling us."

Along with sounds of dissent, now there were some interested looks and even a few sighs of acceptance in the room.

"But, one change will be that you will have no firearms or weapons of any sort. All weaponry and defences will be entrusted to us native peoples guarding you. The main armouries will be far away from our new town. But, you will all also have two large projects."

"What? What is that?" Many in the crowd now seemed genuinely interested and curious.

"It will be a good challenge for you. A great one: The first is to learn the great river you will live along and the countries and peoples beside it. You will need to help us make shallow draught ships that go up and down to and from its mouth; to open a trade to and from its delta to all the many seas; to make a part Europe on this side of the Ocean, but only on the terms you can work out with us protecting native peoples. We will decide what we can then best take from your way.

Some whistles of wonder were heard in the crowd.

"The second project is to make a great story, together - you and the surrounding first Nations."

There began questions about that, but then, a man, a great merchant man, and member of the appointed New York colonial Council, Nicholas Bayard was caught sneaking out a side door.

"Bring that man here," shouted Many Axes in the English he had learned in the past twenty years of war and peace, leaping up from his chair.

The struggling man was brought to the stage.

"What were you doing, sir?" demanded Many Axes brushing even Water Bear aside and Magic Walk's attempt to translate

The man spoke easily. He was in a cold fury,

"I was ridding myself of this wild scheme of yours. Nothing can save such an act of the Devil." He looked down at the Dutch clerics and his looks were returned with fearful ones.

Many Axes put a hand to a second of his axes.

"Let me give you a chance in this. Answer me: what do your warriors marching into war, know?

"They serve their King," the man instantly replied.

"But what is the coup – do they know what the King wants, or why he wants it?

"Of course not. We do not try to know how the King thinks. We – the warriors as you call them - only know that the King, who only answers to God Almighty, gives direction and we follow, whether the English or the Dutch, through our Governors or our letters patent companies or other means that are granted by the King. "

"So you warriors know nothing, except the commands of the King?"

"Not one thing!"

"That seems to me an empty warrior, not capable of coups and counter-coups."

"I have no idea what you mean by 'coos' or whatever you say. Except that it is devilish traitorous nonsense!"

"Well then, we have given you a chance to speak your case and by your own words and by the law of your own lands, and ours too, since you are guilty of treason against this new country being created, you will pay for your grievous offence through the only remedy that treason everywhere warrants, but in this case will be mercifully short."

Bayard made a whimper as Many Axes took and raised his heaviest axe and split the shorter man's head vertically in two, down almost to his neck.

Amid the screams that followed this horrendous act, Many Axes finally shouted down the audience into a new silence.

"So, do you deny your laws? Your laws would have me bring this man back to be skinned alive and then drawn and quartered as he dies in far greater horror than my one axe stroke gave him. We are merciful compared to your law for a traitor."

A few seemed to agree.

"But, let this man's split-in-half head tell you twice over: There is no escaping your fate. Here, in this great room; or on the treks inland the first beginning even tomorrow; or there when you reach it that new town you will help us make along the Michissippi, if you feeble folk can get there. It all must be done. Let no more of that Dutcher or English stubbornness see my axe! There is no escaping your Orendan fate!

Many Axes took out his last axe – at which move many near the front fell strongly back – and buried it deeply in the wooden floor.

"Let this be where the last axe falls. Not on any other man's head, if you but follow the much better fate we have given you."

"He is the leader?" someone weakly cried out.

"Yes – now all of you see that it is so?" replied Water Bear, sweeping his arm toward Many Axes.

Another silence followed.

Finally Many Axes again arose.

"Oh, I am the leader of this, though reluctantly. It comes from the dream of this Water Bear who warned us just in time. You should all know this. Let Water Bear tell you the dream and how it is coming to life among all of us. Before that, though, let this mess be cleaned up. Copper Star: ensure that we bury the man: let his last angry nonsense rest with him forever in that cemetery at the Dutchers' church."

Even as the body of Bayard was being removed, Water Bear began to recount the dream that was now commanding everyone.

As he concluded with the friendly fish, he looked all the first rows in their eyes: "You see, from Many Axes' buried axe on the floor, we want the best of you, not the worst, just as we want the best of us, not the worst. Your people will continue, whatever our fate. So too, will ours. If there is to be a mixed people's fate, we will require that of you, not just our people. If there can be a mixed people, we will take you as us, in leading that new way!"

There were murmurs in the crowd. Water Bear sensed that some of them were seeking more understanding. He nodded to Many Axes.

Many Axes again spoke.

"This Leisler, here, has been one of your own leaders. He seeks a change, but he didn't know what change and descended into errors. If he chooses, he shall again be helpful to you."

Many Axes sat down, and Water Bear resumed.

"I will deal with some questions among you. What questions do you have, Leisler, so that we may start to answer them here and now?

Leisler was slow to rise to his feet. Looking around carefully at the crowd, not knowing how they would react because of his futile rebellion. He said carefully,

"Let you first be clearer, pray sir, on the matter of who goes which way on the morrow: who shall return by ships and who shall be marched inland?"

Water Bear answered, "I think there will only be one small line to the broken ships hopelessly leaving for England. All others will be helped to prepare for the trek to their new life inland.

Many now nodded.

"But let there be no doubt about one thing. The eventual inland line must be a full mix of you, for we value all. It cannot just be those who do work for others. It must include the best builders, the best traders and the best dreamers, including Leisler here, and your religious leaders, as well. If necessary, we will have to cut out those from the lines of the foolish cowards who would flee to those broken ships, if, as I doubt, there will be too many.

"I see." replied Leisler.

The crowd was quiet.

"If it is to make us continue a European life, how shall our tools and heavy goods needed for that be transported and their commercial ties and arrangements be secured; what of the law itself, sir?"

"Ah. Those are very good questions. All the goods that make things: well, they will be moved by our ships to the mouth of the great Michissippi River. The trade of things will depend, in part on the means you shall help devise to bring all useful things into and out of the new Orendan settlement"

"But will there be a framework of laws?

"The laws will be a good mix of yours and ours. It shall be based as much as possible, on a council each year of yours; a council each year of ours; and, a council of both of ours and yours of which this, let it be announced to all, is the first. That mixed council shall be known as the Manhattanate, its first meeting here is this very meeting, renamed for the Manhattan village of the Lenape it was."

"May we have our city land registry, our libraries," said an official. "Our churches?" said two clerics at once.

"Those too are good questions. Fear not your property rights, your books or your religions – let them only try to challenge the vision of Water Bear. We think they will soon share his vision too. And perhaps adopt some of our way as we shall no doubt adopt some of your way"

Many Axes rose again and looked pointedly at Leisler. "About the laws: the courts will have to be worked out, but courts there will be in both our eyes. As to the other things, I'll say now: why not? Is that all? Does your silence say we have concluded this meeting?"

Leisler replied, "That would be too soon, Many Axes. It may well be we can do these things, if you, in turn, vow, to give us your own more welcoming thoughts, we may be able to make a good life under our God too amongst your peoples, even if far away from our own peoples, if that is what we must do."

"Well said! All who adopt that attitude will have seen the last axe fall."

Many Axes looked out at the crowd and then turned to Water Bear

"And you, Water Bear?"

Water Bear added, looking out also to the crowd,

"How well you do in that new town, all of you, is very much and will always be on our mind. A success in this humane experiment will make us all stronger; the price of failure will be terrible. The snakes will remain in all our stomachs!"

He paused for effect, and continued, looking again at each group represented in the room, and unable to hide a smile,

"And, doubly blessed be all of you, for you will be sharing that great new town with a nearly equal number of captured Roman Catholics from New France, with their own church, language and customs also guaranteed."

A huge commotion ensued, until Many Axes arose, smiling this time and all became quiet again.

"Exactly, you grasp your greatest challenge exactly since they too are a part of your fate at that new place: you must and will share your "industrious" fate with the papists!" said Many Axes in clear enough English for there to be more cries of "Oh" and Oh no." He laughed loudly at the again clamorous audience.

And then a new shout rang out, "Let us abandon our fears and make of it a grand new city!" cried out Van Pammister and his claque. "God will be with us!"

Enough others gave cheers of support joined the chorus that Many Axes, Water Bear and Magic Walk looked at each other, heartened.

It surprised Water Bear that the horrible execution of the Dutch objector now seemed so much in the past. Magic Walk sensed his thoughts. She approached him and whispered the truth of what Many Axes had done, "Husband, you have done well with your steady voice. Many Axes with his one mighty blow, has reduced to a trickle what might have been rivers of blood before this Plot is done."

As the latest uproar died down, Smith emerged from the back of the room and strode to the platform, amid boos and calls of "traitor," especially from the front benches.

He mounted the platform and addressed the room with a voice even louder than they, surprising the audience with his force.

"Welcome to Manhattan. Know you that I am indeed your traitor – not Leisler here, the honest and responsive man who tried to find a way for you through the stupid interregnum and whom you fine gentlefolk were vilely set upon a course of murdering as a traitor, and, as a traitor, would have drawn and quartered the man beyond pain we can imagine whilst still alive. Let me tell you why I am your traitor. Then, discover your fear of what is next here, and prepare yourselves and your families for life or death!

He eyed Many Axes, who nodded, and thrust an arm forward, and the room became silent.

"Let me make to you all, five points, as if I nail them to that large outer door."

His listeners whispered, thinking of Martin Luther.

"Point One: You have been denied in this colony even the freedom of your own constitution - the Dutch, by conquest; the English by the Duke Proprietor's abuse, then that King's abuse, and now the new King's likely abuse of the very English liberties you are entitled to enjoy. The French have no liberties at all, that I can see, except what they boldly take in the wilderness – a lesson for all you!"

There were some murmurs of agreement through the crowd.

"Point Two: You are all so busy with your lives, you have missed the less imperfect state of the native folk around you, who would seek, and even now give greater freedom in their towns and villages to the many who seek this place from corrupt Europe."

"Point Three: You are, as we have told you, utterly crushed in military and naval defeat, by a clever plot executed almost perfectly by these surrounding people, who would now take you into their midst so that you, and they, may try to find your combined excellences with them, a most civilized offer by these victors over you.".

"Point Four: The freedoms you will have will keep you very busy. They will include the freedom of your religions, and the freedom to pursue English and Dutch commerce and craft of all kinds, but also the responsibility to share those excellences with the surrounding peoples, whom you will learn to live and share yourselves with."

"Finally, Point Five: I will give you the plans for your Orendan treks inland. There will be three, with as many as 5,000 each, men, women and children. The first will move out tomorrow, via Montreal. The last two, in the next week will move straight west. In all of this you will not lose the claim you have to property here. Stonemark, step forward and explain."

The crowd were startled as the third guard in the line along the right hand side of the room stepped forward. Stonemark was the only one of the fifty who could speak passable English and Dutch, and who understood exactly what he was to say. He had been selected for this by Magic Walk, as part of her arrangement of the events of the day, who sensed this would make one of the biggest impressions of the afternoon among the crowd.

Stonemark said, "All the documents and maps pertaining to the existing right to a property in the entire Manhattan Island, and surrounding shores to the east, but not including the New Englander settlements further east on the Long Island, whom we have decided not to include in this hostaging inland, have been gathered up and will be stored and organized as records of claim against those of your fellows who will come across the great sea and attempt later to claim your rights. This action here, and again in New France, will, we hope, discourage further opportunistic colonizing by your cousins in New England, in the other colonies or across the sea, for a goodly time, Three of your leaders, not including Leisler, will be selected to vouchsafe the documents we amass on your behalf are the only true documents we have taken from New York for the areas concerned and are stored in the new location as we gathered them here. As for personal property within those lands or otherwise, this will be carefully recorded and stored to be fairly redistributed per present holdings in the new town to which you are all headed."

Stonemark stepped back.

Smith resumed, noting the surprise and at least initial acceptance of this arrangement rippling about the room, again especially along its front benches.

"Return here, all three hundred of you, for your instructions on the morrow as to who will first depart, so that you may safely inform all the rest. Let those of you here who refuse, fill up the broken and doomed ships going back to Europe, and we will find replacements going inland. The first snow is near inland and the abandonment of New York will be rapid. The New Englanders will be given no chance to reverse this new thing God has favoured you with."

"Good day," Smith concluded.

Smith stepped away from the front of the platform, and let some remaining sputtering against him die away. The stage emptied of the Orendan leaders, and the armed braves then moved the crowd out of the hall.

The next morning, thousands of New Yorkers came together, from all manner of life and in all manner of dress though the warmest they could find, clutching belongings they hoped they might carry inland, the strangest of which were a portrait of the last Governor and included the equipment for an entire hair dressing and barber salon. They were the large majority who wisely decided not to attempt the return to Europe. They converged on the 'Bowling Green' north of Fort James where the cannons had already disappeared. All these people and families were surprisingly ready, with what small possessions, trade tools and record making appurtenances they could carry, to begin the trek inland to their new Orendan fate. All the rest of the essential stuff from New York was now being stripped from the city and would be shipped to the mouth of the Michissippi on Smith's ships.

Chapter 26

Two weeks after New York had fallen to the Orendan forces, the settlements of New France suffered the same fate. Less military action was necessary for Many Axes' forces to do this after the Battle of Cohoes Falls had so disastrously depleted the forces in New France as well as in New York.

Many Axes had marched into Montreal and then Quebec, largely unopposed. He left the first trek of 1500 New Yorkers on the south banks of the river. The residents of the New France towns, were by late September, 1691, either facing being forced to march inland at the beginning of winter or being bundled into what everyone knew would be badly overcrowded ships at the wrong time of year that would sail back to France with poor chances for those on board surviving.

Many Axes and Smith and their aides had worked hard together to further the overall Orendan logistical plan to move captured heavy goods from New York and eventually Quebec by sea on Smith's ships and any other ships he could muster and pay for with the colonial booty, from the Caribbean. The ships with the heaviest goods and larger gunnery would have to go to the mouth of the Michissippi and the goods would have to be stored there until some means could move them further north or an Orendan settlement could be made at that tricky place, already flanked by a small settlement started by the d'Ibervilles's brother. Smith had already tested the New England colonies to determine their ability to intercept him at sea. They could not now do so alone, and d'Iberville's fleet had disappeared, possibly, some said, back to France.

Goods of smaller bulk or weight, including most of the captured musketry, would be moved by sea around the New England settlements, to Quebec, and on to Montreal and from thence, by large freight canoes which would move the goods with the people on the first trek to Niagara, via Lake Ontario, or up the River of the Odawa and across to the waters of the northern lakes, then down to the Michissippi and from thence down to the new Orendan settlement.

The future city there had been named St Lis, by the mistaken omission on a rough map of the "o" and "u" from the St. Louis name which had been proposed for the place by the French explorers through the area. The error was sent on a more refined map bound for Europe that Many Axes approved, knowing full well of the implication of the wrong spelling and chuckling as he gave the approval to the map.

In the month during which New York was emptied, the colonists of New France were made to face the same options as the New Yorkers: join the great treks inland, or take over-crowded ships back across the Atlantic. The hostaged people from the colonies could move with their lighter goods through the winter, a movement of the hostaged peoples that was deliberately expected by the Orendan leadership to test and firm the will of everyone – trekkers and native escorts alike – on the idea for the new Orendan settlement along the Michissippi.

As the last day ended when the ordinary citizens of New France had to make their choice, Laliber had to confront his once friend, the sub-Intendant, Emil de Merleau, on the mountain overlooking Montreal.

He looked down at the town and saw puffs of smoke, either signifying the remaining few pockets of resistance to the Orendan forces or where material was being torched to prevent it from falling into the hands of any re-colonizing Europeans who might return up the River of Canada.

The settlement of the praying Indians, the converted Christian Iroquois across the river at Montreal remained untouched, because the Orendan leaders, aware of Laliber's own uncertainty, were not sure what its fate should be. Its small population feared for their lives, despite learning that Laliber, Dancing

Pipes and even Many Axes had insisted they be spared the treks to St Lis or take them, as they decided among themselves.

Many Axes and several of his allied Chiefs, Laliber, and Water Bear's deputy, Copper Star stood together on the mountain above Montreal speaking of the situation. They had decided that Laliber would have to persuade de Merleau, the sub-Intendant, to take the true reports of the successful Orendan plot back to France, just as Smith had arranged for the same reports to be sent back to England.

The group turned silently when they were approached by a small party escorting the last officials of New France, led by de Merleau. Most had a defeated and fearful expression, but de Merleau in his first words showed that he was still embittered and bold enough to be defiant and sarcastic.

"So this is how you choose to serve God, Laliber, in league with these devils who are no doubt contemplating which of us they would eat first. Would you yourself partake of a rib first, or a leg?"

"I would not talk of such things Emil, or they might come to pass. One talking as you in New York had his head split down to his back bone."

"That would split us here in New France no more than you have done already."

"Emil, you must try to see the larger purpose in what is taking place."

"I can see only one purpose, a cursed and fallen priest, and that you are intent on working a great evil against all the forces of good that the French have brought to this wild country."

"You make of it a French thing. Yet, it is the dream of an Odawa, far out there in the wilderness. I think you would be better to reverse the order of good and evil in this land."

De Merleau squirmed in his tethers. "Such shit," he grunted.

"Listen to good sense, Emil." Laliber looked firmly at de Merleau.

"We are indeed delicately balanced on the scale of good and evil. The events of this day, too, may tip the scale either way. You must choose your words carefully. Listen well, to the proposition that we will make to you. For it will be largely on your shoulder that the fate of New France will fall."

"Nonsense, you cannot put the burden of this temporary uprising on me."

Many Axes intervened. "It is more than a temporary uprising, sir!"

"Yes," said Laliber. "The events of recent weeks have made clear two very significant changes have taken place in this New World. Firstly, that a determination has been made by many of the woodland Nations to take upon themselves the powers of the European colonists. They will do, in the interests of their long term survival, whatever is necessary to achieve this Orendan purpose even as it changes their own customary behaviour in many things. In this, they follow the dream of Water Bear."

De Merleau began to protest, but Laliber impatiently spoke over his protest.

"Mark me: it is now disclosed that the great plan of Orenda has been successful at every stage as predicted in the dream and that following the plan creates an opportunity to come on their own path to an ordered existence of their own, with or without us. That path of their own is always necessary for a truly Christian state to prevail. Emil, hear me, what happens here does not exclude the Christian faith."

"More nonsense!"

"Well, you must surely know that New York was taken and is temporarily occupied by Water Bear himself and other chiefs. Smith determined that d'Iberville's ships laid off from the New York and Smith's devious fleet surprised and fired, sunk or captured the English naval forces at Graves End. The entire European colony there, as well as the smaller one here in New France, is now delivered to us and is experiencing the wisdom and initial decisions of the new Great Council of Orenda - what we have called the Manhattanate – which had its first meeting in the colony there, renamed Manhattan."

De Merleau answered this instantly. "All these things I do not accept. You are all caught in a frenzied foolishness to think these things can last. I will never accept it. They are but a temporary success. All who have participated in them shall live to rue their treacheries and deceptions by which these temporary reverses to God's purpose and to the King's purpose have come about. Your mess of allies will more likely set upon their poor hostages and then upon each other than create anything useful here. It is evil at work here I say, and it will not have the ultimate triumph!"

"Spoken boldly, Emil," Laliber replied, equally quickly.

Many Axes had heard enough of this to take up an axe.

Laliber stayed him. "No, please be still, Many Axes, this parlay has not finished."

Laliber turned again to Emil.

"But come now, it is to the more immediate disposition of the Quebec colony to which we must address ourselves. How see you the fall of New France itself? Must this continue to be a bloody battle to the last resisting man and woman and child, and, I cannot guarantee, the last fingernail in a stew; or shall it be an intelligent recognition by the authorities in Quebec that vastly superior forces surround them and that they must finally accept some terms?"

De Merleau shrugged. "I cannot speak for Quebec, from which I was temporarily away from here in Montreal when this nonsense occurred. That would be for Governor Frontenac. I have no doubt that all in Quebec must find the turn of events as loathsome as I and that it is their duty to God to resist such pernicious forces for as long as is possible. There are no terms from the Devil that will tempt us."

"But, Emil, Frontenac when he was captured at Cohoes Falls, asked simply to be able to execute the Intendant and then to take his own life. That has been done."

"Oh no – how can I accept this news? God help us!" De Merleau crossed himself and knelt.

"You speak to me of the Devil, Acting Intendant, indeed, Acting Governor - for indeed this is the position now thrust upon you de Merleau - as if the Devil is exclusively at work on one side of this struggle. I say: do not keep up this one-sided harangue. The Devil has been working too long unchallenged on all sides in this new World. "

Laliber looked at Many Axes, who strongly affirmed the statement.

Many Axes now added, in broken French "That Devil of yours has kept my villages playing children's games. You shall all pay for that. How can you expect not to pay for such offensive games you foolishly had expected us to accept?"

De Merleau was silent for the first time. Then he looked directly at Laliber.

"Laliber, if I cooperate with you in any way this day you must promise me one thing: if ever a French doubt enters your mind, you will simply stop trying to influence events and let them take their course."

Laliber threw up his arms in frustration.

"You far overestimate my role."

De Merlot pondered for a moment.

"So, what is it then of which we must talk?"

Many Axes caught Laliber's eye and indicated the two should be alone for a moment and pointed to the path leading off in the direction of the cliff.

They took the path together and soon emerged at the cliff face at the mountain's heights. Before them, the wide plain of the great river of Canada spread. The mountains far to the south were being enveloped by huge white clouds. Many Axes had already told his captains those clouds were the symbols from the spirits: they were the sails of Orenda's bright future and the sails of the fleet that would soon ply the southern seas to protect the seminal Orenda midway along the Michissippi at the new settlement's main point of contact with the outer world at the mouth of the great river.

Many Axes was not now in a metaphorical mood. "I understand not this last talk with that man. We all know it is necessary to disorganize the European for a time, but that it will only be temporary unless something greater happens. We have learned that from the dream. We agree that we must create a new people here. Some mix of our people and the French, English and even Dutch. We want you to help Orenda at this moment with this Frenchman. But where are you headed with him? It seems you only talk in anger. Remind me of what we do here. "

Laliber considered this.

"I say again, strongly: let those who foolishly wish to return to France from here, be permitted to do so. Emil himself must be among those who should soon make that departure carrying our terms of a peace to his King and my private documents even to Rome explaining clearly the course we have set upon here. Believe me, this will help our cause. But this man de Merleau must be well and truly set upon the course we would put upon him. Have patience with me in making that so."

Many Axes said, "I will give you little more time: perhaps only a little more than it takes for that cloud to move across the lowering sun. Do what you can, but do so before the last sun shadow of the day crosses this mount, or I cannot guarantee the fate of either of you. The chances this man will even see France again, let alone proffer your documents without himself altering them we think are as little as the eagle carrying the bear to his nest.

Laliber again signaled patience, and they returned to where de Merleau was held.

Sensing one last possibility of influencing Laliber, de Merleau again spoke up.

"And what role is there, then, for you in all of this, Jesuit? Or, should I say former Jesuit? How can you possibly think there is a consistency of purpose in what you will be forced into to maintain some peace among the savages or the freshly warring colonists themselves, let alone some useful link with civilized Europe? What will your own presence add to the pursuit of such heretical ends, other than to fool them into an ultimate disaster? Or not fool them at all and end with you upon their fires?"

"My presence adds a great deal, as I continue to pray about it. First, I am a witness and a kind of sanction as a Frenchman. That is the first meaning of the dream: that it must be of two sides, not one. Secondly, God has only given to me, among the Europeans, excepting Smith in New York and lately, Kastler, the physician in Quebec, the knowledge and the will to see that an inner light as brilliant as our own burns among the woodland folk. It only for us true friends who sympathize with their existing soul to help kindle it further with our own virtues."

"I still doubt any such mix is possible," said Emil.

Laliber said, "I acknowledge that it will be as much a struggle within the savage himself as with our own efforts to help them stay within the bounds of balanced progress in this world, which the Jesuit in me always seeks. The new settlements must not lose their pure Native soul to the immediate needs of an ordered social life, nor fall back to a disordered existence destroying the best of the European soul. This an equal challenge to all those mixing in the new settlements."

Emil turned away, realizing a leap over rock face was his fate should he not agree to accept terms of a peace.

"Will you now agree to take our true terms to France and on to Rome as we ask "

"Yes. Alas, the bureaucrat in me sees that someone credible must inform His Majesty directly and truly of this horrible business, though I will be cursed for it".

Many Axes looked severely at Laliber. "Tell him how small is your own role, priest."

"Many Axes reminds me that, as part of your duty, you must assure the King and his Ministers that my own role is not the greater force in what makes this happen. There is a native force here now, which attends its own spirit and has made up its own mind upon which our God can smile' It is a Native dream being played out, one that this rigorous Jesuit firmly believes our Christ and even our Church will be a part of. This is far greater than my own personal influence. I act only to ensure the best part of both sides' emerges has a powerful presence in these countries. Nothing of Christian or for that matter French genius will be lost."

"Yes, I understand your desire for this. But surely you must realize the chances of them taking that interpretation from a blaspheming priest is unlikely. Your role cannot be denied. You interpreted the dream."

"All we say is do not make my role in this the thing His Majesty, or for that matter Rome most closely attends to and takes from it. Let them read the documents that will give the true emphasis."

De Merleau shrugged.

"Now let us turn to practical matters. We have given to you, the Acting Governor, the best ship returning to France. It will likely make its way back to France even in the worst conditions of this late season. You are to take, in these boxed writings, the truth of what has happened here first to the French Court. Your only course is to ensure these materials arrive unadulterated in any way. You will cheat God and history if you do otherwise. They must think that by their pure undisturbed state, you are a mere messenger: that you have not influenced these events, other than your own strong resistance to them, which the material faithfully reports."

De Merlot was beginning to indicate acceptance of such a role.

"If the French Court refuses this truth, then, on to Rome, though they must understand that we will then be forced to cut the French part out of the Orendan scheme, and our future trade. After Rome has had a chance to deliberate the profound message in these documents then the Pope must understand that, failing some acceptance of the Orendan fact, the Roman Catholic part that I sense from my prayers will then be cut out of the Orendan scheme. If the English, in their turn, deny what Smith sends to them, then they too must be given to understand that the English and the Protestant part will be cut out next, unless Smith and his forces would give them the whole continent on Orendan terms alone, possibly even without our God. As you see, much is at stake in how those capitals respond to the true news that you bear from the New World.

"But if all whites are cut out, then there will be no mixed people, Laliber."

"Possibly. But then Europe and the remaining colonies here will simply face the wrath of a united, more civilized and implacably hostile Native people time and again. Do you understand this, Emil?"

"Though I am stunned by it, I do see the direction of the news that you want me to deliver, whatever my own beliefs."

Laliber saw the change in Emil, and turned to Many Axes, who seemed relieved.

"Exactly, Emil. Here is the core packet about the new Orenda. Guard it with your life, though you may yourself doubt its truth."

Emil accepted the packet and was about to leave.

"But before you go, Emil, you must tell me of Antoinette."

"Why not. I have all but abandoned her to that damned Kastler who promises her he will find my lost Jacques. He fools only her – he must be very taken by her to make such a foolhardy promise. She gives me all the daughters to take back to a gentler France, but not herself. I don't understand her anymore. She seems little upset by these recent Orendan events that anguish everyone else in New France. Perhaps she has simply resigned herself to accept the fate of God has in store. She takes the view as have you that we have brought it on ourselves. I think perhaps in her case that may be partly true."

Emil teared up as he talked. "Perhaps she may see some good in it. I know how the two of you spoke when you were last at our Island. I cannot forgive her that she kept your confession from me. Had I but known, I'm sure I could have reasoned with you. It was then not yet a decision but a movement toward a decision."

"No, Emil. Do not delude yourself on this point. You must realize that it had become impossible for the two of us or the two of you to speak the whole truth to each other on many important matters. That was very much of your own doing in reacting so strongly to the grievous loss of your son, Jacques, to the Iroquois raiders. Tell me: is there any word at all?"

"Nothing at all of small Jacques have I heard. I am now myself resigned. He is either with God or forever lost to the savage ways."

"Nothing can be lost from God in those savage ways, Emil. Especially, that Orenda now gives those ways a new Godly direction."

"So Antoinette says. I wonder what might have passed between you two that night. I trust, given your vows you did not renew your old love," de Merleau said, shaking his head in bitterness.

Laliber looked at his erstwhile friend and spoke honestly.

"I cannot deny we held each other and struggled with a temptation that night, Emil."

"Oh mad God," cried out de Merleau, clutching his head, startling the others standing near the two men. "And me: not touching her since. Now there is yet another - that man Kastler for sure. Have I not been cursed enough?"

Laliber had to think quickly.

"I am sure she has striven to be chaste in your absence. Let it be. You must not lose heart - it is the run of all events here that God allows much of his purpose here by accident of contact. If you take the larger truth from here, I swear to you much of it is God's truth, though you bear more of the burden than most."

De Merleau, swallowing deep breathes, calmed himself.

"There are other letters in that packet you hold. To others who may try hard to understand."

"You no doubt refer to our circle from La Fleche. So says Antoinette, but it is beyond my own simple soul."

After a moment further in thought, he concluded, "What I can do, now that all else meaningful to me seems lost, is force myself to deliver your difficult news, purely, to all of Europe, though heaven knows what horrors I will face in delivering this news to France, Rome and England, as is your wish, Father Paul. Lord knows, it is likely the last time I can call you that."

Knowing they could not give it more thought together, the two withdrew from the cliff and returned to Many Axes and the other Chiefs to make the final preparations as the day ended.

The next day, Emil and his miserable company departed Montreal, for Quebec. A day after that, a cannon boomed on the heights as the last ship left Quebec for France and gained the main river. In the woods beyond the French settlement, a solitary beaver was startled, slapped his tail and slipped beneath the water. He made his way through the water to his winter home under the great wooden lodge he had built for his family.

Chapter 27

T hree months later, a pale winter dawn brought a change in the wind in the lower great lakes.

The erratic gusts through the night that had chased away the previous day's blizzard had become a steady blast of icy arctic air from the north-west.

Along the north central shore of Lake Ontario, it was as if the elements were seeking a final solution to the human misery stretched out over half a league upon the snowy landscape beneath them. As if it was trying to freeze and to deny any new physical or mental energies among the trek's dwindling once four thousand souls.

It was the twenty-first day of the delayed first of the three great treks inland from the European colonies that had fallen to Orendan forces in the late summer of 1691 in the monstrous plot against New York and New France.

The late winter into 1692 had been unforgiving. It had already taken a terrible toll on this trek. Hundreds had died. And, while a forced movement of peoples is common enough in human history, there had been nothing quite like this movement.

The thousands of hostaged European colonists being moved inland to the middle of the continent was no simple displacement or destruction of a conquered people: in this case, the overall vision, not just the convenience of the conquerors, depended upon the spirited survival of the conquered.

At least there was a sun this particular morning in early March. It was the first sun in over a week. But few had emerged from what protection they had managed to fashion against the previous day's storm. The cold now cut deeper than ever, and the winter sun, though it dazzled the woodlands, was too weak to moderate it. Few of the early morning fires along the long line of hostages were large enough to give much warmth.

The line was now stretched thinly between several large fires. Most remained huddled under overhanging stream banks or in hastily made lean-to's, too hungry, too weary or too numbed in the bitter cold to care anymore that only their continued movement with whatever fire wood and provisions they were given by their captors or they could forge for themselves could save them in such conditions.

This trek had merged nearly three thousand from Quebec and Montreal with fifteen hundred from New York, leaving very few back in the French colony, scattered in smaller places beyond their now emptied main towns.

The European colonists on this last trek were currently escorted by a group mainly made up of 300 well-armed Mohawk and Seneca forces, until the trek would reach Toronto, "Where the Trees Stood in the Water", and then Niagara Falls. The guardian tribe taking over in Toronto would be mainly the Seneca, more populous than the Mohawk now were, though the fearsome reputation of the Mohawk among the European colonies made their role in these treks more important than their more numerous and equally warlike western brothers.

Of the thousands of colonists who had survived the Orendan war, many preferred the hostaging inland to the prospect of a sea voyage back to Europe. Their likely death at sea in what many correctly, as it turned out, anticipated would be ill-fated voyages of those colonists jamming the mostly poor ships available returning to Europe, where they would once again be impoverished and crushed under the boot of their betters. It was not an option preferred by most over the hostaging option. Even some of the merchants had been won over to the possibility of regaining their wealth with the prospects of new trade along the Michissippi to the southern Gulf.

Many Axes had argued from the beginning for the winter endurance test forced upon the palefaces. It would ensure the hardiest, most spirited group and possibly the luckiest – even better he said - would survive. Those he said, would be the most able to make a life in the Orendan settlement and would be all the more willing to do so, given the severe hardship of the trek, compared to which, survival inland in the Orendan settlement would seem a desirable fate.

The sun had now fully risen. Despite the intense cold, there was an improved spirit among the Mohawk and especially the Seneca guardians, many of whom were considering themselves settling as the first Orendans, to differentiate themselves from any of their brothers in their own or other tribes who doubted Heno's Plot. They not only welcomed the brilliant sunshine; they knew they would today reach their first destination where they anticipated many warm fires, a large new supply of stored food, good ice fishing and a successful winter hunt in this flat country to replenish the food supply. Many Axes had ordered it all to happen before and they believed in him on this last trek.

But such was the desperate plight of the trekkers, few perceived this lightening of attitude among their captors. There was an equal stirring only among a few of the hardier souls here and there along the lines of the colonial trekkers.

Two such hardy souls were now moving with an advance group of Mohawk within a few leagues of a few advance Orendan mixed settlements already set up temporarily at Toronto. The pair trudged along on makeshift snow-shoes through a ravine protected from the strong winds that cut in from the Lake Ontario shoreline.

The taller of the two men was Daniel McCardle, red-haired son of the first Irish Roman Catholic family in the St. Lawrence valley, arrived in Quebec twenty years before. He had survived Cohoes Falls only by being spared by a native chief in his almost successful furtive attempt to retreat the futile front lines. The second was Louis Jolie, also middle age, a thick-set French Protestant Huguenot, whose family had found its way to Massachusetts Bay and then New York after the persecution and expulsion of those Protestant peoples from France in 1685. Jolie too was given a chance to heal his wounds on the battle field by his native captors. The pain of his healing shoulder made him think he had earned a better future.

The two men were from as different backgrounds as an Illini and a Nipissing. But, they now shared a common fate. In fact, their different personalities much more than their differing ethnic, national or religious backgrounds made them care strongly in their agreements and differences on many matters. McCardle's continued speculation at God's reasons for the Orendan defeat of the colonies particularly irritated Jolie, whose experiences in life had stripped him of all religious belief.

They were talking of this now as they struggled to gain higher ground and a view back over the other advance encampments being broken all the way back along the ravine valley to the lakeshore.

Jolie looked around and shouted into the strong wind.

"What say, McCardle?" he shouted in French they both understood. "Do you hear the rumours that it is no more than today's travel to the place they call 'Toronto?' Does that physician share any news with you?"

"Kastler gives us good leadership, but has no news for me".

"I know we are a mix too, but how can a man of that German name be a leader of any French?"

"Oh, he is Alsatian. It is all mixed German and French there. He speaks several languages, like us. I heard that he has the ear of some very important people in France. He supplies the King himself with exotic plants and flowers from these countries and studies everything, even this Orendan plot, like a science."

"Well, that makes me think of Leisler, our own leader, up ahead there now again with his sharp moustached Dutcher goatee, also German born, though Dutcher seeming. He was, before all this, a New York man wealthy from land transactions who, then as Captain of the Militias, led us through the time between King James to William and Mary. And yet, when the new Governor Sloughter arrived Leisler was destined to a traitor's death. He told me what his fate would be as a traitor. I will never forget his words. He, and his son in law, Jacob Millburn, who is also with us on this trek, would be hanged by the neck and being still alive their bodies would be cut down to the earth and their bowels taken out and then, they being still alive, those bowels would be burnt before their faces; and finally, their heads struck off and their bodies drawn into four parts and buried in four different places.

"Yech! Such drawing and quartering must be the Devil's own work, since it does not seem to lessen the number of traitors. "

They were silent for a time.

McCardle said, "I can only say this trek in the fiendish cold must end soon, or they will have few hostages left to be hostaged wherever we are ultimately headed. Whatever befalls us in the new settlements, God cannot smite us more fearsomely than He has in the last half year."

Jolie replied, "You yourself have said that God is all-powerful. I have heard it in your prayers these many weeks. He could surely correct this tragedy if He wished. But, if my humble experience is a guide, God has an infinite pail of woes to pour upon us."

As Jolie said this, both men reached the heights above the ravine. McCardle, resisting this latest temptation to argue God's purpose with Jolie, looked back along the struggling line of captives.

"I cannot deny we make up a hapless lot at this stage, Jolie. But, can you not resist your dark humour even now, looking upon this sorry sight?"

They were silent for a time, before McCardle continued.

"If the rumours are true that we are so near our first destination, then we must take heart. There are others, too, among us who have made the same vow as we, that if we but make it to the new place, we will make something of it."

Though he was looking at a strange fate around him, he concluded,

"No fate is so strange as to be lost from God's eye."

Jolie engaged that thought easily.

"I share your resolve, my friend, but not your reason. I would say rather that God has surely abandoned us to this devil priest and his savage acolytes. Do they not say that it was the Jesuit alone who interpreted the native dream and thence stirred up this horror? The savage has not the wherewithal to do so. Nor can those few of them who may have the mind for it keep it up for long. They know no constant purpose. It will be our blood, along with the Jesuit's, soon upon the ground, unless we can turn a thing or two where we head. But, look, the devil himself now approaches."

The man approaching them up the slope was indeed, Laliber. He was once again as gaunt a figure as he had been aboard the ship that had brought him first to Quebec when he was at death's door. The clothes he now chose to wear would not have identified him to anyone in Europe, for he was dressed in his own strange combination of buckskins and leggings and his robe, now rolled and cinched around his waist as a thick black sash as if to signify a new form of priesthood.

Many Axes had ordered him and Laliber agreed not to wear his black robe on the treks in order to lessen a false and unwanted image of the European influence behind the Orendan scheme.

But now, as he approached two of the emerging young leaders of the hostaged third trek of colonials, his thoughts were angry ones about his own still elevated reputation among the hostages as the cause of the Orendan turn of events. He struggled to control the annoyance as he spoke to the men.

"Do not turn from me, for I bring you news. It is the will of God to give and to take away. I would therefore have you consider two facts. First, we are within this very day from our first destination at Toronto. But, second, I am afraid I learned as I passed along the line this morning that at least two score more have perished this past night."

"They are well rid of their earthly suffering," muttered McCardle.

"For me, I can say that it should be a matter of joy that so many of those who set out from New France and New York will surely live to settle in the Orendan settlement on the Michissippi. Most on the other two treks to the west trek survived to reach the Michissippi. The conditions they faced were not as severe as you have faced this last part of winter. By the strong will many of you have displayed, there can be no doubt God has an Orendan purpose for you here if you but seize it."

Jolie was quick to respond to this, despite the cautions of McCardle.

"What delusions, Jesuit, if you still be that. No man, least of all you, can take it upon himself to pronounce God's unknown will. But, if it is your cause to see us to the Orendan settlement, and that is what your savage allies truly want, so be it for now."

The two men stared at each other.

Laliber replied as brightly as he could.

"Those are words spoken with spirit. That is what is needed here."

"So, you speak as the great leader?"

"No. You will not find your great leader in me."

"Then in whom?"

"In yourselves and in your Native guardians and then you will experience the power and sway of Many Axes."

Jolie spat upon the snow.

A short while later, in the early afternoon, the leading trekkers approached close to the Toronto settlement, which they could just make out from several plumes of smoke rising from its snow covered long-houses.

They all could see a snow cleared field beside the town's longhouses. On the field were fast moving waves of men, mixed of their own and the first nations, many running with a netted stick, moving as a small ball was passed rapidly from stick to stick. Receiving and defending players collided in full run, sometimes bloodily and wrestling each other to the ground. The ball was passed from one to another and to another again, and then, with terrific force played against a net guarded by a keeper who might prevent the goal.

They watched the ever changing swarm of players move up and down the field, following the small ball as it was whipped about, making ever-changing patterns like a thick roost of birds rising in the sky.

Jolie studied the movement. "I see that the requirement is to run fast, to where the ball in flight is expected, to catch it in those netted racquets, then to turn it to the goal."

Laliber, still near him, was enthused at the man's interest. "But, watch carefully. The art of the game is not just catching the ball, or holding it. That leads to broken bones, bashed heads and worse as they all pile on." As he said this, two bloodied and dazed players left one side of the field.

"There you see! The ball is in the air, into that man's stick, and just as fast out again and all that way up the field, to that tall man. All in one move, so the tall one can catch and turn it and whip it past that one defender to the goalkeeper who sees it not in time. And see: he does!"

Huge whoops and shouts went up from the goal making team, amongst them the now sulking players on the losing team, some beating their own, others, beating the winners with their racquets, as they gathered again at midfield for the next toss of the ball from the presiding chief.

McCardle shouted, "They hate to lose, Jesuit. Like us. Fun enough, though dangerous fun."

"Yes. The Iroquois villages play it best. But it is catching on with some of the white folk, too." It was the first time Laliber had used "white" instead of "pale face."

McCardle then ran to the field, beckoning others of the newcomers to follow, though none did. He ran into the midst of a mob of players and a wounded Iroquois tossed him a stick with the ball in it. Another stick smashed his wrist, but he somehow managed to flip the ball out to a white fellow, who ran through suddenly open ground all the way to the far goal and hurled the ball beyond the goal keeper's reach.

Now a new whoop went up, erupting from many on the field and all of the scores of people watching along the sides. It was the first paleface's goal of the day.

Another goal and then another yet was scored. All causing increasingly explosive shouts and yells from everyone, until the sun began to sink and the game had to be called.

Smith, who had been in the village for the winter, after testing the waters of the lower lake, approached the incoming trek's leading men. He was wearing new buckskins, but was looking weary. He hailed Laliber.

"That was the best game yet! But listen to me, priest: Many Axes' summons you to the great Falls. I myself, will go the opposite way, back to the oceans and around to the Michissippi that way. You must go immediately. Come. Bid adieu to your new friends there."

"New Friends? Ha. Hardly that," said Jolie, who was listening in.

Laliber turned to someone he indeed might have befriended, McCardle the Catholic still searching for God's purpose. "It seems I must go. Attend to that lacrosse game. Learn to play it with them. It is an exuberant sport. It engages us all. Something whole villages can participate in. It will be good for all of us."

"Enough!" said McCardle. "Be gone, foul Jesuit. We believers know a heretic."

"Enough indeed" said Jolie, marvelling that it was now he holding back McCardle from striking Laliber, as Copper Star and some warriors ran to protect him, looking menacingly at McCardle.

They watched, as in their mind, the key European and Jesuit conspirator headed down to a large war canoe on the thinly iced shore awaiting them with six Iroquois paddlers at the ready. Soon they were well off shore, into the ice-free water.

After a time, McCardle turned to the Huguenot as they both watched the canoes head west.

"I know why I hate him, but why did you bate him so?"

"Because I too hate him too - without him and that Smith, both crazed people of our own blood leading them and trying to divert the trade to Europe down the Michissippi, those savages would be lost and we would regain ourselves and our freedom and our way back to our own settlements."

"So, that is all you think this is: a conspiracy of errant Europeans?"

"Of course! Do you begin to change your mind because I played well in a rowdy and terrible game? What else can there be to explain what these primitives have seemed to have done. I have heard they themselves speak of this. They are angry that it seems even their own dream of reversals is made to actually happen by two Europeans before their Many Axes came along."

Copper Star listened to this and then bid them and their several compatriots to return to the warmth of the fires.

Copper Star then headed rapidly to the shore, entered a waiting canoe beyond the near-shore ice held for him by two strong Odawa paddlers and headed after Laliber, toward Niagara.

Chapter 28

On Many Axes' summons, Laliber spent the last two months of the winter uneasily in a small camp near the chief at Niagara. Both men were working out in their mind the widening exaggeration of the priest's role in Heno's Plot. Though only a few hundred yards apart, what little contact they had in this period was awkward.

The two treks directly from New York were wintering in the mountains to the south, under the watchful eye of the Susquehannock whose chiefs had made a peace with Many Axes. They had then been well armed to allow protected passage of the treks through their own lands. As those treks would make their way to the Michissippi, the guardian role would be taken in turn by the Shawnee and then the Illini who now equally relished a role in the Plot.

Through the late winter, Water Bear led the preparations for the northern trek to resume its movement west out of Toronto. Like the other treks, the native-colonial mix of people had spent the last part of winter surprisingly well. Magic Walk had heard enough talk that she concluded the main motivation of the trekkers was to get to the ultimate destination with life, limb and what possessions they had or could be brought by Smith's ships up the Michissippi for them to start a new life. Water Bear decided to count on this continued cooperation. With lessened concern about losing rebellious trekkers along the way, the 3500 hostages would take the most direct land and water routes west through a series of leapfrog movements. The necessary flotilla of large and small canoes was assembled in Toronto.

After the trek resumed out of Toronto on the first warm April days in 1693, Water Bear and Magic Walk diverted to Niagara. They had heard little of how Laliber and Many Axes were faring. They joined the other two Orendan leaders on the far side of the river just after the river was clear of its groaning rafts of winter ice. They were walking northward to join Many Axes and Laliber through the oak forest along the river's high banks.

Around them in the flanking woodland, warriors from several nations secured their progress. One Seneca warrior, just behind them, carried the new flag of the Orendans - a white slash above a black slash on a red background: the sign on Water Bear's face two years before at the trading island after he had finally interpreted his dream.

When they had reached the other side of the river, close to the thundering falls, they made a camp. In the distance even closer to the falls, they could see the encampments of Many Axes and Laliber. They were told that for the first time since Laliber's arrival, the two men had agreed to meet and were in deep conversation.

"Let us join them," said Water Bear.

"No," said Magic Walk, "let them see if they can work some things out alone first."

They agreed only to send warriors over, bearing the new flag with their greeting that they would join the other two in a day or so.

Earlier in the day, Many Axes began the talk with Laliber.

"So, it is good that you have learned enough of our language that we may talk alone."

Laliber shrugged. "My God gives me a gift with languages that your spirits gave more completely to Magic Walk."

"We rest these nights above mighty Niagara where Heno, Orenda's guardian spirit at the falls, awaits us.

"I have been here twice before. Heno and Orenda together make much noise at those great falls. As you say of that place, the lesser spirit is the guardian of the greater. Perhaps that will play out in our own moment here."

Now Many Axes shrugged. "Perhaps it will; perhaps not. I do not think the others truly know our challenge. The spirits and the chiefs are always at each other, eh? It makes for much wasted energy, so it seems we must try to make a peace."

"I think," replied Laliber, "it is more you who must make a peace. I have learned that your spirits do not easily release the chiefs from a once known and balanced way. But mine releases me not at all. It is my estimate that you can change more readily than I and must do so."

"Well, it is my thought that the upsetting spirit here is indeed you palefaces and your own spirit."

Many Axes threw a stone into the river.

"Anyway, we do not need to discuss such large things at this moment. You and I know, priest, we must speak mainly of the false news: too many now believe that you have tricked us into a plot ordered by your Pope. I say we spend this moment to see what can be done to correct this falsehood once and for all."

"I too would welcome a conclusion to the false allegations about me as if I were the leading power in the scheme. But do you truly seek more thoughts on this?"

"Why do you say that?"

"Are you not considering an easy way out of this falsehood?"

"Well, you must tell me of this. If you mean would I simply have you dead and gone, you make of me a boy hardly grown. No. We will not have a martyr's mischief. I want none of your bloodied Brebeufs here. Water Bear well tells that story. That is what we must together avoid, for it builds a wrong story of Orenda."

Laliber was not sure where this was headed.

Before they could continue, several Seneca approached from their distant fires with food at the midday. They were given a leaders' meal of pheasant, fish and corn cake, served by several clan mothers who had come in, who now believed Many Axes had achieved a unique level above all chiefs and thus deserved their faithful service. They also thought themselves to have earned a right to listen in on his talk.

Many Axes thanked them and chased them all away. Then he sent a message for Water Bear to join them the next morning.

It was a warm morning. The two were seated in loose clothing when Water Bear joined them, explaining that Magic Walk, with a touch of morning sickness, had held off.

Many Axes immediately posed a question.

"Water Bear: tell us what you have heard from the medicine men about the recent events. "

Laliber saw the direction of Many Axes question.

"Is it your concern that no medicine man is among the native leadership, whereas I am, their French equivalent?

"Yes, that is a good part of my concern. Exactly, priest. In this equal Orendan mix, we have not one of the medicine men in the leadership. So, now answer my question, Water Bear."

Water Bear chose his words carefully. "The medicine men and all our chiefs too, think you have led us well and will continue to do so. The medicine men remain convinced that Laliber is somehow a part of the dream, though they know not what part."

"They do not resent the possibility that his medicine is more powerful than their own?"

"They do not admit that, but that does make them strongly deny that Heno's Plot was powered by the black robe."

"What of the talk among the colonists?"

"Many indeed still say that this is a black plot, surely driven by the Jesuit here for some popish purpose."

Many Axes turned to Laliber, "What do you say to this, priest?"

"I have heard this talk first hand. You seem as determined as the false speakers to put me in such a role. I indeed am a Jesuit sworn to my Pope, the

Holy Father, to find a new way in this New World that will lead to more souls finding Christ. God has spoken through me and has taken me even beyond his Holiness in Rome in this. I make no determination of my own as to whether my own church, as it is, is needed or not in this. I hope only that when the true Orendan spirit emerges at St Lis and back here among the people, many more will find their way to Christ than do now and will not be denied such."

"That is exactly the concern expressed by my own people: you think this is a Christian village we make."

"That it might or might not become. But I am prepared to put the accomplishment of Orenda first before what can be any new flourishing of Christianity here. I do not confuse some of the inspiration I and my Christian God have for Orenda with what drives those, you above all, whose own spirits and practical powers will make it happen in the first place. I do not deny other large forces and spirits in the dream. If they can become composed in the new Orenda settlement, they can and will face the possibility of a co-existence with the Christian God. I say so be it. I have done much on my own side to try to declaim the view that this is fundamentally a Jesuit plot under the cover of a temporary savage uprising. I urge you not to feed the cheap blaming of Jesuits for all things bad as is the stupid habit of my European side."

"I still struggle with the thought that you could put much Christian content into the Orendan mix that is uncertain and unpredictable. There is too much talk of the 'mystery' of your Christ, something Magic Walk tells me that is a hidden story and cannot be known."

"Has not my Christ been steady in what I seek from Orenda – the release of native spirits first and then their mix with our own spirit?"

Many Axes could not disagree with that.

"The mystery that is Christ is not mischief. I can say that very strongly. If you accept the best European side of the mix, you must also accept that Christ will have his strong influence, but that our entire influence, as yours too, Many Axes, will be an unpredictable mix. I think you are the rare leader who, like the middle tree of the Longhouse Confederacy can bend to the unpredictable winds this way and that, without losing the main strength. Is there not some agreement we could pen together?"

"The people caught in this Plot tell me they want one leader. I am that leader. Smith and Water Bear fit easily into my leadership. They have not my strong will to lead the new Orenda settlement inland nor wish to. Smith is our protector at sea, but he is not the leader on the land, nor does he want to be. Magic Walk is exceptional but not yet, I think, the equal in leadership of my aunt, Dancing Pipes."

"Since I am the leader, I look around to see who saps any energy from the Plot. I always see you. The native brothers also sense that your dark role is an uncertainty and therefore a still unknown part of what the dream of Water Bear foresaw. Those widespread thoughts cannot continue. I can think of no other way to stop this weakening talk. You must face Heno's Test, here, at the falls."

Laliber looked directly at Many Axes.

"So, tell me of this test."

"This is a test that Heno, the spirit who lives behind these falls and helps empower Orenda to give us energy. The test offers the people caught up in divisions a way to determine whether one's fate is here and now or beyond, with the spirits, by daring to go over the falls."

He watched Laliber nod slowly.

"The brothers who have tested these waters know there is no test over the main falls. That is sure death. But, it seems the record we have of tests shows there is an equal chance to survive the falls over at that gentler place, there, the chute between the shore and the closest rock outward from the shore." He pointed along the shore.

Laliber saw where Many Axes was pointing.

"Who should remain alive, below, after daring to go over, has Heno's blessing and may continue in this world, honoured by the people."

"And what if they do not survive?" asked Laliber.

"It is enough they took the test. They will be remembered well."

Laliber was silent.

The mothers were already approaching with a midday meal.

Many Axes arose and said, "We have let the morning go by. Let us eat together now and then consider these things again alone through the night and meet again in the morning."

Water Bear took some of the meal back to Magic Walk with news they would be at the falls for another night.

When he turned to his blankets that night, Laliber prayed. He thanked God for bestowing his grace and enabling Laliber to restore his faith. He began thinking through scripture for a call from Christ. Nothing had yet come to him before he fell into fitful sleep.

At one point he got up, unrolled his robe and put it on. As he lay down again he thought how amazing it was that he was once again so comfortable in Christ. He again whispered some prayers of thanksgiving for God's grace and fell back asleep.

Just before the dawn he came sharply awake. He had dreamed of his time in La Fleche, delivering his paper on Saint Isaac the Syrian, Bishop of Nineveh, and the words of that Saint had once memorized as an acolyte after the death of a friend. He had said, "Why do you trouble yourself in a house that is not your own? Let the sight of a Dead man be a teacher for you concerning your departure from hence.

With that, Laliber accepted both the nearness and the meaningfulness for others of his own death.

Many Axes woke him. "So, you are wearing your true garments, Jesuit. Come greet the white clouds of the morning in your black robe. Water Bear over there will no doubt see such a contrast as good!"

Laliber waved aside his morning meal.

Water Bear followed Many Axes and Laliber as they walked to and stood at the edge of the wide river foaming its way toward Niagara Falls. He was looking at two of the people, himself another, who would change a whole continent.

Magic Walk, sick throughout the previous day was determined to join the men this morning, but again had waited for a morning sickness to pass. Whereas Water Bear was much troubled at Laliber taking the test of the falls, she was not. "Maybe he, and we, could use a miracle," she had said as they fell asleep in each other's arms.

Now he watched Laliber nod in understanding of the test.

"God gave me good Christian reasons last night for me to take Heno's test. I will take it. But first, I want first two promises from you."

Initially relieved Laliber had made a decision, Many Axes now frowned.

"What are they?"

"First, that you will admit all European essences to the Orendan mix: that must also include the science of Kastler our physician, which we Jesuits have learned to teach, without losing spiritual energy. Say that boldly far and wide, so that it is freely permitted, including our religious faiths and our science in its Cartesian or newer ways. Even as you would admit the powerful mysteries of your own peoples to the mix, we must then allow those different mysteries to mix together well as the people move forward in this life."

Many Axes took a moment to get the gist of all these words and then nodded.

"We have talked of this. You have our promise that the mix of our peoples' genius must be equal and must move into the future equally."

Many Axes turned to Water Bear who nodded his acceptance.

Many Axes turned back to Laliber. "What is the second promise you wish me to make?"

"If I take this test, you will inevitably turn to thinking whether you should take it yourself. If you do you must think hard. It will remain your choice to do so or not to. Is it not best that you survive the test by never taking it? You are surely the irreplaceable leader to guide and ease the painful Orendan birth. Even though we cannot deny that our new Orendan people require great acts by its leaders to be matched on both sides of our mix, I think it would be too much a loss at stake if you let your warrior side fool yourself into seeking my own fated challenge."

Hearing this, Many Axes could not stop his surging anger.

"First you suggest I would consider we both take the test and then you seek my promise not to take it. How can I promise to think hard on that? I will become feverish with opposing thoughts."

"It is difficult matter to think through but I know that you will compose your thoughts on it, Many Axes."

Water Bear was now also angry. "My chief, it is only the priest's role that is questioned, not your own. But, now as I think of it, you will also think of it. If you think a pure blood of our side must take the test, as part of the Orendan commitment on both sides, let me substitute for you."

Many Axes took Water Bear in his mighty arms and began squeezing him, so strongly that Water Bear could not speak further. "Learn by this that what is intended to test me, does not test anyone else, Water Bear. You fail to see this challenge. It is mine alone. No one substitutes for me. Spit out that thought!"

Laliber looked out at the surging waters,

Laliber finally said, "I would prefer to believe that my survival or not would be a matter of agreement between my God and your spirits."

"Let only one last promise be made by you, Many Axes."

"A third one; what may that be?"

"It is another part of your first promise. The Pascalini Machina, the wonderful wooden numbers machine Kastler has even now taken to the St Lis settlement. It must also be treated there by the mixed people as a dream: a thing to be interpreted to make other wondrous things, ever better performing than it already does, in calculating who owes and who pays. Make a study of it, Many Axes. Do you promise that?"

Many Axes shook his head in disbelief.

"So I will do, it is surely meant that the machina is to help make better stories not mere sums. Now that would make our lives rise to the spirits!"

"So then, make it a story machine!" said Laliber.

"And now it is well I meet God's test at these falls. May Christ bless Orenda! I am gone over the falls!"

He crossed himself, leapt into the rushing river and was swept away.

Many Axes watched Laliber rapidly disappear from view. He was without expression. Yet his thoughts were burning within him.

Water Bear said, "Maybe he has half a chance." But, then he said, as he thought about it, "It might not be half chances each time."

Many Axes was calculating his own chances. He had been told a heavy man would likely careen from the dividing rock to the gentler chute which some survived.

Magic Walk was now arriving. She had witnessed the last exchanges between the priest and the chiefs. She hurried up to where Laliber had jumped into the river. Then she whirled and yelled at Many Axes.

"I have seen what happened. The priest is true to his own spirit, to himself. He is still Laliber. It cannot be the priest alone over the falls, Many Axes. That is not the Orenda mix we seek! Many Axes must be Many Axes. If it is not to be you, or Water Bear it must be another of our Plot – let that be me."

She strode forward and was about to throw herself in the river but Water Bear grabbed her away at the last moment and held her firmly though she struggled to free herself.

A small crowd of native witnesses had gathered at the falls. They watched and saw the flapping black robe flash past them. They covered their mouths in awe – some later said the priest seemed to fly above and beyond the chute. Then they all hurried off to the bottom of the great falls.

Many Axes had found no comfort in figuring his chances. Who knows the chances? They do not direct me. His only thought now was how to balance the priest's test with his own fate here as the leader of the Orendan scheme. He could not stop thinking about the other option spoken by Laliber but as the great leader, why should he follow him? He must surely avoid the test, so to be assured he would lead. Even Laliber thought Orenda cannot survive Many Axes' death. Surely, that had seemed the obvious choice.

But now Magic Walk had intervened. It angered him.

He turned to Magic Walk, still struggling to break Water Bear's firm grasp.

"You would have gone over the falls for me," he yelled to her. "Yet, Water Bear tells me you have been sick in the mornings. I can tell: you hold a baby. Why do you want to kill another baby? You must control that too wilful side. I know the story of what happened to your first one. You would now risk the next one you carry in your belly? That is the first child of Orendan chiefs. How can you be so careless?"

That angered Magic Walk more than he. "So, you think I only carry babies. I may be a woman, but I am also a leader. Orenda has become my first child to make, before all others, just as it is yours, barren man. The cause made by all Orendan leaders followed by all our countries is greater than this new baby inside my belly: that was made only by Water Bear and me. Learn to accept a women leader as one of you."

Many Axes glared at her. Her reference to his failure to beget a child was an even greater provocation than her severe speaking to him.

But, Magic Walk would not let up. "I challenge you, Many Axes. Someone of us must follow Laliber down the falls! The very idea of Orenda is that the leaders of our peoples and their people must equally share the great tests it thrusts upon us. Our side must be up to that." she demanded.

Many Axes was left looking out at the coursing river, searching for a decision of his own about the dream and its requirements.

Magic Walk smiled in triumph. She knew Many Axes was again thinking it through.

Water Bear hated this. He tried to hold Magic Walk securely, but knew he could not grasp her abdomen tightly. He covered her mouth with his hand. Then he shouted, "Do not listen to Magic Walk! Laliber said your pride should not make you take the test. He said that he feared for us that you also would take the test and would not survive it to lead us."

Magic Walk pulled away Water Bear's hand from across her mouth and managed to counter, "But, maybe he counted on you not to lead in a dishonourable way."

Many Axes turned and said,

"And he might equally not want me to share his martyrdom. I can guess, but I know not, nor care of the fate of Laliber. I know he will always smite his own God and Heno one way or the other, as he has me. The question is can I avoid the test now, and lead effectively, in my own mind?"

Water Bear shouted, "I tell you, Many Axes, as did the priest, it is only important that you lead."

"Yes, lead."

Water Bear looked around.

"We are watched by some. There is a clear expectation that you will emerge, no matter what has happened here."

"Do they want me to take the test?

"It is not expected. I say no. They want no foolish risk to their leader's life."

Magic Walk again escaped Water Bear's clasp over her mouth.

"Hah. I say yes lead and yes take the test."

Many Axes could not ignore that.

He felt strongly out of balance.

"Unhand her, Water Bear. She speaks some of the truth to me, which I must consider."

Magic Walk immediately spoke.

"It is not like you to remain in your thoughts for so long. There cannot be an untested hero on our native side. You know it."

This seemed again to free him. Many Axes now knew even more strongly that he alone must again take charge.

"Yes, you are right. I now know. I see that the test of the falls for me is a fool's way in this whole story. Here is my instruction and my reason for it. There can be no middle way at the start of this swallowing of the pale faces. Nothing must suggest it, especially anyone in the middle. Only I am strong enough to ensure such a thing at St Lis. I now welcome Magic Walk as equally strong, but that she is and must be a woman. Her time as a grand chief is not yet. Mine is now."

Magic Walk did not answer. She now stood free beside Water Bear and had crossed her arms deliberately not replying.

Water Bear could say no more. He could see both Magic Walk and Many Axes were as powerful as he.

"Well, do you see why I must deny myself taking Heno's Test? Only I can guarantee that Orenda will have pure parts to start the mix with, whatever we and the spirits make happen afterwards."

Many Axes, his mind now made up, continued, "I am to St Lis. Make sure the Jesuit is tended to below. If he survives, send him to Dancing Pipes who sympathizes with him and if he survives past that, have Smith send him back to France, if the priest so wishes. I will keep my promises to him, but I want no more of him inland. If he does return somehow, so let it be. By then, his complicating influence upon me will be too late."

"What if others may have the same thoughts as Magic Walk?"

"As for others, we face what talk we will face. Let anyone dare to speak against my story do so if they must. Let all voices speak."

Magic Walk looked away, feeling defeated.

"As for St Lis, I alone know what is to be done!"

Water Bear began to ask another question, but received no reply.

Many Axes had already left Water Bear whose arm was again firmly around Magic Walk, this time to give her comfort. The great chief was striding rapidly away.

He strode almost to the edge of the woods

Then he stopped.

Water Bear watched the great Chief, wanting to be sure that he was indeed going inland.

Then he saw Many Axes turn sharply toward the river.

Water Bear groaned as he saw Many Axes begin to run toward the river.

Water Bear started to run, but he knew from his angle and distance he could not intercept Many Axes. He could only watch as Many Axes dove into the surging river and within a few moments, disappeared over the falls.

"You see," yelled Magic Walk, whom Water Bear had left behind.

Water Bear could only answer, "I know I see Water Bear has foolishly taken Heno's Test. What else should I see?"

He returned to Magic Walk.

"He is the purest and best of our side. He challenges the too certain way. But he has gone down the safest chute. The one with no rocks at the bottom. Let us find him laughing at us at the bottom. "

She and Water Bear headed to the path down to the bottom of the great falls. She pushed him forward. "Why are you astonished after so much time with him? Many Axes would not have been Many Axes and declined the Test after the priest took it."

He impulsively grabbed hold of her again and held her.

"What do we say to the others headed down there?"

As she searched for words, she wondered at Many Axes' bold resolution of his inner conflicts. Many Axes was like her, in that way. So unlike Water Bear, more often silenced by the various sides of things, waiting for circumstances, a sign from the spirits or her own firmness to give him direction. So unlike the Laliber: constantly reinventing himself, debating endlessly within his own soul the conflict between his faith in a pure god and some hopeful new way forward in this impure world. So unlike Smith: though successful and decisive in this world and like Many Axes having constantly to make decisions for others, but a strong man becoming weary of doing so.

She looked up at Water Bear.

"Let's spread Heno's news. A guarantee from the darkest spirit."

He looked at her questionably.

"What news?"

"Orenda will be!"

"How do you know that?"

"Because, Father Laliber knew it and now even the jealous spirits are dancing it…"

She broke free of him and looked back, her voice rising to a defiant shout,

"Many Axes is still Many Axes!"

The End

Made in the
USA
Middletown, DE